Gilbert Elliot Minto, Emma Eleanor Elizabeth Minto

Life and Letters of Sir Gilbert Elliot

Gilbert Elliot Minto, Emma Eleanor Elizabeth Minto

Life and Letters of Sir Gilbert Elliot

ISBN/EAN: 9783744666466

Printed in Europe, USA, Canada, Australia, Japan

Cover: Foto ©Raphael Reischuk / pixelio.de

More available books at **www.hansebooks.com**

LIFE AND LETTERS

OF

SIR GILBERT ELLIOT.

VOL. III.

LIFE AND LETTERS

OF

SIR GILBERT ELLIOT

FIRST EARL OF

FROM

1751 TO 180

WHEN HIS PUBLIC LIFE IN EUROPE

APPOINTMENT TO THE VICE-RO

EDITED BY HIS GREAT

THE COUNTESS O

IN THREE VO

VOL. III

LONDON

LONGMANS, GRE

1874.

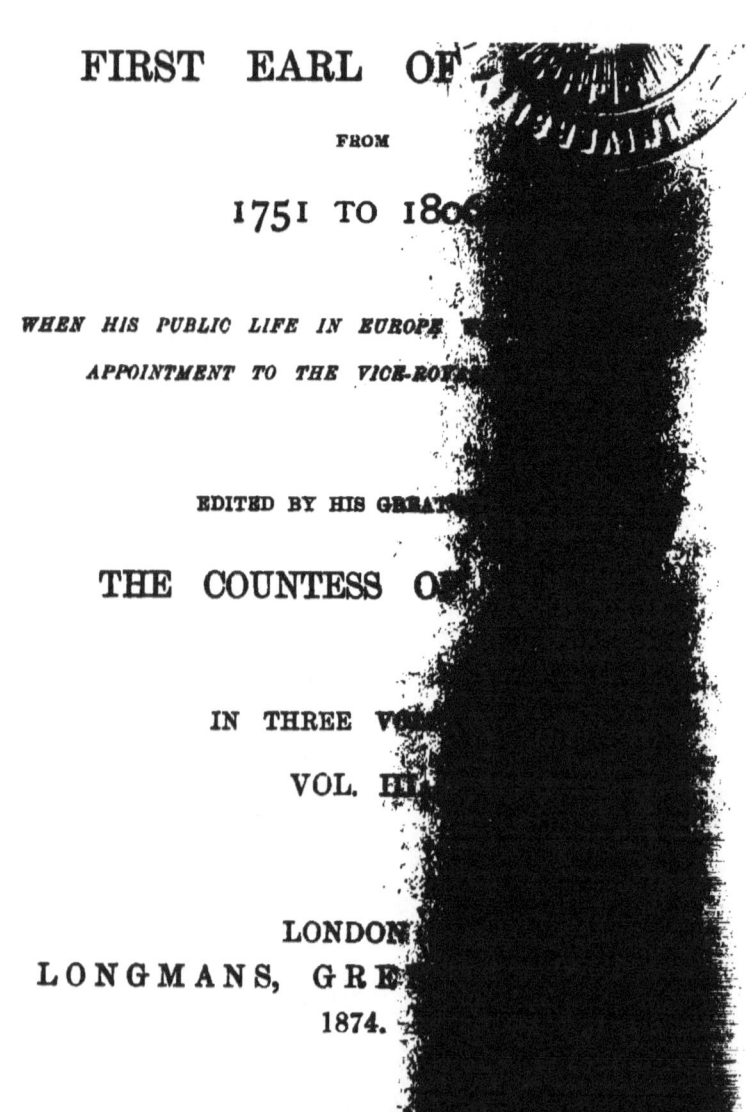

LIFE AND LETTERS

OF

SIR GILBERT ELLIOT

FIRST EARL OF MINTO.

CHAPTER I.

It was announced to Sir Gilbert during the autumn that the King intended to confer on him the honour of a peerage. Early in October he went to London to kiss hands.

'October 5, 1797.

'I am to kiss hands on Wednesday or Thursday next, and I propose to set off for Minto on Friday the 13th. I dined at Lord Spencer's yesterday. There were Lady Spencer, Lady Pembroke, Lord Pembroke, Windham, Canning, Lord Malmesbury, Elliot and I. The Duke of Portland was also there; and it is impossible to say what he reports of the King's favour towards me, and the satisfaction he expressed at this measure. The King said over and over again that there was the greatest propriety in it, and that he did it with the greatest pleasure; that I had earned it, and should be of the greatest use in the House of Lords.

'I dine to-day with Lord Hood at Greenwich; Nelson and his lady carry me there.

'Nelson looks better and fresher than I ever remember him. His arm is, however, by no means well, owing to some awkwardness in the operation. The ligature has not come away, and they are afraid that it has taken in the artery or even a sinew. They must wait till it rots off, which may be a great while. If they should attempt to cut it (it is two inches up the wound), and they should cut the artery, they would be obliged to amputate again higher up, which is not easy, for the stump is very short already. He suffers a great deal of violent pain, and takes opium every night. He is impatient for the healing of the wound that he may go to sea again. He writes very tolerably with his left.

'Gilbert is the only person to whom I have found it necessary to make an apology for our new honours. You know he said to me some time ago, that he hoped I would not have a peerage, or *any of that* nonsense. When Mr. Reed told him of it, he said, "Well, if it is so, it must be so." However, he will be reconciled to it I have no doubt; if he were not, I should certainly have missed my aim, for his interest in it is more material than either yours or mine.

'I propose to have the Moor's head for crest, as a memorial of Corsica.'

Shortly after this letter was written, Lady Minto, as we must now call her, joined her husband in London, and in the course of the autumn they took possession of a villa at Roehampton, to become henceforth their home during several months of every year. Besides its own conspicuous merit, this locality had a peculiar charm for them as associated with early memories, and as bringing them into the immediate neighbourhood of their most intimate friends. Within no great distance were the villas of Lord Malmesbury at Park Place, of Lord Palmerston at East Sheen, and of Mr. and Mrs. Legge at Fulham. Close to Park Place was the 'Lavender House,' a charming retreat belonging to Mr. and Mrs. Culverden (Lady Palmerston's sister), and closer to Roehampton, in Bushy Park, was the 'Pheasantry,' where Mr. and Lady Katherine Douglas made 'a mere box contain a larger number of jolly individuals than could be found packed within the same space in any house in Europe;' the 'jolliest' being the hostess, with her pleasant sisters,[1] who all inherited more or less of their father's wit and humour.

And in all these houses were to be found at times, not only the genial personages to whom they belonged, but a floating population of occasional visitors from Town, who brought the freshest news and talk in exchange for fresher air and verdure. Among those who thus met under the chestnut trees of Sheen, or among the flowery shrubberies of Fulham, or the more am-

---

[1] Lady Ann and Lady Charlotte North.

bitious heights and slopes of Park Place, were some
whose names are known to fame—as Windham, Francis,
Canning, Frere, the Ellises, both George and Charles —
and many more who in their own day made *la pluie
et le beau temps*, but are long since forgotten.

The correspondence reopened when Lady Minto went
to Scotland in June 1798.

‘ Friday, June 8, 1798.

‘ The news from Ireland to-day is bad.[1] Col. Walpole,
with a body of troops of about 400 or 500, has been
defeated by the rebels. Col. Walpole is killed, and our
loss is about 150 killed and two pieces of cannon taken.
Gen. Loftus with another corps fell back to wait for re-
inforcements, in consequence of Col. Walpole's defeat.
The account adds, however, that the next day, viz., the
5th inst., a general attack on the rebels in Wexford was
expected. I trust they will be defeated when an army
is fairly got together ; but in the meanwhile they are
in great strength, and have possession of a very strong
country. Some French officers, it is said, have been taken
by our troops and hung. Windham called on me last
night in York Street, and fixed a party to dine at Mrs.
Crewe's at Hampstead to-day with Pelham ; and this
morning he sent me a note to put it off. Pelham says
Windham is an idle fellow, for when he came to town he
tried to see him, but was told he was gone with Lady
Salisbury and other ladies on the water. The next day
he found Windham had come up to town to the House
of Commons, but had returned to bring the ladies to

---

[1] The rebellion in Wexford broke out in the last days of May.

town.   But that he would certainly be in town that
evening for—(Pelham supposed a Cabinet), for—he was
engaged to the masquerade!'

'June 9, 1798.

'I am in a thousand hurries owing to the Cock-pit,
and am an hour too late for Putney Park,[1] where I dine.
The news from Ireland is a great defeat of the rebels,
who are said to have lost from 2,000 to 3,000 men.
I don't know what our loss has been, but Lieut.-Col.
Dering, of the Romney Fencibles, is killed, and I fear
two other lieutenant-colonels; 5,000 men are going
immediately, among them a brigade of Guards.   No
other news that I know of.   The burning of a French
frigate which came out of Havre, by our frigate the
" Hydra," was in the papers ten days ago.   She was
blown up in the presence of a body of French cavalry
drawn up on the shore, and she contained brass artillery
and stores, probably for Ireland.'

'June 11, 1798.

'The only event to-day is unpleasant.   An insurrection has taken place to-day at Antrim, in the north
of Ireland.   The *North* was thought quite secure.   The
insurgents intended to seize the magistrates.   Their
design was defeated with the loss of 22 men killed on
our side, and P. O. Neil, and a brother of Lord Scar-
borough's, a Mr. Lumley, wounded.

'I go to-morrow to Henley to see the Palmerstons,
and have slept every night at Fulham; it is very quiet

---

[1] The residence of Mr. and Lady Jane Dundas.

and very sweet with flowers and shrubs. Windham is constantly there, so that I see a great deal of him. I was yesterday in the evening at Sir Andrew Hammond's, next door, and saw Lord Duncan and his daughter. They are both magnificent creatures. She very handsome, but colossal. Nelson is actually gone to the Mediterranean with only three sail of the line. Lord St. Vincent had detached nine more to join him as soon as Sir R. Curtis arrived with his reinforcement. They have not yet heard of these ships having joined Nelson, but I trust they will before he attempts anything. I had this from Admiral Gambier, who is a Lord of the Admiralty, and let it out incautiously, for I believe they wish to keep the exact state of the affair back till they hear of Nelson having the whole of his squadron with him.'

' Saturday, June 16, 1798.'

' On my return from Henley yesterday, I found Elliot just arrived from Dublin,[2] and he returns to-day. He came to press for troops from England, and for their immediate departure, as it was not yet known at Dublin

---

[1] On the day on which this letter is dated, June 16, Mr. Dundas brought down to the House of Commons a message from the King, announcing that several regiments had freely tendered an extension of their services to Ireland . . . . several Militia regiments went over accordingly. Lord Stanhope's *Life of Pitt*, vol. iii. p. 146. Lord Cornwallis landed in Ireland on June 20.

[2] Lord Cornwallis wrote to Mr. Pitt, October 17, 1798 : —' Mr. Elliot, who is well known to you, has been much in my confidence, and there are few persons who can give a more just, and who will give a more dispassionate, opinion on the state of this wretched country.'—Cornwallis's *Correspondence*, vol. ii. p. 419.

that the troops lately sent were going. You would think it odd if you were not used to them, that Lord Cornwallis should be setting out this day for Ireland to take Lord Camden's place, and that Lord Camden does not *yet* know a word of the matter. It is true that he had expressed an opinion that the business of Ireland being now entirely military, a military Lord-Lieutenant might be desirable, unless a Commander-in-chief were appointed in whom entire confidence might be placed, which I imagine is not the case at present. It would seem still more extraordinary that this measure should be taken not only without the Cabinet's having any knowledge of it, but even without the knowledge of the Duke of Portland, in whose department Ireland is. The news come this evening is more favourable than what you will see in this day's papers. The rebels in Antrim are not agreed among themselves, and it appears that some bodies of them have offered to submit on promises of pardon. It is hoped that by the troops sent and being sent from England, the rebellion may be crushed by a vigorous effort in the present state of it. But it is too precarious not to cause grave apprehensions. I went to the Lavender House yesterday, the prettiest and most charming little settlement I ever saw, and walked up to the house at Park Place.'

'Tuesday, June 26, 1798.

' I enclose a printed bulletin sent me by Elliot, which arrived to-day by the post, giving an account of the defeat of the rebels at Vinegar Hill on the 21st, since

which a further account has arrived by express of our
troops being in possession of Wexford on the 23rd.
General Moore (my friend) marched from Cork towards
Wexford, and being opposed on his way defeated the
rebels and arrived at Wexford, but did not enter the
town ; he encamped on a height which commands it and
was advantageously situated near it. In the meanwhile
General Lake, after the action at Vinegar Hill, followed the flying rebels to Wexford. They offered to
treat for a surrender of the town on promise of security
to their lives and property, which was rejected. The
rebels then murdered about seventy prisoners or hos-
tages and threw them over a bridge into the river ;
and they retired from the town, which General Lake
took possession of; the rebels were hemmed in between
General Lake and General Moore on the sea side, so
as not to be able to escape, and it is supposed they
went there in hopes of obtaining a capitulation.

'I give you this account as I had it from Pelham,
and if not quite correct in all particulars, it is so in
every thing that is material. Lord Camden is expected in town to-day. He is already in the Cabinet
without office.'

                                        'June 27, 1798.

'I hope there is a fair prospect of suppressing the
Irish rebellion for the present. These are times in
which a short distance from evil must be reckoned a
great advantage ; and it is indeed an advantage to
gain time. I find that serious thoughts are entertained
by Government of bringing about a *union* with Ireland

similar to that with Scotland. It is thought by the
friends of this measure, that nothing else will prevent
the constant return of hostility and contention between
the two countries, and it is thought not impossible that
the terror excited by the present civil war amongst those
who have property to lose, may induce them to accept
of these means of future security at the expense of
national pride and private ambition. Lord Cornwallis
has instructions, after the rebellion is quelled, to sound
Ireland on this question. It is a very great and I
should suppose doubtful question, and I think it extremely improbable that it should be carried through
either in England or Ireland; all this either is or
ought to be extremely confidential and secret, but it
will probably not remain so long.'

'June 30, 1798.

'I am out of spirits and dejected to-day. like one
that has done a wrong thing that he is ashamed of.
I let yesterday pass without speaking, and I not only
intended to speak, but this is positively the last possible opportunity this year. There is nothing to be said
except that I deserve a severe flogging infinitely
better than poor Gilbert, who you will see by the enclosed letter has had it. There is also nothing to be
said about him, for he certainly earned it, and I take
for granted they all made their minds up to that consequence of the resolution they had taken.[1]

'There were as usual no strangers yesterday on the

[1] A celebrated rebellion at Eton had been terminated by a wholesale
flogging of the school.

Irish questions. All I now say is that I *must* do better next year. I go to-morrow to the Princess of Wales' breakfast at Blackheath.'

'June 28.

' Our breakfast yesterday (with the Princess of Wales at Blackheath) proved extremely agreeable, though it was so *prudent* that I was within two of being the youngest gallant in company; my juniors were Tom Grenville and Lord Goodyer. The Princess made herself extremely agreeable, seemed delighted herself and contrived to satisfy all her guests. These little indulgences seem to be the consequence of some late interposition of her family, who desired formally to know the cause of the extraordinary treatment she received. The Prince, however, does not see her, and the child comes only when Lady Elgin chooses; she was there yesterday, and was led about by Lady Elgin in a leading string; though she seems stout and able to trot without help. The Princess of Wales seems to me very undeserving of such strange neglect and repudiation. Her countenance is remarkably lively and pleasing, and I think her positively a handsome woman. Nothing can be more unexceptionable than her conduct. Tables were laid in a little strip of garden under a row of trees, and providentially there was no violent rain, though it thundered all day. A slight shower, which drove the white muslins for a few minutes into the house, was only an incident enlivening the feast. After it there was music in the house, and I did not get away till two o'clock.'

This was the first of a series of meetings, at the second of which the Princess opened herself fully on her domestic grievances, and before the summer was over, Lord Minto found the amount of confidence reposed in him somewhat irksome. With his usual sympathetic kindliness, he did his best to make his influence of use by invariably urging 'conciliatory measures' on the part of the Princess, 'whose wifely duty was submission.' Though alarmed and distressed by her indiscretion, he could not but feel compassion and sympathy for the position of a woman cut off by no fault of hers from all domestic ties and interests, and of a Princess not only deprived of the honours, dignities, and gratifications belonging to her high rank, but debarred from the frank enjoyment of social pleasures that would have been within her reach in any station of life but her own. He could not blame her because in circumstances which demanded extraordinary qualities these were wanting, while he recognised in her the existence of many good gifts, which had she fallen into better hands might have sufficed for her own happiness and that of others.

'July 7, 1798.

'I probably see the Jersey devilry in the stronger light for having passed yesterday with the Princess of Wales, and seeing the most extraordinary sacrifice to the devil that ever was made. She dined at Lord Hood's, who asked nobody but me. I am in the highest favour, or rather the most intimate confidence imaginable, and you are right in supposing that there seems a natural attraction between me and all royal distresses.　I should fear the Princess may give her confidence too incautiously for her own interests, as my acquaintance is certainly not of a standing to warrant so unreserved a reliance on my discretion as her conversation implied.　She refused to play at whist from a desire to continue our talk ; and after setting the rest to play, she continued, till eleven at night, unburthening herself of all her wrongs and sufferings.　She is really *not discreet*, but she is, on the other hand, certainly all nature, and seems to have a good deal of character and firmness.　Lord Thurlow is her chief adviser at present.　There was nothing of any sort she did not seem disposed to relate, being restrained only by the doubt of the notion I should conceive of her. Another day's acquaintance will leave no scruples.'

'July 12, 1798.

'Windham's marriage is actually true, and done two days ago.　It seems there is an etiquette which requires that Cabinet Ministers should acquaint the King with their intention to marry, and the King appears to have been his only confidant.　He mentioned her age, which is forty, and said she was now twenty years older than when their attachment commenced ; but, he added, that ought not to prevent the marriage, or that ought not to be objected to her, as it *was no fault of hers* that the match had not been earlier.　He is as odd, I think, as most people.　However, I have great hopes of the marriage improving him, for he will not now be dodging with the world and playing at whoop with all his friends. I will not condole with you upon the occasion, as you have only to strike up a great friendship with Miss Forrest that was, and get him to take a house near Roehampton. I hear she is brown, with dark eyes, good teeth, and past forty —my idea of perfect beauty.

'I was last night at a children's ball at Sheen, which Anna Maria would have liked as well as I did, though I was not to be pitied, being the only man in the midst of the Duchess of Devonshire, Lady Bessborough, and Lady Melbourne, all attending their daughters. The house was full of little girls; amongst them, however, Lady Georgina Cavendish was pretty nearly an adult. She is a true compound of her father and mother, with the drawl of the Cavendishes and the peculiarities of manner belonging to her mother's family.

'Lord Palmerston went to Vauxhall with a Francis party, and literally found no one but themselves. One cannot conceive how Lord Palmerston would get through Lent without the oratorios.'

'Saturday, July 14, 1798.

'I dined at Blackheath yesterday, and was shown on my arrival to Miss Hayman's round tower in the garden, where she had been ordered to show me part of the correspondence between the Prince and Princess, Lord Malmesbury, Lady Elgin, &c., relative to their separation, the child, and other similar matters. It appears that they lived together two or three weeks at first, but not at all afterwards as man and wife. They went to Windsor two days after the marriage, and after a few days' residence there they went to Kempshot, where there was no woman but Lady Jersey, and the men very blackguard companions of the princes, who were constantly drunk and filthy, sleeping and snoring in boots on the sofas; and in other respects, she says, the scene was more like the Prince of Wales at Eastcheap than like any notions she had acquired before of a princess or of a gentleman.

'There seems some idea that Opposition, with whom the Prince seems now connected, mean to attempt some ostensible reconciliation, in order to diminish the Prince's unpopularity. Her motive, perhaps, for showing me the correspondence was to prove that she should not be to blame if she refused such offers. However, I give no encouragement to such ideas, and urge strongly the propriety of complying; but I do not suppose anything of the sort is in agitation. The company at dinner yesterday was only Lord Thurlow, (Lord Hood was asked, but was not able to come,) and her ladies, and Mrs. and Miss Crewe. Lord Thurlow is her principal champion and adviser. We had a pleasant family dinner in a quiet uncourtly way. After dinner the ladies played and sang, while the Princess entertained me mostly on the old topics on the sofa. We also played two games at chess, in which I beat her without any mercy, and told her afterwards that she saw I did not play like a courtier. She said she believed it was not my custom.   There was a little supper, and we parted at twelve o'clock.

'My Princessly history is only for yourself, for I confess I think her confidence in me is more natural than discreet.'

'Bcckenham: July 19, 1798.

'I have been a man of Kent all this time.   On Tuesday I wrote you a line from Eden Farm ; on that day I transferred myself to the Bennets, where the Palmerstons were also, and on Wednesday everybody in the parish was to dine at the Duchess of Hamilton's ; but an invitation to dine at Blackheath broke all that private plan up.

' The company had not well recovered their lamentations on the loss of Wednesday, before the Princess and Miss Hayman arrived on horseback, and meaning apparently to stay half an hour, but it ended in their staying to dinner and till supper-time.   The evening was rather long, particularly to me, for the Princess got into one of her confidential conversations, and as she spoke extremely low I was kept in a state of straining attention, both as to the ear and to the brain, for several long hours, while a very large company sat round in a circle doing nothing, not speaking out, and looking on with fatigue and impatience.   When the carriage drove off, Bennet took off his coat and flew about the room, huzzaing and capering for joy; however, he went to dinner yesterday and was comparatively tame.   We were a small and pleasant company ; the men, Lord Auckland, Lord Gwydir, Bennet, and

I; the ladies, the Duchess of Hamilton, Lady Auckland, Lady Palmerston, Miss Hayman, and Miss Garth.
After dinner we strolled in the park, played chess and
backgammon. Pozzo di Borgo has been with me all
this time, till yesterday, when, as he was not asked to
Blackheath, he returned to town. The Aucklands and
everybody who have seen him are extremely pleased
with him, and this always gives me pleasure. I go
to-morrow to Bulstrode, and shall be at Beconsfield
before I return to town. This wandering life has its
uses; and indeed when my own house tumbles down,
as it did on the 7th of June, I see nothing for it but
going into the fields and getting shelter where I can.

'One of these days I am going to Long's at Bromley,
and with him to Holwood to see Pitt.'

'July 26, 1798.

'I have seen Windham and his bride, and am quite
delighted with her. She is a tall showy woman, something in the Siddons' style of figure and dimensions,
with a remarkably sensible as well as pleasing countenance and an engaging manner. He seems the most
delighted bridegroom that ever was. I met them
yesterday evening, taking a conjugal walk round St.
James's Park after dinner, just as the inhabitants of
Park Street have done before. I dine with them to-
morrow.

'The Speaker is very full of a good story which he and
Mr. Pitt have got against Windham: how on the day of
marriage he not only forgot the wedding-ring, but
forgot the way to Reigate. Whether he arrived there

at all or not, I do not know, as we could not press for
particulars which he reserves for the first interview
with Windham himself; he assured us they drove
about most of the night in search of a habitation, and
I rather think did *not* get to Reigate.'

During the recess of 1798, Lord Minto was consulted
by the Princess of Wales, through the intervention of
a common friend, as to the course she should adopt if
overtures of reconciliation were made to her by the
Prince. It was strongly urged on the Princess's part,
that the idea of any *rapprochement* between herself
and the Prince was painful to her, as she felt per--
suaded that it would only be desired by him to serve
purposes of his own, in which her happiness and comfort
would have no part, and that it could only be made by
the sacrifice of the enjoyments of quiet and independ-
ance which she owed to the privacy of her life. Lord
Minto's answer was that of a true friend and wise
counsellor.

' It is perhaps a great deal to say on any question so
interesting, that I have never arrived at anything like a
doubt, and that my first feeling has been confirmed by
all the deliberation I have since bestowed on the subject. I think it quite essential for the future happiness
of the Princess that a proposition for reconciliation
should not be defeated by any obstacle or resistance on
her part. If you ask me whether I think such an event
likely to produce that sincere and cordial union on
which domestic happiness depends, I should frankly own

that I by no means reckon on such fortunate consequences. I must acknowledge that not hoping to see
the expected offer founded on any sincere motive either
of affection or justice, I cannot disguise to myself the
possibility of the Princess finding herself not only
deprived of some great comforts which she now enjoys,
but even subject to some great vexations from which
she is now exempted, by such a change in her situation.
Is all this answered, you will say, by the commonplace
observation, that she is a Princess and not a private
gentlewoman? I believe I must even reply that this
same commonplace will be found more conclusive than
all the more agreeable sentiments that can be opposed
to it. In contrasting the elevated situation of the
Princess of Wales with her private comfort, I do not lose
sight for a moment of her happiness. If I were merely
to weigh against each other the two sorts of enjoyment, I
should prefer for her the simple pleasures of a private
life to the splendid gratifications of her own rank.
But she is Princess of Wales, and can never change or
be divested of that character except to assume that of
Queen. What follows? Let the Princess of Wales's
happiness stand, if you please, on the same general
foundation with that of all other women, and indeed
with all human happiness whatever—that is to say, it
must not be in contradiction with any clear duty; and
this for two reasons. First, in such a case, conscience
breaks in as a mar-plot, or *trouble-fête,* and spoils the
sport. In the next place, the opinion of the world we
live in, which, let me tell all the cynics of the earth,

is an indispensable ingredient of all sublunary happiness, is missing, and the dish becomes flat, if not bitter. A reconciliation is a thing which so much affects the general security and happiness of this kingdom, as to require the sacrifice of some portion of private and personal comfort. But the moment you come to consider the matter on the footing of Duty, and of the general sense of the world concerning that duty, you will feel, with me, that the question of substantial interest and happiness is also decided. Nothing can be more certain than that the Princess has no other chance, even for a tolerable share of comfort, than by keeping constantly not only in the right, but so much on the right side of right as to be completely out of reach of that left-handed wisdom which generally accompanies malice, and which is sure not to miss a blot.

'Lastly, even an ostensible reconciliation would give a chance, however slender, of an impression being made at length on the Prince by the sight of so much merit, and the recollection of the unprovoked wrongs for which she would be making so different a return.

'Had this letter been intended to meet the Princess' eye I should have thought it necessary to be more reserved in manner, but not less decisive in its matter. I should be ungrateful if I did not feel most deeply the great condescension and goodness with which the Princess has distinguished me.'

All sorts of petty annoyances were heaped on the Princess at this time. She was urged to submit to the appointment of a lady in waiting of whom she disapproved—she was refused the nomination of one she liked.   She was not permitted to live either in London or in those quarters in its neighbourhood where she herself desired to have a residence.   Though her child was established in a house at Blackheath, the Princess rarely saw her alone, and expressed herself afraid to insist on so doing, lest any fault of temper or manner, afterwards detected in the child, should be traced to her.   The Royal Family treated her with marked neglect, and the Princess had irrefragable proof that wishes of hers, simple enough to have obtained immediate gratification had they been made known to the King, were purposely withheld from him—a policy which he himself described, when he became aware of it, as ' *much too bad.*'   When attending the Queen's drawing-room, the Princess was not even certain of receiving from her husband the acknowledgment of a bow ;[1] and all this time common friends, or enemies, of both made it their business to envenom the situation by retailing to each party in turn the malevolent observations they

[1] An odd scene took place at the drawing-room. ' The Princess was there, so was the Prince. He came very near to her, which never was the case before, but did not bow, which likewise never was the case before ; but His Royal Highness says she on her part did not try to catch his eye. The King spoke to the Princess about the Countess d'Almeyda, who was a new appearance at court, and said he thought she could not be handsome as she was not fair. The Princess curtseyed, and archly said she wished others of His Majesty's family were of the same opinion. Her manner of saying it made the King laugh very much, but he said he wished so too, and thought the contrary a proof of very bad taste. She looked remarkably well.'

had been able to make on the conduct or expressions of
the other.

The Princess had been thrown into a violent state of
irritation by a current report that the Prince, having
broken through some later ties, was endeavouring to re-
establish his relations with a lady to whom his early
devotion had been notorious. Meeting at this crisis a
friend and companion of the Prince, she said to him
that 'she hoped *her husband* would not feel *her* any
impediment to the reconciliation he was so desirous for.'
A few days afterwards, the same gentleman informed
her that he had delivered 'the message' to the Prince,
who said: 'Did she say so? Indeed she is very good-
natured ;' and the Princess was not long in hearing that
she was represented as having taken an active part in
the reconciliation referred to, to the great disgust of
the Prince, who commented to her informant, a
gentleman of his household, on the indelicacy of the
proceeding. 'Indelicacy, indeed!' said she, 'and I
wonder who could say such a thing or suppose I could
ever have thought it; all I said was that I hoped I did
not stand in the way of his happiness.' It was remarked with regret by those who frequented her society
that she was apt to prosecute enquiries concerning the
movements of the lady in question which it did not
become her dignity to know; the feeling actuating
her on such occasions being probably much the same
as that which prompted Cleopatra's interest in Octavia.
Nor were there wanting circumstances in this case
which might almost have justified her in asking,

with the Egyptian Queen, 'What says the *married* woman?'[1]

A more cruel practice than that of reporting the gusts of ill-humour to which each party occasionally gave vent towards the other, consisted in confidential communications to the Princess sometimes bearing the character of messages from the Prince, calculated to excite her hopes of a change in his feeling towards her; the effect upon her being such as to prove to the by-standers how much mortified feeling lay at the root of the bitterness, necessarily increased by the disappoint-ment too surely following on every ray of hope.

The Princess had formed a strong wish to become possessor of Lord Downshire's villa at Roehampton, and was actually in treaty for it, when she was informed that the scheme, as 'displeasing at Windsor,' must be dropped. 'Last night Jack Payne returned from Windsor, where the Prince has been, and is to be for some time; he brought the unqualified declaration that the Princess must not approach that neighbourhood. Indeed, the Prince did so far qualify it as to say: "Assure the Princess it is not *my* fault." The Princess bore the disappointment with great good humour, though her first observation was, "Whenever I am treated in this manner it is satisfaction to my conscience. It proves that I have not injured the Queen and the Prince in anything I have been provoked to say of

---

[1] Many years later, the Princess, then living at Kensington Palace, said to Mr. Hugh Elliot, who was sitting by her at dinner, that 'the only *faux pas* she had ever committed was her marriage with the husband of Mrs. Fitzherbert.'

them."'   Two or three days later the following scene
occurred and was related by the same correspondent,
a lady attached to the household of the Princess of
Wales :—

'Enter Princess of Wales with a book. " Here, my
dear, read, read ; tell Lord Minto directly that I am
in love with his friend Mr. Burke. He has drawn the
Prince's character exactly, exactly ; read it, read it."
" A man without any sense of duty as a prince, without
any regard to the dignity of his crown, and without any
love to his people ; dissolute, false, venal, and desti-
tute of any positive good quality whatever except a
pleasant temper and the manners of a gentleman."
"Ask Lord Minto if it is not quite like him, and tell
him, too, that I am delighted with Mr. Windham. He
is so charming since he is married, and now I can
speak to him quite easily ; but Lord Minto must not
think that I forget absent friends or prefer Mr. Windham, for I do not."   And then away flew Her Royal
Highness, leaving me to tell you that Mr. Windham
gratified the Princess by his warm encomiums on you,
and his strong opinion that you were of all men on
earth the most proper to be chosen as a confidential
adviser.'

Whether stimulated thereto by her newly-formed
friendships with Burke's friends, or by the desire to
learn more of George Prince of Wales in studying his
predecessors, the Princess gave herself up at this time

to the perusal of Burke's works, and derived not a little
malicious pleasure in imparting her enjoyment of them
to Lord Thurlow.

Lord Thurlow was at this time a frequent visitor at
Blackheath : on one of his visits the Princess talked to
him of the writings of Burke and of her great admiration of them.   He replied that Mr. Burke was a man of
genius without wisdom. The Princess then particularly
praised the letter which he wrote for the Prince of Wales
to Mr. Pitt during the King's illness.   Lord Thurlow
said he did not recollect it. She promised to send it
to him, and did so with a letter from herself.   To this
he made a short reply, in which the following passage
occurs : ' It would make a long story to lay before your
Royal Highness in exact detail the circumstances of the
period, without which it is impossible to form a judgment, and with which your Royal Highness would be
the readiest to discern his Futility and Folly.   The
Prince, he believes, is satisfied that his affairs both
then and now would have been in a different situation
if he had followed sounder advice.'

CHAPTER II.

ONE of the first duties of Parliament, when it re-assembled in the autumn of 1798, was to congratulate the hero, who was now called to the Upper House by the title of Lord Nelson of the Nile, on the great victory of Aboukir.[1]   In the debate which took place there on this occasion Lord Minto had the satisfaction of bear-ing part; the last words of his speech express his peculiar claim to add his tribute to the general meed of admiration.

'There is one other point of excellence to which I must say a single word, because I am perhaps the man in the world who has had the best opportunity of being acquainted with it.   The world knows that Lord Nelson can fight the battles of his country, but a con-stant and confidential correspondence with this great

---

[1] The battle of Aboukir or the Nile was the first blow given to the notion of Republican invincibility. 'His victory gave a new impulse to Europe; and from Constantinople to St. Petersburgh, for the first time since the commencement of the revolutionary war, it was felt that France was not invincible.' Under the influence of the Queen and the Hamiltons, the King of Naples had defied the strict injunctions of the Directory by admitting the English fleet into his ports; and without the repairs and assistance thus obtained, Nelson's further course would have been impossible; his triumphant return was hailed by court and people with transports of enthusiasm.—Alison's *History of the French Revolution.*

man for a considerable portion of time has taught me
that he is not less capable of providing for its political
interests and honour, in occasions of great delicacy and
embarrassment.　In that new capacity I have witnessed
a degree of ability, judgment, temper, and conciliation,
not always allied to the sort of spirit which without
an instant's hesitation can attack on one day the whole
Spanish line with his single ship, and on another a
superior. French fleet moored and fortified within the
islands and shoals of an unknown bay.' [1]

The winter of 1798 was a time of arduous toil and of
intense anxiety in Downing Street.　In addition to the
measures in progress for a new Continental War, they
had to devise others for the pacification of the dominions of the Crown.

The moment had arrived for the introduction of 'a
new comprehensive and healing measure,' an Act of
Union between Great Britain and Ireland ; but the
question remained undecided as to whether the scheme
should comprehend the removal of Roman Catholic
disabilities, or should be simply a union of the existing
legislatures.　Lord Cornwallis was profoundly impressed
with the necessity of adopting the first course.　To
this the Irish Protestant party was violently opposed,
and the Irish Chancellor and Speaker came over to
England to urge their views on Mr. Pitt.　Some of the
transactions which ensued are related by Lord Minto

---

[1] Speech of Lord Minto in the House of Lords, on the occasion of the
vote of thanks to Nelson for the victory of the Nile.—November
21, 1798.

on the authority of Mr. Elliot of Wells, himself, as we have seen, a member of the Irish Government and in the intimate confidence of the Executive.

'London : November 19, 1798.

' Elliot has given me full information on the Irish business.[1] It seems doubtful whether the Union will be proposed.   Pitt was clear for it till lately, but seems to have been shaken by the Irish politicians who have come to London on that subject.   The question is whether the Catholics are to partake in the new united Government.

' Lord Cornwallis is very strong in their favour.   The Irish Junto violent the other way ; and it is not thought certain whether the measure can be carried in Ireland, that is to say, in the Irish Parliament, against the sense of the Junto.   Elliot will not vote in the Irish Parliament for the Catholic exclusion, and on that account thinks it necessary to quit Ireland if that

---

[1] A month earlier than the date of this letter Mr. Elliot had written from Dublin Castle as follows :—

' If the Union is to be formed on the principle of excluding the claims of the Catholics, I shall most indubitably withdraw myself from all connection with Irish politics ; and I have explained myself most unreservedly on this topic to Lord Cornwallis, who is himself perfectly free from the prejudices of the Protestant faction and wishes the Catholics to be admitted to their share of the benefits of the British Constitution. One of my objects in going directly to London is to have some conversation with the Ministers on this very important subject, though I do not expect to do much good, and I am apprehensive Pitt is much under Protestant influence.   Though I believe an union has become a topic of general conversation, it is not yet avowed by Government, and I must therefore beg you not to quote me.'

measure is adopted by Government; and I believe he is right.[1] Pitt seems not determined, but Lord Grenville is supposed to have taken his side against the Catholics, which is the opinion at Court. The Chancellor is with the Irish Chancellor and *against* the Catholics. Windham and the Duke of Portland and Lord Spencer *for* them. In short, the Cabinet is divided, and so many difficulties will arise that although the Union would be a desirable event for both countries, yet Pitt not being bound to undertake it may probably fly from all the embarrassments attending it. He will be very well justified by the declaration of the Irish members of the Irish Government that it is not possible to carry it. But Dundas says he shall abide by Lord Cornwallis's opinion on that point, and he may very likely think it right to try it.'

'November 24, 1798.

'The Irish Union is still intended, but Pitt has given way to the Protestant party and engaged himself to leave the Catholics in the same situation as at present. This is against the opinion of Lord Cornwallis, who thinks, however, a union desirable on any terms, and will therefore probably consent to propose it on

---

[1] Mr. Elliot's opinion of the mischievous effect wrought on Mr. Pitt's mind by the representations of the 'Irish Junto' is supported by the expressions used by Mr. Pitt himself in a letter to Lord Cornwallis, wherein he gives his view of the course likely to be adopted by the Speaker, who, according to Mr. Elliot, 'was one of the most unscrupulous and determined enemies to the measure,' and so proved himself by his subsequent conduct. The letter is published in Lord Stanhope's *Life of Pitt*, vol. iii. p. 160.

the conditions agreed to by Pitt. Elliot is still in a
degree of doubt whether he will retain his situation
being determined not to vote against the Catholics;
but he is much pressed to return both by Lord Cornwallis and Lord Castlereagh, and I think may still go.'

'November 24, 1798.

   'Douglas [1] has been hard at work on the Union and
has written and collected two volumes of manuscript
on the subject. This has been done with the privity
of Pitt, who, as Douglas says, approves very much of
what he has done. He is all in the Protestant politics
in Ireland, and I conclude therefore Pitt is so too.
Pitt has acted a strange part in this Irish business, and
I hardly see how he will get out of it. I should not be
surprised if it led to Lord Cornwallis's resignation.
He is, in fact, not supported, and the Irish faction are
listened to just as our factious friends were from Corsica.
To avoid the danger of a rupture with Lord Cornwallis, which would certainly do more to shake Pitt
than almost any other event could, I think it not unlikely that the Union may be dropped altogether. I
think Elliot improved and strengthened in his mind
and talents. Nothing can exceed the degree of estimation in which he is held by everybody who has acted
with him. Lord Cornwallis and Lord Castlereagh are
as anxious to keep him as Lord Camden and Pelham
were.

   'Lady Nelson has given me a letter from Nelson to

<hr />

[1] Sylvester Douglas.

herself to copy for you. It is so fine that I asked leave to copy it.[1] It relates to a storm which appears to have been the true reason of his not coming up with Bonaparte at Malta.'

'Monday, November 26, 1798.

'Elliot has determined not to return to Ireland to stay. He is writing to Lord Cornwallis to-day to say so. His motive for this resolution is the determination of Government to exclude the Catholics in the Union. He will not vote with them on that point, and thinks he should do harm by staying and voting against them. This business has been most strangely managed here. Lord Cornwallis will be perfectly disgusted with it, and Government here are throwing upon him the exclusion of the Catholics, though they know that his opinion was exactly the contrary. Elliot is acting on pure and honourable principles, and on every view of the matter is right.'

'Sunday, December 2, 1798.

'Yesterday we all dined at Colonel Dillon's. In the evening came M. and Mdme. de Boigne, the D'Osmonds, Pozzo di Borgo, and a number of emigrants. M. de Boigne is by no means so old nor so shocking as I expected, though very unlike a match for Adèle.[2] He

---

[1] The letter referred to is given at length in the Despatches of Lord Nelson, by Sir N. H. Nicolas, vol. iii. p. 17.

[2] Madame de Boigne, daughter of the Duc d'Osmond, was for many years a *marquant* personage in the society of Paris and of London, and there are many who retain reminiscences of her, and of the somewhat formidable circle over which she presided, both in her *salon* at Paris and in her pretty marine villa at Trouville.

does not look above fifty, and is a tall, stout, hale-looking man, with a coarse rough sort of favour, and very much like one's idea of a foreign sergeant become an officer. The contrast with his wife is no doubt striking, for she is the smallest and most delicate piece of Sévres china I ever saw unbaked, and extremely beautiful in that way ; which, however, seems fitter for a mantel-piece than the home of a Swiss grenadier. I am told that M. de Boigne's good health and constitution gives great discontent to all her family, who are languishing for a chance of his death, and speak of it without reserve or I think much decency.

'I went with Windham to Blackheath yesterday. We saw Princess Charlotte, with whom the Princess seems to be on the best terms. She is a fine, lively, thriving child of three years old. I am extremely glad that you are so well satisfied with my having spoken in the House of Lords, and have always great pleasure in the *mention honorable* of your council, which is a great reward and a great motive for well-doing. But I still expect the whip and spur, both on that subject and on that of application to the Ministers. I must nevertheless conform myself, on both those subjects, to my own judgment, feelings, and even constitution. With regard to speaking in the House, I know I cannot persevere too much in that practice. With regard to the other, I shall do what is necessary and reasonable ; but I shall not force myself too much on that point in opposition to feelings which are fit to be listened to. There is so much disgust and humiliation in the sort of importunity which is required even for obtaining rigorous justice, that it approaches very near to meanness to submit to it. What I must aim at is to set myself on higher ground by obtaining a larger share of public and Parliamentary consideration. While I am a mere suitor even for justice, I shall probably be treated as such, and nothing diminishes real weight and estimation so much as that posture. Indeed, too much anxiety and earnestness in pursuits of interest lowers, in the end, even one's own character and estimation of oneself. In all this there is a medium, and I should wish neither to fall short of private duties nor to overshoot them, so as to sacrifice a just sense of personal dignity to matters of interest. I have, in the meanwhile, little or no doubt that I shall in the end be placed more in my own form than I have hitherto been. I shall decline no exertion or sacrifice that consists in personal labour, privation, or even hazard. If by such means any prospect of improving the fortunes of the family should occur, I shall not reject or neglect it; but I really cannot go further.

'A state of expectation and anxiety on such subjects, if too much indulged, not only degrades us in the opinion of others, but does really and truly give a sordid cast to the character, which I cannot bear to acquire or seem to possess. Your wishes and expectations of exertion on my side are most natural, and I am always concerned to disappoint you.''

---

¹ The latter part of this letter was written in answer to one from Lady Minto urging him to apply for employment either at home or abroad.

‘ Friday, December 7, 1798.

‘ Our dinner at Blackheath consisted of Lady Jane Dundas, Lady Charlotte Greville, and Lady Mary Bentinck. Some men, among whom was Tom Grenville, disappointed her (the Princess of Wales). Princess Charlotte was in the room till dinner, and is really one of the finest and pleasantest children I ever saw. The Princess of Wales romped with her about the carpet on her knees as I might have done with *Princess* Catherine. Princess Charlotte, though very lively and excessively fond of romp and play, is remarkably good and governable. One day she had been a little naughty, however, and they were reprimanding her. Amongst the rest, Miss Garth said to her, “ You have been so very naughty I don’t know what we must do with you.” The little girl answered, crying and quite penitently, “ You must *soot* me,” meaning shoot her—but they let her off rather cheaper. Our dinner was pleasant as could be.’

‘ December 1, 1798.

‘ I have been attending the boys these two days to the play; the last night to “ Lovers’ Vows,” in Lady Palmerston’s box. Another German, sentimental, Jacobinical play, meant to recommend the frailties of ladies as amiable and interesting, and to exhibit the

---

She reminded him that abilities such as his are not given ‘ to fust in us unused ; ’ and that having abandoned a professional for a political career, he owed it to himself and to his family not to let this drift away from him for want of such exertions as were alone required to place him in a prominent position.

vices and ridicules of rank, and the virtues of the poor. It is also intended to level ranks and fortunes, and legitimate with illegitimate offspring. The heroine is a young girl who falls in love with the tutor, and proposes herself to him in a way that is intended to recommend to all ladies in their teens that charming frankness and disinterested love. The proud baron is brought to consent and to join their hands. The " Stranger " is the most stupid thing I ever saw.

' Talking of the " Stranger " last night, Mr. Wallace was violent against the moral of that play ; but I stuck to my text of pardon from mortal to mortal of any possible offence, truly repented of, still more of pardon from man to woman of frailty. I swore that I should certainly forgive my own wife for any impossible frailty or offence, and that I could not conceive the possibility of parting from, and giving up to misery, one for whom we had true affection ; that the world might be right, as I think they would, to exercise a strict discipline, but that neither husband nor father could be required to abandon or destroy what he loved. Wallace was furious, and said he thought he should shoot his wife through the head if she should be unfaithful in any circumstances. This is carrying morality a good way, and I cannot help thinking it would require a great many infidelities to make up the guilt of one murder.'

'December 10, 1798.

'Yesterday in the morning I went with Pozzo di Borgo to visit the Prussian Chargé d'Affaires, who is a great friend of his, and a very sensible man, well informed on the affairs of the Continent. They have not condescended, however, to give him any intimation of Tom Grenville's mission to Berlin, and he will probably not have an opportunity of even seeing him. This is an ungracious and clumsy way of doing such business. After breakfast this morning Elliot and I walked to Roehampton, where I got some books. Elliot has received letters from Lord Castlereagh which must now determine him to return to Ireland. It seems that the leading Catholics themselves think it most advantageous to their future views to waive any new concessions on the occasion of the proposed Union, and not so to embarrass that measure as must in the end prove prejudicial to them.'

'Eden Farm: Saturday, December 15, 1798.

'I came here last night with Lord Auckland from Blackheath, where we had one of the grand dinners. The Prince and Princess of Orange and one of their sons, Lord and Lady Grenville, Lord Thurlow, Lord George Cavendish, Sir John Stepney, Lady Elgin, Mrs. and Miss Lisle. I sat near Lord Grenville, who gave us the news which you will see in the papers of Bonaparte's death and the probable destruction of his army. It seems likely to be true, and Lord Grenville appears to believe it. But it still stands on the authority of the Turkish Government.

'. . . The Princess (of Wales) tried hard to get a private word or two with me; but, being of the modest sex, I was so coy she could not accomplish her whole purpose, though, after all, I thought too much was done for discretion. She told me that she had received two days before a letter from the Prince, desiring her to dine at Carlton House and inviting her to settle there for the winter; and that she had declined. I told her she was wrong, and begged her to reflect seriously on any step she might take if similar overtures were renewed; but she said she was a very determined person when she had once formed an opinion, and that her resolution was fixed on this point; that she knew I should think her a very wicked woman, but that I did not know and could not imagine all the circumstances; otherwise I might agree with her. She seemed very eager, and talked with so much action and earnestness that I was in the horrors all the time, knowing all the eyes that were upon her. I told her we must not talk any more, and she acquiesced, but asked me to come to a small dinner next week. I shall persist on my text of the necessity for not refusing the Prince's offers of reconciliation. It is the only advice I can give. At the same time I confess I think that his character and her inclinations are so impossible to alter, that the experiment will fail if it is made, and, I fear, leave her so far worse than she now is, that the blame of their separation may probably enough be laid at her door, on grounds sufficiently plausible to deprive her of the sympathy and interest which at present accompany her retirement.

'Prudence is totally wanting in her.   When her subject engages her, her eyes and countenance speak louder than many people, Mrs. Robinson for example, could bawl at the top of their voices.   The Prince has got 40,000*l.* from Germany.—Lord Castlereagh has arrived and Elliot's departure is fixed, sore against his wish. I saw Lord Cornwallis's letter to him, which is very pressing but expressive of the most real confidence and of the highest opinion of him.   Indeed Lord Cornwallis will want all the friends he can muster, for there is not one of the Irish Government, from the highest office down to the common clerks in the Postoffice or Custom House, who is not open-mouthed against him in public and in all companies.   This might signify less if he could depend on support here; but Elliot thinks Pitt quite indifferent if not worse about him, although his mission was Pitt's own measure exclusively, since it was done without the knowledge of any other Minister.   It seems difficult to get through such an arduous measure as the Union in this state of things, considering especially that these Irish Members of Government are in their hearts, and perhaps with their hands, privately against the Union. The Catholics are taking a most moderate and sensible line. . . .   Elliot thinks, however, that Lord Cornwallis will undertake and try to push it through under all these disadvantages, but that he may not improbably be left at some bad step in the mire by Ministers in England.'

' December 18, 1798.

' I have had a long conversation with Dundas about himself. He got again on his old objections to a peerage. He talked very freely of his views, and said he would almost ask advice. · That he is determined not to stay in the House of Commons after the end of the present Parliament; that he shall have served the public forty years, and that he is entitled to repose ; that his determination is taken and nothing shall induce him to change it, though his age is not great, being no more than sixty. I presume the late alarms about his health enter into these speculations. That it became a question whether he should accept a peerage, and by that means exclude his descendants from the House of Commons. That for his own part he should prefer a simple retreat with his own name ; but he could, nevertheless, suppose it possible that after a life dedicated to public affairs he might, even in his retreat, wish to have an opportunity of taking his share in the House of Lords on any great affair that might arise. That his son was not ambitious and had not turned his thoughts to political pursuits, so that his exclusion from the House of Commons would not disappoint any views of his. But that a grandson might have another taste, and he always felt a peerage to be a disqualification for the most flattering and important situations in this country, and that, besides, it excluded the eldest son from the profession of the law. I gave, however, my advice for the peerage : I allowed that his own personal consideration would not be affected by it ;

but urged that it would place his descendants in so advantageous a position as to consideration, and even as to political views, that nothing but the most soaring ambition, and the determination to be first minister,[1] could well be frustrated by it ; and that when the day came for his retreat, I thought the country would like to see him retain at least the hold of public life which a seat in the House of Lords would give him.   He ended by saying there were three years to consider of it.'

'December 20, 1798.

'Elliot went to St. James's yesterday to take leave. I never saw anybody more averse to what he is going about.   Indeed that country is always disgusting to those who do not resemble them ; and at present the Government is in a state which I have learnt to think possible, but which the public cannot conceive.   Lord Cornwallis, sent there in a moment of extreme peril to counteract the mischievous violence of an Irish party ; that party instantly listened to in London ; Lord Cornwallis's measure sacrificed to their views ; and Lord Cornwallis, now charged with the most arduous undertaking imaginable, with every man employed by him in open and indecent opposition, and with the total desertion by Government in England.   The Duke of Portland and Lord Cornwallis are not on writing terms,

---

[1] It is remarkable that in 1798 the peerage should have been considered as likely to prove a disqualification for the Premiership.   In the following half century no less than seven peers held the office—Lord Grenville, Lord Liverpool, Lord Goderich, Lord Grey, Duke of Wellington, Lord Melbourne, and Lord Derby.

though the correspondence is properly in that office. Dundas is, however, entirely on the side of Lord Cornwallis, and he was so warm on the question of including the Catholics, that he had declared he should withdraw from the discussion of the Union if they were to be excluded.   Lord Cornwallis has, however, entreated him and prevailed on him to acquiesce on that point—at least, to attend the measure, exactly by the same arguments which he used to carry·Elliot back to Ireland, viz., the desire of the Catholics themselves to waive their claims on the present occasion.   Elliot showed me Lord Cornwallis's letter to him, and Dundas read me his.   Dundas spoke strongly on the way in which that business has been managed in London, and seemed to feel that Pitt had been guilty of some duplicity in ascribing the exclusion of the Catholics to Lord Cornwallis's opinion that it was impracticable to carry the Union otherwise, at a time when he was in possession of Lord Cornwallis's positive declaration that it would be as easy to carry it the other way, and that the measure would be deprived of half its value if that Catholic point were not secured by it.   Elliot thinks there is some dryness between Dundas and Pitt on this subject ; but I don't think that will last, even if it is so now.   Elliot and Pelham are just come in.   They came from Burlington House, and the news to-day is that Minorca is certainly taken.

' The Directory has declared war against the King of Naples and Sardinia.   The correspondence between General Mack, an Austrian general commanding the

Neapolitan army, and Mr. Championet, the French general at Rome, is published in the French papers. Championet complains of the Neapolitan troops having entered the territory of the Roman Republic. Mack answers that the conquest of the Roman territory took place after the treaty of Campo Formio, and contrary to its tenour, and requires Championet to withdraw the French troops from the Roman territory, protesting that he shall consider his refusal to do so, or the entrance of French troops into the Tuscan territory, as a declaration of war. The continental war, therefore, seems once more begun.'

'Reigate :¹ Monday, December 24, 1798.

'We like ourselves so well that we have all determined to stay till Wednesday ; and you would like us as well as we do ourselves, as you will allow when I name the party— Elliot, Windham, Pelham, and I. I send you some verses I have written to Emma Crewe : to understand them you must know that she has always expressed a most unnatural preference for youth, and that she gave in general to Windham and me very much the same reception as Susannah did to the more ancient elders, though we certainly did not put ourselves so much in the way of deserving it. However, the idea of her beauty making us still young is the subject. There is nothing very new in the political world. As to Italy, though I am glad to see the war recommence and the French driven from

---

¹ Mr. Elliot's country residence was situated near Reigate.

Rome, and although I trust these measures are concerted with the Emperor, yet I confess I am impatient to see the Emperor act, or at least declare war; for I have no great confidence in that court; or, to say the truth, in any other. The French have gained an immense, and perhaps irretrievable advantage by the possession of Piedmont. It must cost the Emperor campaigns to take from them all those strong places, and the passes of the Alps; and before he comes to that he has Mantua and Lombardy to recover. On the other hand, Leghorn in our hands is a capital point. You will be sorry to hear that poor Sir W. Hamilton [1] has lost his collection of vases, which he had embarked on board the "Colossus," lately shipwrecked at the Isle of Scilly. It will go far, I think, to break his heart, and I am really most heartily grieved at his loss. There seem to be apprehensions of a renewal of the disturbances in Ireland. An Irish Directory still subsists in Dublin, and they are organising a fresh insurrection. Lord Cornwallis has countermanded his daughter Lady Mary Singleton, not thinking Dublin an eligible residence for her.'

'January 1, 1799.

'Tom Grenville has returned after being nine days in very bad weather. They could not get into the Elbe for the ice. I understand he is coming to town, and I know the frigate is coming to the Nore; so that his mission, it is to be hoped, is not pressing.

[1] ' Sir W. Hamilton was wont to say that his wife was the only woman he had seen who had all the lines of his vase.'—*Lady Elliot to Sir G. Elliot*, 1795.

'I cannot think without uneasiness of the extreme cold of your journey.[1] I have been lamenting over the poor wretches who have no fire or even home to go to in such weather; and that is exactly the case with my wife and four of my children. But Joseph (the man-servant) seems most to be pitied, and if the weather continues so intense you should take a chaise for him. I can perfectly understand the fatigue of mind, at least, attending a travelling nursery, to which, I am afraid, I should oppose less patience than you. As for the children, pleasure is a pellisse that defies frost and snow till it gets old and threadbare, which is not the case with them.

'I dined on Saturday with the Aucklands, and Dr. Heath[2] came after dinner. He talked favourably of Gilbert, and particularly of his character. I said I was quite satisfied about that, and only wished him to get on in his studies. He also spoke favourably on that point, but I humbly conceive he knows little of the matter. I showed him great civility on the Auckland plan, and carried him home in my carriage.'

'January 7, 1799.

'I carried Windham yesterday to Blackheath. It was extremely pleasant. Our party was the Speaker, Tom Grenville, Windham, the Cholmondeleys, and myself. The Speaker seems smitten with the Princess's nature and good nature, and will be one of the knights of the round tower. I had several confidences in loud whispers before watchful eyes, which mean nothing and

[1] From Minto.   [2] Head master of Eton.

worry me not a little. The Speaker, though no genius, is cheerful and conversible, and very civil, which always makes good company.[1]

' January 9.'

'I went yesterday to Lord Grenville, and made my offer of service on the Continent, if it should be thought advisable to employ me on any special mission. He received the matter civilly enough, but of course without saying anything positive on the subject. He talked freely and fully enough on Continental politics, which I confess I think in an unpromising state. Naples engaged in these hostilities not only without concert, but contrary to the advice of the Emperor, and with a declaration that he would not support them. Lord Grenville seems to think the King of Naples justified, even in these circumstances, in beginning the war, because he could not avoid it in the end, and he might make it more advantageously by attacking than by waiting for the enemy. He also hopes to force the Emperor into the war by the necessity of preventing the conquest of Naples; but I confess it seems to me otherwise, and Naples was so sure of immediate defeat, single-handed, against France, that it is only a means of depriving the Allies of the assistance to be derived from Naples if the war really becomes general.

'I have seen Austria play the fool or rogue for so many years, that I can't expect much from her.

'Lord Nelson and I are asked to meet Pitt at Lord Darnley's.'

---

[1] This and the following letters are addressed to Lady Minto at Park Place.

'January 21, 1799.

'I have heard a good deal of Lord Camelford's business. The Chancellor has taken the lead in treating the business as a puerile 'vivacity, rather meritorious than criminal. The fact is that he fell into company with the captain of the "Hoche" in England, and passed himself on him for a disaffected person and a friend of France. He obtained by these means a letter from him to the Municipality, I think, of Paris, stating that the citizen who would present that letter was one of the most ardent friends of the French Republic; that he had occasion to confer with one of the Directors (Barras), and that he expected the Municipality to forward him immediately to the Directory *pour le salut de la République*. He was taken actually embarked for France with this letter upon him. Langley, you know, was hanged for intending to embark with a printed paper, not a bit stronger, in his great-coat pocket. The defence is a declaration of Lord Camelford's own concerning his motives, which he alleges to have been merely a curiosity to see Paris in its present state, with a sort of general idea of procuring information that might be useful to this country, but not with a view to any particular service that he had in contemplation; that he only meant to stay a few days and find his way back; that he had long had this curiosity, and thought the present interval, while his ship was not on active service, a favourable opportunity. The only evidence to support the defence is that of a Swiss gentleman of good cha-

racter for loyalty, who proved that Lord Camelford had
communicated, some time ago, a scheme to him of attacking South America, and had meant to employ him
in it, and that he had also proposed to employ him in
the south of France to obtain information and communicate with him in the Mediterranean, so as to enable him to strike some blow there. For this purpose
he had actually advanced, or lodged at a banker's for
this gentleman, 3,000*l.* of his own money, which he let
this gentleman believe was furnished by Government.
On this the Chancellor was for discharging him at
once; but Pitt, it seems, had scruples, and Windham
took a part in opposing that measure.   The question
came to be whether he should be tried for high treason,
in which case his treasonable *intentions* must be
proved, or whether he should be tried on the late Act
which makes it felony to go to France, whether your
intentions are good or bad.   The Attorney-General
declared he could not prosecute him for high treason,
because it was evident that his intention was not treasonable, but just the reverse, *very loyal*; and that it
would be improper to try him for felony, because then
the proof of his good intentions could not be brought
forward, since they would not prevent his coming
within the provisions of the Act, and this would be un-
just.   As he could not be tried with propriety, and yet
was guilty of a capital offence, it followed that a pardon should be given him, which was accordingly determined.   But it was at the same time declared in the
minutes of council that it would not be advisable to

employ him again in the Navy.   He is certainly mad.
I dined yesterday at Mr. Wickham's : a foreign party,
the Duke de Bourbon, Duc d'Harcourt, Évêque St.
Pol de Léon, Cazalès, and who but Baron de Rolle who
was sent for from Edinburgh [1] to speak to the character
of the Swiss gentleman who was examined in Lord
Camelford's favour.   I dine at the Duke of Portland's
to-day.'

' January 24, 1799.

'Lord Malmesbury and I have settled to come together to Park Place on Sunday.   You will see the
debate in the House of Commons in the papers.   The
House of Lords was silent, and despatched the business soon enough to let us dine at Blackheath.   The
party was Lord Malmesbury, the Lavingtons, Sheffields
Jack Payne, and I.   Lord Malmesbury has been uneasy
all along at being asked, especially with Jack Payne,
who we know has been in disgrace ever since he brought
the Princess to England and restrained Lady Jersey's
impertinence on board ship.   Then the Queen's visit
to the Princess at Carlton House yesterday added to
Lord Malmesbury's uneasiness, and he frequently said
he believed she had gone there on purpose to enquire
about this dinner.   One of the first things the Princess
said at dinner was that the Queen had asked her if she
staid in town, and she had answered no—that she had
company at dinner at Blackheath.   The Queen asked
who, and the Princess said, Lord and Lady Lavington,
Jack Payne, and Lord Malmesbury.   This was dreadful :

---

[1] The Baron de Rolle was attached to the French Court at Holyrood.

however, it may be the less fatal, as the Prince lately
met Jack Payne for the first time since his disgrace
and spoke to him with great cordiality and affection.
The principal turn of the conversation was a good-
natured attack and defence between the Princess and
Lord Malmesbury concerning the vigilance and duenna-
ship of his proxyhood.'

' January 25.

' The Irish papers are full of violent resolutions
from several fresh counties.   However, I understand
Government expects to carry the question in the House
of Commons by about sixty majority, which is all that
can be desired.

' Canning's last speech on the Union was less successful than the former.   I am told it made no impression
at all.   Pitt's voice, it seems, failed him in the course
of his speech, but he rallied and recovered his usual
powers.   He is thought, however, to have been led by
this incident to use some expressions of diffidence in his
strength, which I have not heard exactly reported, but
was something of this sort, that he would employ his
remaining strength, or power, or faculties in carrying
through this measure.   It was one of his very fine
speeches.'

' Saturday, January 26.

' The question on the Union was carried in the
Irish House of Commons by *one* vote, and the Address
was afterwards carried by a majority of two.   The
majority in the House of Lords was considerable for

the Union.   The measure is, no doubt, lost for the present; however, it is not given up, and all hope of carrying it even this session is not abandoned.   It is still intended to proceed in England with the preliminary measure of a declaration by Parliament in favour of a union ; and the resolutions will still be voted.   At least, such was the intention of the Cabinet to-day.   There were some members who were to support the Union that went away during the debate, which lasted till one o'clock after noon of the next day.   There were eighty speakers ; almost a hundred of the House were absent.

' Shocking news from Italy.   The Neapolitan troops have begged to be excused everywhere.   They have fled and deserted uniformly.   The Royal Family have embarked for Sicily, and the enemy must now be in possession of Naples.   I am most sincerely grieved at this event.   Europe seems ripe, or rather rotten, for destruction.   I should not be surprised to see my Queen in a straw hat in England yet.'

Throughout the spring Lord Minto and Mr. Elliot continued to exchange letters in which the question of the Union was the chief topic discussed.   Lord Minto's views are mainly to be gathered from Mr. Elliot's letters, as his own have not been preserved ; but from the tone of Mr. Elliot's it is clear that both correspondents considered the determination of Mr. Pitt to drop Catholic Emancipation out of the Government measure as a lamentable concession to the Protestant faction. In their minds two propositions appear to have been indissolubly connected.

I. That Protestant ascendency should be abolished, and the Catholics admitted to equality of political rights and privileges with their fellow-subjects.

II. That under the circumstances existing in 1799, this could only be done with safety and justice by incorporating the Irish Parliament with the Imperial Legislature.

It is obvious that when the first proposition was dropped, the policy of the second became more doubtful. 'It is doubtful,' wrote Mr. Elliot, 'whether the measure of union under such circumstances will not be worse than none.'[1] Lord Minto thought differently. Though holding as strongly as his kinsman the opinion that Catholic Emancipation should be conceded in the treaty of union itself, it was his conviction that, failing this, it would be secured at no long distance of time, by a measure which he believed would draw closer the bonds of union between the two countries. But as his opinions are stated at length in a speech made by him

---

[1]   *Mr. Elliot to Lord Minto.*

Chapel House : January 1, 1799.

I sleep here to-night and hope to get a stage beyond Shrewsbury to-morrow. If I felt zeal about the enterprise in which I am embarking, I should go without reluctance ; but as the inclusion of Catholics and the modification of tithes are relinquished, the measure of an union stands so denuded of advantages, that I have much doubt about the policy of it. Such a subservience too has been displayed by Government here to the dominating Irish faction, that I do not believe Ireland would gain much in points of equity and impartiality of administration. Thus bereaved of all trust and confidence, I am also without the ardour which ought to accompany, or rather to urge me into, such a conflict.

in the House of Lords (March 19, 1799), we shall endeavour to give an abstract of them here, premising that it is scarcely possible to do justice by so summary a process to what was, in fact, an elaborate disquisition on the relations of the two countries. The speech was one of those which commanded most attention at the time, and congratulations poured in upon him from all sides.

Lord Minto began by the assertion that the British Islands, viewed simply in their natural relation to each other, must of necessity form one State for their mutual security and happiness.

Assuming this as granted, he passed on to an exhaustive examination of the various kinds of connection which might exist between them, dwelling especially on a federal connection, as 'in the variety of opinions entertained on this question of union with Ireland, some have been supposed to lean towards a connection of that nature.' But he explained himself to have been influenced in an opposite direction by recent examples of the rapidity with which federal states may be disunited to their summary overthrow; instancing the United Provinces and the Swiss Cantons, and pointing at the threatened dissolution of the grandest confederacy the world ever knew, that of the Germanic Bund. His own experience of the 'occasional confederacies of mere allies' had tended to strengthen his objections to federal government. 'We shall frequently observe them more occupied in the internal jealousies and competitions of the confederate states, than in promoting the common cause; and especially in moments of common danger and exertion, they will often discover a greater apprehension of contributing a grain too much in the federal scale, than a grain too little for the success of that object which is the only rational motive for exertion at all.'

Coming to the form of connection actually existing between the two countries, he said: 'We have a common Prince with separate Parliaments. Ireland claims a sovereign independent government, and that claim is freely admitted by our own; while we exercise nevertheless, with the acquiescence of Ireland, an open ascendency and control in every one of its concerns.'

In an earlier portion of his speech, a closely-reasoned argument had been made to show that such a 'partial connection of Government between two unequal countries is not a permanent condition in which they can settle;' that 'it is not a stationary point, but merely transitive and progressive, is but a stage or resting-place, tending either to total separation or to perfect and entire consolidation and union.'

Experience of 'the grievous and abhorrent union of nominal independence with real subordination,' producing discords ever tending to separation, had determined the union of Scotland with England.[1] The

---

[1] 'I will venture to assure your lordships, and to speak for my neighbours as well as for myself, that at this day we see without humiliation or regret those towers and beacons which were very necessary appendages of our independence at least before the union of the crowns, when we had a predatory enemy within ten miles of us; we behold, I say, without mortification or concern, those badges of imperial dignity mouldering and in ruins on our rocks, while we can see the plains below

true touchstone on which the virtue of connection and of mutual engagements may be proved is their efficiency in strengthening the empire in a crisis of difficulty, 'in repelling danger from without, in reconciling the minds of the nations within, and finally in cementing and perpetuating their union.'   Despite, however, the indubitable fact that 'the Irish Government, the Irish Parliament, a great portion of the property of Ireland, of its gentry, and even of its people, had made exertions of courage, activity, perseverance, spirit, as well as of fidelity and honour, in fulfilling the engagements of their connection with us, and in the protection and defence of their country, which challenge the thanks of Great Britain and the approbation of the world,—'in spite of such undoubted facts there was in existence an extensive and desperate conspiracy, aiming avowedly and distinctly against the connection of Great Britain and Ireland.   'The grievance which they have risen to redress is that connection, the course which these manifestoes proclaim, the standard under which they muster and fight, is Separation.'

After an eloquent exposition of the miseries which would be produced to Ireland by separation, he arrived at the most important part of his speech, that in which he urged union as the only escape from ' the horns of a

covered with crops, which he who sows is now sure of reaping; and while we can extend our views of national instinct and dignity, and all our public feelings, whether of pride or of affection, not only beyond the little range of hills that we look upon, but to the remotest extremities of the habitable globe.'

dilemma that, allowed to exist, would gore and lacerate their country—namely, Protestant or Catholic ascendency.

' Ireland is a divided country, but unequally divided as to property and numbers ; the least numerous class possessing the property and the power ; but the most numerous entertaining, and indeed cherishing fondly and tenaciously, claims on both, I mean both on the property and the power. . . . Everyone knows the firm and immovable basis on which their mutual hatred stands, the irreconcilable nature of its motives, its bitter, malignant, and implacable character. In this frame and temper of mind, however, towards each other, one of these portions of Ireland claims and exercises what is felt by both to be a species of dominion over the other. I believe it is hardly too much to say that there are two nations in Ireland ; two Irish peoples ; the one sovereign, the other subject. The sovereign class or caste of Irishmen claim their sovereignty as of right, and ground it on an old title of conquest, confirmed, as they contend, by possession, acquiescence, and prescription. They claim also the federal support of Great Britain in maintaining this dominion on the solemn grounds of fidelity to implied compact, compensation for sacrifices and reward for services.

.   .   .   .   .

' I must confess that I have always felt this point as constituting a true and proper dilemma. On the one hand, I cannot admit the ascendency of one part of a nation over another part of the same nation, to the extent and to the purpose claimed in Ireland, as capable of assuming any character deserving the name of right.

. . . . . .

'On the other hand, that part of Ireland which we would wish to redress, claim not only political equality in the government of their country—a claim in which I 'confess I cannot help sympathising with them—but they are known to entertain and nourish yet more fondly and anxiously, though perhaps not yet so loudly or distinctly pronounced, claims of a very different nature. We cannot be ignorant that the first application of those rights with which we should be disposed to invest them would be the perpetuation of a great wrong; and that at bottom that wrong was, perhaps, the true and constant object of their actual demand, and would be the practical result of its attainment. The Catholics of Ireland not only claim a participation in the civil franchises enjoyed by their Protestant countrymen, but they foster claims on the property of Protestants, the present possession of which they treat as mere usurpation; and these claims are of no trifling extent. We know the aspiring character of their church, or, if you please, of all churches, or of all bodies and descriptions of men. We must above all recollect what is, perhaps, more urgent than all the rest, that the Catholics, besides their claims civil or religious, have passions to gratify, passions long irritated, long restrained, and not on that account the less vehement or dangerous.

. . . . . .

'I am not more clear therefore in thinking the Catholics entitled to a fair participation in the civil and political franchises of Irishmen, than I am in feeling that the Protestants ought to be protected and defended in the security of their property, their religion, and their persons, against every violence which the Catholics might be disposed to attempt when they have passed from their present state of subjection to that of authority and power. The dilemma, therefore, has hitherto consisted in this : the Protestants could not be supported in that ascendency which seems necessary even for their protection, without derogating from what may appear to be a natural right of the Catholics. The Catholics could not be supported in their claim of equality, without transferring to them that ascendency which equality of rights must draw to the larger body, and which from that moment must expose the Protestants to dangers from which they ought to be protected.

.   .   .   .   .   .

'I do sincerely think that this divided and double condition of the Irish people requires something of an *imperial aula*, a legislature founded on a broader and more liberal basis, to administer impartial laws to all, and to reconcile security with justice. While one of these parties must judge the other, in whichever hand the *fasces* may be placed, I fear there is only reason to expect violence in the suit, and if not injustice, at least slow and imperfect justice, in the decree.

'If the Union, therefore, permits a hope of meliorating the condition, and extinguishing the discontents, of a great majority of the people of Ireland without exposing the rest to danger, . . . I must confess myself, on that account, a warm friend to the measure ; and I am free to confess that if these were not to be the consequences, I should expect very little advantage by it. I am desirous, therefore, of declaring for myself, that I shall think the Union much more perfect, much better adapted to all its beneficial ends, if the just claims of the Catholic Irish are provided for by an express article of the treaty itself.

' After having thus declared my own mind, and distinctly pronounced my own judgment on this great leading point, I think it right to add that if any political peculiarities of the present time should render it impracticable to express those wholesome provisions in the written treaty itself, I would rather restrain my wishes for the accomplishment of this desirable end, than expose this great transaction to needless and unprofitable hazard by unreasonable pertinacity or impatience.'

The speech concluded by an examination of the competence of the English and Irish legislatures to pass an Act of Union. In the case of the union with Scotland ' a separate Parliament existed in both countries, and the respective Parliaments were the parties in the treaty ; that treaty was negotiated under the authority of the two Parliaments ; they sanctioned the conclusion, and they constructed finally and irreversibly that happy system, under which we now live secure, at the distance of almost a century.'

In a letter from Mr. Elliot to Lord Minto at Vienna, dated August 14, 1799, the following passage occurs:— ' It is impossible to describe to you the effect which your speech on the Union has produced in Ireland. You have acquired by it a great name and reputation, and even a considerable interest in the country. It has obtained us several *real* and *sincere* proselytes, and those who from other reasons than conviction have been induced to take another line, attribute their change of conduct to your speech. The latter circumstance you will perhaps not think very complimentary to the merits of your speech, but nothing can prove more forcibly the estimation in which it is held than its being resorted to as the general and ostensible ground of conversion. The Union certainly is rapidly progressive in public opinion. The Catholics are favourable to it, which I think very important. We are also gaining strength in Parliament; but the measure cannot be accomplished unless the English Government are very liberal both in patronage and in the money which must be given in compensation for the disfranchised boroughs. The Government of Ireland has hitherto been a monopoly, which we have now to purchase.'

In these words all is said that can be said for the means employed to effect the act of union. A monopoly of power was purchased from one section of Irishmen, with the honest intention of using that power for the benefit of all sections of Irishmen. Whatever may be said as to the immorality of the course, it was not that worst immorality which corrupts the pure. Under the system to be abolished corruption had been the rule.[1]

Lady Minto joined her husband in London, in January 1799. No more letters were consequently exchanged between them until they were again separated by his departure on a special mission to Vienna, which took place in July. But, in order not to interrupt the narrative of his proceedings at Vienna, we shall place here some correspondence addressed to Lord Minto at various periods of the year relating to the Princess of Wales.

Up to the summer of 1799 there had been nothing in the Princess's conduct to justify censure. The most

---

[1] Many hard things have been said as to the immorality of the means by which the Union was brought about; a most severe indictment having been drawn up against those partaking in its 'infamy' by one of the most gifted of Ireland's living sons. But no moral judgments are wholly just when passed on facts viewed apart from the general condition of the times in which they occurred. To us it seems that corruption was the rule, instead of the exception, in all the dealings of politicians from Walpole to Pitt. Jobbing was universal; immense patronage was at the command of an administration and of many private individuals. If, therefore, the necessity of buying out the borough-mongers had prevented the Union, the birth of a new virtue would have been ill-timed. Peerages were no doubt bestowed wholesale; but though the days of such gross corruption are past, we have heard it said that even in our time, strangely pertinacious requests are made by those who think their services or support worthy of reward; and applications abound for ribbands, blue, green and red, and for caps with balls which might be more appropriately caps with bells. The crime which England has to deplore was the failure to the Catholics, if not of pledged faith, of hopes encouraged and believed. If, indeed, Pitt kept the promise to the ear, he broke it to the hope; but then again it should not be forgotten that the influences brought to bear upon him were Irish ones. It is noteworthy that the great Irish leaders Flood and Lord Charlemont had both opposed the Catholic claims.

constant frequenters of her society were elderly statesmen with their wives and connections, with whom
the Princess dined, and worked, and talked, doing
nothing worse than leaving those who were tedious to
her to wait in-doors for the carriages which were to
carry them back to town, while she walked in the Park
with more interesting companions, making confidences
of her wrongs to the embarrassment of the gentlemen,
and draggling her skirts to the horror of her ladies.

But in 1799 some more lively elements were introduced into the society of Blackheath ; and the Princess,
with high spirits and no acquired prudence or discretion,
allowed the tone of the society to become so lax and
free that dignity, if not decorum, was placed in peril.
Little games were instituted after dinner and kept up
till the small hours of the morning.   Of those invited
to dinner some were made to stay supper, and others
till sandwiches appeared, which they apparently did
at cock-crow.   Those who cared for her became
seriously distressed at the opportunities recklessly
given to malignant observation.   Fortunately for the
Princess, the most distinguished and agreeable members
of the society had her interests at heart, and were infinitely more sensitive to the dangers she incurred than
she was herself.   With men such as Grey, Canning,
Frere, Spencer, and with such ladies as those of the
North family, she was safe enough ; and they confided
their consternation to Mr. Pitt, who, though alarmed,
was, it was surmised, a little amused, and not a little
curious to see for himself what went on.   He had not

long to wait; and a certain Sunday dinner at Blackheath in August 1799, at which he was present, de-
serves to be reported.

'The Chancellor, Mr. Pitt, Mr. Dundas, Mr. Douglas
and Lady Katherine, Lady Charlotte North, Mrs. Crewe
and Emma Crewe, George Canning, Mr. Frere, and Mr.
Long dined here last Sunday; and we *did* play at musical magic. Mr. Dundas was made, by the power of
harmony, to kiss Miss Emma's hand, on his knees.
Lady Charlotte was to present the Queen of Prussia's
bust to Mr. Pitt, and make him kiss it, which, after
some difficulty, he performed. The Princess was to
tie Mr. Long and Mr. Frere together, and make each
nurse a bolster as a baby. Mrs. Crewe, with all her
caution, was the most frisky in the company, which
amazed some of us much; but the most charming part
of all was that of Mr. Dundas. I do not think he could
be tipsy, for I sat by him at dinner and saw no excess,
but he squeezed the Princess's hand in the tenderest
manner possible, called her angel repeatedly, and said
he hoped no one but himself would know how much he
loved her. What can the old thing mean? It diverts
us extremely; but he is in high favour, and the Princess dines with him on Saturday to meet the Premier.
He was charming on Sunday, and Lady Cholmondeley
and Miss Garth, to whom he was beau, were captivated.
When Blindman's Buff was proposed to him (not in
earnest, I believe), he said, " I will endeavour to shut
my eyes all I can, but I cannot promise the rest of the
world will do the same." The playful manner of his

saying this delighted the Princess.[1] Amongst other
things, he told us that at seven that morning a gentleman arrived at Holwood in a post-chaise and four. Mr.
Canning's servant flew into his room, saying, " Sir!
Sir! here is a great naval victory, and nobody here to
hear it ! Shall I bring the gentleman to your bedside ?"
The house was soon up, and the gentleman told Mr.
Pitt he had travelled all night from Brighton, that his
name was Jenkins, and his business not about the
navy, but the army, which he had a plan for recruiting. He had been reading " Pizarro," and was persuaded
that Rolla's first speech was irresistible ; that he had
read it to numbers at Brighton and to all he met in
the way. Every soul felt its power and had enlisted.
Here he produced a list of all their names, and insisted
that if empowered he could soon raise 200,000 men.
Mad as he was, Mr. Pitt could in no way get rid of him
but by an appointment to meet him in town to-morrow.
Jenkins will, it is supposed, be made into *Jenkinson* ;
the plan given to Lord Hawkesbury, and printed as a
second part of the March to Paris. Mr. Pitt asked for
your verses on Easter Monday, on the favourable representation of Mr. Canning, and praised them as much as
you could desire.'

Lord Minto, though at Vienna, was again urged to
exert his influence with the Princess, who then kept
up a correspondence with him, and in his reply he

---

[1] There was point as well as playfulness in Mr. Pitt's remark, as he
was well aware that a game of musical blindman's buff had been played at
an after-dinner party some days before, to the great consternation of
some of the *convives*,—members of the present party.

says:—'Her spirits will naturally give the preference
to lively society and cheerful pleasures; and I have
always felt it to be a great source of uneasiness to her
true friends, that the eye and opinion of the world
afford very little control in a case where they are so
important. It is not that she undervalues the general
opinion or applause of the world; on the contrary, she
is fonder of it than she perhaps knows herself. But
she has a great contempt for the common observation
of what is called the world, that is of strangers, on the
particulars of her conduct and manners. It has required a constant exertion to enforce these observ-
ances, and it has often been impossible to act up to
one's own notions and feelings on these points without
hazarding a diminution of the influence which one felt
to be useful to her.'

No stronger proof of the unnatural dulness and re-
pression in which her life was passed could be found,
than is afforded by the references in this correspondence
to the occasions that gave play to her natural spirits,
and were afterwards cited as evidence of her indiscretion.   A fine day tempted her to gallop over to Roehampton to pay an impromptu visit to the Palmerstons, when a cricket-match between the servants
and the gentlemen detained her and her lady in waiting tolerably late. 'Nothing could be more gay and
good-humoured,' but it was a 'frisk' not to be often
repeated.   Again, a great deal was said about a party
at Sheffield Park,[1] when the Princess went to visit Lady

[1] Lady Anne North had married Lord Sheffield in 1798.

Sheffield, a new and favourite lady in waiting; the
true account of a day there was thus written by one of
the party :—' She was in great spirits and very happy.
Tom Pelham was delighted with her ; she drove with
Lord Sheffield, in a little chaise, full gallop over roads
considered till then impassable, and Tom Pelham drove
in a kind of tandem, which held four, in the greatest
fright possible.   Lady Margaret [1] groaning, Miss Vane
with a face four yards long, Lady Charlotte [2] laughing,
and Lady Sheffield, on a little pony, crying in expectation of seeing them all scattered over the road with
broken arms and legs.'

But if the severity with which such innocent ' frisks '
were viewed in certain quarters had the effect of increasing the recklessness which became daily more
apparent in the conduct of the Princess, it could not
be denied that there was in her an innate want of discretion, while less than any other woman in the country
was she subject to the criticism, or guided by the example, of her equals ; an influence perhaps not sufficiently taken into account as a power for good.

The Queen seems to have held entirely aloof from her,
and to have confined her supervision of her daughter-
in-law's life to the willing reception of every tale that
was brought against her.   The Princess, meanwhile,
was one of those characters who, without any high
principle of their own, are quick to detect the least
want of it in others.   The somewhat conventional

[1] Lady Margaret Fordyce.
[2] Lady Charlotte North, afterwards Lindsay.

virtues of the Queen she held in contempt ; nor was she backward in seizing occasions to show it.   Having been scolded for inviting to a breakfast a lady about whom rumour had been busy, it happened that not long afterwards a much more notorious offender was proposed to her as a member of her household.   The Princess quickly replied 'that while she did not conceive it wise to enquire too closely into the characters of those she met in public and in general society, she must draw different rules with regard to her intimacy.'

In the course of 1799 the Princess became as anxious for a reconciliation with the Prince as she had been formerly opposed to it.   To an intimate friend she gave as the ground of the change, 'that finding the comforts of her private life to be disturbed by the comments of every observer, and that she could not as she had hoped be *forgotten*, while she indulged herself with innocence and propriety, she had now only two things to look to : the one a sort of reconciliation which would give her the sanction of a husband's presence ; the other, if that failed, retirement to her native land, where an income, trifling here, would afford her everything she wished, with the friends of her youth.   This project is at the moment fixed in her mind.'

A letter written by Lady Minto after a visit to Blackheath describes her at this period, and not unpleasantly.

'Spring Gardens: October 14, 1799.

'I returned last night from two days' visit to Blackheath, where I was received with the utmost affection,

and was literally never out of her sight, except while I
was asleep. Breakfasted alone with her by her bedside,
and sat there without stirring from ten till near two.
She invited everybody she thought I could like to meet
—Pitt, Dundas, the Speaker, Windham, and a great
many others, amongst whom were Lord Clive and Lord
Eldon. They spoke in the highest terms of your
speech, and Lord Eldon said he regretted much he had
not heard it and would have given the world to have
been able to make it.

'Our good friend at Blackheath told me they all speak
very highly of you, and absence does not lessen her interest in your concerns. I never saw anybody so kind
as she is or so warmly interested in the credit of those
she loves; she looks to your return with great impatience; and there seems some reason to think she
may soon require the advice of a real friend; for there
has been a sort of sounding by means of Jack Payne,
and a proposal from Mrs. Fitzherbert, of seeing her,
saying she had such power over the Prince she could
do what she pleased with him. The Princess replied,
most properly, that she would not see Mrs. Fitzherbert,
and that if the Prince ever knew Mrs. Fitzherbert had
proposed it, it would only give him offence. Jack
Payne likewise asked her if she would object to dining
with the Prince at Carlton House. I do not know
exactly how she received this, but she told him that if
the Prince came to Blackheath, she would receive him
with the utmost civility, and never hint at anything that
had formerly passed. On the whole, I think that up to

the present time, her conduct has been properly digni-
fied ; but I agree with her that if she goes to Carlton
House she ought to know on what terms and what it
would lead to.   For my own part, I believe it is her
present popularity that leads to the measure, and much
might be done by proper management, but not in the
way the Paynes set about it ; and so I told her, and she
seemed to agree.'

It was actually proposed to the Princess by *a gentleman*, that H.R.H. should receive a visit from the said
lady, in order that she might exert her influence with
the husband on behalf of the wife.   No wonder that
on being told this by the Princess, ' George Canning
started from his chair in indignation at such impu-
dence.'

CHAPTER III.

LORD MINTO was appointed Envoy Extraordinary and Minister Plenipotentiary to the Court of Vienna, in June 1799. In the following month he set out for his destination, and arrived there in the first days of August.

A sudden outbreak of illness among the younger members of the family prevented them and their mother from leaving England with Lord Minto, and they were left behind to follow as soon as the children should be able to travel.

When that time arrived, events, to be presently related, had momentarily disturbed the relations of Great Britain and Austria, and a rupture seeming imminent, Mr. Pitt advised Lady Minto to postpone her departure. But before the political horizon was restored to serenity, an unusually severe winter had set in. For months the Elbe was blocked with ice. Even the communications by messengers were stopped for a considerable period. Lady Minto therefore did not join her husband until the spring of 1800.

'I never felt more unwilling to part with you, and more heavy-hearted,' he wrote to her a few hours after their separation, 'nor have ever felt that I left you more forlorn and melancholy. If burdens are diminished by being shared, you may feel lighter already, for I have felt particularly depressed with all your evils present and to come. We must not be ungrateful to the post, and to the sublime arts of reading and writing, without which we might as well die at once as part. It is certainly the very first of comforts and blessings to those who, like us, must so often have our bodies at a distance, that our hearts and minds may be within hail of each other.'

Though deprived of the comforts of family society, Lord Minto was fortunate in his travelling companions, for he carried with him, as members of his suite, Pozzo di Borgo and Mr. Bartle Frere. The features of the former were too well known to Lady Minto to require special portraiture in her husband's letters, but of Mr. Frere there are frequent notices, all in terms of strong regard. ' I like him extremely. He is clever without pretension, modest without bashfulness, cheerful and gentle at the same time. He seems anxious to learn and try everything, and he takes a quiet interest in everything that is going on, which I think a pleasant quality.' Again : ' Frere is a very lovable character.' On their way to Vienna they halted at Brunswick, where Lord Minto, as a trusted friend and counsellor of the Princess of Wales, met with a warm reception, and was touched by the anxiety and distress manifested by her parents in speaking of a position at once so desolate and so dangerous.[1]

---

[1] The Duchess of Brunswick also gratified him by the keenness of her sympathies as an Englishwoman, and by wearing a ' Nelson cap '— whatever that may have been.

At Dresden, too, the travellers spent a few days with Hugh Elliot, His Majesty's Minister to the Court of Saxony.

Eighteen years had stolen away since Lord Minto, passing through Berlin on his way to St. Petersburg, had first seen his brother in his newly-assumed character of ' Benedick, the married man.' Even then, to a discerning glance, there were symptoms in the matrimonial sky of the clouds soon afterwards to burst—a dreary time, of which the tale has been told elsewhere.[1] On this occasion he found his brother in a home of happier auspices, with a wife no less beautiful than her predecessor, and endowed with a more happily-constituted nature.

Of Vienna, of its scenery and society, Lord Minto's first impressions were, as indeed they remained to the end of his sojourn in Austria, eminently favourable. ' Wooded hollows, rocky glens, corn lands and vineyards, hills and water, make charming scenery. The people, who are very well-looking, are all thriving so far as the eye can judge. They are much better lodged than ours, and show a spirit of neatness about their dwellings equal to ours or very little inferior to it. But though agriculture seems to have reached considerable perfection throughout Germany, I observe that the land is universally very foul and full of weeds compared with ours.

' I am very kindly and cordially welcomed into the

---

[1] Memoir of the Right Hon. Hugh Elliot, published in 1868.

society here. I have seen Baron Thugut [1] twice, the last
time alone, but I went only to improve my acquaintance
with him, and abstained intentionally from business
till I have a full right to begin. He is remarkably
pleasant and even humorous in conversation, and enjoys
it extremely. I like both the Emperor and Empress [2]
extremely well. She has the reputation of being remarkably plain, but her manner is good and agreeable. The
Emperor gives audience to every person of whatever
rank who desires it ; and there were in the ante-room
at least 100 people of both sexes, and of all ranks from
princes to washerwomen, waiting for their turns. He
begins at six in the morning and stands till two o'clock
in this occupation. This is once a week at present, but
oftener at other seasons. This with the thermometer
at 93° ! '

'Madame de Thun, who has been so long the centre
of the society of Europe, and is a plain, agreeable, sensible woman, with three agreeable daughters, all married,
is unfortunately very ill, and her family is alarmed
about her ; but even in this situation her lodging in

[1] Baron Thugut, born 1739, a man of no family; created a baron by
Maria Theresa for diplomatic services, succeeded Prince Kaunitz in
1794 as first minister, was accused of always separating Austrian
interests from those of the Allies, but was distinguished by the energy
and courage with which in 1795 he persisted in resisting the progress of
the French arms, after Prussia and Spain had signed a separate peace.
By a secret article of the Treaty of Leoben, 1797, the removal of Thugut
was insisted on. Francis II. gave him the portfolio of foreign affairs
when at the beginning of 1799 the second Coalition was formed against
France. In 1800, just before Marengo, he signed a treaty of subsidy
with England: he finally retired after the peace of Lunéville, 1801.

[2] Daughter of the King of Naples.

the Fauxbourg seems still the only rendezvous for society at this time of year. She is extremely agreeable, and talks incessantly and pleasantly and cheerfully even now. At this time of year, however, Vienna is empty, and in truth for those who have neither business nor family there are parts of the day altogether unprovided for. The morning is soon over, for the hour of assembling for dinner is half after two, and you sit down to table at three, never later. Immediately after coffee, afternoon visits are made, which are over by seven or eight o'clock; at this hour some may go to drive in the Prater. From this time, if you don't frequent the theatre, you must come home, for the day is done abroad. This will do mighty well when we are all together, and in truth it suits me very well now. The three daughters of Madame de Thun are most pleasing women, in the best style of English gentlewomen. The eldest, Madame de Rosamowsky, is married to the Russian Ambassador, and is famous for her bad health and cheerfulness since her youth. The second, Madame Lichnowsky, ill married to a worthless Pole, is uncommonly sensible and clever. The third, Lady Guilford, married to the son of an Irish earl, a pleasing man but ruined and melancholy; yet she is the happiest of the three, having a husband she can like. There is also in the family a first cousin, Madame de Kinsky,[1] very ill married too, but herself uncommonly handsome as well as good and sensible. . . . Madame

---

[1] Née Comtesse Dietrichstein.

de Thun is the centre of all this and of a numerous society accustomed to frequent her house, and it will probably be all dispersed by her death. All this family talk English, or at least understand it perfectly.'

At a somewhat later period (September 1799) Lord Minto wrote :—' There are certainly a sufficient number of well-bred, pleasant people here, especially of women, to afford you an agreeable private society, besides the world in which you must live a good deal. But I don't think you will find the world very fatiguing. The female style of this country seems very good, like the good specimens of English gentlewomen. I hardly know whether there is much gallantry or not. I believe they have that reputation, but the manners appear to me very decent, and there is no need to be inquisitive about the rest. The Thun family are all as pure as they are superior in other points. Pozzo di Borgo seems to succeed here more than any of my suite both among men and women. They have all the highest idea of his talents and like his looks and manners. . . . I have assisted lately at a most noble *chasse* at the Prince Nicholas Esterhazy's, three posts from Vienna. We were eighteen sportsmen and 1,000 attendants. I was myself attended by three peasants carrying on their backs each a stand with seven guns, and I had three servants to load for me. We killed in the forenoon upwards of a thousand pieces of game, and, strange to say, I shot like Robin Hood, and killed 120 pieces of game, viz. pheasants, hares, partridges, myself. We dined with a beautiful princess and re-

turned to Vienna. It is really a royal style, and a thing
to do *once*. . . .   What you will enjoy here is the love
of country life, at least in summer.'

Such were the social conditions under which Lord
Minto entered upon his mission to Vienna.   To appre-
ciate the political situation, far less smiling, we must
review the events of the previous year.   Naples, as we
have seen, began the war with results which did not
increase her military renown.   The army refused to
fight, the King fled to Sicily, and his kingdom became
a Parthenopean Republic under the sponsorship of
France.   But as the presence of Nelson had caused the
momentary intoxication that proved fatal to Naples,
so his great victory of the Nile (August 1798), by cut-
ting off Bonaparte and his army from the soil of
Europe, stimulated the great Powers to a second Coalition for the renewal of the war.   Before Christmas
1798, a treaty of alliance was signed between Great
Britain and Russia for the purpose of putting a stop
to the encroachments of France ; and Austria, with
the finest army and best equipped artillery in Europe,
was prepared to take the field.

By the middle of August 1799, France, whose
generals had given the law to half the capitals of
Europe, and seized her ports and harbours from Ham-
burgh to Naples, was driven from all Italy save the
state of Genoa, was held at bay behind the Rhine, and
retained of all her conquests Switzerland alone.   The
genius of Bonaparte being withdrawn, there was no
reason to doubt that the god of battles would still be

found with *les gros bataillons*. Mr. Pitt therefore conceived the moment to be come for a combined movement upon France herself. Acting on Burke's doctrine that the true objects of the war were the subversion of the existing Government of France, and the restoration of Europe to the *status quo* before the Revolution, the British Government urged on their allies a plan of campaign embracing the expulsion of the French from Switzerland, the advance of the allied forces into Franche Comté, and the raising of the Royalist standard at Lyons. This course, it was said, would ' enable the French people,' who were represented as weary of their present rulers, ' to declare themselves openly against them.' What was to be done if they declared on the other side was not specified. But in proportion to the rapidity and extent of their successes in the field had been the development of certain seeds of mistrust among the members of the Coalition.

The very knowledge of the course chalked out for her by the tenacious policy of Great Britain had brought Austria[1] to a temper in which it was thought not im-

---

[1] Austria by no means shared in the English sympathies for the Bourbon dynasty. When in the spring of 1800 the Duc de Berri visited Vienna, he was very coldly received by the Austrian Government, who, as is well known, had not, like that of Great Britain, recognised the claims of the French Princes. Lord Minto, however, felt it his duty to show the Duke all possible respect, and for some weeks he resided under the roof of the English Legation. The fact of the Prince's connection with the reigning house of Austria had so little weight at Vienna that in his conversation with Baron Thugut, Lord Minto could only bring him to the admission that attention to the Duke was right on the general grounds of misfortune being respectable.

probable that she would negotiate a separate peace with the Republic, if by so doing she could obtain the territorial aggrandisements she coveted in Italy; and to prevent this consummation was the special object of the mission undertaken by Lord Minto. Austria, like old Paoli in Corsica, suspected everybody else of views and combinations similar to her own. She was jealous of the Anglo-Russian expedition in Holland, as having possibly ulterior designs on the Low Countries. She was more jealous of the Russian successes in Italy and Piedmont, as thwarting her Italian projects; and above all was she jealous of Prussia, who was lying by, and 'keeping green,' while her perfectly appointed and disciplined armies under the Archduke Charles were called on to make a campaign in Switzerland for objects which were none of her seeking.

Thus it came about that from the 1st of June to the middle of August, this self-same Austrian army and its illustrious chief lay within entrenchments before Zurich, in a state of entire inactivity, though superior in numbers to the French, perfectly equipped, and in first-rate condition.[1]

The most various speculations were afloat in England on the influences which rendered the Archduke as immovable as the Lady in ' Comus.' Some blamed the Aulic Council; others Thugut's jealousy of the

---

[1] During this time they were not without amusements at head-quarters: ' It happened occasionally,' says a visitor to the Archduke's camp, ' that *French musicians* were invited to complete any deficiency in the Austrian bands which enlivened the ball-room.'

military fame of the Archduke; others, again, the latter's jealousy of Suwarrow. English agents and generals buzzed about the camp in vain. Less fortunate than the fly on the coach-wheel, they could not even delude themselves into a belief that the coach moved, while they had an uncomfortable consciousness, altogether wanting in the experience of the fly, that their principals would ultimately be called on to pay for the wasted load. At this conjuncture Lord Minto arrived at Vienna ; but before he did so, the discourtesy shown to Lord Mulgrave,[1] who had been sent to the Archduke's head-quarters to concert the plan of campaign, and the avowal of an intention to transfer the Archduke's army from Switzerland to the Lower Rhine, provoked Lord Grenville to add some categorical questions, in his most imperious tone, to the general instructions already delivered to Lord Minto. Lord Minto was desired to express His Majesty's great dissatisfaction on account of the reserve adopted towards Lord Mulgrave and the general conduct of the Court of Vienna towards His Majesty, particularly respecting the transference of the Archduke's army to Mayence. . . . Lord Minto was to observe that England and

---

[1] Lord Mulgrave, an officer of rank, had been sent, at the request of Baron Thugut, to the head-quarters of the Archduke professedly to concert with him the operations to be commenced in Switzerland. On his arrival at Zurich he learnt that Baron Thugut had not authorised the Archduke to enter into any discussion of his plans of campaign, and Lord Mulgrave was told by His Royal Highness that he should repair to Vienna where alone he could obtain the information he desired.

Russia were not to be expected to co-operate in plans of which they disapproved, and that England would not furnish troops for the execution of plans decided upon without previous communications and concert. His Majesty required concert in the plan of campaign, and fresh communications with His Majesty's Ministers as a matter of right, which the King would not waive. If such discussions were declined, Lord Minto was desired to declare all hopes of concert relinquished.[1]

Lord Minto to Lord Grenville.

'Vienna: August 9.

' I therefore acquainted M. Thugut with His Majesty's very earnest desire that the plan already settled with His Imperial Majesty should be persisted in. I represented it as a point on which the King felt a real solicitude, founded purely on his conviction that the most important object of the campaign and that

---

[1] Notes drawn up for conference with Baron Thugut, from a despatch of Lord Grenville's, August 31, 1799.

'The objects, if not the existence, of the Coalition,' said his instructions, 'are believed to be endangered by the manifest desire of the Court of Vienna to retain the power of entering into separate negotiations with the enemy, and to look for the security of future peace rather to the extent of territorial acquisitions than to any change in the system of government in France . . . . The rapid progress of the successes of the Allies has made it extremely important to ascertain, without delay, the extent to which this principle is likely to operate, and the possibility of establishing with the Court of Vienna, either directly or through the medium of Russia, a system of communication and concert as to the means both of prosecuting the war with vigour, and of ultimately terminating it with advantage and security.'

which presented the fairest hopes of obtaining in time the blessings of a secure peace, was the deliverance of Switzerland; and that His Majesty was not more persuaded of the importance of delivering Switzerland ultimately, than he was of the extreme danger and mischief which must result from any extreme delay.

'. . . I observed that the world had reason to conclude, from the long inaction of the Austrian army in Switzerland, that the Archduke's present force was deemed insufficient to advance ; that the Russian force under M. de Korsakow was inferior to that now employed in Switzerland, and that their progress must be yet more difficult.

.   .   .   .   .   .

'On my observation respecting the importance and urgency of expelling the French from Switzerland, he admitted the importance of that object generally, but not exclusively to the prejudice of the German or Italian war ; and to the remark I had made of the inaction of the Archduke's army having been attributed to the insufficiency of its force, he answered that the Archduke had not stopped for want of numbers nor from the impossibility of advancing, but because the loss attending success must have been necessarily great, and the hazard of some disaster considerable in the circumstances under which Massena must have been attacked in the country which he now occupies: That the Emperor could not at this period of the war expose that army to a great loss or considerable hazard, but that an army of equal force would be suffi-

cient to accomplish that object where there did not exist
the same motive for caution. Your Lordship will have
observed that M. Thugut considers the remainder of the
Swiss campaign as an arduous and hazardous enterprise ;
and for that reason amongst others would transfer this
service from an Austrian to a Russian army.

' M. Thugut says very distinctly what your Lordship
had already penetrated as his principal motive, that the
Emperor wishes to have the Archduke his brother
(who was Governor of the Netherlands), and an Austrian
army in such a position as to stand connected with the
English and Russian expedition in Holland, and ready
to enter the Netherlands when events shall render it
expedient. . . You will feel that with this substantial
motive at the bottom of his mind, he must be perfectly
inaccessible to any arguments it was possible for me to
urge in favour of the Swiss operations.

.   .   .   .   .   .

' Your Lordship will now be enabled to judge
of M. Thugut's motives for committing Switzerland
altogether into the charge of His Majesty and the
Russian troops.

' Some of his reasons do not appear to be void of
foundation, judging of them independently of the particular views of Austria; but there are many others which
come so home to their own feelings and interests, as to
supersede in their minds all other considerations, and
leave no hope whatever of shaking their resolution.
1st. The Russian troops which are now chargeable to
them in Italy will be employed usefully in the war with-

out expense to Austria. The operations and designs of
that Court in Italy, and particularly in Piedmont, will
be delivered from the immediate control of Russia and
England through Marshal Suwarrow ; a hazardous war
in Switzerland will be thrown on Russian troops instead of Austrian ; a prospect of retaking Mayence and
Ehrenbreitstein will be opened, and it is known that M.
de Thugut has a strong personal feeling on that subject, the reproach of having given them up lying still
at his door. Lastly, a secret uneasiness and jealousy
concerning the issue of the English and Russian expedition in Holland, as it may affect the Low Countries, has evidently a great share in their determination, and will draw them inevitably towards that
quarter.'

In a private letter to Mr. Wickham of a later date
Lord Minto wrote that in his opinion the desire of
Baron Thugut to keep his army to fight another day,
was the governing motive for the inaction of the
Austrians. ' I will freely confess what I believe to have
been the real and operating motive in Thugut's mind
for the calamitous, and perhaps irretrievable, fault he
committed in arresting the progress of the Archduke
since the first occupation of Zurich. The reason he
gives appears to me so bad that I think he would not
avow it so distinctly as he does if it were not true. His
grand policy in war is to spare his army. This is a
sort of policy which seems to me perfectly to defeat itself, for the army which does not conquer the enemy is
in the meanwhile destroying and conquering its own

master. But this is really his system in all parts of the war, and I do assure you he has seen the progress of Suwarrow with more apparent terror than he has ever discovered at that of the enemy. He argues very openly on that point, and tells you of the difficulties he has to encounter in forming the army; of the 80,000 recruits he must now provide for it; of this being the seventh campaign of the Austrian war; of Prussia's recovering herself fresh and green to profit of her weakness, and of the necessity to preserve a force for such occasions.[1] In his disposition to indulge this sort of economy in war, he saw before him in Switzerland a campaign which must cost many men. He expected the arrival of the Russian army; he thought it would come sooner and be more numerous than it has proved; and he satisfied his ill-understood policy by lying by for the unhandsome advantage of throwing the loss and the hazard of the campaign on the troops of another nation. This is, I am persuaded, the real account of the matter. I venture to give you the trouble of reading all this, though I hardly know that it leads to any political consequences : but I wish you to know as correctly as we can discover it, what sort of person the whole business of this empire hangs upon. For it is with him, and through him, that all the good, bad, or indifferent we can look for from Austria, and all its power, must be accomplished.' [2]

[1] 'The mutual jealousies of Austria and Prussia afford one of the greatest obstacles in the way of future arrangements, as they have already opened the way to all the calamities of Europe.' Despatches of Lord Grenville.

[2] Lord Minto to Mr. Wickham : Vienna, September 14, 1799.

These sentences explain the motives that governed Lord Minto's conduct towards Baron Thugut during the whole of his mission. Frequently disgusted by the narrow selfishness of the Austrian Minister and justly offended by his duplicity, Lord Minto nevertheless considered 'this particular old man' as the sole channel through which the Austrian counsels might be directed to an efficient co-operation in the war.

There was but one statesman in Austria; or if others there were, their influence is not discoverable in this correspondence; whence we receive an impression not unlike that produced by certain famous pictures, where the foreground is occupied by a couple of figures, while around them shadowy forms, with crowned or dishevelled heads, are seen rising and falling in misty distances.

A discovery made about this time, August 1799, of the crooked policy of Austria, was a somewhat severe trial to the English Envoy's purposes of conciliation.

In the course of August Lord Minto informed Lord Grenville that Baron Thugut proposed to make a full and precise communication to the Government of His Majesty of the Emperor's policy on condition that the communication should be held to be strictly confidential. 'Your Lordship,' wrote Lord Minto, 'will naturally anticipate the objections I suggested as likely to be made by His Majesty. I represented the close and cordial union between His Majesty and the Court of St. Petersburg; and the repugnance which His Majesty must feel at entering into a secret consultation on matters interesting to all the Allies, and indeed in general to Europe at large, in such a manner as industriously to exclude the Emperor of Russia from any share or even knowledge of the proceeding. It is my duty to report the solution offered for that difficulty by the Austrian Minister, viz. that of perfect and entire secrecy ; alleging that it was possible by care and attention to keep the secret, and that no ill consequences would follow from the exclusion of the Emperor of Russia if he should remain ignorant of such transactions having existed at all. I observed that it was difficult to depend on the degree of secrecy which was necessary ; and that if that difficulty was removed, there would still remain His Majesty's own sense of the attention and confidence due to the Emperor of Russia. M. de Thugut could not but feel the force of these objections, but as he persisted in his desire that the proposition should be made, it is my duty to transmit it to your Lordship.'

A little later the marriage of the Archduke Joseph with the Archduchess Alexandra Paulowna, solemnised at St. Petersburg, was made the occasion of similar overtures from the Court of Vienna to that of St. Petersburg ; the chief objects of the negotiation being to create a jealousy between Russia and Great Britain, and to procure the aid of the former Power in carrying out the Austrian views in Germany and Italy.[1]

---

[1] Other objects there were, however, as :—1. The exchange of the Low Countries for Bavaria if possible. The Low Countries to be a kingdom in the House of Bavaria. The Archduke Joseph to be hereditary governor of Bavaria, and the sovereignty to be vested in the Empire. Piedmont and its dependencies to be united to Lombardy. The greatest part of the Legations to be annexed to the Emperor's dominions. Parma to be also annexed. An alliance, offensive and defensive, to be negotiated between Austria and Russia as against Prussia. Active ope-

No wonder that Lord Minto 'found it difficult to continue his relations with the Austrian Minister on a footing of courtesy,' after the discovery of so much double-dealing. But while the honesty and uprightness of his whole nature recoiled from the statecraft of Baron Thugut, he nevertheless perceived in him a sincere and courageous desire to maintain the reputation and European position of Austria ; and to this sentiment he addressed himself as the 'best means to clear the way in this wood of suspicion.'

Many subsequent conferences were held on the topics broached by Lord Minto in his first interview with Baron Thugut. But it was not till after ' much general fencing,˜some fluctuations, and a good deal of ebb and flow of condescension, according to the course of events,' that their final results were notified to Lord Grenville as follows :—

' 1st. A full concession has been handed to Lord Mulgrave, and he will be admitted to the councils of the Archduke.

' 2ndly. The march of the Archduke to Mayence and the withdrawal of his entire army has been countermanded.

' 3rdly. A promise has been made that the Archduke shall remain in Switzerland, until that country can be safely committed to the Russians; that the army of the Archduke should remain on the Upper Rhine to support, if necessary, the Russians.'

rations to be suspended against France till spring in order to bring about these projects.

Unhappily, while these engagements were being entered into at Vienna, the Archduke was actually commencing his retreat; and to the infinite disgust and exasperation of the British officers, the reason given for the movement was the pressure laid on Austria by Great Britain and Russia, to whom therefore were directed the indignation of the Austrian army, and the resentment of the Swiss abandoned to the undisciplined forces of Russia.

The despatch just quoted, announcing the concessions made by Baron Thugut, was written on August 11; on the 15th a sudden attack was made on the Austrian outposts before Zurich, which, though repelled, served to cover far more important movements in the Grisons and on the St. Gothard. On the same day Mr. Wickham received from the Archduke himself the information, that in consequence of orders transmitted from Vienna he was about to commence a retreat with his entire army from Switzerland, leaving the defence of that country to his Russian auxiliaries, whose habits made them more formidable to the Swiss than to the enemy. These orders the Archduke represented as imperative, and as having been dictated under pressure from the Courts of St. James's and St. Petersburg, the former Government being mainly responsible for them.

Language such as this repeated by the officers of the staff, greatly excited the feeling not only of the army against Great Britain, but also of the Swiss, who believed themselves sacrificed to political combinations instigated by her.

'I confess,' wrote Lord Minto to Lord Grenville, 'I had been much hurt with the disappointment in the expectations which had been given to me so positively, as your Lordship knows, and so repeatedly of the Archduke's remaining in Switzerland. But your Lordship will imagine the impression made on me by the account I received from Mr. Wickham of the motives which were alleged for his quitting that country—of its having been ascribed by the Archduke, on the authority of the Cabinet of Vienna, to a cause so entirely false as the positive and peremptory demand of His Majesty and the Emperor of Russia, at a time when I had so recently obtained, by long and urgent solicitation, a positive promise and, as I conceived, an actual order to the contrary. This very extraordinary misrepresentation became matter of real offence towards His Majesty, and seemed, even on personal grounds, to require that clear and formal notice should be taken of it.' Lord Minto, in the same despatch, enclosed a copy of the official note containing the embodiment of his sentiments on this transaction, addressed by himself to Baron Thugut, whom he subsequently represented as 'seeming disconcerted in some degree by the strong statements I had made of the false motives attributed to the retreat of the Archduke from Switzerland. He declared with much warmth that if the Archduke was the author of that assertion His Royal Highness had greatly misrepresented him. . . . I do not say to your Lordship that this assurance, warm and positive as it was, has satisfied me concerning the real state of the facts, but

in the meanwhile it may be considered as a formal dis-
avowal of such an assertion on the part of the Court of
Vienna.'

In another despatch he says, ' I have no doubt that
Dietrichstein was instructed by Thugut to tell the lie to
the Archduke which he believed.' By the second week
of September the Archduke's army had retired from
Switzerland, and the deserved chastisement of these
misdeeds was close at hand.

The news of the Battle of Novi, gained by Field-
Marshal Suwarrow over General Joubert, followed by
his march to Genoa, together with further intelligence
of the successes of the Allies in the southern part of
Italy, increased to intensity the impatience of the
Austrian Government for the recall of Suwarrow from
the south to the north of the Alps. While he was urgently desired to effect his junction with the Russian
corps already in Switzerland, these were left unsupported, and the fatal results are too well known.

Massena took advantage of the retreat of the Archduke to fall on the small forces of Korsakow and
Hotze, and having routed them he interrupted the
advance of Suwarrow, and drove that gallant leader to
the disastrous retreat which destroyed his army, closed
the Swiss campaign in disappointment and disgrace,
brought about a rupture between the two Imperial
Courts, preserved to Bonaparte the stronghold of
Switzerland as a basis for his subsequent operations
in Italy and Germany, and so paved the way to
Marengo and Hohenlinden.

'The immediate causes of these misfortunes have undoubtedly been the restraint laid on the Archduke by the Cabinet of Vienna, after he obtained possession of Zurich, and the subsequent orders to depart from Switzerland as soon as the arrival of even part of the Russians should make it possible to do so, and in opposition to the sentiments of the Archduke himself, as well as to the ardent wishes of his whole army. This determination neither to advance in Switzerland when it would have been easy to do so by Austrian force alone, nor to co-operate in that measure with the Russians, when such a reinforcement should again have insured success, has been, I say, the immediate cause of our disappointment.· It is rendered yet more discouraging and alarming for the future, when we observe that these mischievous errors naturally result from a vicious system, and from a set of false general views and opinions prevalent in the Austrian Cabinet.'

Lord Minto was repeatedly assured by Lord Grenville of His Majesty's approbation of the tone and position assumed by him throughout the transactions which have been described. He himself says, ' It is a consolation to me to know that no exertion of the most brilliant talents could have effected different results. The question was really settled before my arrival.' [1]

---

[1] Lord Minto to Lord Grenville.

CHAPTER IV.

THE state of irritation produced by these events in England had occasioned the postponement of Lady Minto's journey to Vienna, and she wrote to Lord Minto on the subject as follows :—

'October 16, 1799.

'Mr. Pitt, Dundas, Windham, Canning, and Frere all agree I should remain for the present where I am. Mr. Pitt was extremely civil, and assured me that as soon as he received your despatches he would himself inform me what to do ; but his expression was, "I should not be surprised to hear Lord Minto had ordered his chaise and had left Vienna." I assured him you were not likely to take such a measure unless you had received particular directions so to do, as you were patient and long suffering, and *never in a passion*. He replied that he could conceive circumstances in which it might have been necessary ; and said that he much feared your appointment had been made too late ; that had you been sent sooner, there was reason to think much evil might have been prevented ; that perhaps you might only quit Vienna for a time, and return there ; but that during the present uncertainty I should not set out.

'It will be a satisfaction to you to know that your conduct is highly approved of; and even were your mission to fail, you have gained all the credit you could have wished by its success.'

Many interviews took place between Lord Minto and Baron Thugut, before the latter was brought to an unreserved explanation of his general policy, though, as Lord Minto wrote home, 'Until these points are ascertained, the Allies are as much occupied with each other as with the enemy.' When they were ascertained, the result can hardly have been satisfactory.

It is hardly necessary to describe in any detail the views professed by Baron Thugut on the territorial arrangements which should result from a general peace. Some of them, more or less modified, became the subject of full discussion at the Congress of Vienna, and were embodied in the conditions of the Peace of 1815: but as forcibly illustrating his own sentiments and those of his Government on certain political questions of general interest, a few extracts are here given from Lord Minto's despatches.

'First, then, with regard to the settlement of France and the operations of the Allies in the interior of that country, Baron Thugut seems to me considerably behind the rest of Europe in appreciating the importance and pre-eminence of that great object, as forming in the present period the prime, and comparatively the only, interest of the belligerent Powers as well as of the rest of the world, and the true governing principle of the war. He covers his indifference, and perhaps disinclination, to this part of the subject, under the suggestion that events are not yet ripe ; and that what remains, both of the Swiss and the Italian war, keeps the measures to be pursued on or beyond the frontier of France still at a distance.

' I have also perceived a stronger inclination to divide France and perpetuate the distractions of that country, than to re-establish either Monarchy or any other steady government. He argues, indeed, very coolly and explicitly on the policy of securing the tranquillity of Europe by this mode of weakness in France. I need not trouble your Lordship with my replies on these topics, as my sentiments are known to you, and those of the King have been too clearly expressed to impose on me the duty of doing violence to my own opinions or feelings concerning those very shallow and inapplicable notions of common-place policy in the present extraordinary conjuncture. I told, indeed, Baron Thugut yesterday, very plainly and firmly, that I was perhaps the man in Europe who was the least disposed to sympathise with these opinions. He expresses on all occasions a great distrust in the supposed strength of the royal party in France. . . . It is easy to perceive that he has a strong prejudice against the King of France and the French Princes, whom he considers as personally obnoxious to the French nation, and whose personal want of popularity he deems an obstacle to any system of which their

restoration is a part.   He expresses also a strong disinclination to concur in an explicit declaration for the
restoration of Monarchy, and hints at a preference for
more general and indefinite terms, such as the re-establishment of order and of good government.   But he
couples with this backwardness a contradictory sort of
courage and consistency in thinking that if a declaration in favour of Monarchy is made at all, the Allies
should engage to maintain it at all *risks.*'[1]

In a private letter to Lord Grenville (September 25,
1799), Lord Minto says :—'It is impossible not to see
that Thugut's principles and opinions concerning the
war and its objects would lead to a peace with the Republic as soon as he had secured the territorial acquisitions at which he aims.   He is decidedly and avowedly
against entering France to co-operate with the Royalists;
and he is constantly saying that they will either make
the counter-revolution themselves, or divide the kingdom into a number of sects and factions and secure
the tranquillity of other nations by their own dissensions.'   On the question of directing the war against
the system of government in France, the sentiments of
Austria appeared to be that her interests, if not those

---

[1] M. Thiers in his History says that in 1799 and 1800, England was
reckoning on the dissolution of France by internal factions.   It appears
from this despatch that this was Thugut's object and that it was repudiated by Lord Minto ; his opinion was that until a regular government on recognised principles was established, every faction in France
would be interested in prolonging a state of anarchy, and, believing that
such a government might be constructed by the monarchical party, he
thought the Allies should give it their support.

of public morality, would be better served by the transference of the Italian conquests of France to herself than by any intervention on behalf of the French Royalists.   As to the territorial acquisitions she had in view, it appeared that they extended to the whole of Italy, excepting only the states of Rome and Naples. 'The Legations will, I am persuaded, be retained by Austria.   Venice will certainly continue subject to her. I am not yet master of the designs on Tuscany.'

Lord Minto in one of his early conversations with Thugut, having introduced the subject of the restoration of the King of Sardinia to his 'dominions in Piedmont, less,' he confesses, 'with the view of obtaining a concession on that point, than in the view of learning something of the views entertained by the Court of Vienna on the subject,' he had no sooner mentioned this subject than he perceived he had touched on a very delicate string.   'M. de Thugut's manner changed instantly from that of coolness and civility to a great show of warmth and some sharpness.   He became immediately loud and animated, and it would therefore be the more difficult for me to follow the order and even relate the matter of his conversation.' 'I am quite aware,' says Lord Minto a little further on, 'that this strong display of passion may very well argue a cooler and more deliberate sentiment, but disguised under the appearance of warmth;' and before the close of the interview he arrived at the conclusion that it was the intention of the Emperor to retain the whole of Piedmont and Savoy.   'I should not think I expressed myself too strongly by saying that this Court would probably make it the pivot on which their whole system would hereafter turn, and that they would, in the choice of their Allies, choose that Power, or those Powers, which should concur or acquiesce in this view. It seems to me as if a determined opposition on the part of Great Britain and Russia to the acquisition of Piedmont might probably throw Austria once more into a connection with the French Republic, and become a motive, as it would furnish a pretext, for a separate peace on that condition.'

Great offence had been given to Austria by the invitation to return to his dominions issued by the Emperor of Russia to the King of Sardinia; a course adopted in conformity with the wishes of the King of Great Britain. Thugut affected to deny to Russia the position of an ally, and treating her as a mere auxiliary, considered Marshal Suwarrow as an Austrian general commanding His Imperial Majesty's troops by commission from him and subject to his orders. The conquest of Piedmont he therefore looked on as that of an enemy's country, and the establishment of a provisional government under Suwarrow as an insult to Austria.

The possession of Genoa and Nice was pointed out as a necessary barrier to the advance of France in that quarter; but nothing in the whole discussion is so remarkable as the exposition given of the Austrian Minister's view of Papal rights:

'With regard to Rome, Baron Thugut declares that

the Emperor will authorise the immediate election of a new Pope, who shall be established in Rome and put in possession of the territories which it is intended to leave to that Prince; but that the Emperor proposes to keep the *whole of the three Legations*. This, he says, will connect him with Tuscany, which may revert to the Emperor by failure of the heirs of the Grand Duke. Little territory of value would be left to support the Papal dignity, on which, however, much of the future tranquillity and happiness of Europe may be thought to depend. I should hope that this article might admit of modification, and that the acquisitions of the Emperor might be restrained to the left side of all the branches of the Po.'

Again : 'Speaking of Rome, he expressed a strong wish and opinion that the election of the new Pope should be made at Rome rather than Venice, in order to avoid the cavils which any imputation of irregularity in that proceeding might furnish to Spain or any other Power not disposed to acknowledge the new Pope. It appears not unlikely, however, that the election is already made at Venice. At the same time *Baron Thugut argued strongly on the possibility of doing without a Pope, and of each sovereign taking on himself the function of the head of the national church as in England.* I said that as a Protestant I could not be supposed to think the authority of the See of Rome necessary, speaking on that question generally ; and that if all the Catholic inhabitants of Europe could at once be converted to the same opinions, I should see no disadvantage in the abolition of the Papal power. But in the present state of religious opinions, and considering the only alternative which I now saw in these matters, viz. the subsistence of the Roman Catholic faith or the extinction of Christianity itself, I preferred, though a Protestant, the Pope to the Goddess of Reason. However, the mind of Baron Thugut is not open to any reasoning of a general nature when it is put in competition with conquest and acquisition of territory: and he has more than once said strongly that, though the Emperor would not object to restore the Pope to the sovereignty of Rome, he could not consent to its being vested in any other Prince, alleging that the Emperor derived his very title from that territory, and was styled Emperor of the Romans. Childish as this reasoning may appear, it is pretty pregnant and accounts for Baron Thugut being in his heart a Protestant.'

While such were the views of Baron Thugut, Lord Minto was disposed to look upon the existing state of things in Italy as favourable to his old plan of the formation of an Italian league, for purposes of common defence, to include all the Italian states from Sardinia to Naples. At his desire Count Pozzo di Borgo drew up a paper stating the military and other resources of the different Powers; and in this paper it is suggested that if such a federation could be brought about, Rome should be selected as the proper place for the seat of the Federal Government.

'Le nom de Rome ajoutera quelque chose à l'éclat des résolutions. . . . Ceux qui ne sont pas informés de la disposition des esprits dans ce pays se tromperaient s'ils affectaient d'envisager cette observation comme indifférente.' The observation becomes a very striking one when taken in connection with the fact that it emanated from an Italian, and that the mind about to rule the 'Thrones, Dominations, Princedoms, Powers' of Europe was also that of an Italian, no less alive than Pozzo to the power inherent in mighty names. In giving fresh life to those of Rome and Italy, Bonaparte gave shape to the vague aspirations of his countrymen, while his intellect, too mighty to be localised, recognised the illimitable extent to which the spiritual power of Rome might be expanded.

A despatch of Lord Minto's, written a few months after the one last quoted, contains the following statement :—

'When Bonaparte lately passed through Vercelli (in Piedmont), which is the residence of Cardinal Martiniani, he made the strongest professions to the Cardinal of his attachment to the Catholic Church, and authorised his Eminence to acquaint the Pope that he was determined to restore the Catholic Apostolic and Roman religion in all its purity throughout France. He even discussed a number of points in the detail of this measure, such as the restoration of the orthodox bishops. He said this would be one of the great difficulties. That he could not undertake to recall every emigrant bishop without regard to his conduct, but that he would by no means force the acknowledgment of the constitutional bishops, whose fate should be left to the decision of His Holiness. . . He said that if the Pope should agree with him he would restore the whole of his dominions. But it is not clear whether he meant to include the three Legations, or only those territories that remained after the treaty of Tolentino. It is added the Pope was inclined to believe this profession.'[1]

We thus arrive at a comprehensive view of the opinions entertained at the time in influential quarters concerning the Pope, and when presented in tabulated form, they will be found strongly marked by national characteristics.

The view of the German . .	to do without him.
Of the Englishman	to prefer him to the Goddess of Reason.
Of the Italian	to substitute for the papal chair a mirage of the ancient throne of Rome.
Of the Gallicized Italian . .	to evoke, from what seemed to others an effete superstition and a decrepit sovereignty, a mighty spell, and to control it according to the custom of his adopted country.

' La maxime de la France est de le regarder (le Pape) comme une personne sacrée mais entreprenante,

---

[1] February, 1800.

н 2

à laquelle il faut baiser les pieds et lier quelquefois les mains.'[1]

'When I,' wrote Lord Minto to Lord Grenville, ' seemed struck with the extensive scheme of aggrandisement which he, Baron Thugut, had opened to me, and amongst other things observed the consequences it would naturally produce in Prussia, by furnishing to that court a motive for falling on the smaller states of Germany in order to keep pace with the growth of Austria; or by inducing it even to attempt checking the progress of Austria by active alliance with the French Republic; he seemed first disposed to defy Prussia and to rely on the superior power of the Emperor for restraining that rival; but when I represented the doubt which must exist concerning the part which Russia would take in a contest between Austria and Prussia on such grounds, he seemed disposed to compromise the matter with Prussia, and to admit of her taking something also, *provided*, however, it *were not too much*.'

The designs of Austria on Italy produced a peculiar irritation against the Italian Jacobins, and perhaps influenced Baron Thugut's conduct in the crisis related in the following despatch. An advance having been made, after the capitulations of Capua and Gaeta, into the Roman territory by the troops of the King of Naples, with English forces under Commodore Trowbridge, these troops had proceeded to within a short distance of Rome, when the garrison of St. Angelo

[1] Voltaire.

capitulated. The articles of capitulation were first tendered to and refused by General Frölich, in command of an Austrian force, and were afterwards, when modified in the most important points, accepted by Commodore Trowbridge, to the great disgust of Baron Thugut.[1]

The capitulation produced a curious conversation between the Austrian Minister and the British Envoy, described in the following despatch :—

'Vienna : October 20, 1799.

'My Lord,—In pursuance of the views mentioned in my last despatch, I desired a conference with Baron Thugut this morning. After some preliminary conversation he produced a letter, which he termed a very extraordinary one, from Commodore Trowbridge to General Frölich, written in answer to one which he had received from the Austrian general, in which the latter told him that he did not acknowledge the capitulation granted to the French at Rome, and that he should attack them on their march. Commodore Trowbridge had replied that he should consider such an act as

---

[1] One of the articles of capitulation permitted the free return of the French and Italian troops serving in the garrison to the French army in Italy. The 'Italian Jacobins' were peculiarly offensive to Austria. When the report first reached Vienna of an advance of the Neapolitan troops towards Rome, Lord Minto asked Baron Thugut if the Austrian troops in the north would not support it. He considered hesitatingly but said if they did, the first measure to be taken would be *to disarm* the *Aretini*, who were committing great irregularities, and even appropriating to themselves stores and treasures belonging to the Grand Duke. 'A jealousy of these Tuscan patriots,' wrote Lord M., 'has certainly been strongly manifested here, since their first rising. A similar uneasiness prevails respecting the march of the Neapolitan troops to Rome.'

a violation of the friendship which subsists between the Emperor and His Majesty, and as an open rupture between the two Courts. Baron Thugut seemed disposed to treat these sentiments as wild and unreasonable, but I could not refrain from interrupting him most warmly, and exclaiming that Commodore Trowbridge was most perfectly and entirely right; that I hoped most earnestly no such rash proceeding had been resorted to, as it could not fail of producing the most fatal consequences. That our debates and controversies in that room, which had been unfortunately but too frequent, were to be lamented, but that they were of little moment when compared with such an act as this, which must amount not merely to a violation of friendship, but to a rupture by a *voie de fait* that must lead to instant reprisals and scarcely admit of reparation. He seemed much surprised and staggered by these strong opinions as well as by the unusual earnestness and warmth which I discovered on the occasion, and he immediately receded from his first tone of complaint against Trowbridge's answer, to soften the matter by saying that, although General Frölich had used that expression he had not acted upon it, and nothing of that disagreeable nature had passed. I said that I was very much relieved by that information, and that in truth these were vivacities which people sometimes indulged themselves in during the first moments of warmth or disappointment, but that led to consequences too serious to be often carried into execution. He said that General Frölich had not threatened to attack the French garrison when they were under the protection of an English escort; but I replied they were under a much more sacred escort in that of the good faith and honour that had been pledged to them by a British officer.'

After some 'captious reflexions' on the part of Baron Thugut, the controversy was allowed to drop, the matter being considered as settled and the capitulation having been observed.

The failure of the attempt to effect a secret understanding with Russia, and the prospect of a probable rupture with that Power, naturally inclined Austria to draw nearer to Great Britain. At the close of the year Lord Minto was able to inform Lord Grenville of the final settlement of a dispute which had subsisted almost three years, concerning an unratified convention.[1]

The second campaign of 1799, though the latter part was chequered with disasters, was in the main a successful one on the part of the Allies. But to the score of France was to be marked the events of the 18th Brumaire, which gave the control of her armies, resources, and policy to Bonaparte, and the rupture between Austria and Russia, whose alliance, long threatened by mutual jealousies, blew up at the close of the campaign.[2]

After the secession of Russia from the Coalition,

---

[1] One of the causes of delay appears to have been Baron Thugut's difficulty in understanding the nature of stock.

[2] The Archduke Charles in his Memoirs ascribes the dissolution of the Alliance to 'those general causes which prevail when two great and rival nations enter into a coalition for military ends.'

Great Britain and Austria redoubled their efforts to prosecute the war with vigour. 'To stimulate the languid dispositions of the German Empire,' says Alison, 'a vigorous circular was, in the beginning of December 1799, sent by the Archduke Charles to the anterior circles of the Empire, in which he strenuously urged the formation of new levies, and pointed out the hopelessness of obtaining any durable peace from France, stimulated by revolutionary excitement and led by a chief athirst for glory. Nevertheless, the author of the circular was known to feel no confidence in the issue of the approaching contest, now that Russia was withdrawn on the one side and Bonaparte added on the other.'

It was speedily known that the Archduke had earnestly advised the Austrian Cabinet to treat for peace, and that for this step he had been deprived of the command of the army in Germany, which was given to General Kray. The removal of the Archduke was viewed with great regret in England.

Lord Grenville to Lord Minto.

'(Private.)   'Cleveland Row: March 28, 1800.
                              (Received April 10.)

'My dear Lord,—You will easily suppose the impatience which we have felt while the ice has locked up all communication with the Continent, especially as the French have been all the time spreading continual reports of negotiation with Austria, the death of the

Emperor, &c. The thing which strikes me as the worst in the whole of our present situation is Thugut's obstinacy in removing (from private pique and jealousy) the Archduke Charles from his command. It is impossible to hope that Kray will create the same confidence in the army, or that he will dare to act with equal energy against the French, or against the factious in his own army. I conclude, however, that the step is now irrevocably taken, and we must make the best of it.

'The Egyptian capitulation is a most mortifying event, and may well put a less peevish man than Thugut extremely out of humour with his allies. I am almost as much grieved at the discredit which this affair throws on Sir Sidney Smith, as I am at the thing itself, for he had deserved so well of the country by his conduct at Acre, that it is a cruel thing to have to condemn and to disavow him. Thugut will, I doubt not, be very angry that we do not annul the capitulation. I really think that, *very* strictly speaking, we have a right so to do; but I am sure you will agree with us, that for such a country as this, the bringing the public faith, even into any sort of question, is a thing not to be done even for such an object as this would have been. What we are doing in the Mediterranean, as well as the powers which you and Mr. Wickham have received for pecuniary exertions in the Empire, must at least prove to Thugut that we are heartily bent on assisting his efforts. But I fear it will all end in a separate Austrian peace, whenever Bonaparte feels himself sufficiently pressed to give the conditions, whatever they are, which Thugut means to require.

'We have received the account to-day that the Union resolutions have passed the House of Lords in Ireland. Nothing now remains but the Address, which was expected to pass without a division. We shall have the whole here before Easter, and proceed upon it immediately after.'

CHAPTER V.

FROM Lord Minto's letters to Lady Minto we learn that his first interview with the second great leader of the allied forces was not calculated to comfort him for the loss of the most brilliant and popular of the Austrian generals.

'Prague: January 3, 1800.

'I am here to see Suwarrow on business, and am not sorry for the opportunity of seeing one of whom one has heard so much and such extraordinary things. Indeed it is impossible to say how extraordinary he is. There is but one word that can really express it. I must not on any account be quoted, but he is the most perfect Bedlamite that ever was allowed to be at large. I never saw anything so stark mad, and as it appears to me so contemptible in every respect. To give you some little notion of his manners, I went by appointment to pay my first visit, which I was told would be only one of ceremony. I was full dressed of course, and although I did not expect him to be so, I was not prepared for what I saw. After waiting a good while in an antechamber with some aides-de-camp, a door opened and a little old shrivelled creature in a

pair of red breeches and his shirt for all clothing,
bustled up to me, took me in his arms, and embracing
me with his shirt sleeves, made me a string of high-
flown flummery compliments which he concluded by
kissing me on both cheeks, and I am told I was in luck
that my mouth escaped. His shirt collar was buttoned
but he had no stock, and it was made of materials, and
of a fashion, and was about as clean and white, as you
may have seen on some labourers at home. On his arrival here he was waited upon by the Commandant at
the head of all the Austrian officers, and received them
exactly in the same attire. His whole manner and
conversation are as mad as his first appearance, and indeed those about him seem conscious of it, for nobody is
suffered to see him alone. He is always attended by
one or two nephews, who never take their eyes off him,
and seem to me to keep him in the sort of subjection
that a keeper generally does. They discover at the
same time the greatest anxiety lest his extraordinary
manner and still more extraordinary discourse should
detect him and discover his real situation. This is
mixed up with the extreme of exterior submission, and
with an appearance of looking up to these eccentricities
and all the nonsense he talks as the inspiration of an
oracle. He pretends, or thinks at times, that he has
seen visions ; and I have seen an official note written,
or rather dictated, by him to Mr. Wickham, in which
he says his Master, Jesus Christ, has ordered him so
and so. His head wanders so much that it is with the
greatest difficulty he recollects himself through two

sentences, and in order to accomplish this he is always clapping his hand before his eyes, and applying to his nephews for a word, and for the subject he is speaking on. What he says is not by any means intelligible, at least it requires a great deal of thought and ingenuity to get a meaning out of it. His writing is exactly like his talk. In the midst of all this there is a sort of wild obscure meaning that seems to wander through his mad conversation, and there is a great deal of that sort of sagacity or cunning towards his own personal objects which is characteristic of madness. With all this he is the most ignorant and incapable officer in the world; does nothing, and can do nothing himself, hardly ever knowing what is going forward; never looks at a map, never visits a post, or reconnoitres the ground; dines at eight in the morning, goes to bed for the rest of the day, gets up muddled and crazy for a few hours in the evening; and has owed his whole success in Italy to the excellent Austrian officers who served under him. He is not so mad as not to know that, and accordingly he refuses positively to trust himself with a Russian army alone, or without both Austrian troops and Austrian officers. In difficulty and danger he totally loses his head and lets himself be led very submissively; the danger over, he begins to vapour and take all the honour.

' Such are heroes, and thus the world is led, and such is fame and name. This is a correct picture of this mad mountebank.

' I cannot help wondering at his having gained Lord

Mulgrave and several other Englishmen. They were mostly cured, however, on further acquaintance; but Lord Mulgrave, who saw him but twice, came away an enthusiastic admirer. This is all most strictly confidential. I am come, in spite of all this, to keep him in Germany and to arrange a great Russian army on the Rhine. A Russian army ought to be terrible to the enemy, for it is dreadful to its friends. It is like a great blight coming over a country. They live entirely at free quarters, to the utter ruin of the country-people. The officers are as bad and pay for nothing. The Grand Duke Constantine himself would not pay for his post-horses, and beat the waiters or landlords if they presented a bill for his dinner or lodging. The common soldiers, however, seem to make up for everything by courage and hardiness and obedience in the field.'

'January 6.

' We all got up yesterday at six in the morning to attend Suwarrow at Mass, on their Christmas-day. We saw him crawl on all fours to kiss the ground, and hold his head on the ground almost a quarter of an hour, with various other antics. The vocal music, however, was good and entertained us. After Mass we dined at about nine o'clock, and sat till twelve, by which time all our heads were splitting. Before dinner Frere and Casamajor were presented to him. The latter being extremely tall, and Suwarrow very short, he jumped up on a chair to get at Casamajor's neck and kiss him. He began before we sat down to dinner by drinking a tumbler full of rosolio or strong liqueur, the heat of which seemed to take away his breath. It is the sort of thing that people drink thimblefuls of. At dinner he drank a variety of strong things, among others a cupful of champagne which went round the table ; and as the bottle was going round, he held out his beer tumbler and had it filled again with champagne. The bottle was set down by him at last. Afterwards a servant filled him a large tumbler of something which I did not know, but I presume it was not water. You may imagine that he got fuddled pretty early. He talked incessantly and unintelligibly, becoming more and more inarticulate. As I sat next to him, and that most of his conversation was addressed to me, I was really bored to death. I got home about half-past twelve and went to another great long dinner at the Governor's, at two o'clock, after which I paid formal visits to ladies I had never seen ; altogether it was a long day.'

'Vienna: March 8, 1800.

'January 31 is still the latest date from England, and I am now in the melancholy apprehension that you must wait till the equinoctial gales have blown over, which may make it the middle of April before you sail and almost the end of May before you arrive. We shall have been separated very near a whole year. I cannot at all express either my regret for the past or my impatience for the future, and indeed it is as well I should not enlarge on feelings which you are

sharing with me. Be assured only that through all
my own disappointments my principal concern has been
for your labours, anxieties, terrors, inconveniences,
regrets, and privations. . . . The grand point, however,
is to avoid danger, and I trust you will not think me
less a coward than yourself on this one point. I am
now saying, the *month after next* I am sure of seeing
them, and persuading myself to be resigned to this
longest term as likely to be the earliest. Thank God
it is really coming, and must come. If I could be
allowed to forget the date of the letters I am writing every day, the months might pass less tediously;
but my time is cut into days, and those days even into
many parts, so that I contrive to make it pass as
slowly as I can. I cannot in the meanwhile complain
of anything but the absence of what I wish; for if you
were here, the way of life is by no means unpleasant of
itself, and the great degree of favour in which I stand
with everybody, whether in business or society, is very
gratifying. I have set you a task which few could
perform; I mean to answer the expectations that are
formed of you, and indeed something of the marvellous
is looked for from all the party. However, in this one
case I am not afraid of fame outrunning the truth.
The names, complexions, and qualities of all the children are as familiar here as if they had come with me,
and people will be calling Anna Maria in the street as
they did at Bastia. George[1] comes immediately next

[1] Lord Minto's second son, George, had arrived in England in November, rejoining his family for the first time since he joined the

to Nelson in maritime estimation. There are a number of children of all ages who will be happy to romp in English and German; and I must confess that in Catherine's[1] absence, I have consoled myself with an absolute mistress of her own age, who cries after me and sometimes calls me papa. The lady's name is Miss Emma Meade, Lord Guilford's youngest daughter, who has just cut a tooth without crying; indeed she never cries, and is always entertained with my jokes, which are chiefly practical ones.'

'Vienna: March 23, 1800.

'The mercury was nine degrees below freezing point this morning, and I have no hopes even of a letter till ten days after the thaw, whenever it comes. I still reckon, however, on your sailing about April 10, and arriving here by May 15, which is fifty-three days

---

' Britannia ' off Corsica. A letter from his mother described the joy of the meeting, which took place under Lord Malmesbury's roof.

'Park Place: November 18.

'George arrived here three nights ago, and I was really overcome with joy. He was slightly wounded on August 11 in the neck and back by some splinters, so as to be knocked down and to be insensible for some time, but did not choose to be named among the wounded, lest we should be uneasy; he will pass for a lieutenant next June. Gilbert and John came on Saturday. Gilbert says he has never been in his right mind since he first saw the arrival of the "Goliah" in the papers. The meeting has really been a sight to see; nothing can be beyond the universal affection and delight. George is so much grown I did not know him. A little backward in his education, because he says the schoolmaster was wounded in the action, and has not been able to give them any instruction since.'

' His youngest child, born 1797, married in 1827, Sir John Boileau, Bart., of Ketteringham, Norfolk.

hence, and by meeting you at Prague, if possible, I may have the happiness of seeing you once more in forty-nine days ; a happiness it seems to me impossible to express—it is *just excessive*. I fall on every shift I can to shorten the time, but without any success. It would run off quick enough, God knows, if I had nothing to wish for, but I have the unfortunate knack of carrying whatever is really on my mind through everything else that I do.

.   .   .   .   .   .

' This delay in our correspondence ever since January is uncomfortable in public affairs as well as in private. If anything amiss happens it will be entirely the work of Jack Frost and the frozen Elbe. I have letters from Nelson and Lady Hamilton. It does not seem clear that he will go home. I hope he will not for his own sake, and he will at least, I hope, take Malta first. He does not seem at all conscious of the sort of discredit he has fallen into, or the cause of it, for he writes still, not wisely, about Lady Hamilton and all that. But it is hard to condemn and use ill a hero, as he is in his own element, for being foolish about a woman who has art enough to make fools of many wiser than an admiral. He tells me of his having got the Cross of Malta for *her*, and Sir William sends home to Lord Grenville the Emperor of Russia's letter to Lady Hamilton on the occasion. All this is against them all, but they do not seem conscious. Acton, who has married his brother's daughter of thirteen years old, is no longer the Queen's friend.'

'March 25.

'At length I am made happy by your *estafette* from Cuxhaven. I now look with confidence to the joy of meeting and being again all together, for we must part no more. I should have wished extremely to meet you at Dresden, but that is quite impossible, for I cannot be absent from Vienna for two or three days without the greatest inconvenience and impropriety. I am sure you will be much pleased with Mrs. Elliot and the children, and I cannot tell you how much I should have desired to be one of this meeting. You will enjoy the gallery and the china and the environs of Dresden. I hope you will like my brother's boy Henry. It is time that Catherine should come, for Emma Meade's love and mine is more notorious than ever. You will find yourself here in the midst of old and sincere friends whom you never saw in your life. I assure you that yesterday's *estafette* produced a grand rumour at Vienna. We did all but illuminate for you. You really have been expected with grand impatience, and it is impossible to say how kind everybody has been in my vexations and disappointments, or how kindly they are all disposed towards you and the children. Gilbert's two last compositions in verse and prose are in circulation, and have been copied by many fair hands. Anna Maria has several intimate friends, and arrangements are made, or making, for giving her up masters, and admitting her to hours of other peoples.

'I shall have a country-house by the time you come.

It is not the perfectly beautiful thing I wanted, but on the whole you will be satisfied. The view extremely pretty, and the country full of pretty walks and rides.

' The whole of our intimate society are in a moment of the greatest distress. Madame de Thun is still alive, but really expiring : we expect to hear every morning that she is dead. I do not by any means wish you to see her, and it is impossible not to wish it were over, for her own sake and that of her daughters and friends ; for the lives of some of them are really threatened by this anxiety and misery so much prolonged. I think she cannot last till you come, and your arrival will afford a relief and a comfort even to her daughters, strange as this sort of anticipated cordiality may seem to you.

' It will really be provoking if you miss the spring, which I am told is beautiful and delightful here. It is expected every hour. Pozzo continues to be the most universal favourite with men and women, and is more desperately in love than anybody I ever happened to see even in a looking glass. It is profound and serious. The lady married and virtuous.

.   .   .   .   .   .

' You will like Lady Guilford extremely. She is fun itself, but kept down, poor soul, by affliction for her mother and anxiety for her children and her future lot. God bless you.' [1]

[1] Lady Malmesbury, writing to Lady Minto not very long after her arrival, says, ' So poor Lady Guilford died in your arms ; a shocking and affecting scene ; but you will have been glad to be of use and comfort.'

Lady Minto joined her husband on the 2nd of May 1800, and his anticipations of her pleasure and delight in the home he had provided for her and in its beautiful environs were amply fulfilled. Like her brother-in-law, Hugh, like her staider husband, Lady Minto fell at once under the spell of Vienna. The beauty of its scenery, the ease and charm of its social life, and the unusual attractiveness of the individuals forming her intimates, captivated her. In spite of the ' John Bull ' tastes and preferences she professed, she loved her Viennese life, and left it with regret. Lord Minto describes their settlement at St. Veit not long after her arrival, in a letter to Lady Palmerston :—

(Extract.)   ' St. Veit: June 17, 1800.

' I should wish to give you a notion of our present life and conversation. We are from Vienna about Roehampton distance from London. Our house stands on the side of a hill rising above a plain dotted with villages and villas, and watered by the Vien. From the river the view is beautiful. Mountains covered with wood, valleys and dells, and a magnificent park of the Emperor's. The hill above us rises into vineyards, and is crowned by the Emperor's park. Our house was once a monastery, and is now the Bishop of Vienna's palace ; it is extremely spacious ; the garden in the old style ; straight walks and parterres, with temples and water-spouts and cascades ; but there is gravel, and grass, and shade. Our studies are French, German, and drawing ; and the boys carry on at the same time their studies with Mr. Reed. Gilbert will learn fencing, and dancing when we return to town. They all ride. There is good fishing, and we have open carriages of various fashions and capacities. One of them carries eight of us. The drives, rides, and walks are beautiful beyond description. Our human society is tolerably large, but you will allow it to be good. Besides our eight selves we have James Harris, Mr. Frere, Mr. Stratton, Pozzo di Borgo, and Mr. Reed. If at any period of our stay at Vienna there should be an interval between Harry's school and college which you think might be filled up abroad, there is no safer or better place for young men than this. The manners, conduct, and character of their society are really uncommonly good ; and as I have a fatherly feeling for them all, perhaps you might venture to trust him to my care ; at least while he is too young to become really my son by marrying Anna Maria.[1] Our children *font fortune* here.'

To the ' Home Society' had been added, before Lady Minto arrived, an outer circle, as constant to its nucleus at St. Veit as his belts to Saturn ; and it included the pleasantest members of Viennese society.

[1] In one of his letters to Lady Palmerston, Lord Minto says, ' You are right in thinking Harry a real and great favourite with me. He has good sense and good humour, two trifles which I happen to like in young and old. I wonder where he got them ? '

Lady Minto to Lady Malmesbury.

'September 19.

'The society here is as easy as possible, and nothing is thought odd or strange, so that one may do as one likes. There is no gossip, but a great deal of good nature and a great desire of obliging. The society we have at our elbow at Hacken is certainly the best here. Madame Kinsky is universally beloved for the very uncommon sweetness of her character and her real desire to serve her friends in every way possible, besides being admired for her beauty. She is uncommonly handsome with engaging manners, and perfectly free from self-consciousness. Princess Lichnowsky is extremely clever, but reckoned satirical. I don't see it; she sees things as they are, not *en beau*, and likes a little ridicule. Madame Rosamowsky is most uncommonly clever, and her conversation is in such perfect language it might all be written down. She is in great poverty, and her health always as bad as possible, though her spirits are good, and she lives just like other people. Her husband is banished by Paul to his estate, but he lives in hopes of his being allowed to return here.[1] She says she is very fond of him, which people say is in reality impossible. They have all excellent hearts, but their heads are full of romance; every individual here has a story which might make a novel.'

At a later date she wrote, 'I begin now to know a

---

[1] One of the first acts of Alexander was to reappoint him to Vienna.

certain number of people here very well. There is a Polish Madame Potocka whom I like very much; very sensible, clever, well-informed, and gentlewoman-like. The Poles are, as you know, all romantic to a degree, and so are many of the ladies here. They are much to be liked for their good humour and good manners; but reason and reflection are pretty much banished, and in general their conduct is governed by the fancy of the moment, or by some high-flown notion, novel-like, inexplicable to our roast-beef understandings. There is a round-about, much-ado-about everything, which I sometimes long to cut short by advising the plain common road, instead of which they all prefer a bye-path. The German plays are always before my eyes: the greatest absurdities they contain I see realised every day; and as I see the whole merely as a spectator, I am amused by the contrast to ourselves.'

Among the most welcome of the frequenters of St. Veit were the various members of the family of the Prince de Ligne. In the early days of their acquaintance, Lady Minto wrote,[1] 'We had the Prince de Ligne, the Princess, Princess de Clary and Princess Flore, his daughters, with several others, to dine with us yesterday. He is very constant to us, very clever, but too odd to be understood at first by everybody. I like the whole family, especially Madame de Clary, who is very fat and looks stuffed with good nature. He has now nothing to live on but his pay; but they bear their misfortunes gently, and never grumble or complain.

[1] To Lady Malmesbury.

'We dined the day before yesterday at Dornbach, Marshal Lacy's. He sent his little low chaise to meet us, and we drove the whole way, about an hour and a half, through the most beautiful woods. His place is as beautiful as a place can be—Dunkeld magnified, and yet only three miles from Vienna. In the afternoon we drove round it to a hill on which he has built a number of huts, each containing one, two, or three rooms, like a little encampment—the most delicious thing in the world. His appearance answers to his character—mild and sedate. He is now seventy-four, is much bent, and shows age. Our neighbours, Madame de Kinsky and the De Thun ladies, were with us. Their house is within half a mile of us, and I believe there are not five minutes in the day in which some of our family are not with them. James [1] and Gilbert ride and walk with them every evening, and are much better employed in this way with agreeable women of fashion than sitting three hours, as in England, after dinner, till their understandings are all muddled. Fortunately it is no *bore* here to be *civil* or *amused*; and people may confess they are pleased and happy without fear of disgrace, and show civility to women without being accused of being in love with them.' [2]

[1] James Fitzharris, eldest son of Lord Malmesbury.

[2] This passage has a reference to a letter lately received from Lady Malmesbury, who wrote that she had taken a French lady to a ball in London, and that the intolerable manners and incivility of the men had astounded her. In her answer to the letter above given, Lady Malmesbury said, 'Cobentzel's place is all you say, perfectly beautiful, and I remember it as well as himself. I thought it so Scotch, and him a perfect *gentleman*. Indeed, Joseph had the merit of detesting courtiers,

' It is the rage here to spend summer in the country ; but no one can comprehend the delight of rural life in winter. We dined at Cobentzel's yesterday, a lovely place at the top of a high mountain full of glens and hills, with an extensive view, quite into Hungary. I, who can see nothing, saw the Castle of Presburg with my naked eye. He is a charming little old man, who has laid out every walk himself in the best taste, *quite Scotch!* He was Joseph's friend and minister, but is quite unlike a courtier, and as fond of a farmyard as myself; we talked farming and are great friends. His cow-house is quite a curiosity, like an immense stable, but clean as a parlour, with separate apartments for heifers and calves—quite a suite. He says this is the hottest summer he has seen for years.'

Social pleasures in a town, and above all in crowded assemblies, were far less to her taste than the easy meetings on the lawns of St. Veit. Like Madame de Staël, she thought ' les grandes réunions une habile invention de la médiocrité pour annuler les facultés de l'esprit;' but she conformed her tastes to her duties, and was struck by the magnificence of the Viennese nobility—dinners at Prince Stahrenberg's and Prince Colloredos', where thirty people were served by fifty servants, and assemblies where the women were covered with jewels like the drawer in a jeweller's shop, but pretty in the midst of the blaze.

or what Miss Carter calls *Royal methodists*. She says they are a sect who follow kings and queens as the Methodists did Whitfield, worshipping and kissing the train of their garments.'

'People in general well-dressed and more Grecian even than in England; no pockets, and as lank as possible; no hoops, even at Court. They all wear muslin, but with gold or silver.' And great was the traffic in gold-spangled gowns and turbans carried on between London and Vienna under the auspices of Lady Malmesbury and of Lady Minto. Nothing pleased her more than a *fête* with fireworks in the Prater: 'it was splendid, and the evening such as you never see in England; and I assure you I have seen nothing here that does not surpass my expectations.'

CHAPTER VI.

DURING the spring of 1800 Lord Minto was employed
in strenuous endeavours to promote a better understanding with the Austrian Government, and to rest it
on a more secure basis than verbal assurances of good
faith. On the withdrawal of the Russian army, Baron
Thugut proposed that England should subsidise as
' many German troops as possible' to be added to the
Imperial army, and should also afford such . pecuniary
assistance to the Imperial treasury as would enable the
Emperor to continue the war. The undoubtedly distressed condition of the Imperial finances could alone
have brought Baron Thugut to make a demand which
would necessarily have the effect of giving to Great
Britain a control of the conduct of the war, as it would
entitle her to a principal share in the determination of
its objects.[1]

---

[1] It was obvious to those who had opportunities of watching the
proceedings of the great continental armies, that subsidies to German
troops were a less questionable proceeding in the interests of morality
than the previous subsidies to Russia, which had contributed to
bring a horde of demi-savages on the populations of Italy and
Switzerland. In spite of the brilliant campaigns in both countries, it is
affirmed over and over again in the correspondence of the times that the
doings and misdoings of the Russians filled their allies with dread ; that
the Archduke shrank from co-operation with them, lest the discipline of

The discussions on this subject between Lord Minto
and Baron Thugut occupy a large share in the official
correspondence; but we shall take the liberty of
summing them up in the following dialogue:—

Austria. If I am to dance to your music, you must
pay the piper.

England. So long as I lead the figure, and you renounce a *pas seul.*

So far all was clear.   Unluckily, a third party inter-
vened in the person of the First Consul, whose para-
mount object was to break up the Coalition, by inducing the great Powers to enter into separate negotiations for peace.   Rumours of a correspondence between
Talleyrand and Thugut were rife long before the latter
could be brought to admit the fact; and grievous were
the perplexities of the English envoy during this
period, and wonderful the distinctions drawn by the
Austrian Premier between official and private language.

'Knowing how lightly and loosely he will indulge

his armies should be destroyed.   In the Austrian states Thugut would
not hear of them.   Austria was to be compassionated for the auxiliaries
pressed upon her.   'The Royalist Army' (the corps du Prince de
Condé, composed of emigrants) ' is no favourite in Austria.   The idea of
our Government was to employ them with one of the Austrian armies,
either on the Rhine or in Italy.   But this Court will not listen to such a
proposal.   The truth is that this corps, as at present constituted, must
encumber any army engaged in active service; and I do not think it
can be made serviceable till a great change is made in its constitution.
Till the old and infirm are allowed to enjoy their provision in tranquillity, and the charitable part is separated from the military one, they
never can be anything but an encumbrance.'   The corps consisted of
7,000, of whom between three and four thousand might be considered
efficient.

himself in conversation, and how little he considers himself as committed by anything short of official communications, I wait for such information as may enable me to contend with the Austrian Minister, who has at present that advantage and latitude in argument which his exclusive possession of all the facts may be expected in his hands to afford.'[1]

'I have always found reports circulating in the public of Vienna more unfounded, and even ridiculous, than even those of other towns; and, what is perhaps peculiar to the Austrian Government, that persons in office, even of the highest class, are as ill-informed as the public. I am not sure if this observation might not be extended to the highest office of all, I mean the Emperor himself. His Imperial Majesty gives a considerable portion of his time to public duties, but in fact does not give a regular and steady application to public business. He is by these means subject to every impression that those who transact business wish to give him.'

The English Government grew very impatient of the procrastination and vacillation of the Austrian Minister. Convinced that he was lying by to watch the course of events, Lord Grenville's despatches grew more and more pressing, while Lord Minto was of opinion that influence would be obtained over Thugut by convincing him that Austria's interests were safer in

---

[1] Private letter to Lord Grenville.

a British than a French alliance, and not by plying him
with categorical demands, which, by evincing distrust,
only produced angry or evasive replies.

'What would men have?' said Lord Bacon; 'do
they think those they employ and deal with are saints?
do they not think they will have their own ends, and
be truer to themselves than to them? Therefore, there
is no better way to moderate suspicions than to account
upon such suspicions as true, and yet to bridle them as
false.'[1]

Profoundly convinced of this truth, Lord Minto accepted, as a fact beyond suspicion, that the Austrian
Minister would prefer Austria's interests, as he understood them, to the interests of the Coalition, and took
his line accordingly.

To Mr. Wickham.

'Vienna: April 11, 1800.

'. . . . I have been doubting every day for some
time past whether I should not have to submit to you
the propriety of suspending your present important
labours. I am relieved, however, by my last conferences, and have resumed the hope of settling and signing such a preliminary engagement as may afford us
security for the campaign, and justify the liberal confidence with which we are making sacrifices and exertions on the footing of an alliance which still stands

---

[1] Essay on Suspicions.

on the anxious ground of Austrian reciprocity in the liberality and sincerity which directs the conduct of our Government.

' You will think it strange that Baron Thugut should make such an unnecessary and gratuitous sacrifice of character, and should expose the Emperor's affairs to so much voluntary inconvenience and hazard, by shaking the confidence and alienating the friendship of the only ally that remains to him in a case where he had every motive to give us satisfaction and none whatever to withhold it. Can anyone tell why he was several weeks before he communicated his first correspondence with Bonaparte, or why he has so long refused to acquaint me even with the purport of the last; since both the answers were perfectly fit to be shown to us, and the last as reported by him is exactly iu the spirit we should ourselves have desired? We should often do too much honour to his eccentricities and perverseness if we ascribed them to any deep and designing policy. He is more governed by passion and caprice than a man of his character generally is; and I think, besides, that he has a natural and constitutional predilection in favour of the wrong and especially the ungracious way; as Burke said, " a fond election of evil." Like all passionate men, however, he comes round if a little time is allowed.'

The discovery of some of the secret views of the First Consul, by the means of an intercepted correspondence between himself in Egypt and the French Directory, provoked Thugut to an explicit statement as to the estimation in which he held that personage.[1]

'February 22.[2]

' The last intercepted correspondence from Egypt has produced a similar effect on the mind of the Government as well as of the public of this country. I was so fortunate as to receive very lately a printed copy of that correspondence. On reading some passages of this publication to Baron Thugut, I was struck with his exclaiming, " Then this is a nation (meaning the French) which we should exterminate." When I said the extermination of a nation was impossible, even if it were legitimate, but that I agreed with him in thinking that the Government and system which made that nation fit for extermination should be destroyed and rooted out, he said it was what he meant. In another place he said, "Then Bonaparte will turn out to be a *misérable*, instead of the great man he has passed for." I cannot refrain from adding to these testimonies of Baron Thugut's present sentiments an anecdote which he related to me last night, and which he introduced by saying that your Lordship would have made good use of it, if you had happened to have known it, in your speech on the 28th of last month.

' When the preliminaries of Leoben were to be ex-

---

[1] 'He (Thugut) does not differ much in opinion with us of the instability, and even danger, of any peace made with the present Government of France, but he says that he cannot, as our insular condition may enable us to do, throw away the scabbard.'

[2] Lord Minto to Lord Grenville.

changed, a copy was delivered by the Austrian Minister to General Bonaparte, who delivered another purporting to be the counterpart. When it came to be read, very essential variations and alterations were observed in that which General Bonaparte had delivered. This extraordinary circumstance having been once observed, produced violent remarks and clamour on the part of the Austrians; and the purpose having evidently failed, General Bonaparte coolly produced a third copy, quite ready and correct, which was accordingly accepted. Low and impudent, and therefore incredible, as this fraud must appear, Baron Thugut assured me that it was true and that he possesses the evidence of it.'

But the successes of the French arms and their threatening attitude in Italy did still more, by exciting the fears of Austria, to incline her towards her English ally.

After many projects and counter-projects had been prepared and thrown aside, the negotiations crystallised into a treaty, signed on June 20, by which treaty the two sovereigns ' engaged mutually to support their forces by land and sea, in concert and co-operation with each other; the Emperor of Austria engaging to make no separate peace for a certain period in consideration of the succours which His Majesty has furnished, and is to furnish.[1]

Up to the actual moment of signing this treaty,

---

[1] A subsidy of two millions.

Lord Minto could feel no absolute security of attaining
the desired end. While private letters from Lord
Grenville were urging despatch on the ground that
Baron Thugut, by delaying to put the relations of the
two countries on a distinct footing, was playing the
game of the French party in Great Britain, and that
Parliament would require positive information as to
these relations, the 'dilatory habits of Baron Thugut,
without any particular purpose or design,' seemed invincible. The treaty, when at last signed and sent to
England, contained in certain articles, treated as secret
because relating to territorial arrangements contingent
on the events of the campaign, a departure from the
previous draft accepted by Lord Grenville. The responsibility of this measure Lord Minto took upon
himself; and as the motives which guided him are
shortly stated in a private letter to Mr. Wickham, it
is given in preference to the longer explanatory despatch sent home.

To Mr. Wickham.

'St. Veit: June 25, 1800.

'I sent the treaty to England last night. I have felt
that this is one of those occasions on which the individual
is bound to risk everything; and the ill consequences
of delay were so great, and appeared to me so extremely
probable, that I shall regret no private discomforts if
they should chance to be the price of so great a
public benefit. I labour under one disadvantage, however, which is merely casual; I mean the necessity I

have been under of sending this treaty unaccompanied
by a full explanation of my motives for assenting ultimately to many points which are objectionable in my
own eyes, and for signing contrary to a wish which
Lord Grenville had expressed to see the project first.
. . . Here, therefore, I have occasion for personal
confidence, and the judgment formed in London of
this question must depend almost entirely on the degree of that confidence which I may happen to possess.'

It had been stipulated in the secret articles that the
Emperor should retain certain conquered territories in
Italy as indemnification for the expenses of the war.
These were, besides certain portions of the territory of
Piedmont and Genoa, the three Legations, the territory
of Lucca, and the Valteline. 'The claim to the Valteline is admissible for military necessities ; that to the
Legations is mischievous, for the Catholic Powers
should support the Church. Bonaparte is already holding out promises of restoring Catholicity in France.'
'The territory of Lucca is a new demand,' wrote Lord
Minto, 'and is founded, I think, simply on the desire
of acquiring and the power of doing so. I confess one
cannot see without regret another independent un-
offending state merge in this great Empire; nor the
people of the Republic of Lucca, who were extremely
happy under their own Government and distinguished
among the Italians for industry and simplicity, exposed
to all the demands of a foreign sovereign. I distinctly
intimated to Baron Thugut that these were measures

which could not be viewed with approbation by Great Britain, though they might be received with acquiescence.' But the moral sense of the ambassador was more sensitive than that of his chief, and Lord Grenville in his reply, says : ' With regard to the three Legations, the Republic of Lucca, or the territory of the Valteline, it is certainly very superfluous to enter into the question of right upon any of those subjects. The Austrian Government has unquestionably the power in its own hands to retain these acquisitions as conquests made from a hostile Government; and the only consideration for His Majesty's Government is, whether an arrangement of this nature in favour of Austria is so far repugnant to any British right, interest, or engagement, as to induce or justify His Majesty's opposition to it.'

The conclusion was obvious—England acquiesced in these plans of acquisition. The moment had arrived, foreseen by Lord Minto when he wrote in the previous year to Lord Grenville :—' The question will no doubt arise, how far Great Britain would be called upon to assert the principles of justice and protect the smaller states, which these great military Powers are seeking to devour, by great risks and sacrifices of her own.'

But the truth was that neither risk nor sacrifice on the part of any one Power could control the action of the others ; and the force of circumstances was leading them all to adopt, or to countenance, measures as far removed from justice as those they opposed.

'I confess I have,' wrote Lord Minto, 'gone much
further than I naturally like or approve in recommend-
ing the acquiescence of our Government in the acquisitions which Austria has proposed to make in Italy at
the expense of so many small states and sovereigns.
But it seemed impossible to reserve any part of Europe
from the French Republic without leaving to Austria
some salvage, as it were, of the re-capture.'

In another letter he writes of these and other arrangements as savouring too much ' of the system of
spoliation, which the true and sound haters of the
French Revolution (the character of which is to take
off all restraint from the passions of the multitude
within and of its Government *without*) should abhor
and reject.   If I ever think favourably of these things
for a moment, it is on the compulsion of the present
danger, which is greater than any other can be, and
threatens more radical and calamitous changes, both
municipal and external, in every part of Europe than
any schemes of partition could do.'

However ready to fight the battle of the sovereigns
and states of Italy, Lord Minto was not disposed to
conceal his opinion of the conduct of some of the
Princes who looked to the support of England. Thus
when Mr. Paget, His Majesty's Minister at Naples,
wrote to him by the Queen's desire that she conceived
his sentiments towards herself and her family to have
undergone a change, he took up the challenge, and replied :—

To Mr. Paget.

'Vienna: May 28, 1800.

'My dear Sir,—What you tell me of the opinion entertained at Palermo, that I am less kindly disposed to the
Court of Naples than I was, gives me great concern.
I conceived a very early respect for that Court from the
spirited and courageous part which it took in opposing
the French Revolution; and I have always felt the
warmest sympathy for the misfortunes and perils to
which that conduct had exposed them.   These sentiments were very much heightened by my short residence
at Naples, where I received from the King every
demonstration of favour and regard which could excite
my gratitude or my zeal for his service.

' I had an opportunity of observing the extraordinary
endowments of the Queen, and verifying all I had
heard of her great understanding and high spirit. . . . I
should also say that I was not less struck with General
Acton and the many indications I observed in him (few
as my opportunities were) of a manly and enlarged
character and understanding.   He was at that time in
most perfect harmony with the Queen.   I cannot judge
of the causes which have led to their estrangement, but
I may be allowed to lament it.

' These are the impressions I brought away with me,
and which I cannot lightly renounce, and it will be
with great pain that I shall set about learning a new
Neapolitan lesson.   I must at the same time confess
that several points in the latter period of Neapolitan
affairs have given me great concern; and they have

appeared to me so unlike everything I knew of the minds of those who used to preside in the councils of that kingdom, that I could only suppose some change of court politics had weakened or impaired the influence which used formerly to prevail.   It is in this manner that I accounted for the delay in returning to Naples, a thing impossible to reconcile with the clear understanding and high character of the Queen.   I presumed therefore that she had lost some of her influence and authority, which I very much lamented ; and you have surprised me extremely by informing me that the Queen opposes the King's return to his capital, and even with warmth.

'The abuse of power which has been sanctioned at Rome is another great error, to say no worse, in a moment when it was necessary to court the sympathy of other nations for the oppression under which that Court was itself labouring from those to whose power they succeeded at Rome.   This also seems so unlike the Queen's character and influence, that I have hitherto ascribed these abuses to a diminution of her influence.   The display which has so long been made of weakness and cruelty united, by the severities exercised at Naples while the sovereign himself could only be viewed as a fugitive, is equally remote from my notion of the Queen's heart and understanding.   If these measures were really the Queen's, no personal partiality, however sincere and warm, could reconcile me to them or prevent a great change in my feelings and opinions.

'But I cannot part with all my first impressions while

it is possible to attribute the faults I have described to a more probable cause—the influence of some court intrigue or some personal weakness in other quarters. I may therefore very sincerely say, that if it is in my power to render any specific service to the Court of Naples (not inconsistent with my proper and peculiar duty), I hope they will give me an opportunity of proving the constancy of my attachment.

' My peculiar duty, as all the world must know, is to entertain a cordial union between Great Britain and Austria, and to keep the latter staunch to her course and firm and steady in the prosecution of the war. Naples is as deeply interested as any other country in the success of this object, and will therefore understand the necessity and propriety of those confidences which are found necessary for that success.

' I am sorry to say that the most cruel and scandalous depredation has been committed by the Neapolitans at Rome on private property, and particularly on that of the families best affected to the cause in which Naples was engaged. I may specify the case of Cardinal Albani, who was plundered by the French because he was attached to the cause of the Allies. But they had not time to remove and to carry off their plunder. It seems scarcely credible, but the wreck of this property has been seized by the Neapolitans, who say it was French property, and it is with great concern I must add, the Court has justified this robbery.

' I assure you that it is difficult to imagine how much prejudice has been thrown on the cause of

Naples by this and a few other measures which are not
calculated to excite the sort of sympathy for their own
situation which would have been useful to them.   For
it is impossible to feel so deeply for the calamities of
those who would themselves glean from the ruin of
others what that very rapine had left in its haste
behind it.   The prolonged severity in the executions
at Naples, and the absence of the Court from a miserable country which requires its presence so much, are
other disadvantages under which that Court labours in
the esteem of the world.'

Intercourse with the Neapolitan Court had fatally
damaged the high renown of Nelson, to what extent may
be seen in Lady Minto's letters to Lady Malmesbury.

'July 6, 1800.

'I am to be at Vienna *before four, after dinner,*
to-day, to pay my duty to Duke Albert, where I shall
see the Palatine daughter of Paul.

'Mr. Rushout and Colonel Rooke, whom I knew in
Italy, are here.   Mr. Rushout is at last going home.
He escaped from Naples at the same time as the King
did in Nelson's ship, and remained six months at
Palermo; so I had a great deal of intelligence concerning the Hero and his Lady.   They waited, when
they quitted Naples, two days for the King's dogs and
guns, and after they had been a day at sea, Nelson sent
back a sloop for some more guns of the King's from his
country-house on the sea near Naples.   The first edict

the King gave on his arrival at Palermo was, that it should be death or the galleys to shoot in a certain district which he allotted for his own sport. Nelson and the Hamiltons all lived together in a house of which he bore the expense, which was enormous, and where every sort of gaming went on half the night. Nelson used to sit with large parcels of gold before him and generally go to sleep, Lady Hamilton taking from the heap without counting, and playing with his money to the amount of 500*l*. a night. Her rage is play, and Sir William says when he is dead she will be a beggar. However, she has about 30,000*l*. worth of diamonds from the royal family in presents. She sits at the Councils, and rules everything and everybody.'

'July 10.

'Mr. Wyndham arrived yesterday from Florence. He left the Queen of Naples, Sir William and Lady Hamilton, and Nelson at Leghorn. The Queen has given up all thoughts of coming here. She asked Lord Keith in her own proper person for the "Foudroyant" to take her back. He refused positively giving her such a ship. She has three frigates of her own lying at Leghorn, but she said she could not trust them, and he told her all he could do was to give her a frigate, for he did not know what occasion he might have for a ship of the line. She is very ill with a sort of convulsive fit, and Nelson is staying there to nurse her; he does not intend going home till he has escorted her back to Palermo. His zeal for the public service seems entirely lost in his love and vanity, and they all sit and flatter each other all day long.

'When Lord Keith refused the " Foudroyant," the Queen wept, concluding that royal tears were irresistible ; but he remained unmoved and would grant nothing but a frigate to convoy her own frigates to Trieste. He told her Lady Hamilton had had the command of the fleet long enough. She was still at Leghorn. It is said that much of the cruelty at Naples is owing to Lady Hamilton, and that if she were to appear there she would be torn to pieces.'

CHAPTER VII.

THE battle of Marengo took place on the 15th of June, and became known at Vienna on the 24th; and from this period events hurried rapidly on towards the final defection of Austria from the Coalition.

The news of their defeat had filled the Austrians with dismay; their confidence in a different result from the collision of their army with that of France had been very high, and was justified by the fact that victory was never more nearly grasped by those she finally deserted. 'All the world here knows,' wrote Lady Minto to her sister, 'that the day was lost by the cavalry all turning tail and falling back on the infantry, who behaved incomparably. Yet the cavalry are remarkable for their valour; so it was not cowardice; but the day would have been theirs had they done their duty.'

'Nobody at Vienna,' wrote Lord Minto (despatch, June 28), 'has ever had a competent knowledge of the French forces in Italy. It appears that Suchet's part of Massena's troops had joined before the battle, and Baron Thugut considers the French to have been about 40,000 or 45,000 strong on that day. Kray, he admits, has completely lost the confidence of his army.[1] I have

---

[1] General Kray concluded an armistice in Germany with Moreau on the 11th, on terms so disadvantageous as to cause great dissatisfaction

requested Baron Thugut to point out in what manner we can most successfully assist the Emperor at this moment. . . . 'I have taken this moment to tender, and indeed to press on Baron Thugut, the payment of the generous present which His Majesty has made to the Emperor, of 150,000*l*. towards replacing the losses occasioned by the first reverses in Germany.' In the meanwhile, Bonaparte proposed an armistice, offering terms of pacification on the basis of the Treaty of Campo Formio, and addressing an autograph letter to the Emperor of Austria. The letter is given at length in the history of M. Thiers, but with the omission of a paragraph as characteristic of the writer as any other it contains :—'Donnons le repos et la tranquillité à la génération actuelle. Si les générations futures sont assez folles pour se battre, eh bien ! elles apprendront après quelques années de guerre à devenir sages et à vivre en paix.'

General St. Julien was despatched with the Emperor's answer to General Bonaparte. It was calculated to gain time without committing the Emperor further than to a desire for peace and acquiescence in the proposal to treat, which was absolutely necessary for the extension of the armistice to Germany and its prolongation in Italy.

at Vienna. Nevertheless, the terms demanded of him had been still more extravagant, requiring with great pertinacity that the fortresses of Ulm, Philipsbourg, and some others should be put into their hands. The Austrians apparently would have been willing to make peace in Germany and continue the war in Italy ; a course in keeping with their usual views of their duties to their allies.

The treaty just concluded between Austria and Great Britain precluded the possibility of ' any material step being taken towards a separate peace between France and Austria until His Britannic Majesty should have declined to share in the negotiations for a general one.' Baron Thugut assured Lord Minto that ' no permanent or solid peace could be made by Austria with the inordinate power now embraced by France; that a Cisalpine Republic and Austria could not co-exist. But he hinted at the possibility of a temporary peace, to be accompanied by a secret understanding with His Majesty for the early renewal of the war ; to which I replied that I conceived it not to be consonant with English policy to subscribe a peace with one hand, and an engagement to make war on the same power with the other. On the whole the prospect is no doubt discouraging, as the events which have led to our present difficulties are afflicting in the extreme. But although the prospect is discouraging, it is not desperate. There is a sufficient hope to justify and to call for exertions ; and it would be a culpable despondency to despair of Europe even under the present accumulated misfortunes.'

At this conjuncture the restoration of the Archduke Charles to the command of the army was felt by many, and especially by Mr. Wickham, to be an object of first-rate importance, earnestly to be urged on the Austrian Cabinet. In reply to Mr. Wickham Lord Minto wrote :—

' St. Veit : July 2, 1800.

' I have not neglected to profit by your suggestion

concerning the Archduke Charles, but at present at least it will not do. And in reality I cannot help yet having my doubts on the whole view of this measure. I can conceive the improvement it would make in the army; but a commander-in-chief not only at variance with but in a state of the warmest and bitterest party opposition to the Cabinet, appears to me a state. of things not free from danger. If the Archduke is really indispensable for saving the Empire, he ought to be appointed; but the Minister should be changed at the same time, for the opposition of the head and the arm cannot achieve anything great. Now if Thugut, with all his faults and enormities, were removed, I believe I should not express myself too strongly by saying Talleyrand might as well be appointed in his room as any other. Prostration to France would be the certain consequence.'

The Archduke was the head of the ' peace party,' which, counting many adherents in the Imperial family, was animated by a strong feeling of resentment against England, who was forcing the sword into their hands. ' No doubt,' said Lord Minto, ' the prolongation of a state of war is fraught with misery to the populations among whom it exists; but the choice at the present time is between misery with national independence, and misery without. For myself I cannot hesitate between the alternatives.' [1]

[1] There was misery enough everywhere. The following extracts from Lady Malmesbury's letters show how the war was affecting England:—

' It is necessary to remind or apprise your Lordship of the universal jealousy, envy, and indisposition which pervade Europe, I believe, towards the supposed monopoly of trade and specie enjoyed by England. We are represented as making war, and inciting all other nations to join us, merely for its profits.   This is the favourite topic of our enemy, and it is matter of real wonder to observe the success with which this in- genious absurdity has been propagated; it is current here among all ranks and has complete possession of the Austrian people.   Baron Thugut has to struggle with the peace faction, and to fight a battle for every measure that relates to war and to England.'   ' I can neither answer for his retaining his present situation nor for the conduct of his successors.   Few can have more reason than myself to complain of certain points in the character and temper of this Minister, but I

' Riots are going on all over the country on account of the *rise* in the price of corn and bread, notwithstanding the excellent harvest we have had. . . . In London it was mere mobbing, and the Lord Mayor has done marvellously well, notwithstanding he is a sad blackguard. Our Henley ladies, headed by Mrs. Bellas, the hangman's wife, have carried their point; for after seizing the butter and selling it them- selves at 1s. a pound one day, they threatened so furiously against the next market, which is to-day, that they alarmed the gentlemen and farmers, who held a meeting on Tuesday, and agreed to bring a regular supply to market and sell it at 25l. the load; so the ladies conquered, forty women in all.'   Park Place : September 12, 1800.

¹ Nothing could exceed the dexterity with which the French excited or fomented the suspicions entertained towards England.   Cardinal Ruffo was persuaded that her sole object was Egypt and the exclusion of the trade of Italy from the Mediterranean.   Nevertheless, the people of Austria and of other countries too brimmed over with enthusiasm for England's naval hero.

confess I should look on a change as exceedingly unfortunate in the present position of Europe ; and knowing that the measure of the disgust which he ex-
periences is almost full, and that every drop may make
it run over, I am more careful to avoid provocation
and to manage the feelings and temper of this person
than perhaps can be well thought necessary at a distance.   I confess that on this account I look with uneasiness to the arrival of the Queen of Naples.   Her
inveteracy against Baron Thugut is not to be doubted.
He is well aware of it.   He has more than once declared that if he perceives the slightest marks of the
Queen's influence in public affairs, he will not remain
four-and-twenty hours in place.' [1]

When shortly afterwards the Queen arrived, she
found herself treated with great reserve ; but neither
prejudice nor ill-will directed towards England could
prevent the population from testifying their enthusiastic admiration for Nelson.

' You can have no notion of the anxiety and curiosity
to see him,' wrote Lady Minto to her sister. ' The door
of his house is always crowded with people, and even
the street, whenever his carriage is at the door ; and
when he went to the play he was applauded, a thing
which rarely happens here.   On the road it was the

---

[1] M. Thiers says, in his *History of the Consulate*, that the Queen of
Naples went to Vienna with Lord Nelson and Lady Hamilton *pour soutenir
le parti de la guerre*. It appears from the correspondence of Lord Minto
that this was not the case. The Queen was eager for peace until she
discovered how disastrous to Naples its conditions were likely to be,
and was always opposed to M. Thugut, who led the war party.

same. The common people brought their children to *touch* him. One he took up in his arms, and when he gave it back to the mother she cried for joy, and said it would be lucky through life. I don't think him altered in the least. He has the same shock head, and the same honest simple manners; but he is devoted to *Emma*; he thinks her quite an *angel*, and talks of her as such to her face and behind her back, and she leads him about like a keeper with a bear. She must sit by him at dinner to cut his meat, and he carries her pocket-handkerchief. The aigrette the Grand Signor gave him is very ugly and not valuable, being rose diamonds. The crescent which he wears with the order is very handsome; but he is a gig from ribands, orders, and stars. He is just the same with us as ever he was; says he owes everything to Lord Minto; that but for the " interest he took about him he should have had no reward for his services in the first action, nor have been placed in a situation to obtain the second." '

Modesty and vanity were curiously mingled in Nelson's character, both probably having their root in the same simplicity of nature. He was as grateful to those who had shown him kindness as if his genius could have failed to make itself known without their aid; and the titles and decorations, the honours and praises lavished on him, delighted him all the more because his utter want of self-consciousness prevented him from weighing them in the balance with his great achievements.

On July 9, Lord Minto received instructions which enabled him to inform Baron Thugut of the King's willingness to take a share in the negotiations for a general peace, and these became henceforth the subject of copious diplomatic communications. What, then, was the amazement and dismay of Lord Minto, when on August 7 he learnt from Baron Thugut, whom he found 'excited, feverish, and ill,' that General St. Julien, notwithstanding his total want of powers, had brought back from Paris, whence he had just returned, a protocol, signed by himself and Baron Talleyrand, for a treaty of peace on the basis of the Treaty of Campo Formio! But the German territories which that peace gave to the Emperor were in this case to be compensated by equivalent acquisitions in Italy. The left bank of the Rhine was left to France, Kehl, Ehrenbreitstein, and other fortresses on the right bank were to be demolished, and no fortress to be constructed within three leagues of the river on that side!

Baron Thugut might well be 'feverish' and account for it by the agitation and vexation which this new disgrace had brought upon him. The wording of the protocol, it is said, was such as to clear the Austrian Government from any suspicion of having furnished in writing, or by word of mouth, the grounds on which their agent acted. They not only repudiated these 'turpitudes,' but expressed their conviction that only temporary insanity could have accounted for the conduct of General St. Julien, who on his side was reported to say that M. de Talleyrand had drawn up and prepared the minutes for signature, and had informed him that it was agreeable to the constant usage on such occasions to do so. General St. Julien had also been of opinion that the conditions would be agreeable to the Emperor, in which possibly he was not wrong, for at every stage of this phase of the war the Imperial policy was an Austrian, never a German, one. This curious episode concluded by the disgrace of St. Julien,[1] the repudiation by the Emperor of the terms proposed and agreed on between Talleyrand and St. Julien, and by the consequent determination of the French to resume hostilities on September 10.

'September 2.

' Thugut expresses great regret that this event had not happened a fortnight later, when the new arrangements that are carrying forward in the army might have been nearer completion. . . . Here he can with difficulty acquit himself of a great fault. I mean the unnecessary delay and protraction of those measures, although he had every reason for despatch. . . . That fault has been founded partly in the constitutional slowness of the Austrian Government, and partly in a tone of feebleness which pervades the Cabinet and restrains the better spirit of the Minister : their fear, as is always the case, has magnified their danger. They were afraid of provoking the enemy by putting themselves in a con-

---

[1] ' Baron Thugut treats this act as more disastrous and mischievous even than the convention of Alexandria, and he told General St. Julien himself, that he had deserved to be dismissed from the service and imprisoned twenty-five years. He disavows the whole proceeding as absolutely null.'—*Lord Minto to Lord Grenville.*

dition to resist him, forgetting that the continuance of their weakness was the greatest provocative that can be given to an enemy ; and so it has proved precisely in the present instance. The Archduke John will set out immediately for the army ; his principal adviser will be General Lauer, and the Emperor himself has determined to show himself at the head of his troops.'

Lady Minto to Lady Malmesbury.

'Vienna : September 7.

'You will all be in great surprise in England to hear that the Emperor is going to take command of his army himself as the best measure for doing away party spirit and evil dispositions. I confess it is a proof of spirit I did not think he would have been brought to. The Empress wept, but sued in vain. The Palatine is gone into Hungary to collect troops, and there seems an activity *not* German. I wish it may last, and that it had begun sooner.

'I told Nelson I wished he had the command of the Emperor's army. He said, " I'll tell you what. If I had, I would only use one word—*advance*, and never say *retreat*." He speaks in the highest terms of all the captains he had with him off the coast of Egypt, adding that without knowing the men he had to trust to, he would not have hazarded the attack: that there was little room, but he was sure each would find a hole to creep in at.

'I never looked towards peace as likely from the late

armistice. Bonaparte will never grant one that can be
of any duration till he is well beaten; and when one
thinks how near that was at the battle of Marengo, one
is half frantic. I am therefore not for " peace:" and
as to " goodwill towards men," that is like all general
maxims. I can never feel. it towards such a devil as
Bonaparte.'

The Emperor's resolution to join the army had been
the result of the urgent representations of Thugut, who
owned ' qu'il lui avait fallu livrer un combat' to decide the Emperor to this step. It was a measure Lord
Minto observed ' such as might have been expected to
operate a favourable and sudden change on the spirit
both of the army and the nation, which are far gone in
those fatal maladies of military indiscipline and apathy,
accompanied with the decay of public spirit and the
prevalence of party passions in the country at large,
which precede the dissolution and fall of empires, or at
least of military ones.' The best hope for restoring the
affairs of Austria was, in the judgment of her Minister
and of Lord Minto, ' the infusing of a better spirit into
the German army.' Unhappily the measures of the
Emperor destroyed what expectations had been raised
on the encouragement to be received by his presence.
On the eve of his departure from his capital he despatched letters to Paris and to Moreau, asking for a
continuation of the armistice. Moreau assented till
further orders should reach him. ' He seems to have
put himself at the head of his troops rather to counten-

ance their weakness than to inspire them with new courage.' In answer to Lord Minto's comment on these proceedings, Thugut expresses much chagrin, and owned to the Emperor's personal want of firmness and to the influence of the Empress and of the Royal Family. ' In this anxious. crisis,' wrote Lord Minto, ' my great, and I may say sole, confidence is in Mr. Wickham's most fortunate and providential residence at head-quarters and access to the Emperor and his advisers. He will also be a most useful and necessary watch on M. de Lehrbach. My habitual way of thinking and feeling on these subjects may very probably have exaggerated in my eyes the discredit and evil to be expected from the present measures. I must allow the necessity of accommodating at times the clearest principles to the urgency of temporary difficulties ; and if the weakness of which I now complain should therefore be justified and redeemed by subsequent and successful exertion, I shall be very happy to acknowledge my error and the better judgment of the Austrian Minister.'

Lady Minto to Lady Malmesbury.

'September 19.

' We are still in doubt how this second armistice is to end, but daily expect the answer from Paris, which we boldly hope will renew hostilities. The Emperor has shown some vigour in erasing from the list so many of his officers ; and his manifesto is spirited and proper. If he will but *do* as he *says*, his presence and command of the army must have some effect, probably a great deal. The fault of this Government consists in neither punishing those who behave ill nor rewarding those who distinguish themselves; so that there is neither fear of disgrace nor encouragement to ambition.

'I had a visit the day before yesterday from the Queen of Naples and her three daughters. She knows this place very well, as it was her mother's. One of her daughters, Amelia,[1] is called pretty. The Queen talks away incessantly; she hates Thugut, and he hates her. Though he is not free from faults, he is a man of strong sense, which is uncommon here. Nobody that has not lived in this country can suppose the deficiency of ability in the men. The women are quite different; if they could be statesmen things might go on better. Even his enemies acknowledge that Thugut is the only man capable of being Minister; and the Archduke is their only great general.'

'September 25, 1800.

'Although Lord Minto is in town, I begin writing as I know a messenger must go to-day to inform Ministers of a greater act of folly than any the Emperor has yet been guilty of. His presence at the army had the best possible effect; indifference was changed to zeal, and one and all seemed anxious to regain the time and credit lost. The Emperor's army is at least 120,000 strong and the French only 80,000; in short, no moment could have been more favourable for an attack; but instead of this, he first sent a request to Bonaparte to

---

[1] Afterwards Queen of the French.

prolong the armistice, saying *he* would not be the first to break it.   Bonaparte, with his usual insolence, answered that the only terms on which he would grant a continuation of the armistice were, that the Emperor should give up to him and put him in possession of three fortresses—Philipsbourg, Ulm, and Ingoldstadt, which should all be delivered up to him and his troops within ten days.   That if these terms were not granted, he should order an immediate attack.   The request was granted without delay, and three strong places were yielded up for forty-five days' prolongation of the armistice.   Thugut received this news yesterday morning, and was really distracted.   The Emperor arrived in the evening.   Mr. Wickham was at head-quarters, but was never consulted or informed of what was brewing till it was done.   I foresee that, some day or other, this country is likely to fall a sacrifice to its neighbours, and will be split up like Poland.'

To Lord Grenville.

'Vienna : September 24, 1800.

' My Lord,—Your Lordship will easily conceive the concern, and I may add the indignation, with which I learnt to-day the disgraceful transaction of which the enclosed convention is the result.

.   .   .   .   .   .

' M. de Lehrbach did not communicate to Mr. Wickham any step till after it was taken ; and it appears undoubted that he avoided intentionally giving Mr. Wickham any opportunity of delivering his sentiments or of representing the interests and wishes of His Majesty in this important and extraordinary proceeding. His Majesty cannot view without equal surprise and dissatisfaction these proofs of weakness in a prince whose hands he has done so much to strengthen, and who was in the act of receiving a considerable subsidy for a vigorous and concerted prosecution of the war, at the very moment when he was clandestinely and in person making at the head of a very superior army the most abject submissions to the common enemy. I believe I shall not exaggerate if I say there were 120,000 against 80,000.

'Baron Thugut was all yesterday under the greatest uneasiness concerning this event, which he had reason to apprehend, but which was not yet certain. He still retained a slight hope, however, from the apparent impossibility of such an act of infamy and folly. I never saw him, nor any other man, so much affected as he was when he communicated this transaction to me today. His sense of its enormity is not weaker than mine, and his language is the same. I had said that these fortresses being demanded as pledges of his sincerity, the Emperor should have given, on the same principle, the arms and ammunition of his army. Baron Thugut said that he had used those precise words to the Grand Duke this morning, and had added that after giving the soldiers' muskets, the clothes would be required off their backs. I said that a nation or a prince, which avowed a determination not to fight in any case, would find enemies that would, and they must be accounted already conquered. To which he assented.

'On conversing further on this calamitous subject, he said he told the Grand Duke this morning, that the circumstance for which he felt perhaps most in the whole affair was the discredit that might fall on me, as having been instrumental in forming a connection with a nation so little worthy of confidence ; and he became soon after so strongly affected by these and similar views of the subject, that in laying hold of my hand to express the strong concern he felt at the notion of having committed me and having abused the confidence I had reposed in his councils, he burst into tears and literally wept. I mention these details because, while they do credit to his present feelings, they strongly confirm the assurances I can confidently give your Lordship, from a perfect knowledge of every other circumstance, that every part of the feeble measures which have lately been taken was either adopted against his opinion, or executed surreptitiously and contrary to the directions he had given. This latter disgrace is exclusively the work of M. de Lehrbach, who has practised on the weakness of the Emperor and seized this opportunity of setting up a kind of independence of M. de Thugut, perhaps a competition with him, as it has been long his wish to do.

'The Emperor returned to-day, and M. de Lehrbach has also arrived. M. de Thugut is to see the Emperor to-morrow. This morning he seems determined to retire.   If he consulted his own feelings and honour alone he would no doubt have resigned his portfolio to-day.

.   .   .   .   .   .

'The French pressed for the signature of St. Julien's preliminaries, in which case they would not have required the fortresses.   The Emperor states himself to have yielded the latter point in order to avoid the former.   He states himself to have declared that he would only treat for peace in concert with His Majesty. The French negotiator, La Horie, told M. de Lehrbach on the 19th, and even on the 20th, that His Majesty had positively refused to treat for an armistice; yet the contrary was known at Paris on the 7th or 8th, and the *contre-projet* must have been there on the 10th.[1]

'From the clear demonstration of fraud it results undeniably that neither the English nor the Austrian armistice is binding. . . .

'I have not yet heard from Mr. Wickham, who

[1] A correspondence had been on foot in England with M. Otto, agent of French prisoners, on the subject of our taking part in the negotiations for peace in concert with Austria.   The French demanded an armistice with England, which was at first refused; but the French having declared that the continuation of the armistice on the Continent depended on His Majesty's agreeing to a maritime armistice, it was ageeed to purely and solely to save the Emperor from the possible inconveniences of a renewal of hostilities at a more disadvantageous moment.

The King's assent to this proposal was known at Paris on the 8th of September.   A project of armistice had been sent from Paris, but so absurd and unreasonable that it was of course rejected.   Lord Grenville's *contre-projet* arrived at Paris on the 10th; notwithstanding which, the French who treated with Lehrbach, at only five days' distance from Paris, told him, on the 19th or 20th September, that the English had positively refused to treat for an armistice.   The Emperor received accounts of the truth at Lintz on his return to Vienna.

quitted head-quarters on the 20th or 21st early, and went to Cremsmunster. M. de Lehrbach endeavoured to see him *after all was done*, and then hearing that he had departed, he wrote to desire that he would meet the Emperor at Wels, on his way to Vienna; but Mr. Wickham did not come.'

Baron Thugut resigned on the 26th, at a Council at Schönbrunn, in spite of the great concern expressed by the Emperor, to whom, nevertheless, his Minister frankly stated that, considering the late measures to be the commencement of many calamities to the nation and to the royal house, he could not consent to have any share in the execution of a system which led to such consequences.

The Comte de Lehrbach was appointed to succeed Baron Thugut in the ministry of Foreign Affairs.

'Your lordship,' wrote Lord Minto to Lord Grenville, ' will not expect me to give any opinion, in the present circumstances, concerning the future system or conduct of the Court of Vienna. I have a new lesson to learn, and my duty seems to require in the meanwhile, that I should withdraw every assurance I may have hitherto given or every opinion I may have expressed on this subject. The character of M. de Lehrbach is that of the weakest, and at the same time of the most profligate and the most corrupt man in the empire. He is universally hated and despised.'[1] Besides which it

---

[1] Count de Lehrbach had obtained unenviable notoriety as the author of the catastrophe of Radstadt, when the French agents were murdered in an attempt to seize their papers.

appears as if the government would now be altogether conducted by Court intrigues practising on the weakness of the Emperor. No man will be really responsible, and no measure or system will be in any degree to be depended upon. I have received Mr. Wickham's letter and am confirmed in my intention of protesting at an audience of the Emperor, against M. de Lehrbach's conduct in withholding this important proceeding from Mr. Wickham, as well as against the proceeding itself as it concerns His Majesty, his allies, and the general cause.

'This step will not be an auspicious commencement of an intimate and confidential intercourse with M. de Lehrbach, and I cannot conceal from myself and your Lordship that the duties which are rising at Vienna will probably be such as I shall be very ill-qualified to discharge. But this and many other points must be reserved for the present.'

The demand by Lord Minto of an audience for the purpose of remonstrating with the Emperor on his choice of a Premier, was felt, even by Baron Thugut, to be a somewhat strong measure. Lord Minto, however, appears to have been of opinion that 'Honour's bound to plainness when Majesty stoops to folly,' and though ready to proclaim to the world, if so required, his faith in His Imperial Majesty's virtues, he was determined to open his eyes to the estimation in which his Minister was held.

The narrative of these events is to be found at full length in Lord Minto's despatches to the Foreign Office,

but as it is given with more succinctness and less formality in his private correspondence with Mr. Wickham
and with Lord Carysfort His Majesty's Minister at the
Court of Berlin, we prefer to reproduce it from these
unofficial versions.

It is perhaps unnecessary to add that on all essential points there is the most entire agreement, even to
identity of words, between the despatches and the
letters.

'Lord Minto to Mr. Wickham.

'St. Veit: September 29, 1800.

' My dear Sir,—I have this moment come from my
audience.   Baron Thugut's resignation, and a point of
delicacy which prevented his becoming the channel of
such a representation as I had to make, determined
me, even if the importance of the case had not seemed
in other respects to call for it, to apply directly to the
Emperor.   The Emperor received me at Schönbrunn.
I had reduced what I had to say to writing, and I proposed to tender the paper after I should have read it.
However, the Emperor began the audience by observing
on the irregularity of the proceeding, it being contrary
to the established usage for a foreign Minister to communicate on business with the Sovereign otherwise than
through his Ministers.   I represented the endeavour
I had made to do so, and the impossibility which the
present interregnum in his Ministry creates to follow
the usual course.   I explained the manner in which I
proposed to proceed, but acknowledged myself to be

subject to his commands in that respect, and professed my readiness to deliver the paper I held in my hand to any Minister he should appoint, and to request that it might be considered, notwithstanding the form in which it was preferred, as an official note.   After some little consideration he said that he preferred the latter method, and pointed out the Comte de Colloredo, Grand Chamberlain, who was then in the ante-room, to receive it.   This being adjusted, I nevertheless opened the substance of my note verbally, accompanying it by every expression of respect and of estimation towards the Emperor personally which could soothe his mind and tend to soften the asperity that belonged to the nature and substance of the thing.   I distinguished between the sovereign and his advisers on the English principle, and aimed directly and by name at Count de Lehrbach, whose administration I stated was inconsistent with any degree of confidence on our parts and would probably prove fatal to our connection.   Then the Emperor defended his measure with more vigour than I should have expected. He dwelt on its necessity and on its not being even so disadvantageous in a military view, the garrisons being more useful in the field than the fortresses were beneficial.   He said his intention was to lay the whole in all its details before me, and then to leave the judgment to my own candour.   I must not conceal from you that he leant heavily on your retiring as precipitate and intemperate, and said that he had already ordered Lehrbach to come to me with full explanations of that part of the subject, and that he had actually called on me four times without being admitted.

'He insisted on his right to choose his own Ministers, and the impropriety of another prince interfering in that matter. He rejected the English principle of the responsibility of Ministers for acts sanctioned by the Sovereign. To all these commonplaces I made the obvious reply. I concluded by saying that my intention in this step was to prevent the extreme resolutions that might be expected both in England and in all the countries connected with us, by suggesting the only point by which any confidence could be restored in His Majesty's adherence to that system which had been the foundation of our connection. I added that I considered the indication of a total change of system which resulted both from the transaction itself and from M. de Lehrbach's elevation as more essential and more alarming to other Powers than any other consequences of the measure; that I did not look on the mere loss of the fortresses as fatal or irretrievable; but that I was well assured His Britannic Majesty could not commit himself and the resources of his kingdom, nor attach his fortunes to those of Austria, in a system of vigorous war, or of firm and sincere negotiation, while both were to be directed by the Comte de Lehrbach. I retired without visibly gaining ground. In the antechamber I found Baron Thugut with Count Colloredo, and after explaining what had passed respecting the formality of the business, I delivered the paper to Count Colloredo, repeating again to them both that I had been anxious to suggest this only mode of reviving the confidence of

England, before some extreme and decisive resolution might be taken. I then came home to write this letter. I enclose the paper. The measure you will see is not a half one, and you will not complain at least of not being supported. Stout as the whole proceeding is, it is nevertheless deliberate, and not the dictate of the first heat and agitation excited all over Europe by the event to which it relates. I had settled three points as *right*. First, to speak strong truths to the Emperor on the nature of the transaction, believing that he may probably hear them from no other quarter; and whatever may be the degree of his displeasure and resentment against me, I will be answerable for its doing him good and leaving a horror on his mind of doing a weak thing again. Secondly, to protest against the measure for our own honour and for the satisfaction of our allies. Thirdly, to throw away the scabbard with Lehrbach. I was encouraged by reflecting that I could do no harm, since it was physically impossible I could act from instructions, and everything is open to our Government that they may think prudent. If Lehrbach does not retire, I do, of course. Even if he should, the Emperor may retain personal soreness, which may require a change in this mission. I was and am aware of all this, and my resolution has been taken with these consequences before me. I cannot yet venture to predict the result; but my grand motto is not to despair. I am even disposed to hope in this instance. If this empire is still saved, it must be confessed that it is out of the fire.'

Lord Minto to Lord Carysfort.[1]

'Vienna: October 11, 1800.

'My dear Lord,—Mr. Wickham, you tell me, has already acquainted you with the miserable falling off, at Hohenlinden, from the grand hopes and expectations which the Emperor's departure for the army had created. Those hopes were not founded merely on the natural aspect of the thing, but also on the assurances given by his Minister, and in some instances by the Emperor himself, respecting the principle of that measure and the spirit and intentions with which it was undertaken. I believe the truth to be that he did in reality carry with him the best possible intentions, but he fell unavoidably into the hands of the Comte de Lehrbach, whose grand view was to negotiate a peace and who was already in possession of his full powers for that purpose. The means which Lehrbach's temporary situation with the Emperor gave him to pursue his purpose, were probably improved by the general disposition to peace which prevailed in the army, and by the whispers of those who were immediately about the Emperor's person. He was certainly completely misled ; and not only was he taught, by exaggerations of the enemy's force and misrepresentations of the defects of his own army, to believe in the absolute necessity of avoiding the contest by any sacrifice or concession that could be required, but they succeeded, I believe, even in persuading him that, as a military measure, it was advantageous to surrender the fortresses for the sake of adding the garrisons

[1] H.M.'s Minister at the Court of Berlin.

to his army in the field.   The Emperor did not suspect
till he arrived at Vienna that he had done a weak or
discreditable thing. He was not long, however, of learning the truth here. Baron Thugut, whose consternation,
affliction, and indignation on the event could only be
equalled by mine, resigned the next day after the
Emperor's return.   He was pressed to retain his situation, and the Emperor discovered a warm concern and
regret on the occasion.   Thugut held out ; and after
speaking plainly the opinion he had of the measure
and of the fatal consequences of the spirit which had
dictated it, he retired.   Lehrbach was appointed in his
place.   It is impossible to describe the universal dissatisfaction and terror which this change occasioned.
The warmest partisans of peace began to call out for
an honourable war rather than these ignominious concessions, and the bitterest enemies of Thugut were
lamenting his retreat and trembling at the loss of his
advice and assistance in the present menacing crisis. I
may tell you in confidence that I asked an audience
of the Emperor, used very strong language on the
nature of the transaction and on the exclusion of Mr.
Wickham from a due knowledge of it though he was
at head-quarters all the time, and stated distinctly that
the continuation of the concert with England depended
on the removal of Lehrbach.   This strong measure,
though harsher than I like myself and certainly unpleasant to the Emperor's feelings, was nevertheless
necessary to secure the point, and it proved entirely
successful.

'M. de Cobentzel is appointed minister of Foreign Affairs. Thugut retains the direction of the Italian provinces and the title of Ministre des Conférences. He is the only statesman in the Empire who has any degree of nerve or who has a notion of political interests beyond the convenience and safety of the hour, and I cannot but rejoice in the hope of his spirit and opinions still influencing the counsels of Austria since he cannot direct them more avowedly.

'You will easily believe how confidential all this is. I should apprise you that the Emperor and his Ministers are very jealous of its being known or supposed that he has had *la main forcée* in the choice of his Ministers, and especially by the influence of England, that being the *cri de guerre* of the peace faction and indeed of nine-tenths of the population of Austria. I have, therefore, entirely refrained from the communication of this matter, even to the Courts most strictly connected with us, such as Bavaria and Würtemberg; nor do I mention it to any individual however much attached to our cause he may be. The opinion you expressed from the beginning, of the French having no intention to treat, with us at least, seems to be verified. The fraud and falsehood in which their diplomacy is now so conversant should disgust us of treating otherwise than with fleets and armies. They attempted to swindle us out of an armistice under pretence of suspending hostilities with Germany, and they have swindled the Emperor out of three fortresses under pretence that we would not hear of an armistice. All this was transacted in England and

Germany at the same point of time.   At Hohenlinden they stipulated the extension of the armistice to the armies of Italy, and General Brune[1] has demanded new conditions for that armistice under pretence that Moreau could not bind him at Hohenlinden ; and what is still more remarkable, Talleyrand has made the same demand after the convention of Hohenlinden had reached Paris.   But Bellegarde rejected these pretensions and carried his point, and the Government here will also reject such demands.'

The great point of the removal of Lehrbach having been conceded to Great Britain, Lord Minto, in deference to the Emperor's ' very earnest wish,' signified to him through Baron Thugut, consented to take back the paper which at his audience of the Emperor, he had, by his Imperial Majesty's command, delivered to Count Colloredo.

' Your lordship will be surprised, as I was, to learn that the note which I held in my hand in the Emperor's presence, which he had himself directed me to deliver to one of his Ministers who received it in his ante-chamber, and which related to matters of such importance, had nevertheless not been shown to the Emperor. Baron Thugut owned this to me.   This circumstance determined me to convert that paper into an official note, and I resolved at the same time to take an opportunity of softening those expressions or passages, the ungracious sound of which to the Emperor had probably

[1] Commanding the French Army in Italy.

deterred the Grand Chamberlain from presenting it to him.'

To Mr. Wickham.

'St. Veit: October 8, 1800.

' After all, I believe that in the end I shall withdraw these papers altogether.[1]   Thugut, who wishes ardently to recover the confidence of England, and on the other part to prevent anything like soreness and indisposition on the part of the Emperor, urges me strongly to show this degree of accommodation.   The Emperor will consider these papers as memorials in his chancery of a violence done to him in a matter of which he is very jealous of entire independence, and especially independence of England, his subserviency to us being indeed the *cri de guerre* of Austrian faction.   The object is fully obtained so far as Lehrbach is considered. . . . But I shall not consent to this accommodation, unless I receive from the declarations of the new Minister satisfaction concerning the new system; and if I do receive that satisfaction, I shall consider every object of my former measure as attained, and shall be well disposed to everything which can conciliate the Emperor or Thugut himself on matters which are in truth purely of form, and in the case I have supposed will have nothing of substance left.   I have not brought myself to this temper on the question without a good deal of reflection and hesitation; for although few people are

---

[1] The official note of his conversation with the Emperor.

naturally more prone to conciliation, or more convinced of its great powers in all human affairs, yet I
have a horror of real weakness, which we have seen in
the last eighteen years to be the true tap root of all
evil.'

In a despatch of October 10, Lord Minto informed
Lord Grenville that he had, on the earnest recom-
mendation of Baron Thugut, consented to withdraw
his official note on the subject of his interview with the
Emperor.

The sentiments of the British Ministry on these transactions will be seen in the following extracts from Lord
Grenville's correspondence.

Lord Grenville to Lord Minto.

'(Private.)   'Cleveland Row: October 10, 1800.
                           ('Received October 25, 1800.)

'My dear Lord,—I share with you all the grief and
indignation which the despicable weakness of the
Emperor's councils has excited in your mind. The step
is, I fear, irretrievable, even if from this moment
other principles and sentiments could prevail.

'But what hope is there of this from an Emperor of
Germany who has publicly proclaimed his cowardice in
the face of all Europe and delivered himself up, bound
hand and foot, to his enemies?

> Qui lora restrictis lacertis
> Sensit iners timuitque mortem.

'Yet with all this, we have adhered to our system, not

in the hope of much further co-operation from such an ally, but because we will not give the example to Europe of abandoning, even under such circumstances, those to whom we are bound by treaty.

‘ If *par impossible* it were yet a question who should go to Lunéville to treat jointly with Mr. Grenville, we should have a right to require, and most undoubtedly must require, that it should not be Lehrbach.

‘ But it seems more likely that he will go there and patch up a separate peace, and then we must do the same ; for in their present humour, Russia and Prussia would be much more likely to interfere against our objects than for them.　Send us therefore the earliest notice you can, that we may take our measures accordingly.　　　　　　　　　　　　　‘ Ever, &c.’

(Extract.)　　　　　　‘ Downing Street : October 14, 1800.
　　　　　　　　　　　(‘ Received November 1.)

‘ My Lord,—. . . In this great crisis His Majesty’s servants rely entirely on your Lordship, on a point in which their own characters and the public interest are so deeply concerned ; and they confidently trust that you will not suffer any plea, exculpation, or pretext, of any nature whatever, to prevent your transmitting to them, before that time [1] at the very latest, a distinct, and if possible a written, explanation from the Austrian Government on that interesting question [2] the answer to which must be the guide not only of their own

---

[1] The meeting of Parliament.
[2] Whether Austria should or would not treat for peace conjointly with England.

personal language and conduct but also of the measure
to be proposed by His Majesty to His Parliament.
Your Lordship's decision and spirit in the support
which you have given to Mr. Wickham and in the
language which you have held to the Emperor himself
on the late measures, are entirely approved by His
Majesty, and I have only to recommend to your Lordship a continuance of the same conduct, in so far as
the occasion may require it.

' I am, &c.

' GRENVILLE.'

' October 31.

' I have great satisfaction in assuring your Lordship
of His Majesty's fullest approbation of the well-timed
tone of firmness and vigour which you adopted on
the occasion of M. de Lehrbach's nomination, as well as
of the whole of your conduct in that critical and trying
situation.' [1]

[1] Despatch of Lord Grenville.

CHAPTER VIII

As a natural consequence of the partial retirement of Baron Thugut, all hopes were centred in the restoration of the Archduke to the command of the Army.

'Colloredo,' wrote Lady Minto to Lady Malmesbury, 'the Emperor's and Archduke's old friend and tutor, was sent some days ago to Prague to propose to the Archduke (Charles) once more to take the command of the army, which is still called that of the Rhine.'

But on the 16th of October Lord Minto notified to Lord Grenville the return of the Count de Colloredo, with the disappointing intelligence that the state of the Archduke's health made it impossible that he should resume the command of the army. The 'Archduke will continue to superintend the levies in Bohemia, but asserts his inability to serve in the field, and his physicians and surgeons all declare the impossibility of his encountering the fatigue of body and mind attached to the command of an army.' This was obviously a true statement, for shortly afterwards the Archduke was in the greatest danger from a severe attack of the illness to which he was subject (epilepsy); but it is remarkable that, as stated by Lord Minto only a fortnight before the date of this despatch, the Archduke had described himself to Mr. Wyndham, His Majesty's Minister at Florence, as perfectly well and able to serve if required to do so.   ' Mr. Wyndham, on his return to Florence, passed by Prague, and paid his court to the Archduke.   He was determined, he said, to know the truth on a question which had been so much debated, and asked His Royal Highness roundly what the state of his health was.   The Archduke answered, without any appearance of reserve, that a great deal he knew had been said about his health, but the fact was that for three months past he had had no illness beyond trifling indispositions, such as happened to everybody, and that he was as fit to serve at that time as he had ever been at any period of his life.   This is the account of the conversation which I received from Mr. Wyndham himself as he passed through Vienna.   Other persons have given similar accounts of the Archduke's conversation.   The Duke Albert has held the same language ever since his return from Prague.   It is difficult to avoid the conclusion that the Archduke has wished to give an impression to the public, which has already produced infinite mischief, that of his having been removed from the command and retained in retirement by a political intrigue and not by his illness. A determination to make peace may be supposed, in cases that justify it, a good qualification in a Minister ; but I cannot conceive a passion for peace and an aversion to the war to be in any case good or even safe qualities in a general.'

In defiance of three several conventions and of an
existing armistice, 20,000 French troops entered Tuscany and took possession of Leghorn on October 16.[1]
'Alas! they have got beautiful Tuscany once more,'
exclaimed Lady Minto.   General Bellegarde, the
Austrian commander, showed considerable spirit, and
but for the weakness of the counsels at Vienna might
have prevented this catastrophe.   Before it was positively ascertained, Lord Minto sought an interview
with Count Colloredo to urge on him the disgrace of
abandoning Tuscany.   'Very like talking to any other
Lord of the Bedchamber.'   Colloredo modestly dis-
claimed all knowledge of business and referred him
to Thugut, who had no longer the confidence of the
Emperor.   .

Lady Minto to Lady Malmesbury.

'Poor Tuscany has undergone the most complete
pillage, far beyond any place the French have yet
. visited. The money they have levied is about 800,000*l.*,
and they have taken everything precious and valuable
in private houses as well as what belonged to the Grand
Duke.   The Venus is gone.   The Tuscans behaved as
well as possible, but were totally deserted by the Aus-

---

[1] 'If there was a grain of spirit in the Austrian counsels, this single
event of the capture of Leghorn ought to rouse it to action, and the
evacuation of that place ought to be made a *sine quâ non* preliminary of
all negotiation. But such measures are, as Mr. Fox calls it "too strong
for the present day."'—*Lord Grenville to Lord Minto*, Cleveland Row,
October 31, 1800.

trians and left to their fate. It really makes my blood boil. The French invasions of Italy have been positively barbarous.'

' In the meanwhile,' wrote Lord Minto to Lord Grenville, ' the brave and noble conduct of the Aretins on this occasion forms a striking contrast with that of Austria and seems to blazon her disgrace. I must do Baron Thugut the justice to say that he feels deeply and acutely the shame which this dishonourable transaction has brought upon the name of Austria. Arezzo was defended with the greatest obstinacy notwithstanding the deserted and abandoned condition of its people. It was at length carried with great loss to the enemy, and given up to pillage for several hours, while the Austrians were spectators at open windows of these horrors, having afforded neither assistance nor advice. When I learned these particulars I ceased to feel any scruples concerning the strong language of the note which I had delivered on this subject.'[1]

Lord Minto to the Hon. H. Wyndham.[2]

'Vienna: November 14, 1800.

' My opinion of the late transactions in Italy is exactly what I presume yours must be; and I can safely say that my feelings are not less lively than yours on the invasion of Tuscany, and the dishonourable manner in which that country has been deserted by Austria. It is impossible not to admire the noble conduct of the

[1] November 7, 1800.
[2] His Majesty's minister to the Court of Tuscany.

unfortunate Aretins, and our sentiments of respect as well as compassion for them must be accompanied by the resentment which it is impossible not to feel against those who have betrayed and abandoned them. I am very desirous that you and they should know that I did not lose a moment after I heard of the danger to which Tuscany was exposed in giving to that country and to the rest of Southern Italy the support to which they were so well entitled from His Majesty's Minister at this Court. I have not ceased to urge the Austrian Ministers to prevent the invasion of Tuscany, . . . and afterwards to expel the enemy and enforce their retreat within the limitations fixed to them by the subsisting conventions. . . . If I have not succeeded, it has not been for want of application or energy. I believe few Ministers have spoken plainer truths and held stronger language. The measures I have taken have not been without some effect. I have obtained a promise that Count Cobentzel should make the strongest remonstrances to the French Government on their flagrant violation of faith, should insist on the evacuation of Tuscany, and should not treat for an armistice till this is effected.'

The disasters that had overwhelmed Austria had naturally weakened her influence with the smaller states of the Empire, some of which desired to avert the ruin impending over them by timely submission to the conqueror. Angry despatches poured in upon Lord Minto from his colleagues at various minor courts, denouncing the cowardly and selfish policy of princes who were accepting the subsidies of England with one hand and holding out their swords with the other to victorious France.

In these moments when the political thermometer was at fever heat, Lord Minto's calm, candid, and forbearing temper stood him in good stead. Numerous despatches attest the fact, which we shall only strive to prove by extracts from one or two, of his constant desire, in judging the conduct of our allies, ' if nought to extenuate, to set down nought in malice,' and to impress on his colleagues the duty of forbearance towards princes, not only threatened with ruin by their enemies, but galled and smarting under the high-handed and often unreasonable proceedings of their friends.

The Duke of Wurtemberg, who resided at Vienna in the autumn of 1800,[1] was one of those accused of being eager to separate his own from the falling cause of the Empire and of being peculiarly bitter in his language against Great Britain ; nevertheless, he was not only on terms of personal courtesy with Lord Minto, but on more than one occasion had resorted to him for advice ; hence, some remonstrances on the score of the Duke's unfriendliness were addressed to Lord Minto, who replied that the little share he had had in the Duke's

[1] ' Moreau is now living in the Duke of Wurtemberg's house at Stuttgardt. The Duke, his brother, and son are here. The Duke's son has proposed to one of the Queen of Naples' daughters, and so has the Duc de Berri. She has not yet decided which she will favour. The Duke of Wurtemberg is handsome, and they are equally poor.'—*Lady Minto to Lady Malmesbury.*

concerns was owing to his accidental residence at Vienna. ' Besides the natural claim he seemed to have as an ally and relation of our own Court to support from an English Minister in his relations with this Government, it seemed impossible to refuse a patient and even a kind and friendly ear to the lamentations and alarms of a prince whose ruin seems so much a consequence of his relation and engagements to us. . . . It is not to his merits, but to his misfortunes, or rather ruin in a common cause, that my indulgence is directed. I admit also that he is no apostle of our cause, and I can easily believe all you say of the mischief done by his indiscreet and perhaps ill-affected language : yet I have not nerves to resist altogether, or rather not to feel some indulgence for, the cries and clamour of a real *agonie* ; for he is at present struggling in the very convulsions of political death.'

About the same time he wrote to Mr. Drake, who had informed him that the Elector of Bavaria was sending an agent to Paris, for the purpose, as was suspected, of negotiating a separate peace.

' Vienna: November 7, 1800.

'. . . In speaking of a mission to Paris, I should not wish to make it a subject of reproach. Morally speaking, there is perhaps much to be said for the Elector, and I enter perfectly into the exculpatory parts of M. de Monglas' note to you of October 27. With an enemy in possession of his country and driving him by the extremities of military vexation on one hand, and inviting him by every sort of seduction on the other, to their own purposes; with many provocations which I cannot deny Austria to have given; with many motives for alarm in the critical and equivocal appearance of things; and without sufficient assurances or security for protection or safety, much less for indemnification or recompense; I cannot feel anything like resentment against measures which are taken with a view to relief against present sufferings and to future safety.

'But, with all this, there is one view of the matter which seems to arise out of your correspondence, that I confess would very much diminish the charity with which on other grounds the conduct of the Elector might be considered. If he is not driven to the measure by necessity, and if he does not merely propose to avert present ruin by an accommodation with the enemy, but if it is an affair of political speculation and he is carrying himself to the best bidder, I shall think his conduct as dishonourable as I am already convinced that it is in every view impolitic and imprudent.'

On the occasion of Lord Minto's first audience with the Emperor subsequent to the removal of Count de Lehrbach, he was received in the most gracious manner and with more than usual civility. In the course of November the Emperor professed an intention of returning to the army; a measure which on this occasion probably met with small encouragement. Baron

Thugut fairly owned that 'if any considerable disaster should happen, no power on earth would be able to restrain him, in the moment of alarm from some weak or precipitate measure.' At the same time Baron Thugut, in great confidence, mentioned that he had reason to believe an offer to accompany the Emperor on the part of Lord Minto would not be unacceptable. 'I naturally suggested the possibility that the strong measures I had been obliged to resort to on some recent occasions might make me personally obnoxious to the Emperor. But he assured me that the contrary was remarkably the case, and that the Emperor always spoke of me with a sort of regard that was not usual with him. That he always expressed a strong belief of my probity as well as of my friendly disposition.'[1]

The project was ultimately abandoned and the Emperor remained at Vienna. Some extracts from Lady Minto's journals, kept for the benefit of her sister, describe the daily fluctuations of feeling there.

Lady Minto to Lady Malmesbury.

'The indecision of the Cabinet of Vienna is wearing —at all events to me. The general mode of action is from the impulse of the moment, which seems of late to consist only of fear.'

'*December* 4.—The Archduke John attacked the enemy on December 1, near Haag, and obtained a com-

[1] Lord Minto to Lord Grenville.

plete victory, though the enemy fought desperately. The Archduke is not yet nineteen years of age.'

'*December* 7.—All our hopes from this victory are blasted. The Archduke attacked the French, and was entirely defeated by Moreau at Hohenlinden.'

'*December* 16.—The Archduke Charles has at last set out to join the army, which has called loudly for him. The French are now within 14 posts of Vienna.'

'*December* 24.—The Archduke has joined the army and finds it is in the worst state possible. The mutinous spirit broke out and rose to an alarming height. We are now coming fast to the catastrophe and have begun to pack up to remove from hence. All the Royal Family except the Emperor and Empress will leave to-morrow; of course Lord Minto stays with the Emperor. We shall, if possible, send off our plate to Presburgh to-morrow. The Danube is not so much frozen as to prevent the passage of a boat.

'N.B.—We have not got one yet.'

'*December* 27.—Another armistice for thirty days. The state of the Austrian army is beyond description. The Archduke Charles yesterday reviewed them man by man. The sight is said to have been deplorable; and as they passed him he placed seven superior officers under arrest, publicly declaring that they had been the cause of misbehaviour of the regiments to which they belonged. The men are absolutely worn out by

fatigue and hardships. To one of the officers who made
an impertinent reply, the Archduke said, "I am sorry
to see you know neither how to command or obey." In
such a moment this spirited conduct is fine. The young
Prince of Wurtemberg and his regiment were highly
praised for conduct, discipline, &c. The works in and
out of the town are going on as they were before.'

'*December* 30.—Although you will see by the terms
of the armistice that peace however bad is the only
thing left for this country, yet we are going on here
more than ever with all the preparations for war. Day
and night thousands of men are employed in raising
cannon, working entrenchments at the lines, and putting up palisades, and all the appearance there is of ex-
pecting a siege. The Hungarian troops are to be quar-
tered in and about the town and even great part of
the main army. Every house has its allotment ; luckily
foreign Ministers are excepted from receiving such very
disagreeable inmates. All strangers have received orders
to quit Vienna and to remove to a very considerable
distance. Moravia and Bohemia are open to them provided they do not live in the large towns ; and all the
officials are preparing to set off with their papers and
attendants. The reason given is, that from the additional number of troops in the town, provisions and
necessaries would become scarce and dear ; but as papers
do not eat, this reason cannot extend to them.

'The women seem to me to have more ability in this
country than the men.

'Thugut is acknowledged even by his enemies to be the *only* man capable of being Minister ; and the Archduke in the same manner is their only general. Unfortunately they are in high opposition to each other ; and this has caused (by faults in both) all the disasters ; for had the Archduke taken the command two months ago, when he was invited to it, things would not have been as desperate at this moment. It is shocking to think how the little and ignoble passions of man have injured the general cause. Actually half the last levies are little boys hardly able to carry their muskets. Fourteen years' war is enough to ruin any country ; and the number killed and dead from their wounds in this year is quite incredible. Poor creatures ! those that remain are half dead with fatigue and hardships. Many have not lain down to sleep for the last month, but have sat round fires in the open air all night. Their shoes and coats were so much burnt that they were often obliged to march barefooted, and of course their feet were full of sores. Several times, from being driven a contrary way from what they had expected, the baggage missed them, and they were without bread for two or three days together. The French army is also said to be in a bad state ; but whenever anyone disobeys orders he is immediately shot.'

'*January* 1, 1801.—I took an airing yesterday to see the works round the town and in the lines. Thousands of people are employed, but they work in the true German way—smoking and eating and not hurrying themselves with labour.   As long as they can enjoy their tobacco and fried chicken they think little whether the French are far or near.'

'*January* 2.—All the workmen are paid off who were employed round the town.   Peace must take place, and a wretched one it will be.'

Count Cobentzel having been instructed to enter into a separate negotiation at Lunéville, Lord Minto, in a despatch of January 2, 1801, gives the reasons for which he conceives Great Britain should not view the resolution of the Emperor as a culpable violation of the treaty of June :—

'In the fair interpretation of that engagement it must be allowed that the Emperor is bound only to the *bonâ fide* exertion of that degree of vigour which the habits and character of his Government supply ; and that neither the incapacity of his generals, military councils, the disaffection and misbehaviour of his troops, nor even the errors and faults of his Cabinet, are imputable to him as breaches of faith. . . . Though the exertions of Austria in the war have been completely unsuccessful, and her conduct has been marked with extraordinary weakness in a variety of instances, yet we must acknowledge strong evidence of a sincere desire to cultivate a cordial connection with us and to act fairly by us in the performance of her engagements. . . .

'I observe that the delay in the conclusion of the

treaty (June 20) has been generally ascribed to a sort of temporising duplicity of this Cabinet, which is accused of having protracted the negotiation for the sole purpose of watching events. . . . Your Lordship knows that the treaty was signed before the battle of Marengo was known at Vienna. The effect of that calamity would have been exactly the reverse of that which is imputed to it. If the intelligence had reached Vienna before the treaty was signed, it would have been impossible to have obtained the signature. . . . The Government would have trembled at any engagement which might stand in the way of any weakness and ignominy leading to peace. As it was, I have always considered the conclusion and signature of that treaty as an exertion of good faith on the part of Austria, and as a strong testimony of a favourable disposition to Great Britain; for the crisis in Italy was approaching, and the catastrophe was to be expected every day.

'. . . From the day on which the treaty was signed I admit that there has hardly been an hour without an anxious mistrust or which did not require a constant and unremitting vigilance to keep this Court steady to the duties which she owed to herself and to her ally. This diffidence has, however, never been founded on a doubt of the sincerity of the Austrian Government, but in a daily experience of its weakness and pusillanimity; and the more the latter quality is admitted the more we must acknowledge the principle of fidelity which has surmounted the very habit and constitution of the Government.

' Throughout the negotiations of Lunéville the intention and conduct of the Government has been clear, firm, and loyal. The fatal battle of Hohenlinden, the passage of the Inn, the battle of Salzbourg, and the occupation of Lintz by the enemy, failed to shake the Emperor's resolution to treat only in concert with Great Britain. The resolution to treat separately taken on December 22nd was solely the result of the hopeless condition in which the Archduke Charles had found the Austrian army. The troops were literally disabled by fatigue, want, and hardship of every sort from standing against the enemy. They uniformly threw down their arms and fled on every approach of the enemy, however inferior the numbers. The Archduke declared there was no remedy for the disorder of the army, and no possibility of stopping its progress.'

Lord Minto to Lord Grenville.

' January 11, 1801.

' The Archduke Charles has been appointed President of the Council of War. Every measure that has been taken since the armistice has breathed the same spirit of unconditional and precipitate submission, and great as the danger has been, it has evidently been increased, as is always the case, by the fear which it inspired. I cannot help owning that all I have seen in one of these periods which may be considered as the touchstone of character and genius, has not tended to exalt my idea of the Austrian Government in any of its departments.

'Baron Thugut, though acquiescing in the necessity of peace, manifested a disposition to treat that measure as well as the Italian armistice with a somewhat better countenance than was thought suitable to the occasion by every other person—hence, some expressions were let fall by the Emperor and Archduke in their communications to Thugut, conveying an opinion that obstacles to peace would be created as long as he had a share in the direction of affairs. Upon this hint, Thugut retired. . . . He was succeeded by Count Trautmansdorff, a man of family and fashion, remarkable for politeness and for those talents which distinguish a man of the world in society and conversation, a gentleman in character as well as in manners : we cannot look for a spirited or enlarged policy from him, but we shall not have to apprehend a low and dirty proceeding at his hand.'

Lady Minto's Journals.

'*January* 11.—The Emperor told me to-day that the French are destroying the country they are in. The Archduke Charles is placed at the head of the Council of War, and it is supposed by his friends that he will restore order and discipline in their armies. At present it signifies but little. He certainly has been the great original cause of the dissensions. He has long been for peace, and has publicly declared that it must be made at any price, which is not high language for a good general to use before the enemy.

'Thugut has again resigned, being still inclined to fight the battle in words, and if that will not do, to try the army again in Italy. Lady W. Bentinck writes that Bellegarde is in so good a position he is certain of beating the French if allowed to try.'

'*January* 24.—God knows what is to become of Naples. The Queen is much alarmed and furious with this Court—indeed, no wonder. No terms have been made respecting Naples in the Italian armistice, though the promise was absolute, and sent by this Court to Palermo within this fortnight. This breach of faith is a new proof of the Emperor's character, and is a bad presage of the Archduke's influence. It is very difficult for me to believe any of that family wise or great.'

'*February* 3.—The Archduke is for peace, Thugut for war. The Grand Duke will now see that his boasted neutrality has saved him in no possible way. How could the Emperor consent to the overthrow of all his own family with an army of 100,000 men round his own capital? Military intriguers have been at the bottom of all the evil. It seems an odd way of making peace for the enemy to keep his armies in the country, causing every sort of devastation and distress. This is to be the case till the peace of the Empire is concluded, and that will be when it suits the Consul's convenience.'

'*March* 16.—I do not think I ever told you the

economy of this Court. When the Princess of France was married they were to pay her the remainder of her mother's fortune, and on paying it they deducted from it the expenses while she had been here—breakfast, dinner, and supper, an account of which had been kept for that purpose. This is royal hospitality. The Queen of Naples gave the two French Princes 500*l*. each when they left Vienna, which, in her present circumstances, was handsome. She is in despair, and so she may well be, for the way in which Naples is to be protected is in fact taking possession of it.'

'*April* 7.—Thugut came and passed two hours with me before he left Vienna; he looks, I think, desperate, sly, and clever; if he were without the faults that are universal here, *trick* and *cunning*, he would be a great man.'

CHAPTER IX.

ONE of the first despatches received by Lord Minto
in the beginning of 1801 announced the resignation of
Mr. Pitt, the cause of his retirement being stated to
be the determination of the King not to grant the
Irish Catholics the political equality which they had
been led to believe would be the result of the Act
of Union.   In a private letter to Lord Minto Lord
Grenville repeats the statement, adding that Mr.
Pitt, Lord Spencer, Lord Camden, Mr. Dundas, Mr.
Windham, and himself, were fully agreed in the
opinion that their retirement was thus absolutely indispensable.   He then proceeds as follows :—

'Report and speculation will perhaps also have conveyed to you other supposed motives for this resolution ; but I do not fear your thinking so meanly of any
of us as to suppose us capable of assigning other
reasons for our conduct on so great and trying an
occasion than those by which, and by which alone, it
was really actuated.   Though public situations can, in
the present state of Europe, be matter of envy or desire to no considerate man, yet I should be sorry to be
thought to have adopted this step without concern, or
to be either insensible or indifferent to the consequences which may, more or less, follow from it.

' But there was no alternative except that of taking this step or of agreeing to the disguise or dereliction of one's opinion on one of the most important questions in the whole range of our domestic policy.

' You will have heard of the King's determination to form on this occasion a new Administration from among the friends and supporters of the present system. I most ardently wish that he may succeed, and certainly my best aid and support shall be given to those who undertake to carry on the Government on the same principles for which we have been so long struggling. I should do great injustice to my own feelings if I closed our official correspondence without thanking you, in the warmest terms, for the infinite assistance we have derived from your services at Vienna. That they were not more successful can in no respect be attributed to you, but belonged to the fatality which has prevailed in the Austrian counsels and arrangements.

' I beg you to be persuaded that in all situations I shall ever retain a lively sense of your conduct and a sincere desire to cultivate your good opinion and friendship.' [1]

Before the arrival of these despatches from England, Lord Minto had (on February 15) addressed a letter to Lord Grenville, asking for his recall, on the ground that he conceived the separate peace made by Austria to be the natural conclusion of a mission destined

_____
[1] Lord Grenville to Lord Minto. ' Cleveland Row: February 13, 1801.'

solely to prevent such a consummation. How he felt on hearing the news of Mr. Pitt's resignation may be seen in a hasty note to Mr. Windham.[1]

'Vienna: March 6, 1801.

'My dear Windham,—In two words I adhere most heartily and unreservedly to those who have resigned on Catholic Emancipation, and I only wish to be amongst you as soon as possible. I fear, however, there may be a good deal of delay in my return, for I cannot quit my post till I am actually relieved. I have heard nothing distinct on the ground of your late transactions ; but I understand in general that you go out on the Catholic Question, which is enough to decide me independently of my personal preference for the men. I am always happy to find myself by your side. I have conceived, on very certain grounds, a very high opinion and esteem for Lord Grenville, and I have long looked on Pitt as the Atlas of our ruling globe. Our kindest and most affectionate remembrances. Ever, my dear Windham,

'Your most affectionate

'MINTO.'

A few days later Lord Minto wrote to Mr. Pitt.

[1] The Right Hon. W. Windham.

To Mr. Pitt.

'(Private.)   'Vienna: March 12, 1801.

'My dear Sir,—Lord Grenville and Mr. Windham will have communicated to you the sentiments I expressed to them on the first intelligence I received of your resignation and theirs. I cannot, however, refuse myself the satisfaction of conveying directly to yourself my entire and cheerful adherence to the principle on which it became necessary for you and them to retire from office, and my desire to partake in the sacrifices and consequences which an adherence to that principle may require. I have already pronounced my opinion upon Catholic Emancipation ; and independently of the pledge I have given to the public on that important question, my opinion is too much settled, and the matter is too weighty, to have left any choice or hesitation in the part I had to take, even if I had not been confirmed in these sentiments by your concurrence. My situation, however, as a very private individual, was extremely different from yours; and I am persuaded that not only the important measure you took was conformable in general to your way of thinking on the question, but that you found it unavoidable, under all the circumstances, to incur for the public all the hazard to which this unfortunate and most unseasonable change could not fail to expose it.

'The despondency and alarm created in this part of Europe by the dissolution of your Administration has been very striking; but I have already touched on that topic to Lord Grenville, and shall detain you no longer.'

To another correspondent [1] he said :—

' I acquainted you in my last with the change of Ministry in England. Immediately after the date of that event, the King became ill with the same symptoms as in 1788. I have already requested of Lord Grenville a successor at Vienna. I have always considered the Austrian peace as the natural term of my mission, and there was nothing in the particulars of the peace that has been concluded, nor in the circumstances of the times, that offered any inducement to depart from this original intention and to prolong my residence here. I had therefore taken that step independently of any motives which the change of Ministry and the question which gave occasion to it would have furnished. Yet I have so strong an opinion on that point, Catholic Emancipation, and have pronounced that opinion so distinctly, that I have been desirous of declaring my adherence to the Ministers who resigned on that particular ground, and my desire to partake in all the consequences of that measure. I have therefore commenced my correspondence with Lord Hawkesbury by requesting that a successor may be sent to relieve me as soon as possible. . . . The Archduke Charles has had a most violent and dangerous attack of his well-known complaint, but we flatter ourselves that the danger is past.'

[1] To Lord Carysfort, His Majesty's Minister at Berlin.

About a week later, Lord Minto received the following letter from Lord Grenville :—

'(Private.)   'Dropmore: March 6, 1801.
                                         '(Received March 26.)

'My dear Lord,—I received by the last mails your letter marked " private " of February 15, and I thought it my duty to communicate it to Lord Hawkesbury.

' You will have been apprised by the letters you will have received, both from me and from your other friends, of the changes which have been determined on here, and of the circumstances which have prevented any of those changes being as yet actually carried into effect, except those of the Admiralty and of the Foreign Department. I have, however, the happiness of being able to assure you that the King's recovery is advancing rapidly and that there is every possible ground of hope that nothing more will be necessary to be done for carrying on the public business than that the persons who happen to find themselves in the different offices of responsible government should continue to discharge the duties of them for a short period longer. If I had been in that predicament I should have felt it my duty to do my best in it; but I am certainly not sorry that accident had completed my release from a situation in which, under such circumstances, one could not hope to do much good.

' I take it for granted that Lord Hawkesbury will have written to you on what relates to your own situation, and it no longer belongs to me to do so.

' But I trust you are persuaded that I have not

omitted to do the justice I owe to your exertions and
services at Vienna, a testimony which inclination as
well as duty will always make me desirous of bearing
both in public and in private.   I am highly gratified
by the kind and friendly sentiments with which your
letter concludes, and it will be a real pleasure to me to
avail myself of any opportunity to cultivate a friendship
which I sincerely esteem and value.

'Believe me, &c.,

'GRENVILLE.'

The same post brought to Lord Minto a letter from
Lord Hawkesbury.

'(Private.)   'London: March 10, 1801.
                                     '(Received March 26.)

'My dear Lord,—Lord Grenville has communicated
to me the letter he received from you by the last mail,
in which you inform him of your desire to quit your
present situation as soon as a successor can arrive at
Vienna to replace you.   After the able manner in which
your Lordship has discharged the duties of a foreign
Minister during one of the most eventful struggles
which have ever existed, it is with great concern that
I have learnt your determination, and I am confident
that in expressing this sentiment I have expressed that
which will be equally felt by His Majesty and by every
one of his confidential servants.   In the state in which
His Majesty's health has been for the last fortnight, it
has not been in my power to receive his commands on
any points of business.   I have great satisfaction, how-

ever, in informing you that he is now almost wholly recovered, and I trust that a very short time will elapse before he will be sufficiently well to receive his Ministers. As I understand from your letter to Lord Grenville that you wish to prolong your stay at Vienna for as short a period as possible, I will take His Majesty's pleasure respecting your successor on the very first opportunity. I trust, however, you will be induced to remain at Vienna till he shall arrive, and that you will give him all that information which he can expect to receive from no person so well as from yourself.

'The disputes with the Northern Powers are likely in the course of a very few days to be brought to an issue. Sir Hyde Parker will probably sail this day, and I feel confident that the very appearance of so formidable a fleet in the Baltic will bring some of those Powers to reason.

'Believe me, &c.,
'HAWKESBURY.'

No fresh light is thrown on the circumstances which decided the retirement of Mr. Pitt by the correspondence of Lord Minto with his ministerial friends; therefore no more of it will be given; but some letters of Lady Malmesbury's to Lady Minto, break so brightly through the cloudy crisis, that she shall be, just for the moment, our secretary for home affairs.[1]

[1] The following passage in one of Lady Malmesbury's letters of the previous year, October 13, 1800, shows some political acumen :—'I see people's minds turning very much from the present Adminis-

'Spring Gardens : Sunday, February 8, 1801.

'You will of course receive an official account of the event of the day. I (of course) know no more than the public; and as I never get an answer I never ask a question. However, my dominie[1] was induced to own this morning that Pitt had resigned, though whilst it was between 200 *or* 300 *friends only* he would not have mentioned it to me for the world. He says the Speaker is to be the successor, and it is therefore perfectly evident to my mind that the whole *is a farce*, for it is impossible that Pitt's friend and creature should be his real successor, or more than a *stop-gap* till matters are settled and he may come in again.   It certainly must appear incomprehensible to any common understanding that in such a business as the *Union*, and during the

tration, and when peace is made and people are no longer in a fright, I shall be very much surprised if Pitt reigns long. You know England well enough to know that the impetus once given things make a most rapid progress.   The heavy pressure and great real distress of the time, without *raising* the people will *undermine* the Ministry, and more effectually dethrone them ultimately than violent commotions, which, if they fail in their immediate object, generally benefit those they attack.'

In the following month, November 1800, she wrote:—'There is certainly a great deficiency of provisions, and everything continues rising. I understand there is to be a compulsory law about the quantity of bread to be consumed by each person, and you are to be obliged when eating in other persons' houses *to carry your bread with you*, that you may only eat your own allowance. Lady Spencer has reformed bread entirely at dinner, and her guests have a choice of a potatoe or rice in lieu of it. This is absurd. The climate is not the cause of this condition of things, for the summer has been one of the hottest ever known, and the harvest magnificent. The real cause is the immense consumption and still greater waste from fleets and armies, and expeditions which float about and do nothing.'

[1] Mr. Elliot of Wells.

year elapsed since it was settled, all parties should not
have come to a clear explanation, especially on such
a major point as the Emancipation of the Catholics.
It therefore, I own, strikes me in this light—that Pitt
always intended to give it up.

' The story appears to me in the style of the Arabian
Nights. You know every now and then a man puts
himself in a rage with his wife and divorces her ; then
wants her again; but according to the Asiatic laws
she must marry another man and be divorced from
him before she can take back her first husband. So
England is the *Bride* and Addington the *Hullah.*
I trust he will play Pitt the same trick that one gentleman did in the book and refuse to give up the lady.
No subaltern resigns but Canning.

' Did I tell you Emma Godfrey has been robbed
coming to town ? She was coming from Waverley
Abbey with Harriet Francis, and they were stopped
and robbed by a highwayman on Cobham Common
near Payne's Hill, at eleven o'clock in the forenoon.
Lord Stowell says he winged one of the same people
who attacked him, but I doubt *his Lordship only shot
with a long bow.*

' Everybody seems much alarmed at the loss of Bogy,[1]
and I declare I feel perfectly certain it will all subside
and be as if nothing had happened. There was an idea
yesterday that the King was unwell. Lady Jane
Dundas said to Mrs. Drummond that the fact was this—

---

[1] Lord Grenville.

that Ministers insisted that the King had seen and approved their letter to Lord Cornwallis,—that he rather denies having seen the letter, but absolutely declares he never consented or did more than say he would consider. It was (they say) represented to him that the King of France lost his life for opposing the constitutional clergy; and the King answered he was quite prepared to meet the consequences. Everyone says that if he considers it a point of conscience, no power on earth will make him yield ; for fear is as much unknown to him as to Lord Minto.

'Lord Auckland and the Archbishop of Cant (that is the right spelling you know) have been at him. Dundas talks of retiring to Scotland because he can't afford to live here. I don't believe him. I don't think Windham appears much grieved. Of course there are all sorts of jokes. Dudley North asked the other day who was to be prompter.'

'Spring Gardens : Sunday, February 15.

'I write quite in the novel style, in continuation. Another proof of this being only a *trumpery* (temporary) Government is the having made it a bargain with Lord St. Vincent that he should keep the command of the fleet if he accepted the Admiralty. He is to do so and arrived in town yesterday. It was, by an odd coincidence, the anniversary of his victory.

'People seem more and more impressed every day that there is a *dessous des cartes* in the whole business, particularly after the King's fine speech to Mr. Pitt at the levée; viz. "That he had acted with the greatest honour and exactly as he should have expected him to do;" and some people seem to think that Pitt will not be sorry by this means to get rid of a certain number of troublesome people and come in again with a fresh set: but the experiment is a dangerous one; as the possibility of existing without him (who was considered by many as a species of talisman) will break the charm....

'The event of to-day is Lord Camelford having brought Horne Tooke into Parliament for Old Sarum: he threatened to bring in his *black servant*. They say Horne Tooke being in priests' orders cannot sit in Parliament; but it will make a piece of work, which is a bad thing just now. Windham seems in excellent spirits and kissed my hand more tenderly than ever; so I suppose he will, upon retiring from office, return to his old line of gallantry: he is like a bird set free.'

'Tuesday, 17.

'Horne Tooke has taken his seat. I understand Lord Camelford asked him what he could do that would annoy Government most, and he said, "Bring me into Parliament." They say he can sit there. Sheridan made an admirable speech yesterday, I find. Jekyll says that they have got up the "Beggar's Opera" without Macheath—a very good joke.

'This is certainly to be a temporary Administration, a lath and plaster edifice just for temporary uses; and all the world as well as myself seem to be of the same mind that it is a juggle amongst a few, and a dupery for the rest.   As to the sentimental part of the business —of the *outs* supporting the *ins*—it is all a farce, unless it is a juggle.

'London is not gay yet, and I think there will be few balls, at least there ought not.   The Brown Bread Bill is repealed, as they say it don't answer. It certainly was unheavy and unwholesome, not being made like household bread but with all the glutinous bran.'

'February 20.

'Horne Tooke spoke last night to the surprise of his audience, only comically saying (it was on a motion for an enquiry upon the Ferrol business) that he should vote for an enquiry, which would surprise people, as it was evidently his interest to discourage all enquiries, since the next might be whether he was not a parson thirty years ago, and therefore whether he was eligible to sit in that House.   The minority was large—79 to 140.'

'Spring Gardens: begun February 23, 1801.

'The King is *really ill*; he has been unwell for some days, and it is called cold and bile, but now there is, I find, no doubt about the matter.   Everybody goes to enquire.   To-day's bulletin was that he had had a few hours' sleep, but had still fever.   There can be no doubt of its having been brought on by the late events. There seems to be but one voice upon Pitt's conduct, viz. that it was insolent and arrogant in a degree to pretend he could give any assurance of such a measure without the previous consent and approbation of the King and Parliament; and therefore talking of his honour being engaged, when he had no power to fulfil his promises without consent of others, is nonsense. The King's pulse was at 144 yesterday. Farquhar says that so high a pulse must be attended with the greatest danger for life. It yesterday was contrived to make the King sign the Bread Bill, but of course all business and appointments are at a stand. Addington is between two stools, —or rather between the Chair and the Treasury Bench. None of the new Cabinet Ministers are in their places but Lord Hawkesbury and, fortunately, Lord St. Vincent and the Chancellor. Pitt cannot go out as he must deliver the seals.'

'Thursday, 26.

' The King's condition continues the same. There are a thousand different reports, but I know it to be a fact that the first day after he was taken ill he remained the whole day without uttering or taking anything; when he spoke first he said: "I am better, I shall do well now: but I will be true to the Church." I think this very affecting, and made to harrow up even the callous souls of Ministers who have driven their master to this condition. The Prince has hitherto behaved well.

' The Duke of York is always at the Queen's house and is their entire director and supporter; the others have sat up with the King and behave very well.

' This letter must be a journal, for it cannot of course go by post.

' Pitt has been several times with the Prince. Something must be done soon if the situation does not change. I find that immediately after his last recovery, the King told Lord Thurlow that the same thing might happen again, in which case he begged no time might be lost in making proper arrangements.

'George [1] sailed from Portsmouth yesterday to go round to Yarmouth where Lord Nelson is to join the "St. George;" he says the "Elephant" is to be in the fleet. Sweet love, I believe he is not half so much afraid for himself as I am for him. Nelson is third in command in the North Sea Fleet, which is to have forty sail of the line. Lord St. Vincent is at the Admiralty every morning by seven o'clock, and all who wish to see him at his own house must call before that hour.'

'March 2.

'Your letter of the 15th arrived just now. Barring death and *outrageous* accidents, I think I may reckon, as far as I can allow myself to do upon anything, upon passing next winter near you. I don't doubt your regretting the way of life at Vienna. Nobody that has lived abroad, as I feel by experience, can get used to English manners and society; and I grow daily worse instead of better about it. The King has slept and is better to-day, and the Queen has been out for an airing; so I hope in God he will do well.'

.'March 6.

'I begin to think this volume will now go. The King mends; and the Duke of York, who was here yesterday,

---

[1] Her nephew, George Elliot.

told Lord Malmesbury he was quite comfortable about him; he has behaved incomparably, and the Prince very well, which does credit to his governors. Indeed, everybody has behaved well, even Opposition.'

'Friday night: March 6, 1801.

' Pelham, who knows Ireland better than most people, says that neither the moderate or other Irish Catholics are the least obliged to Pitt for the sacrifices he has made for them; that the former declare it was no object to them, and that the latter were in fact doing nothing.

'Adieu: love to all.'

'Spring Gardens: Friday, March 27, 1801.

'Pelham succeeds old Porty, who takes Lord Chatham's place, and he the Ordnance. As Pelham is certainly as good a man as lives, I am very glad. I have long considered honour, honesty, good faith, and good humour to be the only qualities worth thinking about, and that they seldom agreed with brilliant talents—wit and genius.

' There is no doubt that peace is on the carpet, and Addington has nearly avowed it. The King recovers slowly, and is in so irritable a state that having waited a quarter of an hour for Addington the other day he got into such an agitation as quite alarmed them. The Queen had a drawing-room yesterday, and looked like Death, and all the princesses crying and the pictures of Despair.

The foolish Princess of Wales did not come at all. The
Irish have surprised everybody by their speaking in the
House of Lords and Commons; very superior to ours in
general, and full of good sense and *temperate*, which is
stranger.'

CHAPTER X.

AFTER the determination taken by Austria, and acceded
to by England, for the negotiation of a separate peace
at Lunéville, Lord Minto's part in these transactions
was reduced to that of a spectator. The observations
he was enabled to make of the perfidy of the French
Government can only have served to strengthen his satisfaction in having no more prominent part assigned to
him. 'Your Lordship already knows,' he wrote on February 8, 1801,[1] 'that General Brune had made a number
of new demands soon after the conclusion of the armistice
in Italy, and that he had even denounced the armistice
for the purpose of adding Mantua to the acquisitions
already made by that convention. General Bellegarde,
who has uniformly contested every material point . . .
remonstrated with General Brune on this scandalous
violation of public faith, and he was rewarded by very
material success, as General Brune desisted from his
new pretensions and acquiesced in allowing the armistice
to continue. . . . Meanwhile Count Cobentzel was negotiating an armistice at Lunéville, and it was concluded
before the French Government acknowledged that they
had received any information of the convention already

[1] To Lord Grenville.

concluded between the generals. The conditions of the armistice agreed to at Lunéville differ from that of Treviso in requiring the surrender of Mantua, and making the surrender of all the fortresses absolute instead of in *deposit*, as well as in giving up artillery, stores, and magazines to the enemy, part of which General Bellegarde had been able to reserve. Foreseeing, or probably being already advised, that an armistice had been concluded in Italy, it was provided at Lunéville, that if this should prove to be the case, the convention made by the generals on the spot should be deemed valid in preference to that of Lunéville; with the exception, however, of what related to Mantua and the other fortresses, which was to take effect at all events.

'This lamentable and most ignominious peace is thoroughly felt to be so by all descriptions of people, even by the peace clamourists themselves, who are heartily ashamed of it. There have been many errors in the course of the war, but the one grand, pregnant, and systematic cause of the misfortunes which have overwhelmed Austria with almost indelible dishonour and irretrievable ruin, has been a most profligate military faction which has substituted party-spirit in the room of all the duties of soldiers or citizens. That party-spirit, which had its birth in the army, has spread through the whole empire, and has completely eradicated all patriotism, all sense of honour, all political judgment, and even courage, out of army and nation. This is a diseased and unnatural state of things; but the remedy must be slow.'

Peace on the Continent was followed by the Confederacy of the North, directed against the maritime power of Great Britain.

'March, 1801.

'I should conceive,' wrote Lord Minto to Lord Grenville, 'that when the present terror is removed by the conclusion of peace on the Continent, and when the different nations which are now pressed into the Confederacy against England have leisure to turn their attention from the care of their immediate preservation to the pursuit of their advantage, the general laws which prompt and direct the intercourse among men will resume their ascendency, and the violent outrages committed against the general liberty of mankind by the attempt to seclude one of the greatest empires on the globe from the fellowship of Europe, will be found one of those idle and chimerical projects which are conceived by vanity during the intoxication of success, and will prove as impossible to be realised as it is unfit to be so. The mutual wants of nations will break these unnatural and momentary fetters. The trade of England and the necessities of the Continent will find each other out in defiance of prohibitions, and in spite of fleets, armies, and confederacies. Not one of these confederates, whether voluntary or compelled, whether principals or accessaries, will be true to the gang, and I have very little doubt of our trade penetrating into France herself and thriving at Paris.'

In spite of positive assurances given to the Queen of Naples, no terms were made for that country by the

Austrian representatives at Lunéville; but by a secret
article of the Treaty of Peace between France and
Austria, the Neapolitan Court was desired to join the
Confederacy of the North in closing its ports to the ships
of His Britannic Majesty.   Of the articles at large
General Acton wrote to the Queen : ' Les articles secrets
sont autant de violences faites le couteau sur la gorge,
et doivent être cachés à toute la terre; mais le reste
nous met dans le cas d'une nouvelle guerre, et c'est
infâme !'   The Queen was driven to despair by terms
so ignominious :—'though,' said Lord Minto, 'that
little state has made a better fight' (through the
Marquis de Gallo, its agent at Lunéville) 'than this great
empire.'   In her wrath and dismay, she placed in Lord
Minto's hands, under seal of secrecy, the letters she
received from the King, from Acton, and from the
Marquis de Gallo from Paris.   The letters of the King,
though full of ' puerilities,' showed resentment as keen
as that felt by the Queen for the ruin impending on
his family and kingdom.

' I found the Queen yesterday bordering on a state
of distraction.   Her eyes were swollen, and she had
evidently wept much before I saw her, as she did during
the greatest part of my conference with Her Majesty.
Yet her indignation at the acceptance of these disgraceful and ignominious terms appeared even greater
than her affliction and despair at the prospect of the
certain ruin to which she considers the King, herself,
and her family irretrievably doomed.' . . . ' The French
have observed their treaty with their usual good faith ;

that is to say, they have required the strict execution
of all that is favourable to themselves without the
slightest observance of those limitations which are
favourable to the other party. They have begun to
exact and to lay on contributions by their own authority in the countries which their troops occupy. They
have required *pay* and *clothing* to an immense amount,
and they have already extorted no less than forty pieces
of artillery from the Neapolitan Government.'

The letters from Paris of the Marquis de Gallo are
remarkable, as showing the sentiments entertained there
towards ' the Revolution.'

The Marquis de Gallo to the Queen.

' March 26, 1801.

' The Neapolitan refugees are despised and hated in
France, where everything that is revolutionary is now
discountenanced more than in many other countries.
Bonaparte, who is now King, does everything to extin-
guish the revolutionary spirit, to humble philosophers,
and discredit literary men. Honours, titles, luxury,
the clergy, resume their ancient ascendency ; and all
this is agreeable to the sentiments of the whole nation.
The Paris Jacobins and profligate or turbulent characters are more hated, reviled, and pointed at than
in other capitals. In a word, the Revolution is over.

' Your Majesty may be assured that if the Court of
Vienna had shown any firmness, we might have been
saved.'

It was the policy of France on all occasions to

alienate from each other the members of the Coalition. Bonaparte and Talleyrand now affected to be scandalised by the indifference shown by Austria in Neapolitan matters, and Joseph Bonaparte confided to Gallo that had Austria persisted in not signing either peace or armistice without Naples, he had orders to yield the point. ' Your Majesty would not believe in an alliance between France and Austria. There will be war again in a year or a year and a half.'

Another correspondent of the Queen's wrote as follows :— [1]

' Il faut observer l'état de la France, et s'apercevoir que le gouvernement et l'armée sont d'un côté et la nation est de l'autre. Il n'y a plus de république depuis longtemps ; la nation française obéit au plus fort, et elle croit obtenir beaucoup quand le plus fort se trouve le moins tyran, avoir des opinions modérées en apparence, et annoncer une manière de gouverner despotique, parce qu'elle a moins de petites choses à craindre.

' Voilà ce qui est arrivé à la dernière révolution de Bonaparte, qui se trouve réunir les suffrages apparents de la France, parce que la tyrannie du Directoire était extrême, et que Bonaparte seul était en mesure de la faire cesser. La Paix et le respect des Propriétés, voilà le but, l'unique désir de la nation française (car on ne peut plus parler de ses volontés) ; peu lui importe le gouvernement et les gouvernements.'

---

[1] The Duke of Ventimiglia, who appears to have been better acquainted with the French nation than with their language.

'It is certain,' wrote Lord Minto to Lord Grenville,[1] 'that the language of all Frenchmen is much altered on questions of Government and its different forms. We have a commissary at present from Moreau's army, on pecuniary business at Vienna. He speaks as freely as an Austrian would do of the disadvantages of a Republican Government and the advantages of a Monarchy as absolute as that of Austria. He says that they have arrived at a better point in France than they had hitherto attained since the Revolution, but that their Government is still defective ; and he pronounces openly his wish for a monarchical form of Government in France.'

For a few weeks Lord Minto's position was a trying one. The friends of England seemed doomed to ruin. Her enemies were triumphant, and all the diplomatic midges, too weak to injure but not too small to sting, swarmed round him in the sultry hours, affecting condolence and betraying genuine pleasure. 'What will England do?' was the question asked of him on all sides, until England presently answered it for herself, to the entire satisfaction of her sons,—at Copenhagen and Aboukir.

[1] March 23, 1801.

Lord Minto to Lord Hawkesbury.

'Vienna: April 15, 1801.

' My Lord,—I have the honour to congratulate your Lordship on the glorious and important events of March 30 and April 2 at Copenhagen. The death of Paul, and the first measures which his successor had taken, seconding the exertions of His Majesty's arms, seem to promise an immediate dissolution of the Northern Confederacy, and to dispel the cloud which had for some time darkened the North.

' We learnt yesterday the appointment of Count Pahlen, the re-establishment of Count Woronzow, and the removal of the embargo at Petersburg.

' I have learnt with certainty that the Ministers of Paul declared a few days before his death that 20,000 men were on their march to the Ganges and had passed through Georgia. These were to be followed by 30,000 more. The whole march was computed to be seven months, but it was said that this expedition would be far advanced by the end of May. I have forwarded this intelligence to Constantinople, although such an enterprise could never have been deemed very formidable.'

The Ganges! Even at this day, one by no means deficient in military glory, we read those words with a strong sense of the marvellous. What a war *that* was, of which the operations embraced half the globe, from the West Indies to the East, from the Baltic to the Nile, while hostile camps occupied the water-shed of Europe and her river systems were turned into military routes. And not one of all its famous episodes was more dramatic than that to which we have now attained; when a great trembling had seized the thrones of Europe and her realms were about to be divided between the rulers of the earth and of the sea; when the first was young, and to many beautiful as Hope, the Michael whose spear was destined to transfix the hoary serpent of which every coil was an ancient crime; and the other, he under whose sovereignty the cause of thrones took refuge, was himself the king of a 'fantastic realm,' 'whose thoughts were combinations of disjointed things.'[1]

Again, we have recourse to Lady Malmesbury, whose lively fancy brings the events she describes from the region of history into the familiar contact of the social circle.

'Brighthelmstone: April 16, 1801.

' First, and thank God, George is safe. The news arrived this morning, and my dominie begins his letter by that sentence. I have not yet recovered the emotion, and all yesterday I was wretched, for we had the report exactly as it has proved, but with the addition of our loss being still greater. Certainly Nelson is the greatest of all heroes. I grieve for poor Riou who is killed and poor Captain Mosse, whom you remember at Yarmouth. We have no gazette yet, and it is vexatious to be out of town at this moment. I must also regret extremely that the news of the Emperor

[1] Byron.

Paul's death (a blessed event) did not arrive in time
to spare so many thousand lives. Our loss in killed and
wounded is about 900; the Danes, of course, much
greater. Congratulate Lord Minto from me about dear
George. I have no doubt if he survives all these things
he will be a second Nelson. I wish *Lord Minto was
acquainted with him, as he cannot take the same interest we do in him.*[1] I hope to have a letter soon
from himself, dear boy, with all details.

' I trust all the fighting in the Baltic is over. You
will have heard of the death of Paul before we did. It
was quite a virtuous action to kill him, which it appears they did. The new Emperor has written a most
conciliatory letter to the King, and his Minister, Von
der Pahlen, to Lord Hawkesbury, and the ships, sailors,
&c. are all to be immediately released. Think of
Count Woronzow : he received news about a fortnight
ago that his fortune was confiscated for remaining here,
and in a letter Mr. Robinson received two days ago
from him, he set out for the Continent on the 19th
penniless. Instead of which he received, probably the
day he wrote, the good news of the death of his enemy
and his re-appointment to be Minister here.'

'May 5.

' I hear the joy was so great in Russia at Paul's
death, that the postillions who carried the news to
Moscow would not accept any pay for the job, and that

---

[1] In the absence of the family at Vienna, George Elliot had found a
home with Lord and Lady Malmesbury.

the contrast of the habits and faces at his funeral was quite comical.

'Tom Pelham is to marry Lady Mary Osborne. The world is very gay—balls every night. The King is at Kew, and continues mending, having done himself harm by over-heating and fatiguing himself at first. The first time he rode out after his illness, he rode over Westminster Bridge to Blackheath, never telling anyone where he was going till he turned up to the Princess's door. She was not up, but jumped out of bed and went to receive him in her bed-gown and night-cap. He told Lord Uxbridge that the Princess had run in his head during his illness perpetually, and he had made a resolution to go and see her the first time he went out, without telling anybody.'

'Spring Gardens: May 7, 1801.

'Everybody is anxious for Egyptian news, and if Lord Elgin continues to keep so much to himself we shall be long before we get at the whole. Pitt says he is the most discreet of His Majesty's Ministers, as he never reveals what he knows even to the Secretary of State.'

'May 15.

'It is a cruel thing to have such an interval between the news of the 21st in Egypt and the returns. Poor Mrs. Beadon and the Bishop of Gloucester are in great distress, as their only child was wounded in both the actions of the 8th and the 15th, and they have no letter or any idea whether slightly or desperately on the latter day. Mrs. Chester has now lost two sons in this war.

I was told last night that Sir Hyde Parker had already arrived. He is certainly coming, but not, I think, from any quarrel with Nelson. We have taken the Danish and Swedish West India islands, but shall of course have to restore them. Many of the French are going back; there will be none left here soon except the Orleans Princes, who are dancing about everywhere.'

'5 o'clock.

' A frigate has just arrived with the very bad news of the death of poor Sir Ralph Abercrombie; he fell mortally wounded, concealed it and continued giving orders till he fainted; he died the 28th, having been struck by a gun-shot wound in the thigh.

'Spring Gardens: May 19, 1801.

' I received your two letters of April 24 and 30 the same day, viz. on Saturday, and was indeed most truly rejoiced to hear you were relieved from your anxiety about George. I do not doubt Lord Minto's nervousness, but I deny its being possible for him to care as much about George as we do, *who know him, sweet creature!*

' I am more in love than ever with Nelson for his kindheartedness and thoughtfulness at such a moment, and even forgive his foibles in favour of his goodness of heart.

' I think you will now condescend to admire our army as much as our navy. There is a letter in the newspapers (avowedly General Moore's) which gives a much better account than the Gazette, and which I therefore send you. He says, " I understand that the 42nd (Highlanders) did more (this with all the service he has seen) than he could suppose *men* could do." The French certainly took them for *Asiatics* by their dress, and threw away their flints to attack *aux armes blanches*, which exactly suited the broad-sword gentlemen, who utterly destroyed the whole invincible legion of Bonaparte and took their standard. We certainly buried 1,600 men. The discipline of our troops has surprised everyone, for their bravery never was doubted. Mrs. Parkhurst wrote the prettiest remark on Sir Ralph Abercrombie's death to Lord Malmesbury, which I think would be an admirable epitaph : "that he raised a monument of glory and then coolly stepped into it himself." If you recollect that he was wounded at the beginning of the action and concealed it till the end of it, the eulogium is extremely appropriate. Lady Abercrombie is a baroness in her own right, with a pension of 2,000*l*. a-year to devolve to two more lives.

'Nelson is made a viscount. Sir Hyde passed over. The cause is supposed to be his having made repeated signals during the engagement to Nelson to desist from the attempt. I was told yesterday that an officer told Nelson of these signals, to which he replied that he could not see them, for he had but one eye and that was directed to the enemy.

'I feel very sorry for Sir Hyde ; but no wise man would ever have gone with Nelson or over him, as he was sure to be in the background in every case. Peace seems quite at a stand for the present, but the next news from Egypt, if good, will, I think, hasten it very much. Balls are numerous just now, but dull and heavy to a degree. People *forced* to dance like galley-slaves. I think Jekyll's joke about Lord Abercorn very good : that all corn is falling except the Aber-corn, and that is higher than ever. The Exhibition is shockingly bad this year. The panorama of Constantinople very pretty. No marriages but Miss Masters to Lord John Thynne ; none hatching as far as I know. Two divorces coming on next week.

'So Gilbert goes to Edinburgh. I am very glad, for Harry's sake and his, that they will be together, and as he is not a drunkard it is a very good plan for him. As to Jacobinism, it is all stuff everywhere. A boy of nineteen may be seduced by a fair face, or led into gaming, or drinking, or racing, but nobody at that age cares about politics that is worth a farthing. It is, like the love of money, belonging to those who have exhausted or left behind them the light and cheerful pleasures of life. Mrs. Robinson says they learn mathematics but nothing else. The Palmerstons pay 400*l.* a-year to Professor Stewart for boarding and lodging Harry.'

'Park Place: June 1, 1801.

'The Carnegies left us on Tuesday. She, you know, is always quite charming, and I must say the girls are quite perfection. I never saw any that enjoyed so much or so quietly. Lord Malmesbury was as much struck with them as myself, and said he never met with such

pleasant people to be in a house.   She was, of course, in
ecstasies with the place, and so was Sir David.   It is in
wonderful beauty, indeed.   The foliage magnificent; the
beech like emeralds, and the variety of hues astonishing.   The laburnums are fuller of bloom than I ever
saw them, and the thorns are like enormous peri-
wigs.   Hundreds of nightingales singing away.   The
honeysuckles just coming out all over the place.   I wish
we lived within a tolerable distance of each other—we
and the Carnegies—for it did very well for Louis XIV.
to say to his grandson when he went to Spain, "qu'il n'y
avait plus de Pyrenées," but we vulgars find Scotland a
long way from London.

'Lady Carnegie told me that George Baillie[1] is to
marry a daughter of Sir J. Pringle's, nicknamed the
Pocket Venus.'[2]

Lady Minto left Vienna a short time before her husband.   The following letter from him will appropriately close the story of his mission to Vienna :—

'Vienna: September 29, 1801.

'You will be wondering at my stay, but the business
I have had to settle was too material to be slighted;
and having completed it I set out on my journey to
Presburg.[3]   The weather was beautiful; all the cheerfulness of a sunny day, without a feeling of heat or cold.

[1] George Baillie, Esq., of Mellerstein in Roxburghshire.
[2] The beautiful mother of a beautiful race, of whom Eliza, Mar-
chioness of Breadalbane, was the eldest.
[3] To visit Baron Thugut in his retirement.

My boat had a covering of boards with a table in the middle and benches at the sides; on these I had a little library composed of elegant extracts, verse and prose; some of Burke's speeches, and Rabutin's letters. The doors being open at each end, I was perpetually out and in to see the country; and shifted from writing to read-ing, from poetry to prose, with a most agreeable and wanton variety for eight hours. I read the whole of the " Rape of the Lock " part of Goldsmith's " Deserted Village," some Homer, and some Cicero. I have had so few whole holidays, or rather it is so long since I could be sure even of an hour to follow my own conceits, that I enjoyed the *insular* situation of my boat more than other people could understand. The whole course of the river is cheerful and pleasant if not interesting; but the Caltenberg and Leopoldberg, and the Predigstuhl terminated my prospect, backwards, above half the way, and the hills near Presburgh, forwards, the remainder. At some points the scenery is beautiful. After settling myself at my inn, I sent to announce my arrival; but Thugut was not at home. He came to me between nine and ten, and I never saw him so blooming and beautiful. Retirement certainly agrees with his health, and indeed with his spirits. He showed great satisfaction and even gratitude for my visit; and we passed our time so happily in social talk and dalliance soft that neither of us thought of the hour till it struck twelve. The place was most miserable. Next morning he took me in his carriage to see the castle; he was dressed in an old green full-dressed coat with gold lace, and an arm-hat, which

has been squeezed into the form of a triangular pancake
for several years; but the air being sharp on the top
of the hill, he put the pancake on his head and was a
capital figure.   Latin here is a living language, and at
the castle, a seminary for priests, we heard nothing else
spoken.   His society consists of four emigrants.   There
are a few families in the country, but they live like rus-
tics—dine at twelve, play at ombre with pipes in their
mouths, and go to bed at eight o'clock.   It is a horrid
residence for a man like Thugut, but it is impossible for
him to come to Vienna.   People continue to say he is
consulted; but though I daresay he is more or less informed of what is going on, yet it is safe to say he has
no share in the direction of affairs; everything that is
done is in contradiction to his known opinions.   I returned to Vienna next morning, having given him great
pleasure by my visit.'

CHAPTER XI.

WITH Lord Minto's return from Vienna, in 1801,
began the last period of his public life in England, to
be closed five years later with his appointment to the
Governor-Generalship of India. He entered upon it
under circumstances not without resemblance to those
in which he had been placed before his first mission to
Toulon. Again as in those early days he found himself
acting with opposition, and as prominent in its foremost rank as a man could be whose constitutional
shyness led him to avoid an active part in debate.
Though Burke had disappeared from the scene and
Lord Grenville was comparatively a new friend, he
found in his intimate relations with Mr. Windham and
Mr. Elliot a continuity with the past.

As of yore, his fairness of mind and moderation of
temper gave his opinion an almost judicial weight; but
to these natural gifts were now added a wider experience
of life, and a personal knowledge of foreign rulers and
statesmen of the highest value when brought to bear
on questions of foreign policy, momentous in importance above all others. A variety of circumstances
that combined to separate him from Lady Minto during
portions of the Parliamentary Session obliged him to

resume his journal-like letters to her, and the want of a home of his own led to a renewal of those nomadic habits of intercourse with friends and relations which had been the solace of lonely hours in times gone by.

It may be said, without breach of confidence, that among the causes which detained Lord Minto at times in London after the departure of his family were the large demands made on his time and patience by friends who consulted him on their family affairs—a synonym sometimes for domestic grievances—with the sort of unreserve and confidence rarely shown unless to those who are

Prodigues d'indulgence et de blâme économes.[1]

Lord Minto reached London in the last week of November 1801. When Parliament met on October 29 to discuss the Preliminaries of the Peace which had been signed at Amiens on the 2nd, the debates that ensued had more in them of the tone of the trumpet than of the tabor. Though Mr. Pitt came to the rescue of Ministers, though the war party, with Mr. Windham at their head, grossly exaggerated the humiliations of Great Britain, there was no denying that after nine years of war to obtain for herself ' security,' and for her allies the restoration of the *status quo* before the Revolution, she had only succeeded in restoring herself to that condition by the surrender of her subsequent conquests, whereas for peace and security, no guarantees of either were to be found in the relative condition of France and England, in the general

---

[1] Victor Hugo.

circumstances of Europe, or in the character of the
man at the head of the French armies. The prospects
of an enduring peace seemed reduced to a hope in the
moderation and sincerity of Bonaparte, and such a hope
might be fairly termed,—

> Brother of Fear! more gaily clad,
> The merrier fool of the two, but quite as mad.[1]

Since his old friend Lord Pelham was a member of
the new Administration, while his late chief Lord Grenville viewed it with unmixed contempt, Lord Minto
could not fail to hear 'a good deal of people's opinions
and of party matters from both sides.' The verbal
explanations he received on various questions relating to the conduct of individuals were not in all

---

[1] 'We are become of a sudden great *hopers*,' said Mr. Windham, 'we
hope the French will have no inclination to hurt us ; we *hope*, now peace
is come, and the pressure of war as it is called, taken off, that the
French empire will become a prey to dissensions and finally fall to
pieces ; we *hope* that the danger from the Revolution is now worn out ;
and that Bonaparte, now monarch himself, will join us in the support of
monarchical principles, and become a sort of collateral security for the
British Constitution. One has heard to be sure that *magni animi est
sperare ;* but the maxim, to have any truth in it, must be confined, I
apprehend, to those hopes which are to be prosecuted through the
medium of men's own exertions, and not be extended to those which
are to be independent of their exertions, or rather, as in the present
instance, are meant to stand in lieu of them. Of this description are all
those expectations which I have just enumerated ; one of which is that
the French will fall into dissensions. Why, Sir, they have had nothing
else but dissensions from the beginning . . . . As for changes of
government, they have been in a continued course of them. Since the
beginning of the Revolution the government has been overturned at least
half-a-dozen times. They have turned over in the air, as in sport, like
tumbler-pigeons ; but have they ever in consequence ceased their
flight ?'

cases superior in lucidity to those already given in his correspondence from home, of which he had said that 'they were not altogether intelligible'; but two points he found perfectly distinct :—' This Ministry came in on the Catholic question. On this fundamental point I am against them. Their principal measure is the peace. Indeed this measure must also be considered as fundamental in their Ministry, for I have reason to be satisfied that Mr. Addington made peace a condition with the King when he accepted the situation. On this question I am also against them. I shall wait, however, for the definitive treaty, and shall probably not take my seat at present. With regard to the stability of the present Ministry, it is difficult to form an opinion. It is so weak in talents and weight, that it could not well stand precisely as it is ; but it may acquire strength from different quarters, and is in fact trying to do so, but as yet with little success. Tierney is said to be gained, and some others from the late Opposition, which may carry some talent, but little weight. Grey has been solicited, but has declined. This is a secret, and must not be mentioned. Pitt has supported the peace himself, and has silenced several of his friends whose opinions were against it. Among these were Lord Camden and Canning. Dundas is also supposed to be against it. It seems that the Duke of Portland and Lord Rosslyn were both taken at their words pretty quickly, and very much to their own dismay when they found it so. They had said in their first zeal that they wished their situations not to stand in the way of the new arrangements. They were very much commended for their disinterested conduct, and thought no more about it. Somebody who happened to be at a dinner where, it is supposed, they both heard the intimation that their handsome offers were accepted, told Elliot there never were two such pictures of gloom and dejection. I dined at Blackheath yesterday to meet the French princes, and slept at Lord Dartmouth's on the Heath, and was very glad to pass a few hours next morning with so pleasant a man and family. I have been to Windsor and have had a very long conversation with the King, who appeared to me in better and sounder health than I ever remember him, and clearer and cooler in conversation. I never saw him so perfectly well in all respects, and I flatter myself we may hope to retain him for a number of years. Nothing could be kinder or more friendly than the whole of his conversation towards me, and he pronounced quite a panegyric on you, seeming to understand your particular class of merits on the score of conduct and sound plain sense, on which he expatiated. On the peace I observed that his language was rather that of apology than of approbation.' [1]

'London: December 17, 1801.

'I have just come back from Dropmore, Danesfield, and Park Place in hopes of going to the Drawing-room ; but, by accidents in driving, I am too late, and shall omit that duty after all the hurry I have been in to accom-

[1] November 27, 1801.

plish it. I went to Dropmore the day before yesterday
and arrived an hour before dinner. I found only Lord
Grenville, Lady Grenville and Mr. Fisher, formerly
Under-Secretary. I stayed all night, having met with a
kind and hearty welcome. We agreed very well on all
the principal points of the present time, especially the
peace. I took occasion to express my difference with
the present Ministry on the two leading questions—the
necessity of taking my own line on them, and the impossibility in this circumstance of professing anything
like connection with the Ministry; but that my views
as yet extend no further, and that I was not aware of
any public principle depending in the present moment
which could be made the basis of a formal connection
or party in opposition to Government. . .

'He professed an entire agreement with me in these
views, and said we could only wait to see the turn events
might take and the line Government might pursue.
He expressed, however, a strong wish that I should
speak on the definitive treaty, which it is my intention
to do.

'I found them a most comfortable couple, Lady Grenville very pleasing, and seemingly very happy. Pluto[1]
made the conquest of the whole family, and particularly
of Lady Grenville's Italian greyhound; indeed he has
great success wherever he goes.

'I breakfasted this morning in Park Place, where I
found Lord Malmesbury improved in looks and health.

[1] Pluto, a German poodle, which had accompanied the family from
Vienna.

The other day I went to the Old Bailey and sat next our friend, Graham, now a Judge and Baron of the Exchequer. . . . Talking of judges, Lord Alvanley, Pepper Arden, on being made a peer was puzzled to find a title, and while he was deliberating cracked this joke on me.   He said he heard there was a Lord Minto, and he thought he might be Lord Pepperminto —very good.'

Before the family party at Vienna separated, it had been decided that on their return home Gilbert, then in his seventeenth year, should at the commencement of winter enter on a course of studies in Edinburgh. The plan laid down for him at this time by his father included two winters in Edinburgh; the first to be devoted to classics, the second to philosophy and science. Oxford was next to follow, in order that ' history, law, and politics might be studied as the time approached at which he would put his education into practice, and enter into real life.'

In order to make a home for their son, and to give educational advantages to the younger members of the family, Lord and Lady Minto hired a house for the winter in Edinburgh, and then and there were laid the foundations of many a warm friendship, never through subsequent years allowed to cool. With Dugald Stewart and his family, with Playfair, Jeffrey, Francis Horner, John Murray,[1] and Lord Webb Seymour they rapidly fell into habits of intimacy.   The relations of

---

[1] Afterwards Lord Advocate, and a Lord of session, under the title of Lord Murray.

society brought them into daily contact with Campbell,
who had written, but not published, his 'Pleasures of
Hope,' 'a poem people amuse themselves by comparing
with the " Pleasures of Memory," by a banker's clerk
in London;' with Walter Scott, who had just brought
out the first volumes of his 'Border Minstrelsy,' for
whom his ' originality, agreeableness, and lame leg com-
oined to inspire a *tendresse*;' with the beautiful Lady
Dalkeith, charming by disposition and manners no less
than by personal attractions ; and with Lady Douglas of
Bothwell, described as 'equally amusing, good-humoured
and clever.' Some old acquaintances they also found
among the residents in Edinburgh in the winter of
1801–2. The Court of the French princes at Holyrood
comprised among its members several *habitués* of Lady
Minto's society in Vienna, who, with the Duc de Berri
at their head, were thankful to escape from Holyrood
to a house where they could dance, talk, and talk French ;
'the pleasantest of them being Mons. de Puysegur, cheerful with the cheerfulness which belongs peculiarly to his
part of France.' But the most intimate companion of
the young Elliots was their early friend, Harry Temple,
a fellow-student of Gilbert's as we have seen at the
classes presided over by Dugald Stewart; ' he is charming,' said Lady Minto, ' having no fault or failing,
unless it be a want of the spirits belonging to his
age;' yet these, if habitually latent, occasionally
betrayed themselves, as on the solemn occasion of a
party at Professor Dugald Stewart's, where he sprained
his leg by jumping over Mrs. Stewart's Gothic couch

in the middle of her drawing-room; the solemnity perhaps acting on his spirits like the pressure on a spring.

Parliament rose on December 15, when Lord Minto joined his family in Edinburgh, and wrote from thence an account of their way of life to Lady Palmerston.

'Edinburgh: January 10, 1802.

' My dear Lady Palmerston,—Perhaps you may have forgotten that I took leave of you on Friday, proposing to reach Monteviot[1] the Monday after. I accomplished this with ease, although I was obliged to sleep at Oxford the first night, being told that the waters were out, and that I could not proceed in the dark. From thence I went on without stopping, and should have arrived at dinner-time on Monday, if my carriage had not required some repairs at Newcastle. I mention all these interesting particulars to show that we are your neighbours, being but three days and a few hours asunder, and less if we are diligent. I found the elder half of my family perfectly well and perfectly merry in that hospitable mansion. Although I had lost sight of them for less than four months, I perceived a considerable growth in them all; and as I never thought them deficient in anything but inches, I am now entitled to consider them as nearly perfect. There were one or two young neighbours, male and female, and there was abundance of dancing, relieved occasionally by commerce and other round games for the younkers, and

[1] The residence of Admiral Elliot in Roxburghshire.

the Admiral's old whist party in a quiet corner. . . . I found the Admiral and my aunts full three years older than I left them on my departure from England, but in other respects as well as possible. There is not a more perfectly benevolent being in the world than my uncle, and amongst the minor virtues of benevolence he possesses those of hospitality and the love of society in the highest degree.

'This you know,[1] and I pass to Edinburgh, where I arrived on Sunday the 3rd, and found the young brood in as great perfection as their elders.

'I have now seen a week of the Edinburgh course, and I am happy to say that my satisfaction is entire. My utmost expectations, or rather hopes, are fully answered. On Gilbert the spirit of the place appears to have operated powerfully. His mind is really engaged in his studies, and while he is acquiring a quantity and variety of new knowledge, he is fixing tastes and habits which I consider as the true fruit of education, much more than what is actually learnt in this short period. As for myself, having less time to lose than he, I am swilling at this Helicon as fast and as greedily as I can. Gilbert and I start together for college, which is a mile and a half's walk. We sit together at the chemical class, we lounge together the hour that intervenes between that class and Mr. Stewart's, not uncommonly accompanied by *another son of mine*,[2] who is also a young chemist. We sit

[1] Lord and Lady Palmerston had visited Monteviot in the previous year.

[2] Harry Temple.

together at Mr. Stewart's first class, and I attend his
second when I can. I also steal a little instruction
of the private masters under pretence of observing the
progress of their scholars. In this manner I purloin
a little geometry and algebra from Gilbert, a little
drawing from Anna Maria and Harry, and a little
dancing and spelling from Catherine, who has made
astonishing progress in these arts and sciences. I
endeavour by these means to make myself less unfit for
the company and conversation of the learned Vis-
countess and her accomplished daughters. It will be
vain for you to deny your learning, for it is established
on the highest authority, and by those who know better
than you. I went the other day to inscribe myself on
Dr. Hope's list for his chemical lectures, and getting
into conversation with him, he mentioned an experiment which he had made with two concave mirrors
to show that cold was transmitted in the way of reflection from one to the other, and must therefore be a
matter. But the experiment don't signify. I mention
it only because he said that he had performed it in the
presence of Lord and Lady Palmerston. "Her lady-
ship," he added, "is a *virtuosa*, and a very agreeable
lady."

'I have kept another subject for the *bonne-bouche*.
Harry is as charming and as perfect as he ought to be.
I do declare that I never saw anything more delightful.
On this subject I do not speak on my own judgment
alone. I have sought opportunities of conversing with
Mr. and also with Mrs. Stewart on the subject, and

they have made to me the report which you have already heard from others, that he is the only young man they ever knew in whom it is impossible to find any fault.   Diligence, capacity, total freedom from vice of every sort, gentle and kind disposition, cheerfulness, pleasantness, and perfect sweetness, are in the catalogue of properties by which we may advertise him if he should be lost.

'Adieu, dear Lady Palmerston; do not call me German, nor sentimental, nor any other names, if I tell you how much pleasure I felt on seeing you again after my long absence.   I believe, in the case of departures, they who stay behind may often feel it most, but in the case of returns, he who arrives is probably the most sensible of the joy.'

Lord Minto having been recalled to London to attend to his Parliamentary duties,[1] Lady Minto wrote to him of the society in Edinburgh in the following appreciative strain.

'February 21, 1802.

'I quite agree with you that natural character is much changed by education, society, air, and the manner of living, and besides by *fashion*, which teaches people not to act upon their own judgment and opinions, but to endeavour to be like somebody, or anybody.   I see this in all countries more or less.   This country has arrived at the true pitch of comfort and happiness. The people are full of information, are natural, unassuming, and social, but with a great mixture of occu-

[1] Parliament met on February 2.

pation. People meet together to be pleased, cheerful,
and easy. Even the Scotch pride has its uses by
putting the poor often on an equal footing with the
rich. A Douglas or a Scott would consider themselves
on a par with persons of the highest title and rank ;
their education is equally good, their society the same,
their spirit and love of their country possibly much
greater. Almost every family can boast of heroes in
some generation, which excites emulation, and nothing
is so uncommon as to see idle men and listless manners.
All is energy, and everyone has some object in view to
exercise his faculties and talents. I must say, at the
present time I think the race very superior to the
English, who are too far gone in luxury and dissipation
to be agreeable or happy. *Morals* here are certainly
very good, and yet the manners are much more free,
and one scarcely ever meets with affectation and airs.
People meet like friends, and not with a cold bow and
a distant curtsey.'

The chief or only drawback to the pleasant impressions
conceived by Lady Minto of the society into which she
was now thrown consisted in the strength of the political antipathies existing there. 'The Lord Advocate
would hardly praise the " Pleasures of Hope " the other
day when I dined there, because Mr. Campbell had been
thought democratical, which *I* thought carrying prejudice rather far ; and, after all, it seemed only suspicion, though probably a man of genius and talent who
felt a claim to notice from his superiors in rank which
he did not meet with, and with an irritable temper,

might lean to that side of the question. I think genius so rare now-a-days that it should not be depressed.'

Lord Minto at this time was doing his best to set a subscription on foot in London for the publication of one hundred copies of the ' Pleasures of Hope ; ' a somewhat thankless task, for the favoured few who were thrown into ecstasy by the MS., cooled notably on being asked to bring the poem by publication within the reach of the multitude. Lady A. protested she could never remember the name—' Pleasures of *something*.' Lady B., on being asked for a guinea, said ' Pray, my dear Lord Minto, *consider* the times.' ' I *did* consider that I had shortly before given her thirty guineas towards defraying the expenses of a publication by a French emigrant which had failed.' ' Campbell's Stanzas on Painting,' wrote Lord Minto in another letter, ' have made a very favourable impression on everybody to whom I have read them. Lord Palmerston, who is a good judge, and not apt to praise, admired them very much.' In the course of the spring Mr. Campbell came up to London, when Lord Minto hit on a method of producing him in the London world which is characteristic of his tact and delicacy of feeling :—

' Finding that I saw nothing of Mr. Campbell, and thinking I should be able to do more for him if he were more known to be connected with me, I have given him one of my spare rooms, and he came yesterday to be my guest. This will save him a good deal of money, and I shall at the same time be able to make him known to my friends.'

Lord Minto to Lady Minto.

'Stratton Street: Thursday, February 15, 1802.

' I am just come from taking my seat in the Imperial House of Lords, and assisting at the reception of the new Speaker.[1] The room is finer in point of dimensions than the old, but there are no fire-places, which gives it a less comfortable look, as well as feeling ; for it is generally extremely cold, and at times oppressively hot, being heated by flues which are not well regulated. It appears to me also as if the great size of the room must be disadvantageous to the voice, as the size of the other theatres is to the other actors. However, I suppose I must try what can be done with a loud whisper one of these days. I am sorry to find Mr. Stewart's course is so long suspended. I hope it will afford Gilbert an opportunity to advance in mathematics, which it is material to push forward this year, as a necessary preparation for next winter's course. Lady Glenbervie has had a principal share in preparing Fred for Westminster, and has made herself a really good Latin scholar. She reads the best Latin authors, both prose and poetry, with sufficient ease to enjoy them extremely, and it has certainly not made her pedantic. Lord Glenbervie told me this, and I believe it is hardly known to anybody.

' I dined yesterday with Lord and Lady Pelham, and a dumb waiter, and had much interesting conversation.

___
[1] Mr. Abbot.

I do not think he will remain long in office ; he indeed fairly told me he only wished for a proper opportunity to quit it.   He is ashamed of the peace and of the insolent advantage that Bonaparte is now taking of our Government's weakness.   He has a mean opinion of Addington, as everybody must.   He seems to think that the Catholic question might be got over by the moderation and prudence of the Catholics themselves, who would consent to waive it, or by the acquiescence of the King, if he were made to feel that the state of Ireland absolutely required it.   However, these speculations are little to be relied on.'

'Friday : February 19, 1802.

' You will be entertained to hear that the King spoke to Lord Hobart yesterday after I had left St. James's of my having entirely lost *my shyness* and being altered in that respect.   I rather understood that he spoke of this change as an improvement ; I confess I am sensible of what I feel to be a great improvement in my own comfort.   The doing the honours at Vienna the first year and the encouraging reception I met with there made this change upon me, and I suppose I shall soon pass for an impudent fellow.'

'February 20, 1802.

' I saw Mrs. Siddons yesterday in the " Grecian Daughter ; " but it is not a very favourable part, and having lost her beauty in a great degree, her exertions of action, and especially of countenance, degenerate a little towards caricature.   However, she is the only

person on the stage who in tragic parts can give one
the slightest pleasure, if we except Kemble now and
then.

'The fine world is at present engaged in a controversy
concerning the private theatre. You will have seen the
names of the lady patroresses, managers, &c. in the
newspapers. They are exactly the set one should have
supposed, and I confess I am by no means a friend to
this institution, by which our people of fashion, male
and female, are to become actors, stage managers,
dancers, and publicans. The Royal Institution is much
more entertaining than the pic-nic. I attended a very
entertaining lecture last night by Mr. Davy on galvanism; the most curious subject of modern science, and
the most recent discovery. Lord Spencer, Lord Gower,
and Lady Sutherland were there.'

'February 27.

'I have been to another chemical lecture. Mr. Davy
is not an orator; still less so than Dr. Hope; but he
is remarkably clear as well as simple. It is curious
to see ex-Ministers and a number of our politicians
attending these amusements as I did at Edinburgh.
Lord Spencer is a constant student; there are a great
many women, principally matrons with young daughters,
who take notes and carry their syllabus as boys do at
Edinburgh.'

'March 16.

'The pic-nic or private theatricals which have made
such a noise are not very exhilarating; it is a lame
performance, and will be found too great an exertion for

those who act and manage, and too little amusement for those who look on, though a spirit of opposition may carry it through this season; but it will not be revived. Harry Greville, the manager, has got into a paper war with Sheridan, out of which he will not come off best. We had a prologue last night, spoken by H. Greville, attacking the newspapers and the managers of the play-houses and the moralists, &c. tolerably well. Then a sort of little interlude describing the distress of the manager, in which H. Greville was the principal, or rather the only, performer.

'Joe Maddox, that dull man who came with the Margravine to Vienna, but who is the crack actor, just came on the stage, but had little or nothing to say; there were then two French proverbs acted by Frenchmen, and the women's parts by men, certainly not above mediocrity. Lord Palmerston being unwell at home, Lady Palmerston wished to go home early. I took the opportunity of retreating before the pic-nic supper, which I hear was served all over the place where the spectators had sat, removing some of the benches to make room for tables, and a table on the stage, where they sang catches. The house was pretty enough, but the stage too small, which is always the case in private theatricals; there were about two hundred people; no attempt at riot or interruption.

'Harriet has perhaps told you that it is now acknowledged on all sides that the Duke of Bedford was engaged to marry Lady Georgina Gordon. The Duke left a locket of his hair and some papers to be delivered to her by Lord John. The Duchess of Gordon, on the strength of this, has made her put on widow's mourning, saying it is a feather in any girl's cap to have been intended for the Duke of Bedford. Adieu.'

'March 22, 1802.

' I went to Lord Nelson's [1] on Saturday to dinner, and returned to day in the forenoon. The whole establishment and way of life is such as to make me angry, as well as melancholy ; but I cannot alter it, and I do not think myself obliged or at liberty to quarrel with him for his weakness, though nothing shall ever induce me to give the smallest countenance to Lady Hamilton. She looks ultimately to the chance of marriage, as Sir W. will not be long in her way, and she probably indulges a hope that she may survive Lady Nelson ; in the meanwhile she and Sir William and the whole set of them are living with him at his expense. She is in high looks, but more immense than ever. She goes on cramming Nelson with trowelfuls of flattery, which he goes on taking as quietly as a child does pap. The love she makes to him is not only ridiculous, but disgusting : not only the rooms, but the whole house, staircase and all, are covered with nothing but pictures of her and him, of all sizes and sorts, and representations of his naval actions, coats of arms, pieces of plate in his honour, the flagstaff of "L'Orient," &c.—an excess of vanity which counteracts its own purpose. If it was

_____

[1] Merton in Surrey.

Lady H.'s house there might be a pretence for it; to make his own a mere looking-glass to view himself all day is bad taste.   Braham, the celebrated Jew singer, performed with Lady H.   She is horrid, but he entertained me in spite of her.   Lord Nelson explained to me a little the sort of blame which had been imputed to Sir Hyde Parker for Copenhagen; in the first place, for not commanding the attack in person, and in the next place for making signals to recall the fleet during the action; and everything would have been lost if these signals had been obeyed.   Lord Nelson said that he would trust to nobody sooner than to Sir Hyde against an enemy in deep water, but that he is not equal to shoals and responsibilities, and is too much afraid of losing ships to make the most of them.'

'March 25.

'Lord Palmerston continues much the same, but something better in point of fever.   I have a kind letter from the Queen of Naples, very desponding on public affairs.   I had a pleasant dinner yesterday at Lady Pembroke's.   Woronzow is going to Russia for his private affairs, but returns next winter; his daughter,[1] a very pretty and pleasant girl, laments his departure bitterly, and will not hear of not returning to the only country she has the least knowledge of.   People don't know what to make of the peace yet, but there is no doubt it is coming.'

---

[1] Afterwards Countess of Pembroke.

'March 26.

'The singing at the opera last night was the most
perfect thing I ever heard—Mrs. Billington and
Baretti together; and the crowding in the pit was
never surpassed; ladies fainting, trodden under foot,
pulled by the shoulders out of the pit into the boxes
during their fainting fits in order to be got out.'

'March 31, 1802.

'Walter Scott's book[1] has amused and interested me
extremely. I sent it to Pozzo, who wrote me a line to say
that in the introduction he was *en pays de connaissance*,
but that the poetry was unintelligible to him. I lent
it to him on purpose to show him how like Corsica we
were so lately. The peace is in the newspapers. The
town has been very flat and dull upon it, and even
with the addition of the repeal of the Income tax, has
produced nothing like a real demonstration of joy.
There has been a slight illumination yesterday and the
day before, but no general one ; and very few private
houses had lights at all.

'Malta in effect is left in the power of France, as a
Neapolitan garrison *must* obey the French Minister
at Naples, and the Knights of Malta belong to countries
which are in general dependent on France. There is
no provision whatever against the further growth of
France in any direction or to any extent. Everybody
seems low and out of spirits.'

[1] The *Border Minstrelsy.*

Lady Minto to Lord Minto.

'Edinburgh: April 2, 1802.

'We were waked yesterday morning by a parcel of boys drawing the mail-coach through the square and all about the town. The Castle guns were fired and all the regiments fired volleys from the Castle Hill; the volunteers lined Princes Street, and formed a line over the mound to the Castle. The day was beautiful, and the sight very gay. Orders were stuck up for a general illumination to begin at half-past seven, accounts having been received by the Lord Provost of a peace concluded with our enemies, but not saying who the enemies were. There was no play, and Lady Douglas, Lady Montagu, Harry and ourselves drove about the streets to see the sight, which was more worth seeing than anything of the sort I have seen or ever can see again. *Every house* in the town had candles or lamps or transparencies three stories high, and the tall houses in the old town to the tops; the streets were so perfectly light that I should have known every creature across them. The tranquillity of the people was striking ; the streets were as full as they could hold, but as orderly and quiet as if perfectly empty.

'It gave one the idea of a fête, not of a rejoicing ; indeed I do not find any sort of people much elated by this event. Gilbert is quite cast down. Lord Dalkeith went to pay a visit seven miles off, that he might not see the illumination at Dalkeith.

'The weather here is delicious; the hedges getting green and the environs of Edinburgh delightful.'

In a letter written on April 9 Lord Minto mentions Lord Palmerston as still very ill, but in good spirits, cracking his jokes and reading from morning to night. 'One of his jokes to-day was repeating a saying of Wilkes's about the peace, I believe, of 1763—that it was certainly the peace of God which passeth all understanding.' On the following day he became much worse; two days later his son was sent for, and on the 16th Lord Palmerston died. Though it does not appear from this correspondence that he was gifted with the even temper and unselfish disposition which made Lady Palmerston's society so attractive to her friends, he was eminently sociable in his habits, and having cultivated literary tastes, he liked to collect about him people of sense and information. Both in London and at Sheen, his house was the centre of a large circle of friends and acquaintances, now to be dispersed by his death. His family was warmly attached to him, and when the news of the dangerous character of his illness reached Edinburgh, it was a great shock to his eldest son, then residing there. He and his friend Gilbert Elliot, who would not let him perform so painful a journey alone, immediately started for London; but at Barnet they were met by Lord Minto, who, by Lady Palmerston's desire, had gone there to break to Harry Temple the fact of his father's death, which she thought would be more gently done in

tender words than by the sight of the closed shutters
in Hanover Square.

Lord Minto to Lady Minto.

'April 19.

'I went to Barnet on Saturday afternoon. Gilbert
and Harry arrived there this morning at seven. Harry
was not at all aware of the extreme danger, and had
therefore a greater shock than I hoped he might have.
I had taken the greatest pains to tutor both my own
servants and the Palmerstons' not to speak to Harry
before he had seen me ; but Hunter mistook Gilbert for
Harry, brought him up to my room, saying, " Here is
Mr. Temple, my lord," and then ran down to Harry,
and told him the event as a piece of news. It was in
reality the same thing, as I must have told him the
moment after ; yet I was provoked at it, as I had stayed
there two days on purpose to perform the office myself.
I am amazingly happy that Gilbert has come. I expected it.'

'April 23, 1802.

'The Dutch and Spanish ratifications not having yet
arrived, proclamations and illuminations are also de-
ferred. There are great preparations at Mr. Otto's for
illuminations, but the mob perceiving the French word
concorde, took it for *conquered,* and made him alter it.
It was too near the truth to be told by him. He had
also neglected to have a crown, which is added.

'Pozzo di Borgo went this morning to Vienna. He
still considers England as his country, and mine as his

real home, and he seemed not insensible to the first separation since our first meeting in 1794.' [1]

'May 8.

'I gave my notice yesterday for Monday, and have not improved my comfort thereby. Gilbert is very fond of the debates in both Houses, and stayed till two this morning in the House of Commons. He came away admiring Fox very much. I heard Mrs. Siddons read the "Distressed Mother" last night. Nothing remarkable except just at one or two short moments; but she was so nervous and frightened, there was no judging of her powers; she literally *read* the greatest part, almost the whole, without any attempt at more.'

'May 11.

'You will see by the papers that I spoke yesterday; the report in the only paper I have seen (the "Morning Post") is, as usual, perfectly unlike from beginning to end. He (the reporter) has caught a

---

[1] From the time of his departure from England dates the commencement of a series of letters addressed by Pozzo di Borgo to Lord Minto during several consecutive years. In the first, dated August 14, 1802, he says, after many warm expressions of gratitude to Lord and Lady Minto for the kindness they had shown him: 'L'idée de vous quitter sans l'espérance de vous revoir serait pour moi une mort anticipée ; dans les temps où nous sommes on ne peut pas se fixer un avenir avec certitude, et surtout moi, sans dieux pénates et sans patrie; mais au milieu de cet espace qui ne me montre ni but ni chemin, vous êtes le pôle vers lequel je me dirige avec une satisfaction qui me tient lieu de presque tout ce qui me manque.' After his arrival at Vienna he wrote: 'Nos amis ne cessent de parler de vous et de la famille; nous avons des heures pour cela: les élus ont seuls la permission d'y assister. Croyez que nous sommes bien d'accord en vous aimant.'

word here and there, and made declamations upon
them himself. My friends Windham, Elliot, &c., are
of course pleased.'

'May 15, 1802.

'Our debates on the peace have certainly produced a
very sensible effect, and the part we have taken has
done real service. It has made the public acquainted
with the real nature of the transaction, and with the
real danger of the situation in which it has placed us.
It has also drawn from many weighty people, and even
from the Government itself, strong declarations of a
more spirited conduct in future, and of carrying our
concessions no further. This is matter of comfortable
reflexion to ourselves, and the universal approbation of
the part we have acted on this occasion is also satisfactory. . . There were several that voted against us
and spoke for us. . . The Ministers themselves spoke
very much as if they were of our mind. Gilbert attended the debate in the House of Commons yesterday
and came home at six this morning. He was extremely
entertained with Sheridan, who seems to have made
one of his very best speeches, especially in the way of
wit. People are speaking of nothing else to-day. We
seem to have had everybody for us in opinion, and
everybody against us in votes. Ministry and Opposition both against us, so we could not shine in numbers ;
but the honour is the more. I heard Mrs. Siddons
read " Othello " last night—amazingly fine.'

' May 25.

' Windham's speech on bull-baiting was the finest thing and the highest entertainment I ever remember. It is impossible to describe it, but the effect was universal, and fairly drew the House after him, for everybody expected the Bill to be carried.'

' May 29, 1802.

' Yesterday I had a very busy, idle day. In the forenoon I attended Mrs. Robinson's party to the Phantasmagoria, which kept us from one to half-past three in the greatest possible heat and stink of lamp-oil. I then dressed in haste for Pitt's dinner at Merchant Taylors' Hall, where I carried Elliot, and it happened oddly enough that we arrived at the same time with Lord Grenville, Windham, and all the rest of the anti-pacification party, so that we entered the Hall and marched up it in a body as if it had been arranged on purpose. It is an immense hall, and there were near one thousand guests.

' We had a series of toasts, preceded by loud raps of a hammer on the table, and loud notices to charge our glasses. After each toast came a song, and more rappings with hands, feet, and knives. This measure will be talked of for a few days, and then forgot. It is in fact, Canning's, and is in his style.'

' June 3.

' We had a numerous dinner at Blackheath—the Chancellor,[1] Lord and Lady Rosslyn, Lord Alvanley, Lord and Lady Carnarvon, Lord Hood, Dundas, and

[1] Lord Eldon.

Lady Jane, Lord and Lady Hawkesbury, Windham, Tom
Grenville, Elliot, and me, and some more. After dinner,
about ten o'clock, the Princess took Windham and
Tom Grenville out to a dark promenade in the Park
through the long and wet grass, and we all took the
opportunity to set off to London, so that they must
have found a clear house on their return. It was a
medley of company, and the Princess got often on
delicate subjects, such as abusing the Prince to the
Chancellor, and telling Dundas, the whole length of the
table, that they had given up the Cape, but not the
Cape wine, and so forth. Lord Hawkesbury looked
distressed; but there is no sourness in the present
politics and we are all very good friends. Pitt has
been *very* ill, and so gone to Walmer for his health,
where, though better, people are uneasy about him. It
seemed like a return of his old complaint. Dundas
says that he persists in forswearing public life and has
still as much as ever the appearance of being perfectly
in earnest.

'I am glad Harry will have had a day or two at
Minto. He is entirely silent, and at present dejected.
He has too little spring for his age; but his heart and
disposition, and indeed capacity, are good.'

                                        'June 5, 1802.

'At Court yesterday there was the usual mobbing.
I stood two hours in the same spot without possibility
of moving either backwards or forwards. However, in
the end I spoke both to King and Queen. There

were two or three very pretty Irishwomen, of whom
Lady Conyngham was one.   Old Paoli was there.   At
Lord Pelham's we wore our Court dresses, the only
specimen of old manners I have seen.   We were
twenty-two, which in London passes for a great dinner,
and was no more than we always had in Vienna with
company.'

'June 7.

'I went yesterday with Lady Palmerston and Mrs.
Culverden to Sheen.   She was very much affected by
this visit, and I confess it was very melancholy to me.
It was the place which he enjoyed more than any other,
and I had seen her indeed very happy there and surrounded with many comforts, as well as experienced
kindness and many comforts myself.   There is always
something desolate in the breaking up of an old establishment and the stripping of a house that you have
lived in of half its furniture, pictures, books, &c.; but
this is much increased when the occasion in this
instance is considered.   We walked a good deal in the
grounds; the air was sweet and pleasant and everything
fresh and green; and this must have done her bodily
good.'

'Dropmore: June 10.

'I came from Beconsfield to Dropmore yesterday pretty
well. The family were all out airing; so I took a Waller[1]
with me into the woods and grounds, and, after walking round the place, I began my summer by reading
an hour on the grass, surrounded by honeysuckle,

[1] Waller's Poems.

mignonette, and other poetical scents. The party at Dropmore was Lord and Lady Grenville, Lord and Lady Buckingham, their son and daughter, with Lady Camelford and her old friend Mrs. ——. Nothing could be pleasanter than the whole party, particularly the female part of it. Lady Grenville is beautiful, Lady Buckingham remarkably agreeable, and Lady Camelford I was extremely happy to meet. She is always kind to you, and I always feel a great kindness for her on account of your old connection with her. I had a full dose of politics with Lord Grenville yesterday, and with him and Lord Buckingham both days. This morning we all went to Clifden and Taplow— walked over those very beautiful places, and had a fine day for it. To-morrow I go to Park Place. I dine to-day with Lord Fitzwilliam—another chieftain who draws together a greater mixture of the old opposition with the alarmist part of the party.'

To another correspondent he wrote :—' Nothing can be pleasanter than the Grenville family at home. Lady Grenville is beautiful, and nice and pleasant in all ways. Lady Buckingham was beautiful, and is remarkably entertaining. Lady Camelford has long been one of my passions, and Lord Grenville is entirely different in his family from the notion which his general manners have perhaps naturally given of him to the world.

' I dined yesterday at the Harringtons, who are very grateful and kind. All their children are beautiful, the second son extremely so; but he seems as fond of the cut of his coat and his Titus head as Lord Thomas (Clinton) could be. Lady Anna Maria [1] is one of the prettiest creatures I ever saw, with lively and uncommonly obliging manners.

'I took leave of the Princess of Wales yesterday. The little Princess was there—amazingly clever and engaging; she sings French and German songs, plays on the piano, and dances, all extremely well, and only six years old.'

On June 29 Parliament was dissolved; and Lord Minto returned to his home in the North, of which we gain a glimpse in a letter addressed by him from thence to Lady Palmerston :—

'Minto: August 28, 1802.

'My dear Lady Palmerston,—I came back yesterday from my second expedition to Edinburgh, accompanied by my friend Mr. Campbell. This house is now entirely filled. Gilbert and his friends take a good deal of their amusement either on the rivers or on the hills, and in the evening the younger part of the society, including Elliot, form a circle, without candles, and tell hobgoblin stories till supper-time; the conversation is not confined to the narrator, but the whole ring is so vociferous that they have merited the title of Pandemonium. In the meanwhile, *she*, Lady Malm.,[2] and I, retreat upstairs to the library, and form a comfortable fogram party,

[1] Married Francis, Duke of Bedford.
[2] Lady Malmesbury.

pitying the noise and fatigues of youth, which we hear like the distant roar of the sea. We have had a most capital addition to the Hobgoblinites in Mr. Walter Scott, editor of the " Minstrelsy of the Border," who besides an inexhaustible fund of spectres, has a rich store of horrid murders, robberies, and other bloody exploits committed by and on our own forefathers, the Elliots. Mr. Scott is a particularly pleasing and entertaining man.' [1]

[1] A great part, if not the whole, of Walter Scott's *Demonology and Witchcraft* was written by him at Minto. Family tradition also relates that two celebrated lines in Campbell's poem of *Lochiel's Warning* were all but lost for want of writing materials in his room under the same roof.

The story is that while lying awake one night with his mind full of this subject the following lines occurred to him :

'   'Tis the sunset of life gives me mystical lore,
                          And coming events cast their shadows before.'

He rose instantly in order to write them down, and to his disgust found neither pen nor ink in his room, when, fearing they should vanish from his memory like a dream in the morning, he rang up the servants, nor returned to bed till he had *fixed them* on paper.

CHAPTER XII.

In the course of the summer the ambition of Bonaparte had fulfilled the worst prognostications of those who had seen nothing in the peace but an opportunity gained by him to pursue new schemes of conquest undisturbed by a war with Great Britain. Since the peace he had annexed the Island of Élba and the whole of Piedmont; had occupied the Duchies of Parma and Placentia, and had declared himself 'Mediator of the Swiss Republic;' and all this with a pretence of serving moral ends that revolted the honest soul of Windham. 'There is something,' he said, in the debates on the address, ' in the boasted title of pacificator so ludicrous that it excites contempt. It is like the cant slang so much in use with smugglers, robbers, and gypsies: with such people smuggling is called a " free trade," " skipping a hedge," " moonshine," and " running away at night." I remember a set of thieves in Suffolk who called every sort of plunder of the revenue " hiding." So when the consul marches 40,000 men into Switzerland he calls it " settling their affairs." When he invaded Egypt in breach of treaty with the Porte, he called it chastising the rebellious Pashas. If any oppose his measures they are disturbers of the peace, but his soldiers and partisans are all supporters of order.'[1]

In the upper House, meanwhile, Lord Grenville made a spirited attack on the Ministry, and called for a strong system of defence, and for the return to power of the leader to whom Great Britain and Europe looked for the preservation of their liberties.

Lord Minto went to London in November to be present at the meeting of Parliament.

Lord Minto to Lady Minto.

'Spring Gardens: November 22, 1802.

' I arrived to-day and took my seat immediately. The King goes to the House to-morrow. I have had a

---

[1] In the same debate Mr. Elliot spoke with vigour and effect. In reply to the argument that Great Britain's wealth and resources were such as would enable her to sever her fortunes from those of the Continent without injury or loss, he said:—' Some gentlemen argued as if the efficacy of wealth did not consist in its application. They really spoke as if it contained some principle of vitality, as if it had some inherent principle of activity, as if it had ears, and eyes, and hands, and feet. They say, " We have a surplus of near four millions of money." I say, "the French have four hundred thousand bayonets." I tell them " an armed robber is at the door." " Oh, but," say they, "we are very rich." In common sense the answer is " so much the better for the robber."

.   .   .   .

' He could not help reminding gentlemen that our wealth may be our glory or our shame. If wealth was in its due place and was made subservient to the honour, dignity, independence, and security of the country, he trusted that, under the blessing of Providence, it might become the foundation of a towering and durable greatness; but if we betrayed more fear for the loss of it than zeal in defending it, if we did not direct it to its proper objects, it would be no longer the magazine of our strength, but an additional bait to the rapacity of the foe.'

long walk with Lord Grenville and Tom Grenville, but am not more in the secret than I was at Minto. They have not the least knowledge of the contents, and only a conjecture concerning the tone, of the King's Speech. It is not likely that any amendment will be moved, but only a discussion of what has passed since the summer.'

'House of Lords: November 23, 1802.

' The King has made his speech, which is not explicit, as might be expected, on war or peace; but the general impression it leaves is not very pacific. In this House Lord Arden moves and Lord Nelson seconds. There will be no amendment moved by me, as nothing is said in commendation of the peace. Lord Grenville will, however, speak pretty fully on the past and present. My speaking to-day is out of the question.

'Despard's plot was very serious indeed.[1] The King's life was certainly to have been attempted this day, and with too much prospect of success.'

'London: November 26, 1802.

'Lord Nelson has been with me a long time to-day, and I have had a great deal of talk with him on affairs public and private. He seems much of my mind on material points, but especially on the necessity of being better prepared than we now are ; and indeed as well prepared as possible. He told me, if there is war, he is to have the Mediterranean command.

[1] Colonel Despard, executed, with others, for a conspiracy against the King's life.

'Lord St. Vincent is very unwell, more violent than anybody against war, and has declared that he will resign if Ministers dare go to war. His principal reason is, I believe, that the ships are so much out of repair as to be unfit for service. I am convinced that both our own Government and the French will avoid actual war if possible; our Ministers because they cannot face the difficulties of it nor could be trusted to carry it on; the French because they wish to have possession of all we have ceded first, and to carry on their plans of aggrandisement both in Europe and abroad without opposition, till they are as strong as they wish to be for the contest with us. But with these dispositions to postpone the rupture on both sides it seems difficult to avoid it. There appears to be no doubt that orders are sent to retain such of our conquests as are not already given up, which Martinique unfortunately is. These strong orders must have been given in consequence of some provocations from France. On one hand, therefore, France must consider the orders to retain our conquests notwithstanding the engagements to surrender them as a cause of war,—and, on the other, how can our Government recede from those orders unless France recede from the measures we complain of? Nothing seems more improbable than concession on the part of France : accordingly she is going on as rapidly as she can without regard to our representations. Switzerland is to be first disarmed, then garrisoned by a French army which they must pay for that service. She has taken the Duke of Parma's dominions. It is thought at Vienna that Tuscany will

go the same way, and that the King of Etruria will not
be allowed to return from Spain. . . . Everybody here is
dejected, and most people terrified, seeing the storm preparing to burst at last upon ourselves, and not having
courage or spirit to adopt the only possible remedy for
such an evil, which is open resistance.   The only decided
advocates for peace are those who have been considered
for some time as the friends of France.   Fox talks of
abolishing all jealousies between the two nations and
confining our competition to excellence in arts and
manufactures ; just as if there was no room for supposing Bonaparte ambitious or for apprehending any
designs against England.   He is, however, almost alone
in this language.   Sheridan does not attend, because he
will not concur with Fox's present politics.   Tierney,
who has been some time in France, says on the contrary
we must arm instantly, that everything is in readiness
or in forwardness there, and that we have not a moment
to lose.   Pitt stops away; his friends call out for a
change of Ministry, and specifically for him ; and the
impression left on the public now is that Addington's administration is to stand henceforward on its
own strength, unsupported by Pitt.

'On the other hand, a coalition between Fox and
Addington ! ! ! is beginning to be talked of.   Lord
Grenville called for Pitt the other day in his speech
on the Address, and if it were possible to have Pitt
again with his former energy and powers and unham-
pered by all the sins of the late period, one should think
the country more likely to exert itself than in any

other hands; but it is generally believed that Pitt's mind and character are very much weakened, and it is certain that the part he has taken from the moment of his resignation very much disqualifies him for calling on the country for energy. Lord Grenville's, according to my own opinion, would be the best administration. But I feel it would not be a popular one, and on that account it might not be able to carry the country through the burdens, exertions, and perhaps reverses and perils of the war. After all I have written, I can only give you general uncertain views on all points, both of measures and parties. In reality nothing is at all settled, and it is difficult to conjecture the result on any part of the subject; only this is certain, that the public prospect is most gloomy, and the public spirits extremely low.

'I have not yet seen Hugh. The Paynes are in town; Isabella a pretty sylph. I have seen the Chevalier de Sade, who is as dirty, as ugly, as economical, but to me as clever and good-humoured, as ever.'

'December 8, 1802.

'I have been to the levée to-day. The King is in the highest good looks, and extremely sensible; for he told me that Hugh is a great deal fatter than me, for which I desired his permission to cite His Majesty, as Hugh disputes the point violently.

'I have letters from all parts of Europe—very kind one from the Queen of Naples. London never was so empty, except of *emigrés*.'

In the course of December Lord Minto took up his
winter quarters in the forsaken house in Hanover
Square.   Lady Palmerston was in close attendance on
her sister, Mrs. Culverden, lying ill at the Lavender
House ; and her son, who now bore the name his long
life was destined to make familiar as a household word
among all classes of Englishmen, was pursuing his
studies in Edinburgh, whence he wrote 'a most charming letter' to Lord Minto, pressing him to settle himself in the empty house.   The old *côterie* of Sheen and
Roehampton was breaking up.   Illness had done its
worst at Sheen, had settled down on the Lavender
House, and had driven the Francises and the Ellises to
Nice ; and from thence they wrote home melancholy
letters, save when they found cause to mention their
pleasant countrywomen, the Miss Berrys.   A visit to
any of these deserted villas, once so gay, had become an
act of penance. ' I felt like a ghost,' wrote Lord Minto,
' as I wandered through the beautiful evergreen shrubberies of Park Place, where the climate was as southern
to-day as Italy ; ' ' and in every walk where light steps
had been, he met the phantom, called Regret.' [1]

' December 7.

' The plan is altered concerning the House of Lords.
I have had a long conversation to-day with Lord
Grenville, who thinks the motion intended by me will
come better after Christmas, but that notice of it
should be given this week.   I shall do this on Friday.

[1] ' Legends and Lyrics.'

Nothing can be more unhinged than the political world at present.. Lord Grenville says pretty nearly that he has reason to *know* Mr. Pitt is ready to resume the Government very much on our view of the danger, and, I understand, in connection with us. He thinks also that the present Ministry is very much shaken, and that there may be a doubt whether they will meet Parliament after Christmas. But other opinions are that the Grenvilles are too sanguine, and that the present Ministry will either look for accession in some other quarter or attempt to get through the session as they are. As for me, I follow my own opinions on points of public concern without seeing which way they tend in party politics; but I am clear that the weakness of the present Ministry immensely increases the danger to which the country is exposed.'

' December 11.

' I saw Mrs. Jordan last night in the " Pannel." She has lost her beauty by the change in her person, which is now very large ; and this takes in some degree from the grace and cleverness of her action ; but her acting, her voice, and extreme naturalness are as perfect as ever.'

' December 14.

' I don't apprehend that any political changes are very near. Ministry are now supported by Fox and Sheridan, in the absence of Pitt. The flourishing state of the revenue and commerce which Mr. Addington produced at the Budget, the certainty that there will be no war immediately, and the rise of the stocks, seem sufficient to carry him through this session on to the next, unless very unfortunate events should bring on some catastrophe sooner. These I am really afraid *must* come upon us; but it may not be soon according to the present system, for this Ministry seem to have taken their resolution not to oppose anything France may choose, so long as she refrains from some direct hostility against us. It is probable, therefore, that Bonaparte will go on extending his conquests in all directions till he is quite sure of being an over-match for us. It is by no means generally thought that Lord Grenville's expectations of Pitt's coming into Government with him are well founded.'

'December 27.

'We had a Christmas dinner, the day before yesterday,[1] of twenty-eight people, and an assembly in the evening. The principal personage at dinner was Mr. Romilly,[2] whom you may remember my liking very much as a friend of Mirabeau's. He is now nearly at the head of the Court of Chancery, and bids as fair for Chancellor as anybody at the Bar. He is universally respected, and is remarkably pleasing as well as able. Mrs. Romilly is beautiful.'

'January 4, 1803.

'Hugh is to be appointed to Naples in the room of Mr. Drummond, who goes to Constantinople. Mrs. Elliot does not speak Italian, but German will do very well for the Queen. I see Bonaparte condescends to

---

[1] At Mr. Gally Knight's.
[2] Afterwards Sir Samuel Romilly.

attack me in the " Moniteur."   I am in good company
—Lord Grenville and Windham, and, indeed, Lord
Pelham.'[1]

'Dropmore: January 7, 1803.

'The weather has been too bad, too wet, to go out.
There is nobody here but Lord and Lady Grenville and
Tom Grenville.   We passed our time very pleasantly
yesterday in conversation and without any attempt at
cards or other troublesome pastimes.   I do not learn
anything very precise about politics.   It is now generally understood that Lord Hawkesbury is to come to
the House of Lords to strengthen Lord Pelham and
Lord Hobart in debate, which they are certainly in need
of.   Mr. Pitt is to attend Parliament after the holidays.
Lord Grenville says his opinions are more nearly ours
than they have ever been; but he wishes to preserve
measures, personally at least, with the present Ministers.
This, however, will be difficult if he is against them on
the principles of their conduct; and it seems not improbable that he may pass from a mixture of personal
support and public opposition to coolness, and from
thence to enmity, as usual in party.   This is the more

---

[1] January 1, 1803.   At the beginning of the year the *Moniteur* contained a series of observations on the debates in the British Parliament,
in which it was asserted that Germany and Italy were inundated by
secret agents under the orders of Drake, Wickham, and others; that
Lords Grenville and Minto and Mr. Windham, perversely addicted to
war, and insensible to all the sentiments of nature, had endeavoured to
raise disturbances throughout the Continent; but their plans were detected and their agents arrested.   Was there a mother in England,
Germany, Italy, or France, who must not regard with horror Grenville,
Windham, and Minto?—*Annual Register.*

likely, as he will be provoked by the sort of support
Ministers are now receiving from Sheridan and others
who are Pitt's personal enemies. Sheridan told Windham
that he should support the Ministry as much as possible as the only way of keeping Pitt out, which was the
grand point of all. This cannot conciliate Pitt to the
system supported by Sheridan ; however, Pitt is an eel,
and no man can tell what part he will take. We can only
go on following our opinions, and setting all these considerations as much out of sight as possible. Lord Melville is coming to attend Parliament also; but he is
another eel, and winds about too much to be followed or
much attended to, at least by me. I have bought a
strange life of myself in a book called " Public Characters." There are several volumes—mine is in 1801–2.
You never read such stuff; it means to be very civil, but
is thorough balderdash. He says " I was brought up at
a free school; that I was put into the army as part of
my education, and had a company at ten years old; that I
was fond of *gardening*, and very civil to the neighbouring clergy. My uncle, the admiral, who took Thurot,
has been dead many years." It is not worth sending,
but I may bring it.'

'Broadlands : January 21, 1803.

' We have no one here, besides the family, but Miss
Whitworth and her pretty nieces, Lady Russell's daughters : the eldest (fifteen) is beautiful. Lady Palmerston
told me yesterday, after tea, that I must come with her
to play at a game of billiards. I followed her, and found
myself all at once in a theatre, the benches of which were

already filled, the stage decorated, and the last music playing. Briefly, I saw " Three Weeks after Marriage," followed by " My Grandmother," represented in a superior style by the quality specified in the enclosed bill of the play. It was really remarkably good ; Lily and Willy[1] were quite famous. They had got it up very quietly and with great pains, that I should not suspect it, and so had perfectly escaped my vigilance. We are to have the play over again to-night, with an occasional prologue by Lord Minto ; but this is a secret, so pray don't mention it at dinner to-day.

' I have been reading Paley's new book, which I am entertained with, as it contains a number of curious particulars in anatomy, chemistry, astronomy, &c.; but the plan of his book is not new, having been executed by Fénélon and others ; and in the argumentative part I think him rather verbose, not to say a little twaddling. God bless you all.'

' February 2, 1803.

' Politics seem to be very much where they were, except that the expectations of good from Pitt are very much abated. He is now expected to take a feeble, trimming part, not agreeing with Ministers, but supporting them against us. We are, it would seem, a good deal discouraged, and it is in agitation to suspend our active measures on the ground of their inefficacy. The idea is to take some one opportunity of declaring once more our general opinions, and after that to

[1] William Temple; for many years Her Majesty's Minister to the Court of the two Sicilies.

desist from pushing them importunately on Parliament and the country. My motion will furnish that opportunity in the House of Lords ; it will come on about the 15th. I am sorry to hear of so much gaming in Edinburgh. This vice was unknown to any extent in our time, and it alters the whole character of the place. However, I have no fears whatever, on that head, for any of your class, nor of those horrid habits of drinking into which —— has fallen, sinking a good understanding and more gentlemanlike tastes ; but he never aimed at more than amusement even in his better pursuits, and has come at last to this refuge from the tedium of nothingness.'

I have a long letter from the Queen of Naples, giving a curious account of her Spanish son-in-law and daughter-in-law.' [1]

[1] The Spanish son-in-law was the Prince of Asturias. In October 1802 he married Marie Antoinette, daughter of the King of Naples, and at the same time the Prince Royal of Naples married Isabella, Infanta of Spain. The first marriage had been anticipated with dismay by the bride and her mother, the Queen of Naples, whose letters before her daughter left her are very touching. The one alluded to in the text, written after their separation, shows that the double marriages had brought little happiness to those concerned in them.

'Je parle,' wrote the Queen, 'à un père excellent et tendre. Il excusera donc mes anxiétés pour ma chère vive et aimable Antoinette. Elle ne peut s'accoutumer à cette vilaine Espagne, à cet époux, non mari, et de plus totalement benêt et sot. Cela lui fait une peine extrême que je partage bien avec elle. Je tâche de la consoler, encourager, fortifier par mes lettres, mais les siennes me peignent si bien la situation de son âme qu'elles me font toujours verser des larmes. Mon fils commence à s'habituer à sa poupée de chair, mais ni société ni conversation ne se trouvent en elle, et comme il est très-vertueux et n'aime que son ménage, c'est un terrible manque pour le bonheur domestique. Elle a toute espèce de maîtres, mais l'envie d'apprendre, ou pour mieux dire l'esprit de connaître qu'elle en a besoin, lui manque.'

' February 5, 1803.

' I shall soon be as blue as Anna Maria !'[1] Member of the Royal Society of Edinburgh, F.R.S. of London, Student at the Royal Institution, and LL.D.—my title will occupy the alphabet, and make as great a figure as Lord Nelson's stars, or Sir Sidney Smith's crests and supporters. It is singular that I was admitted a Fellow of the Royal Society the day before I received the account of my admission into that of Edinburgh. I wonder I was not F.R.S. sooner, as it costs next to nothing and is entertaining and instructing. It brings one acquainted with a class of people that one has hardly any other chance of seeing. The day before yesterday there was only one paper read that was not very interesting, though you ladies may think it otherwise, being a Treatise on the Human Tongue by Mr. Horne, the celebrated anatomist, formerly friend and associate of John Hunter. He has ascertained that a part of the tongue may be removed without injuring the organ materially for taste or speech, &c. As soon as I receive the official letter from the Secretary of the Royal Society of Edinburgh, I shall

---

[1] The playful charge brought against her by her father seems to have been revived among her acquaintance at a later period of her life, and is thus disposed of by Sir Walter Scott in an entry in his Diary, published in *Lockhart's Life*: ' August 10, 1826. Went to Minto . . . missed my facetious and lively friend Lady Anna Maria. It is the fashion of some silly women and silly men to abuse her as a blue-stocking. If to have good sense and good humour, mixed with a strong power of observing, and an equally strong one of expressing—if of this the result must be *blue*, she shall be as blue as they will. Such cant is the refuge of fools who fear those who can turn them into ridicule '

thank both the Society and Mr. Stewart, to whom 1 am indebted for this favour. I am extremely pleased with the "Life of Dr. Reid." [1] It is, I think, very beautifully written, and is rendered extremely interesting, in two very different ways, by the very pleasing and amiable character of Dr. Reid, and by the account of his philosophy, of which he must be considered as a founder. I have sent it to Broadlands, as I know both Lady Palmerston and the girls are well qualified to understand and relish it. I was yesterday with Mrs. Gally and Mrs. Romilly at a little French theatre where the emigrants have amused themselves for some years past with acting French plays two or three times a week in winter. I was extremely amused. One of the actors was very good and all the rest tolerable. The town is ringing with Monsieur Sebastiani's report on Egypt, published in the "Moniteur." It seems to make a strong impression everywhere—as if nobody suspected that Bonaparte had views on that part of the world before !'

'February 9, 1803.

'There is nothing doing here in politics. We are all resting on our oars; I think, unwisely, for there are right things to be done without the imputation of pertinacity. I think, indeed, that pertinacity, activity, keenness, and especially great vigilance, are the qualities expected of any Opposition ; and, though troublesome to Ministers, they are looked for by the public. The most

[1] By Dugald Stewart.

wholesome and natural state for England is a strong
Government, and *one* strong Opposition. Now, nothing
is strong, nor united, nor active, nor vigilant. The
Government, the Parliament, the people are all loose,
incoherent atoms. This is all France can wish; but this
is so unnatural a state of things here that it cannot
last. It must be ascribed very much to Pitt's equivocal
conduct. This keeps men from taking their line decidedly—I mean all except ourselves, who are simply
proclaiming our own opinions, and hallooing them
into deaf ears, but without any settled or distinct party
or party object. The truth of Pitt, I believe, is that
his opinion is one way and his hampering engagements
another. He cannot do what he feels to be his duty
without encountering the cry of inconsistency and in-
fidelity to his professions. However, his conduct from
the moment of his retreat appears to me too weak and
too little directed by the great interests of the country
to leave him without reproach, and not to sink him
greatly in reputation, as well as to diminish one's confidence in him. Then, in whom are we to confide? I
really do not know; and therefore, as I said before, all
this is so much the better for Bonaparte.

'I dined yesterday with Lord Graves, and met the
Glenbervies, Hugh, &c. I came away at eight, leaving
them all at table, to hear Mr. Davy's Lecture on Heat,
Light, and Electricity. You must allow I am a worthy
member of the learned societies. I wanted to see and
to hear what concerns the *reflexion* of cold, which dis-
concerts the received systems about heat and puzzles us

philosophers. Mr. Davy left it unexplained. Hugh
was declared unanimously by the company yesterday
to be *much* the fattest, and they only wondered at his
disputing it. I am getting dapper, I believe. Is it
attributable to the severity of my philosophical studies ? '

'February 10, 1803.

' Last night I went to a concert at Colonel Dillon's.
Madame de Boigne looks younger and more girlish, and
full as handsome, as determined, and as uncaptivating
as some years ago. She sings perfectly. Many reproaches from the Aucklands for my infrequent appearances there. Hugh had said that the real case was that
I lived with the *Invisible Girl*,[1] but that the effects
would soon be visible. Dined at Mrs. Crewe's with
Harry Greville and Mr. Lawrence the painter, who
repeated an extremely pretty poem of Cowper's, which
will be in the new edition by Hayley.'

'February 22.

'Despard was executed yesterday morning. He died
as great a rascal as he lived. Two people have been
taken up for attempting to seduce soldiers, one of whom,
it was said, was acquitted on the last trial. There is a
portion of bad blood in our veins, and I only hope it
will not contaminate the mass. Pelletier is convicted.
Mackintosh is said to have been more eloquent and
able than it is possible to express. I have not read the
trial ; but if, as Lord Ellenborough says in the charge
to the jury, the pamphlet contains provocation to

A scientific automaton at that time much in fashion.

assassinate, I shall not regret the prosecution, as those are means of which no Government should suffer the imputation to lie upon them.

' Napper Tandy has been challenging Elliot in the French newspapers to meet him at a frontier town and fight. He says he sent the same challenge by the post, and he now proclaims Elliot a coward and a scoundrel for not accepting it. Elliot never received the challenge by post, and is neither Irish nor French enough to pay any attention to that blackguard.

' I met Sir Richard Worsley the other day. He had four most famous pictures, which were taken by the French at Venice most scandalously. He applied to Bonaparte to have them restored ; but that great Consul was pleased to be jocular, and told him they were vastly too fine to be parted with; but he should be happy to show them to Sir Richard at St. Cloud.'

' February 23, 1803.

The object of Nelson's visit yesterday was truly kind. He told me in strict confidence that for some time back there have been great doubts between peace and war, and that still Government is under the greatest uncertainty whether they shall be forced to some hostile measure or not. One of those in contemplation has been to send him to the Mediterranean, by way of watching the armament and being ready if wanted. He says that he is thought the fitter for that delicate service, as on one hand he wishes the continuance of peace, and therefore is not likely to precipitate

matters ; and on the other hand Bonaparte knows that
if he hoists his flag it will not be in joke. He came to
say that under those expectations and possibilities he
had thought of George, and had determined to have him
with him if his command takes place. It must be in
a sloop ; but, with his earnestness to promote George,
that consequence could hardly fail.

'We had a great deal of conversation about Despard.[1]
Lord Nelson seems to have been quite right all through,
and to have behaved with a due mixture of generosity
and private feeling with public propriety. He abomi-
nates and abhors him, and never took a step towards
saving him except by merely forwarding a petition,
which Despard had sent him, to Mr. Addington, which
nobody could refuse doing. He spoke with horror of
his behaviour on the scaffold. Mrs. Despard, he says,
was violently in love with her husband, which makes
the last scene of the tragedy affecting indeed. Lord
Nelson solicited a pension or some provision for her,
and Government was well disposed to grant it ; but the
last act at the scaffold may have defeated any chance of
indulgence to any member of his family.'

'February 28.

'My dinner at Nelson's was entertaining enough. A
great deal of talk about Despard. Nelson read us a
letter written to him by Despard the Tuesday before the
execution, extremely well written, and it would have
been affecting from any other pen. It spoke in a high

[1] Lord Nelson appeared on the trial to give evidence of the high
character borne in former years by Despard.

strain, you may suppose, of his gratitude to Nelson, whose evidence, he says, produced the jury's recommend- ation.   Whether his days were many or few, he said, he would have no other inscription on his tomb than the character given of him by Nelson at the trial; he enclosed a petition for pardon, but said hardly anything on the subject.   Nelson merely sent the letter and petition, just as he had received them, to Mr. Adding- ton, who told Nelson afterwards that he and his family had sat up after supper, weeping over the letter.   Hugh, Charles Greville, and Colonel Graham dined there.'

'March .7.

' I am reading Hayley's " Life of Cowper," and like it much.   I don't know that you will, however.   It is not lively.   It was a dull and, in part, a gloomy life.   He was often insane—perhaps never thoroughly right; but it was a most uniform, innocent, and amiable life, and not a short one.   His letters are written charmingly, with a pleasant mixture of genius, nature, levity, and seriousness.   I dine to-night and to-morrow at Lord Spencer's ; but I shall go this evening before dinner is well over to the galvanic lecture by Mr. Davy.   I should not be surprised if Lord Spencer came too, as he is keen about galvanism.'

'March 9, 1803.

' You will see the warlike message[1] to the two Houses in the papers.   I learnt it yesterday at the Literary

[1] A message from the King to the House of Lords, acquainting them that the preparations in the Ports of France and Holland require pre- cautions on our part.

Club, and immediately wrote you a line which was too
late for the bell in St. James Street ; so I ran, dressed as
I was, in my cocked hat to Charing Cross. . . .   At the
club we had Lord Spencer, Lord Macartney, the Master
of the Rolls, and Dr. Lawrence, and several other politicians ; but nobody knew anything of the grounds of
this alarm ; and the message itself was kept such a
secret that the Chancellor himself seemed to have no
knowledge of it when Lord Hobart got up to deliver it.

'I went afterwards to Sir George's consultation at
Lincoln's Inn,[1] and there resumed my old profession ;
for I made a regular speech and argument on a material
point which Adam and Mackintosh seemed not convinced
upon, and brought them completely round, so that the
point will have been tried to-day, I don't know with
what success ; but, if it succeeds, it throws out the
petition entirely.   From thence I went to a political
consultation at Tom Grenville's—Lord Grenville, Lord
Spencer, Windham, Elliot, Lawrence, and   myself.
They were all as much in the dark as myself on the
history of the rupture.'

[1] A consultation at Mr. Adam's chambers regarding the course to
be pursued in committee on an election petition under the Treating Act
served against Sir George Cornewall. Mr. Adam and Sir J. Mackintosh
were his advisers.   Lord Minto wrote on March 15 that the petition
was thrown out, and 'Adam and Mackintosh say he owes this entirely
to me.'   Mr. Adam told Lord Minto that his speech had consisted
entirely of the topics suggested by Lord Minto at the consultation ; and
in fact that, without that consultation, they would not have tried the
point at all.

'March 17, 1803.

' Nothing positive is known concerning peace or war. It appears, therefore, that the measures taken here did not produce an instant rupture at Paris, and that negotiation was not thought inadmissible. Bonaparte will certainly only negotiate for the purpose of gaining time and completing his preparations. We, on the contrary, may negotiate on a different principle, and hope, if not for security, which is impossible, at least for such an accommodation as may leave a pretence for deferring war. To-day a change in the Admiralty is universally expected, and the general opinion seems to be that Lord Melville will succeed Lord St. Vincent. However, I do not know this from any authority. . . . Pray tell Gilbert I have seen the Duke of Roxburghe, who does not know exactly when the officers must join their regiments ; but the King's warrant for calling out the men is already gone to the country. I dined yesterday quietly at Lady Palmerston's, and sat there part of the afternoon, reading them the first volume of " Delphine," which does not interest me so much as it does many of her readers. It is surely a pity that the female half of the world keep soaking their minds so perpetually in novels, good, bad, and indifferent. It can only make people unfit more or less for real life. The false views and opinions are generally made very amiable ; and nobody minds the poetical justice which is executed on the interesting culprits in the last pages of the book, that being merely the invention of the author, and a judgment from which they may appeal. The virtues, again, are all exaggerated and unnatural, and such as there is no chance, and often no sense, in copying. But here " Delphine " is occupying everybody.'

'March 18.

' I have to-day a private letter from a correspondent at Paris, which says that there has been a great deal of activity in preparing flat-bottom boats and other measures relating to invasion. With the dispositions which prevail towards us in France, and the means of hostility which they have in constant readiness, I do not see how anything short of a war establishment at sea and on shore can really protect us.'

'March 29.

' I dined yesterday at Caulfield's, where I went at a quarter past six, the time appointed, and found the servants in their waistcoats beginning to prepare the rooms. I saw them light fifty-two wax candles in the drawing-room, and admired all the treasures he had crowded into it. There were *six* great Paris clocks, ormolu and bronze, all immense in size and superb in decoration, as the fashion now is. I was a good while alone; and then the company came by degrees—Caulfield himself not till about eight o'clock. I had ordered my carriage at half-past eight, being unwell, and expected it to come for me before dinner was announced. The plate, *service*, *cuisine*, were all in the same splendid style, and he himself did the honours extremely well. The company was mostly young men—Lord Henry Petty,[1] whose manners I like much ; Mr. Lamb, second

[1] The third Marquis of Lansdowne.

son of Lord Melbourne ; two young Pagets, and so forth. I came away as soon as I could, and called at Spring Gardens, Hanover Square, and Palace Yard, before going home.'

'March 25, 1803.

'I am indeed persuaded that a serious contest with France cannot be long avoided; but it is possible this storm may blow over for a time. For my own part I am not sorry for the present little delay; for no one could have imagined the total want of preparation, and the total impossibility of a very sudden preparation, in which this country has been placed. It is too bad to speak of without danger. We had till within the last fortnight at most *one* ship of the line able to go to sea. We cannot have five ready for a month to come. There are some frigates, indeed ; but they are all employed in procuring men all round the two islands, so that at this moment the sea is completely open. Providentially, Bonaparte is not better prepared for naval expeditions. The press [1] has done very little for some time, and there is a want of seamen that one does not at present know how to supply. The hasty and total reduction of all our force, as if it were impossible to apprehend anything from France again, seems a sad infatuation. Economy, revenue, commerce, were the only ideas for which the Ministers could find room in their enlarged minds ; and nothing can prove better how unequal those minds were to the Government in such times than the extreme danger in which they have

[1] The Press-gang.

placed us of total destruction. Bonaparte's absurd, flighty conversation with Lord Whitworth really took place much as it has been represented. He has excited a great deal of ridicule in France; but that will not prevent him from carrying out his designs whenever he is ready. Lord Hood has just been with me, and we agreed that Lord Melville would be the best First Lord we could have at the Admiralty; he has more energy and activity than almost any other man, and incomparably more than any of the present Administration.'

Lord Minto's youngest son, William, came up from Minto in the course of April to join the ' Ardent ' at Sheerness, in which ship he had received his commission as midshipman. The parents felt sensibly the flight of the *youngest bird of the covey*; but of himself his father wrote :—

'April 6, 1803.

' William is all delight and spirits. Indeed, hitherto a sailor's life has proved very pleasant to him. He has passed his time at plays, opera, sights, exhibitions, and conjurors. On his departure he has received more presents than ambassadors do at taking leave. He got his midshipman's jacket home this morning; and my next letter will carry you the account of his being settled in his profession, and of our separation perhaps for some years. This reflection prevents the scene from appearing as smiling to me as to him; but it is impossible not to enjoy to some degree his happiness and spirit, and in parting with him it is a great comfort to

think him so well adapted to the profession he is entering on and so promising in every respect. It is impossible to see a finer boy in disposition and spirit; and
I have no doubt of his turning out well, barring misfortunes which must be barred in every line of life.'

The next letter recorded the journey to Sheerness,
and William's instalment there in the midshipman's
cockpit, 'seeing nothing formidable in being thus
shoved off alone into the ocean.' 'But,' wrote his
father, 'he was not without feelings of another kind.
When Captain Winthrop was going to retire on
Wednesday evening, I said to William, "Now, William,
there is your new master, your new father, and you
must honour and obey him accordingly." Captain
Winthrop was going out of the room as I said this;
and, the moment he had shut the door, William crept
close to me, and said, "Papa, he may be my new master
if you please, but not my father. I don't want to
change fathers." This came quite feelingly, though
very naturally from him.'

'April 12.

I now know [1] with certainty that negotiations have
been carrying on amongst the Parliamentary leaders for
some change in the Ministry. Lord Melville was the
author of these measures. He wishes to come into office;
but is desirous of having Pitt with him, or, at least,

---

[1] On March 21 Lord Minto had written that Lord Melville was gone
to Walmer to see Mr. Pitt, but with what precise objects he was not
informed.

of having his full sanction and concurrence.   For this
purpose, he went to Walmer, and carried overtures from
Addington for a very partial change, or rather accession
to the present Ministry.   Pitt seems to have listened.
He invited Lord Grenville to confer on these matters.
Lord Grenville proposed as broad and comprehensive a
Ministry as possible, not excluding even some of the
old Opposition.   Pitt did not seem prepared for this
plan, but afterwards appeared to think of it more
favourably.   On this footing the thing was left when
Lord Grenville came from Walmer, it being settled
that Pitt should come nearer town, and that further
deliberations should take place.   In the meanwhile
Lord Melville's and Addington's own negotiations with
Pitt are going on, and, I presume, quite separate from
Lord Grenville's, and the more probable result appears
to be the accession of Pitt with Dundas and a few of
Pitt's own friends to the present Ministry ; Pitt being
first Lord of the Treasury and Addington Secretary of
State.   It does not appear what share the King has in
all these plans ; only it is certain that he has none in
Lord Grenville's extensive scheme, nor in any that
could entirely remove Addington, to whom he is particularly attached.   This is all very confidential.'

    (*Confidential.*)   ' Beconsfield : April 13.

    ' Since my letter of yesterday, I have reason to know
that the separate accession of Pitt with Lord Melville
and a few of his friends has been rejected by Pitt ; and
that he is not likely to resume the Government, other-

wise than with the principal members of the old Government, and with a Ministry appointed by himself.
If this be the case, and he adheres steadily to that
resolution, it appears to me that the general uneasiness
which prevails at present, and the alarm taken even by
the present Ministers, must bring Pitt in on his own
terms. The only terms consistent with his personal
honour are those I have mentioned, and they are equally
necessary for the public safety; although, setting all
personal politics aside, I should have considered any
change, and especially the assistance of Pitt and Lord
Melville to the present incapables, as fortunate for the
country, if a more effectual change could not be
obtained. I still don't understand what degree of
countenance the King has given to these arrangements. I don't go to Dropmore to-day, as Lord
Grenville is in town. Our company here is Dr.
Lawrence, Walker King, Elliot, and Windham came
last night. We took a long and beautiful walk to-day
through this pretty country, conversing on the same
subjects which would have engaged us in Palace Yard.'

'April 18, 1803.

'I have seen Lady Hamilton, who is worse off than I
imagined, her jointure being 700*l.* a year, and 100*l.* to
Mrs. Cadogan for her life. She told me that she had
applied to Mr. Addington for a pension, and desired me
to promote it in any way I could; and Lord Nelson,
coming in, made the same request. I promised to do
so.

'She talked very freely of her situation with Nelson

and of the construction the world may have put upon
it; but protested that their attachment had been perfectly pure, which I declare I can believe, though I am
sure it is of no consequence whether it is so or not.
The shocking injury done to Lady Nelson is not made
less or greater by anything that may or not have
occurred between him and Lady Hamilton. Politics
are much where they were. Ministry have lost real
strength by the proof they have given of their own
opinion of their weakness. The negotiation with Pitt
is generally known to have come from Addington. This
betrays distress and dismay. The fact is that the negotiation between Addington and Pitt broke off on
Thursday. Pitt asked two questions: First, whether
Mr. Addington's overtures were expressly authorised by
the King; next, whether he was authorised to propose
that he, Mr. Pitt, should form his own Administration—
intimating that he should require to call in his friends.
Addington answered that he was not expressly authorised by the King; and, with regard to the second point,
that he was neither authorised by the King to acquiesce in Mr. Pitt's forming a new Administration, nor
could he advise the King to adopt that measure. On
this footing the treaty broke off entirely. If Pitt had
been called upon to assume the Government and to
appoint a new Ministry, I rather understand that he
inclined to make a sort of coalition by keeping a certain
number of the present Ministers, in less efficient situations, but in the Cabinet. Lord Grenville, on the contrary, feels the objections that are obvious to such an

arrangement; but I rather imagine that he would consent to it if insisted on.   Windham, Elliot, myself, and
some others think such a coalition ought not to be
assented to at all.   All this *is most confidential.*'

'April 28, 1803.

'I read Walter Scott's "Lay of the Last Minstrel,"
last night, at Lady Palmerston's.   Lady Malmesbury
and Harry Drummond were there.   It was much admired; and, indeed, there are very beautiful passages,
while the whole is in a strain of true poetry.   This
poem will do him great honour, and adds to the classi-
cal as well as to the chivalrous and *Romancical* character
of our country.   I forget whether I told you of my
dining with Fox at a literary club lately, and of his
being an admirer of Campbell's "Pleasures of Hope,"
and a very great admirer of Burns.'

'April 30, 1803.

'The last letters from Paris are very warlike.   Lord
Whitworth held that language to some persons whom I
know, but I am desired not to say so.   He was packing
up for his return; and it seems to be understood that
the last instructions to him were to come away if our
terms were not peremptorily assented to.   There is
always some uncertainty, however, in such transactions;
and the issue must be considered as still doubtful in
some degree, with a great probability of war.   I have
written to Gilbert my opinion concerning activity in
Parliament at this moment.   I think it by no means
advisable; though it seems now intended to proceed

with motions in the House of Commons; but I doubt the propriety of it. We can have no influence in the measures of our own Government; and we shall be accused of disturbing and prejudicing the negotiations actually pending. This is always a plausible charge, and is better justified than usual by the circumstances. However, the forbearance of Parliament on these grounds always supposes some confidence in the Ministers; and, as there is none in the present case, it is the more difficult to refrain.'

'May 16.

'War is entirely decided. Hugh is ordered to accompany Lord Nelson, and they go to Portsmouth tomorrow. This is distressing to Mrs. Elliot and the children, as I imagine it will be long before she can go to Naples in the unsettled state of that country.'

'May 18.

'I received this morning a letter from Lord St. Vincent, desiring that George might go with Nelson, and saying he would find a ship for him in the Mediterranean. George and I, therefore, set off for Portsmouth to-night. Hugh goes at the same time. I have not seen or written to Lord St. Vincent for some time, so that his attention to George's interests is all the more friendly.'

'May 21, 1803.

'I am just returned from Portsmouth. I left sweet George in perfect health, but neither of us in high spirits, on board the "Victory," at Spithead yesterday, ·

at 2 o'clock.   They sailed at 4.   I took leave, as you
may conceive, with a heavy heart; yet everything that
relates to his situation and prospects is exactly all we
could wish.

'Lord St. Vincent is friendly in the highest degree,
and I must be grateful, let his system at the Admiralty
be what it may.   It is certainly a most fortunate circumstance in the prospects of our two sons that I happened to possess the real kindness of two such men as
Lord St. Vincent and Nelson; and that, notwithstanding
my being in opposition to the Ministry of which he
is a part, the First Lord of the Admiralty should, from
personal regard for me, have done more than for anybody in the kingdom.   You will be glad to hear that
the "Victory" is to communicate with the Fleet off
Ushant, and that George and William will therefore
meet.   Hugh is on board the "Victory," and will be
a great addition to the society of the ship.'

'May 24.

'I have no time to describe last night's debate.   Pitt
made one of his grand displays, and made an extraordinary impression—strong support of the war, and
reserving the conduct of Ministers for another day.   It
was remarked that he always called Addington the
right honourable gentleman, and Lord Hawkesbury his
noble friend.   The last joke about Addington and his
brothers is to call them the *Medici* family.'

'London: May 28, 1803.

'I have been writing to George and to Lord Nelson, as there is an opportunity for them to-day. You will see by the papers that the debate was put off last Thursday to next Thursday, when I shall speak, if ever in my life, unless some event or other happens in the interval to supersede that discussion, such as some change of Ministry; but I know no reason to expect it, except that the continuance of the present seems every day more extraordinary, and I believe it is contrary to the real wishes of the country. They have been reporting me First Lord of the Admiralty strongly for the last two days, I need not say without the smallest foundation. I feel much as you do about office. It never was an object of vehement desire to me; and it is less so naturally as I approach the period of repose, and know by experience the vanity of all gratifications of that description. I am perfectly comfortable at present, doing what I think right, without dependence on any man or any party. At the same time, if those with whom I act were to come in, and slight or depress me below the rank that I think due to me, I should be hurt; and, though I feel nothing like passion in my views of that sort, it would, no doubt, be gratifying to fill once in my life a situation of real weight and eminence.'

' May 30, 1803.

' You will see the account of Bonaparte's return to ferocity. The Peploes [1] are among the prisoners; but I apprehend no harm can come to any of them—only a great deal of vexation.'

' June 4.

' Addington is firmly fixed in his seat, to be displaced only by some great disaster, and, therefore, I hope, not to be displaced at all; but I rather wish than expect this, for I seriously think the danger too great to be averted by him. Pitt has now taken a line clearly distinct from us, but it is not less so from Ministers. His friends in the House of Lords and himself yesterday proposed the adjournment or the order of the day on our motions of censure. The effect of this is to avoid a decision either way; the topics used for that purpose the unseasonableness of the moment, when we should rather be employed in preparations for war than in party questions. They not only made no defence for Ministers, but intimated that one reason for their avoiding the question was, that they could not vote against the censure if it came on.

' Accordingly, when it came to the vote of censure, instead of voting against it, they retired. This is not a flattering support of Mr. Addington; but is nevertheless very effectual support, since it divides his opponents and keeps him in power.

[1] Mrs. Peploe was a daughter of Sir George Cornewall's; and was travelling with her husband through France when the English were arrested by order of Bonaparte.

'. . . Tierney has joined them ; Lord Moira joins them also. One pleasant consequence at least, I think, must follow from these public evils; which is, my being able to come sooner to Minto.'

'June 7.

'I spoke yesterday,[1] and was well received by friends and adversaries. There is not a word of mine in the report of the " Morning Chronicle," as is really the case with almost all reports that I have seen of speeches that I have either made or heard.'

'June 13.

'I have just now a troublesome job in hand, to distribute the " Pleasures of Hope " and get the guineas ; the distribution is nearly finished, but the rents are in arrear. I shall have made him out 100 guineas, which has been no small nor short exertion. I met at dinner yesterday Mr. Beckford,[1] with his son and daughter.[2] She is really beautiful, and her manners and character seem equal to her beauty. Her paintings in miniature are equal to those of the best artists. The son is a remarkably pleasing, handsome young man ; but the father is a brute. He is on the footing of barely meeting his son in third places and speaking to him as he might to a stranger; he never allows him to come to his house nor has any sort of intercourse with him. This originated in some hasty answer which the

---

[1] On Lord Fitzwilliam's vote of censure. At Lord Grenville's urgent request this speech was printed. See App. I. for an abstract of it.

[2] The author of *Vathek*.

[3] Afterwards Duchess of Hamilton.

boy made at Florence years ago to some unreasonable harshness of the father, who carries on the quarrel still and means to do so all his life. The sister, who is fond of her brother, probably leads no pleasant life.'

'June 21.

'You will see the plan of defence and the debates in the papers; the plan is an addition of 50,000 men to the militia, with some improvements on that sort of troops. They are to serve in Great Britain and the channel islands, and are to have officers of the line, which is certainly a good point. *But* it is still a militia, not disposable for *general service*, and will increase a thousandfold the great difficulty which has been felt so much already—I mean the impossibility of recruiting the army. It proves that nothing is thought of but defence at home. This is just what Bonaparte would wish—to be left at liberty to do what he likes all over the world, without losing even a colony.'

'July 4.

'I went on Saturday to Mr. Angerstein's breakfast at Woodlands, Blackheath—a beautiful place; and we had also reason to admire the beauty of the female generation. Mrs. Beauclerc and her sister, Mrs. Charles Lock, very striking. The Prince of Wales, Mrs. Fitzherbert, Duchess of Devonshire, Lady Duncannon— in short, all the world, his wife, and his mistress—were there; Francis and Windham too, and other choice spirits.'

'July 9.

'Windham and I went to Lord Grenville to show our ideas about proposing something to promote a very general arming and training of the people; and Lord Grenville desired us to come with Elliot to Dropmore.'

'July 14.

'I dined and slept last night at Sir George Shee's near Holland House—one of my young haunts, having bird-nested in those hedges. Holland House is entirely neglected, and going to ruin. I called on the Romillys, in the evening, close to Holland House. Windham dined with us yesterday; Elliot came after dinner. Lord Malmesbury was in town for a few days and returned to Park Place yesterday. I dined at Francis's with Elliot the day before yesterday. We squired the whole family to Vauxhall, where we had about fifty people. Elliot attends Mrs. Crewe to-night to Sadler's Wells. This is a London summer.'

'July 16, 1803.

'The expectation of invasion [1] is very strong; in the meanwhile, the preparation is alarmingly backward and

---

[1] 'I don't know what to think of Bonaparte's landing. If he does, I think we shall all be in a very bad way—not from cowardice, but from want of knowing how to use our courage. I know you will laugh; but I seriously think that arms should be furnished to the women whose husbands are in the service to guard their own homes, and I am perfectly persuaded they would make use of them in such situations as would make it necessary; and amongst the lower ranks their physical strength is certainly sufficient. I shall keep your "Killing no Murder." I have half a mind to copy it and send it by the post to Bonaparte, it would put him in such a passion.'—*Lady Malmesbury to Lady Minto,* July, 1803.

difficult. I do not remember in my life a season of such real and well-founded anxiety. Mr. Addington alone is smiling, complacent, and confident. I cannot on any account stay longer away from home. My plan is to go to Dropmore Wednesday, Park Place Thursday, and to go on from thence.'

'July 23.

'I went yesterday after dinner to Eden Farm, where I found the Hobarts and Lord [1] and Lady Frances Osborne, with their boy [2] who makes me grand uncle. The sweetness of the air, flowers, hay, all delightful. It is certainly very hard that I am not at Minto, where these and so many other pleasures and delights are at present lost to me.'

Not long afterwards he was at Minto, where he found Lady Palmerston and her family.

[1] Created Baron Godolphin, married Hon. Charlotte Eden, daughter of Lord Auckland.

[2] George, eighth Duke of Leeds.

CHAPTER XIII.

THE extensive preparations for an invasion of England made by the First Consul during the summer of
1803, aroused a spirit of determined resistance throughout Great Britain. Grievously as the country had
felt the burden of a long war, the Peace of Amiens,
considered as the fruit of concessions greater than were
demanded by the exigencies of the situation, had been
generally unpopular. But when it was found that
these concessions were inadequate to satisfy the arrogant
demands of France, an open rupture was welcomed as
a safer and more honourable condition than an armed
peace. The threat of invasion was met by a general
arming of the population. Lord Minto accepted a
commission in the Roxburgshire militia for his son,
and himself took an active part in the volunteer movement which was converting the whole country into a
vast camp. He could no longer write from Minto as
he once had done: ' Though Gilbert lives at least forty-
eight hours a day, shooting wild ducks till evening, and
catching grilse in the Teviot till night, the character of
this place and life is that of the most perfect repose and
tranquillity; one *sails* to *heaven* without the least
occasion to *pull an oar*.' Teviotdale resounded with
the din of arms; and Gilbert was away at Musselburgh

learning his drill.   The assumption of these new duties
had not been made without a sacrifice of long-laid and
long-cherished plans; for Lord Minto had always desired that his son's entrance into public life should be
preceded by a University education, and he was well
aware that to substitute for this the life of camps
would be a severe test to the habits of occupation, and
to the intellectual and political tastes which he sought
to foster in his son.

In the spring of the year Lord Minto had commenced
a regular correspondence with Gilbert Elliot, with the
intention of initiating him in those concerns of public
and private interest which occupied the thoughts of his
parents.   No doubt with the view of guiding his son's
judgment to just and candid conclusions on political
subjects, he wrote fully to him of men and measures,
and invariably in the same spirit of fair and tolerant
criticism.   No bitter or even depreciatory word of his
laid the foundation of an hereditary prejudice; whilst
the first political enthusiasms awakened in his son were
called into existence by the eloquence of Fox and the
brilliant powers of Sheridan.   'You will consider,' wrote
the father to the son, 'what I write to you as the first
proof of that entire and unlimited confidence to which
your age and your character entitle you on all subjects
from me.   I own I look to a cordial and unreserved
intercourse with you as the principal comfort of a
period of life which generally requires comforts, and in
which, however, one such comfort makes full amends
for many of the enjoyments that are gone by.'

On another occasion he, wrote in reference to the
subject of University education :

'I have been of late hesitating between Oxford and
Cambridge, and feeling your own wishes or opinion on
this, and, indeed, on all other questions, to be a principal consideration, I think it best to mention to yourself the grounds on which I have conceived this doubt.
The purposes to be proposed, in your particular case, by
one of the English Universities, can be answered, I
think, equally by either.   As you do not go to college
from school, and are considerably above the age and
standing in life of the greater number of those who
enter at the Universities, I shall look less to the advantages which are supposed to result from the discipline
and tuition of those societies than to other advantages
which are found there, and which belong to greater
maturity both in previous study and in character.   By.
these I mean the opportunities afforded in a college
life to pursue any course of useful study you may
approve of or be advised to choose, without interruption either from the general dissipation, or even the
business and occupation, of what is called the world.
A college furnishes retirement, leisure, tranquillity,
books, and ready assistance in all branches of study;
not to mention the society and conversation of studious
men.   A part of the year passed in this way at your
age, and just in the interval that precedes real and
active life, may be made very precious.   These advantages are, however, to be found equally at both
Universities, or at neither, depending almost entirely

on the tastes, habits, and views of the individual. But, as you see, my notion of the benefit to be derived by you from an academical life depends on your own exertion and application, I confess I should think, at your age, discipline and strict regulations concerning study rather an obstacle than an aid to your progress. After enquiry, I found the regulations as to *time* stricter at Christ Church than at Cambridge. Another principal object, you know, is, to obtain your degree, so as to facilitate the plan I have recommended to you of studying law, and, if possible, taking at least some share of practice at the bar. This point can be ac-- complished at Cambridge in less time and with less confinement in point of residence than at Oxford. I think this, I confess, a great inducement in our case, for I certainly regret the necessity of prolonging the restraints of education beyond their usual period, and at a time of life when they cannot be supposed to sit very easy. This inconvenience, you know, could not well be avoided without suppressing the course at Edinburgh, which I am sure you would not think it advantageous to have done. In these circumstances, however, I think it desirable both for your ease and for other reasons, that the restraints of college should be as few and as light as they can. All these considera- tions point to a preference for Cambridge; there re- mains only one which I think it may be worth while to mention. The studies at Cambridge, and the exercises, and the credit, run principally in the mathematical line. If you find your taste particularly averse to that

study, I should think that circumstance a disadvantage
to Cambridge. I should not by any means wish your
application directed exclusively, or even principally, that
way, though there is a certain proficiency in that science
which belongs to a liberal education ; and the faculties
of the mind, particularly the reasoning powers, are
undoubtedly more trained and improved by that study
than by any other means. So far as this you should
even do violence to your taste and inclination ; but
beyond this, or much beyond this, though my own taste
runs naturally that way, I really think it prejudicial
to push the study of mathematics at the expense of
more practical and equally liberal and noble pursuits.
I should, therefore, not be disappointed if you did not
acquire the honours of the University in that branch,
and should be more gratified by your becoming a good
general scholar, and acquiring a general taste for liberal
studies, and general habits of application. These are,
just at your period, the best preparation for life. The
special knowledge and talents for professions, or for
Parliament, may safely wait for their cultivation a *little*
longer ; yet these also may extremely well be advanced
by the acquisition of general preparatory knowledge,
such as history, constitutional law, and the science of
politics, at college. For my part, I incline to Cambridge ; but you need not scruple to make your own
choice. During the summer you will be at Minto,
where I am confident you will find study and pleasure
compatible with each other ; and for a year or two
restrain the natural tastes of youth so far as to make

your pleasures the recreation of your studies, and not
consider your studies only as the interruption of your
pleasures.'

> The best laid schemes o' mice and men
> Gang aft a gly,

says Burns, and so in this case it proved, for, as we
have seen, the academical plans sketched here were set
aside and were never resumed. The time was one in
which Lord Minto thought it the duty of all men to
make some sacrifice of their personal desires in a public
cause ; and with the dread of foreign invasion before
their eyes, preparation for the defence of hearth and
home was a duty of a pressing kind. For a whole year
Gilbert Elliot remained in camp at Musselburgh, his
visits to his family being confined to a few days at a
time.

In the course of August a public meeting was held
at Jedburgh for the purpose of carrying an address
to the King, assuring His Majesty of the zeal and devotion of his subjects on the Borders. ' Our hearts,'
said the address, ' are firmly devoted to the land in
which our fathers and ourselves were born, and we now
solemnly pledge ourselves to your Majesty and to each
other, that we will maintain with our latest breath and
the last drops of our blood, its independence, its laws,
its religion, and renown.'

At this meeting Lord Minto made a spirited speech
which, addressed as it was to men not unconscious of
the responsibilities resting on those who have an
hereditary right to national independence, was received

with vehement applause, and was ordered to be published and circulated throughout the country. 'Can
we look,' he said, 'in the whole range of our country
upon a hill, upon a plain, upon a river, nay, upon a
glen or a burn, in which we shall not recognise some
memorial of a brave ancestry? This country, placed
as it was for centuries on the very frontier of an enemy
—this people living as they did from childhood to old
age constantly in the advanced posts, as it were, of one
great camp; this country and this people have transmitted to us all some trophy, some monument of
ancient prowess. . . . Are we not the sons, and I trust
not the degenerate sons, of those fathers?'

A few months later, when a false alarm of the French
having landed lighted the beacons on the Border hills,
the Borderers showed themselves no less alert in
their reply to the summons than when the 'blazing
bale' was a sight of daily occurrence. It is unfortunate that no account of that memorable 31st of
January has been discovered in the Minto papers;
though there is an acknowledgment by Mr. Elliot of
Wells of a letter from Lord Minto 'which,' he says,
'I read everywhere; for my Border blood is fired by
your account of the conduct of the Teviotdale and
Liddesdale clans.'[1] The story, however, is published,
and is well known; and we are glad to have heard from
one who remembered it, the impression wrought by the

[1] Since these lines were written I have had the pleasure of receiving
a letter from a lady whose memory retains a distinct impression of that
eventful night: it will be found in App. II., and cannot fail to be read
with interest.

fierce red light on Dunion—the first incredulity, the fierce indignation, the gallop to the trysting place through a river in flood, and the pouring in of men from every hill and every dale, till, when the muster-roll was called, but one man was missing, and he was a lame tailor. As for those who stayed at home, one sentence in a letter from Lady Minto to a friend is descriptive possibly of more than herself and her daughters. 'We sat at the window and watched the fires with sick hearts.'

While such was the spirit of the people the measures of the Government were felt to be sadly inadequate to the occasion. Great and general discontent had been aroused by the contradictory regulations in respect to the allowances for the volunteer force. These allowances were in many cases far too small, and did not provide for great coats, which were felt to be an indispensable part of their equipment. There were likewise heavy complaints of the scarcity and the badness of arms. 'Lord Grenville,' wrote Mr. Elliot, 'had a few days ago pistols and swords for the Bucks regiment of yeomanry which were so unserviceable that he is under the necessity of returning them. I am told too that a fortnight ago the post-captains commanding the sea fencibles on the Sussex coast, stated that a large proportion of that corps was without arms. Ireland cannot fail of being a principal point of attack, and, in point of matured and organised conspiracy, I am afraid it is more vulnerable than it has ever been. The negligence and perverse and wilful blindness to the condition

of that country, both on the part of our own and the
Irish Government, surpasses belief. . . . Lord Cornwallis is the person who should have been sent there.
From his recent knowledge of the country, he would
have made his dispositions immediately; and so I
cannot help thinking too he would have been employed, if Ministers had not been jealous of his Catholic
bias. The consummation of this infatuation in respect
to Ireland seems to be a private polemical correspondence which, I hear, Lord Redesdale has commenced
with Lord Fingal, a leading Catholic peer, in which he
endeavours to prove that every sincere Catholic must
consider the King as an usurper. You may nevertheless rely on it that His Majesty is as fully determined
as ever to support these Ministers, who, by their follies,
are shaking his throne. I confess I do not participate
in the wishes of those bold citizens and country gentlemen who are anxious that the French should come in
a fortnight, that we may get rid of the expense and
trouble of preparation. Greater and severer trials are
coming on us than perhaps this country expects; but
such is the spirit of the people that I am fully persuaded that, in spite of our Government, or the grand
scale of French preparation, we shall, though not
without a long and arduous struggle, frustrate our
enemies.'

'If the enemy is with us immediately,' wrote Mr.
Windham, 'he may, by a landing in Norfolk, and a
march unopposed into Yarmouth, possess himself at

once of the only naval station in the North Sea, and a
port opposite to his best shore.   The Ministers have
now sent an officer to examine this.'

When in the course of the winter a fresh outbreak
of the King's illness came to increase the difficulties
of the Ministers, it was apparent that their tenure of
office would not be much longer endured ; and, soon
after the New Year, letters from Lord Grenville and
Mr. Windham informed Lord Minto of the steps taken
for a *re-cast* of the forces of Opposition by a proposed
co-operation between the Grenvillites and Mr. Fox.
His return to London was urged by Lord Grenville,
and on February 20 he wrote thence to Lady Minto :—

' I had a long conference and discussion with Elliot
and Windham last night.   We did not part till one
o'clock and I could not go to sleep till past three.   The
thing is much as I imagined, but is much looser in
points of positive connection, and in anything like engagement, than I thought probable in such a transaction.
The ground of union, or rather co-operation, is to remove
the present weak, and therefore dangerous, Ministry.
But what is to happen afterwards, in case of success in
that object, seems very much left to chance or future
deliberation.   You will think it odd—at least I do—that
Lord Grenville should have been the most forward, and
almost precipitate in this affair.   I cannot, I confess,
answer all the objections which my own mind suggests
to this measure.   I spoke as strongly as I felt on the
subject to Windham and Elliot, and I think staggered

Windham more than Elliot, who, however, admits the objection, but pleads the necessity of any effort, how. ever objectionable on general principles, to escape the imminent ruin of a weak government at this season of danger and difficulty. It is a real pity that this measure was started when I was away, as I should certainly have restricted it to something much less objectionable than it now is. What I shall do myself I do not yet know; it is a subject which requires cool and serious reflection, and it should be viewed on every possible side before a determination is taken.'

'February 24, 1804.

'The physicians have said for several days past that there is no change in the King's condition; yet I flatter myself his recovery is likely, but perhaps not to be expected quite so immediately; and I should be apprehensive that the pressing nature of business at present may require some expedient which will bring the affair into discussion in Parliament—a thing we should very much wish to be avoided.

'I have had a long conference with Lord Grenville and Tom Grenville to-day. He was anxious, and at great pains to explain and to justify; but I cannot launch into so wide a field so near the post. I expressed very plainly my own impressions and objections; and signified my concernment only in the opposition to the Ministry, and even that properly modified to the present circumstances. This both I and they should have approved, independent of any co-operation from Fox; and so far I can go along with my friends comfortably and heartily.   The affair reduces itself, indeed, rather to a concert *in opposition to the Ministers* than to a connection amongst ourselves.   But it is easy to see that a connection must spring out of concert in daily business.   Ministers seem to me stripped of all support whatever, except just the Treasury influence.   Fox and his party have hitherto supported them ; they will now oppose.   Pitt does not accede to this joint opposition ; not from any objection, as I understand, to the cooperation of Fox, or to concert with him, but that personal considerations make him abstain from avowed opposition.   At the same time, I expect to see him censure measures, and he will certainly *not support* Ministry.   The Opposition will therefore be much more formidable, and may very possibly throw the fruit of the victory to Pitt exclusively, which *I* shall think a great point gained, compared with the present Ministry. All this, short as it is, is most confidential.'

As on former occasions, London society was divided between those who declared the King to be perfectly well and those who reported him hopelessly ill ; to the first class belonged Lady Malmesbury.   ' Harriet [1] is in a rage if you don't believe he is perfectly well when *she* tells you that *she knows* it.   To-day she quoted Lady Uxbridge, to whom she complained that the public was deceived by the physicians, whose bulletins people were absurd enough to believe, in preference to reports coming from the Royal Family themselves ; and Lady

---

[1] Lord Minto to Lady Minto.

Uxbridge said, in that case, the bulletins should be better to-morrow. Harriet calls all the physicians idiots, and says they are only *signing* physicians and have nothing to do with the King. Then why don't they sign what others report? The only favourable thing they have said is that the King is not in danger. She also attributes the reticence to some shabby under-plot of Addington's, and says that the Ministry chose to give unfavourable impressions for some reason or other. They certainly must have some very odd reason if they do. Lady Castlereagh was holding some rather less favourable language to Harriet, but she says she forced her to confess *the truth*, and that he was quite well. I don't wonder at Lady Castlereagh's yielding.

' The reconciliation between the Prince of Wales and the Duke of York is true. It is but very lately that, when the Duke of York called at Carlton House, he was left a good while waiting in the hall, and at last a message came, that after what had passed, the Prince could not think of seeing him.'

' February 28, 1804.

' The explanation in the House of Commons last night gives us the comfortable assurance that the King's recovery is certainly to be expected soon enough to make an intermediate measure unnecessary, and this hope will make the public and Parliament acquiesce in the protraction of the present irregular and distressing interval a little longer.

' Pitt made an attack on Lord St. Vincent last night. He was defended by Fox and Grey. I have heard it remarked that Pitt's manner yesterday was very hostile to the Ministers, and that it was thought somewhat softened towards Fox.'

'March 1.

'The King is said to be better to-day than yesterday. . . . I have had Lord Grenville, Tom Grenville, and Elliot here to-day, to talk things over. Pitt renewed his observations on the want of preparation yesterday, and said he should bring the matter before the House if his mind should not be satisfied on the subject by information or reasons which he had not yet received.

'I dined last night at Uxbridge House, which I had not entered, I think, since I saw the old Duchess of Queensberry there, whom I felt myself looking about for; and, to say the truth, if I had found her, I might have been as well entertained as by the present tenants. By entertainment, however, I don't refer to the dinner; for everything is as sumptuous and, I must say, as civil, as it could have been in the days of the ancients or *vieille cour*; but whether the Duchess was there or not, I could discover nothing of *Gay*. But we had Lady Charlotte, and everybody must prefer live beauty to dead wit.

'Nothing can be more beautiful than the whole race. Lady Charlotte and Lady Graves are in different styles of beauty, but both extremely handsome.

'James and I went to the House of Commons after dinner, where I stayed till eleven and had the pleasure of hearing Mr. Pitt support the volunteers and quiz Mr. Yorke.'

'March 5.

'We had a very pleasant, jolly dinner at Blackheath the other day, where we stayed till one in the morning.[1] Lady Hester Stanhope was the principal personage. We played at Pandemonium games, especially magical music, in a style inferior only to Dalkeith. . . . The accounts of the King are improving. The bulletin to-day is the best we have had at all. The Chancellor has seen him for the first time to-day, preparatory, I imagine, to the enquiries he may expect in the House of Lords. I wish sincerely the reports of amendment may be sincere and prove well founded. But where there are purposes to answer, there is always a degree of doubt; and if the recovery should not be very speedy, the inconvenience will be very serious, and, so far as I see, without remedy.

' The Mutiny Bill expires the 26th inst., and in a few days more there will not be time to pass a Regency Bill before that day; in which case, should the King unfortunately not be recovered, the new bill cannot be passed at all, and the whole army is disbanded. I dined yesterday at Lord Carysfort's with Lords Grenville, Spencer, Carnarvon, Tom Grenville, and others of that kidney. I am going in haste to the House of Lords, where a communication from the Chancellor is expected.'

[1] The Princess of Wales dined at five o'clock.

'Pall Mall: March 6, 1804.

' You will see what the Chancellor said concerning the King. He did not mention his health at all, but said that he had had an audience the day before, and again yesterday, and having explained to him the purport of the Duke of York's Estate Bill, His Majesty had authorised him to acquaint the House that, so far as his interest was concerned, they were at liberty to proceed with the Bill—no allusion being made to his past condition nor to his present recovery; but the Chancellor having given his testimony, by this measure, that the King is in a fit state to exercise his powers in person, everything will proceed of course on that supposition, just as if there had been no interruption to the ordinary course of business. I am extremely glad it has been possible to take this course; provided, however, that the recovery is real, and that some obstacle to the despatch of the serious business now in hand, and approaching, does not arise at a still more distressing period. From experience, we may fairly expect the King to regain his usual state of mind and body for a time at least. At the same time, I must regret one consequence of his present situation: I mean the establishment of Mr. Addington's government. The King's weak health is to him a tower of strength; and that is to the country a great increase of danger.

' There was an interesting debate last night on the Irish Bank Restriction Bill, in which the superiority of Lord Grenville was very manifest. Lord Hawkesbury

is much better than we are used to from that side of
the House, but I thought rather inferior to himself as
I remember him in the House of Commons. The
House sat late enough to make it eleven before I had
dined at the coffee-house, so I went home to bed instead
of dressing for Mrs. Robinson's ball.'

'Roehampton: Thursday, March 8.

'I came here on Tuesday. At Hyde Park Corner I
fell in with Colonel Dillon, walking to Brompton to
visit poor Madame de Polastron, who is dying of a consumption. Monsieur [1] is inconsolable, and having been
told by some quack that she might be cured by breath-
ing the air of a *cow-house*, he is pulling a house down
in order to convert it into a *byre*, to be made habitable
for a lady. He has also bespoke a sleeping carriage,
curiously constructed, to carry her into Italy, though
she is in the last stage of the disorder and cannot quit
her room. While we were talking of these things I
got to Brompton, and then walked on a mile further to
Amyot's ; he was in a soldier's dress, being a private in
the Kensington volunteers, one of the best volunteer
corps near London.

'I have had great pain as well as pleasure in this
farewell visit. The weather has been most spitefully
fine ; the place looking quite lovely, everything coming
out and smelling sweet, and the air goes down like new
milk. I have really had many heavy thoughts on quitting a scene which I like both for its beauty and the

---

[1] Monsieur, afterwards King of France, by the title of Charles X.

recollection of a pleasant time. I do not think it possible, certainly not at all likely, that we should ever be
so well off again in this quarter of the world.

'I shall pass another forenoon here, though I have
little or nothing left to do, so that this operation
may be called *mon agonie*. If I die so hard on the
Roehampton scaffold, what a fine agony it will be when
the French general turns us out at the Lily-Law Lodge,
and drives us down Shepherd's Wood. However, I
think Lieutenant-Colonel Gilbert and Captain John
and their companies will fight a harder battle for
those premises than I have done for these. From
what you say, Scone[1] will be a very perfect thing. If
one might ever indulge vain wishes about fortune, it
would be with me for the pleasure of decorating the
spot one is attached to. I saw at Lady Carnegie's
ball the Dowager Lady Mansfield, who is rather like an
old Palace than a new one ; but as I sometimes *foresee*
the blemishes which are to come out in a handsome
face with time, through the freshness and roundness of
young beauty, so I perceive the traces of youthful
beauty through the cracks and angles of age, and Lady
Mansfield is therefore still a beauty to me. This
faculty of carrying youthful impressions forward into
other periods, and then making a perpetual spring by
one's own authority, in winter or autumn, is a very
happy talent and one which I hope you will be able to
cultivate as well as I—that while you are May to me,

---

[1] Scone Palace, the residence of Lord Mansfield, in Perthshire.

I may not appear January to you.   However, though I wish for this agreeable delusion from you, I neither expect nor wish it from other ladies, and have no objection to their preference of John's soft cheek and downy beard.

'I sat next to Lady Donegal (Dowager) at dinner last night—a very handsome woman—formerly a Miss Godfrey; and I found her conversible and agreeable.'

'March 9.

'The'bulletins go on just as if the Chancellor had not said the King was well.   I fancy he is by no means so yet.   However, time must be allowed for a perfect recovery, if possible.   Lord Camelford [1] is still alive, but there seems no expectation of his living; and Pitt ran the Ministers very close on the Volunteer Bill.   He did not attend the Irish question, but his friends voted for the enquiry—that is to say, against the Ministers.   The minority was strong; but the majority had increased since the former division by a better attendance.   It is thought that the whole force of Opposition, including Pitt, may rise to about 110, or say 100, which is stronger than most Ministers have stood.   Pitt is certainly to attack the Admiralty, and is expected to give notice, perhaps, to-day.'

'March 10.

'I find some well-informed and sensible men thinking very seriously of the invasion.   They consider the means prepared for transporting and landing the troops

---

[1] Lord Camelford had been mortally wounded in a duel.

as well calculated for the purpose, and as difficult to
oppose by the usual means hitherto employed by us at
sea.   It does seem as if we should have prepared something similar to the weapon that is to be employed
against us—that is to say, a great number of vessels
capable of *rowing*, as theirs are.   For if they are
favoured by a calm, we can make no opposition at sea
at all.   It is thought that 80,000 men may come over
in the vessels already assembled at Boulogne.   The
same persons think our preparations on shore very inadequate to resist such a force.'

'March 11.

' Lord Hobart told me to-day he had just been reading a most favourable account of the King—that is to
say, a private account.   The bulletin yesterday was
worded in a more extraordinary manner than usual, and
gave impressions of a greater contradiction between the
physicians and the Ministers than ever.   " We continue to think favourably of the King's recovery," which
seems to convey an *opinion* that perhaps he *may* recover some time hence, but not even that positively.
However, by the language of Lord Hobart it seems
that a real recovery is soon expected ; which will reconcile all differences and let us attend at last to *the*
business in hand.'

'Pall Mall : March 10.

' Lord Camelford was alive at twelve to-day, but
could not survive many hours, mortification having
taken place some time ago.   He suffered great torture
till the mortification relieved him, and then said to

Captain Macnamara,[1] who is a great friend of his, and who has seen him every day, " Is not this a wonderful cure ? " Macnamara told me so to-day. He was left literally alone on the ground, his second and the other parties having thought it necessary to fly for their own safety, and he was brought by a countryman in a wheel-barrow to a neighbouring house.'

'March 27, 1804.

' There is a very strange jumble of men and parties; and I feel comfortable in having a clear line of my own to go by. Without considering who my partners may be, opposition to Addington and to Bonaparte are good points to steer by through all the intricacies of the present political channel. The single consideration that gives me anything like pleasure in the famous coalition or co-operation of which so much is said, and of which I see and perceive at present so little, is the prospect which it affords of obliterating the principal class of animosities and coolnesses in which I have any concern. I have a strong disinclination to differences and quarrels, and a very strong desire to live hereafter, and to die, if possible, without an enmity or even a coolness in the world.'

' Pall Mall: April 10.

' I am sorry to say that the Duc d'Enghien was exe-cuted on the 26th of last month. I had flattered myself, I confess, that this horrid, sanguinary, vindictive

---

[1] Captain Macnamara had been tried for manslaughter in the previous year (1803), having killed his antagonist in a duel. Lord Minto was one of the witnesses to his previous character called by him during the trial.

act would not have been thought politic.   The efforts
of this young prince to restore his family, even if
proved, and even if they were subject to the laws of a
government which he had never acknowledged and in
whose territories he never resided, must be deemed
perfectly justifiable.   I heard Paoli, when the conversation turned upon the Corsican vendettas and private
assassinations, say to his Corsican ragamuffins that
revenge was *la passion des âmes fortes* ; and I suppose
this sort of magnanimity was the catechism he taught
his godson.'

'April 16.

' Mr. Pitt is to oppose the transfer of the Irish militia
to England to-day.[1] On Friday Mr. Fox's motion is
to unite all the various oppositions in the House of
Commons.

'Reports are circulating of the King being worse.
This nation seems to be of the frog family ; they, as
Fontana[2] proved, can swim as well without a head as
with one.'

'April 17.

'The division in the House of Commons last night
makes a great impression—107 to 128 ; only 21 majority.
On this question Pitt came up from Dover to oppose
the measure—the new Irish Militia Bill ; and all
the oppositions joined their forces, which are very
formidable to a Minister.   On Friday Opposition will

---

[1] The opposition to the ministerial measure was based on its in-
adequacy to the national defence.

[2] A celebrated experimental philosopher who resided at Florence.

have a greater number; but Ministry ought to have more in proportion, as 128 cannot be their whole strength.   However, a slackness in the attendance of a majority is as distressing and as bad a symptom as the increase of a minority.   On the whole, it appears that a hearty exertion and a clear unequivocal line on the part of Pitt would, in addition to the more regular Opposition that existed before, shake the Ministry and probably turn them out.   But whether this will be the conduct of Pitt, or not, I cannot say.   The prospect of success is as likely to draw him out, perhaps, as any other consideration.

'There was a grand rumour last night of the Boulogne flotilla being actually out ; but it proves nothing but a little stir and manœuvring.'

'April 20, 1804.

'A very remarkable event happened yesterday in the House of Lords.   The Ministry was in a minority of one vote—30 to 31, including proxies—on a motion of Lord Carlisle's, of little consequence, viz., for the dates at which the accounts of the war with France were sent out to India and received there.   This question came on first, and the division took place very early, before six o'clock ; and as there was a battle expected on the Irish Militia Bill, on which there was sure to be a debate of some length, neither side had come down in force for the first question, and we proved the strongest.   The division on the Irish Bill was also very strong on our side—49 to 77.   The whole force of Ministry was brought down—the Archbishop of Canterbury, who is in a sort of second childhood, Lord St. Vincent, three of the princes; in short, everybody. These divisions in both Houses have shaken the Ministers very considerably. They are evidently much alarmed, and the other parties no less sanguine and exulting. Probably the feelings of both are a little beyond the truth. I think, however, that if Pitt sets his shoulders sincerely and stoutly to the work, he and all the talents and influence of various kinds which are united in opposition to this Ministry can hardly fail of overpowering it. Those who are most likely to know Pitt's intentions give me reason to think this will be his conduct. All Lord Melville's connections are come to town and vote with Opposition. I should imagine these appearances will bring himself also. We are to have another battle to-day in both Houses. Pitt moves the question in the House of Commons.

'The King is, I believe, a great deal better. Lord Dartmouth tells me that he was with him two hours, two or three days ago, and that, except having fallen away, his appearance was remarkably good. If the divisions get closer, Addington must go. In that case, the natural thing is that the King should send for Pitt and let him manage it his own way; the probable consequence of which would be a Ministry on a broad basis— that is to say, including all parties or, at least several.'

'April 21.

'The Prince of Wales is said to have expressed great satisfaction at the prospect of the Doctor's overthrow, which might seem odd, as his members voted for him very lately. The King's health is a very anxious and embarrassing circumstance in the midst of this crisis. He is a great deal better, but by no means equal to take on himself the real direction of affairs, and the agitation may naturally produce some risk of relapse.

'At the same time the situation both of public affairs and of Parliament and parties requires a decision. It appears to me that the state of the King's health will leave but one advice for those immediately about him to give—viz., to desire Pitt to settle it for the best.'

'April 23, 1804.

'As to Mr. Addington, things are much as they were on Saturday, except that he is clearly to stand the battle, which may grow into a campaign. . . . Such divisions as show that they do not possess the general confidence of Parliament afford the regular and constitutional notice to retire. I think this intimation has been made already; but it will be conveyed still more forcibly every day and every week.

'I went to the Duke of Kent to-day. He is remarkably pleasing and gentlemanlike in his manner.'

'Pall Mall: April 24, 1804.

'The division [1] was 256 to 204—majority for Ministry 52, which appears decisive against the Ministers. The appearance and manner of the House were still more

---

[1] On a motion of Mr. Fox, which amounted to a vote of want of confidence.

mortifying and alarming to Addington even than the number of his opponents. I rather understand, however, that they mean to fight it out still longer. There will be another trial of strength to-morrow in the House of Commons; and it is expected that the minority will be still stronger than yesterday. Sheridan voted with Fox, but did not speak; which was exactly what was wished, as his speech would probably have been mischievous. The Duke of Norfolk had been refused the blue riband two days ago, and had resolved to vote in opposition yesterday; but he changed again during the debate, and his members voted with the Ministry, which makes a difference of eight or ten in the result. Lord Dalkeith was much disappointed after coming to town to find that he could not vote against Addington, as he is brought in by Lord Sydney, who objected to his voting against his party. Lord Dalkeith, therefore, stayed away; but explained the circumstance to Pitt, who thought he did right. I have this from Lord Dalkeith himself. We are to have small contests in both Houses to-night; but Monday next is to be the grand battle;—we expect to divide above 90.

'There is a new print of Gillray's, in which the state waggon is drawn by asses, and is stuck fast in a slough. Addington, the waggoner, is on his knees calling out "Help! help!" John Bull points to a number of fine horses who are idle and longing to be in harness. The horses' faces are portraits of the Oppositionists.'

'April 25.

'The minority was 61[1] in the House of Lords last night, and would have been 62 if Lord Ashburton had not gone off to dress for a ball, in spite of all remonstrances, a quarter of an hour before the division. There is the grand battle in the House of Commons to-night on a motion of Mr. Pitt's. The divisions go on increasing. The adherents of Ministry consider the game as up. It is true, as the newspapers say, that Lord Chatham was at Buckingham House yesterday, which could not be on the business of the Ordnance. The King had not been told the state of things in the House of Commons the day before yesterday, when he was present at a Council. The Chancellor professes to have told the King all that happened in the House of Lords whenever he had an audience; but the state of things in the House of Commons had not been communicated to him, nor do I know that it has yet. You may judge by this of the real state of the King's mind even now. Notwithstanding these expectations of an immediate change, I know that Mr. Addington said yesterday to one of his supporters that he should fight the battle as long as he had a majority of one. This he will naturally say to encourage his partisans ; but, in truth, it is not only highly culpable to retain office in such circumstances and in such times, but it appears to me simply impossible to do so ; for the present situation of public affairs requires both vigorous measures and expedition.

---

[1] On the Irish Militia Offer Bill.

Against such an Opposition no vigorous measures can be attempted, and despatch is equally impracticable, when every proposition is contested, debated, and put to the test of close divisions in all its stages. The weakness of this Government was an objection to it when it was at the strongest—that is to say, when it had next to no Opposition to contend with ; now, its inefficiency must be such as to expose the country to the greatest disasters. It is extremely desirable that a strong Government should be settled here before Bonaparte gets out of his troubles.'

'Pall Mall: April 27, 1804.

' The division¹ last night was 240 to 203—majority only 37 ; so that Addington lost fifteen since the last division.   Several did not vote yesterday that had voted before.   There is no new event since yesterday ; but the opinion of the Doctor's being dished, as the elegant phrase is, prevails more generally than ever.   Elliot dined yesterday at Lord Camden's with Pitt.   Pitt was amazingly keen, talking of nothing but the divisions during dinner and discussing and examining the lists of the two Houses after dinner.   He was as sanguine as he was keen and treated the affair as decided.   He looks for the change next week.   Elliot thinks him too sanguine, as he is apt to be ; but he is thoroughly in earnest.   By the lists Pitt thinks us sure of a minority of a hundred in the House of Lords on Monday.   Elliot, who saw the lists, says we are sure of

¹ Army of Reserve Suspension Bill.

ninety-five.   In the meanwhile the King's situation
may prove embarrassing.   As yet there is no reason to
suppose the King less capable to appoint a Ministry
than to do other acts which have been done in his
name.   But in truth nobody except the individuals
immediately responsible for these acts know whether
he was in a state that justified them or no; and
certainly the signing a commission to pass bills requires
less strength and soundness than the very agitating
business which must now fall upon him.   The people
in the Queen's House themselves speak as freely against
Addington as any other people.   I saw a note from one
of the Queen's ladies to-day, in which she says: "As
for the Doctor, I only wish, as the Spaniards say, he
were with Mahomet."

'In the midst of all this everybody goes to see
"Valentine and Orson," and weep over the death of a
bear.   I got Harriet's box this evening.'

'April 30.

'The business is put off at Lord Hawkesbury's desire,
who pledged the private honour of the Ministers that
the motives were proper and sufficient.   He was pressed
to say that it was the resignation of the Ministers; but
he repeated only the former assertion.   This is undoubtedly a change of Ministry.   Lord Hawkesbury
used the word *faction*, which occasioned a warm retort
and altercation.'

'May 1.

'The Ministry is certainly going out; but no one
knows what steps have been taken to make a new one.

Mr. Pitt will be the Minister ; but whether the present ones will try to treat the affair with him before they resign, or whether the King will send for him and give him *carte blanche,* is not known.   Windham's opinion and Elliot's is that Pitt will propose a Ministry including all parties ; but will be prevailed on, partly by the King's objections, partly by the importunity of his own friends, to exclude Fox and Lord Grenville.   In this case Windham and Elliot will refuse to come in, and the elements of a future Opposition will be prepared.   For myself, I shall of course act with those with whom I have been connected all my life in friendship as well as politics, and with whom I have been fighting from the beginning for the victory to be enjoyed by others.   I am not at all insensible to the attractions of power or the private convenience of office ; but it is fortunate for me that my ambition has always been temperate and could never interfere with what I thought my public duty or disturb my private tranquillity and comfort ; at the same time, I am determined to have nothing to do with any opposition to a Minister whom we have been all calling out for, although he may have played us a shabby political trick.   I sincerely think the largest Administration would have been best for the country, but I am sure the smallest Opposition is best in these times.'

'May 2, 1804.

'Public affairs are exactly in the same state as yesterday.   Nobody knows anything.   Mr. Pitt has certainly not seen the King yet. It is thought he may to-morrow. There is reason to think that some message had been carried to him from the King by the Chancellor, and that the King wished to communicate with him through the Chancellor. This will, of course, be declined. The extraordinary part of it to me is, that things should have remained in this state so long and no communication of any sort pass between Pitt and any one of those with whom he professes his intention to act as his colleagues. He has neither seen nor written to nor sent any information to Lord Grenville, Windham, or Fox. And yet there is no doubt that he will propose all these names to the King as members of his Cabinet. I have seen Lord Grenville, Tom Grenville, Lord Carlisle, Elliot, Windham and Canning to-day, and all are equally uninformed. However, by what I do hear I continue to think it as probable an issue as any that Pitt will propose the *broad* plan and make a fair effort to carry it, but give way to the narrower on a strong opposition from the King to the other. The common opinion is that the King's objection to Lord Grenville will be as strong as to Fox; but I really don't know on what authority that is said.'

'Pall Mall: May 4, 1804.

' Mr. Pitt has, in consequence of the communication through the Chancellor, sent a written paper to the King, expressing in very general terms the advice he would offer respecting the formation of a new Ministry, which, as well for the King's personal tranquillity as for the public interest, ought to comprise all the principal persons, and I believe he names Mr. Fox. He has expressed also his hope that, whatever may be the King's sentiments, he may receive them in person and have an opportunity of laying the grounds of advice himself before the King. This paper, of which I cannot give a more precise account and of which the above contains only a general impression, was laid before the King yesterday. At least, so it is understood, for there is still the greatest mystery concerning anything that passes at Buckingham House. Of the King's real state many serious doubts are entertained. Lord Malmesbury has some information, which he seems to believe, that the King has expressed no disinclination to take both Lord Grenville and Fox ; but, unless I know his authority, I should not rely much on this or any other surmise on the subject. I have talked the whole matter over very fully and confidentially this morning with Lord Grenville.'

'May 5.

' Mr. Pitt has not seen the King, and there is no alteration since yesterday. We must trust to winds and tides to protect us against invasion—a greater complication of difficulties cannot be conceived.'

'May 7; at night.

' The House is up; the motion adjourned to Friday without a word of observation, except the Chancellor's saying that the same motive for postponing it existed. The fact is that Pitt has seen the King, who has declared his positive resolution not to admit Fox, but agrees to any other person. To-morrow Lord Grenville and Windham, &c., will declare their resolution, which is pretty well certain. I am to be with Lord Grenville at twelve to-morrow.'

'May 8.

'I told you yesterday the state of affairs. The resolution taken by Lord Grenville, Windham, and every person of any consideration who has acted with them, has been to decline taking a part in the new administration. The ground on which they think this necessary simply is, that they had desired and accepted the aid of Fox and his friends to remove Mr. Addington's administration; and although there was no express engagement concerning the consequences of success, they felt it would be dishonourable to be parties to his exclusion after owing the accomplishment of the common object to his assistance! I went to Lord Grenville at twelve to-day and found Lord Spencer with him; and after hearing from Lord Grenville a detailed account of everything down to this time, I explained the distinction between myself and them in all that relates to connection with Fox, and acquainted them that I had resolved to take the same part as they had done in abstaining from office. I explained to them at the same time my notions concerning the duty of assisting the new Ministry in Parliament, and refraining from anything like systematic opposition.'

If the Ministerial crisis had caused agitation in

London, it threw the country into a state of fierce excitement. At a distance from the scene of action personal combinations are always regarded with less indulgence than by those on the spot; and in the present case the failure of a comprehensive administration was viewed with equal disfavour by the partisans of Pitt and by the followers of Lord Grenville and Windham. They united in condemning a course which, 'for the sake of a romantic idea of the point of honour,' left Pitt unsupported, and more closely allied Lord Grenville with Fox. Letters poured in upon Lord Minto from Scotland, full of bitter invective against the universal desertion of Pitt and of passionate reproaches that he should have been sacrificed to so 'infamous' a connection as that with Fox. Lady Minto wrote that she could not bear to hear the universal condemnation of her husband and his friends. 'Some say Lord Grenville has played to be ruler himself; others that he and Windham have always preferred Fox to Pitt in their hearts. It is plain the object in turning out Addington was not a strong administration, since they refuse to make that, at the cost of the exclusion of one man, and that one Fox, with whom they have never agreed.'

Certain members of Lord Minto's family who were aware of the strong objections he had entertained to the *co-operation*, as it was called, of Lord Grenville and Fox, were not slow in condemning his personal conduct in not separating himself from these new allies, to hold by Pitt; and the notion, though quite unfounded, that his son might share in these views, produced a letter from

Lord Minto to him, so honourable to the writer and containing so clear a narrative of the course of political events during the last two years, that it will be well to give it in full.

'Pall Mall : May 9, 1804.

' My dear Gilbert,—I know that my letters, or at least everything material in my correspondence, is forwarded to you; but I feel an inclination to write a line directly to yourself on the very interesting and singular state of affairs at the present moment. . . . To go back to the origin of things; you know that, on my return from abroad, I brought with me the strong and decided opinion concerning the peace which I have since expressed. I had every reason, with the rest of the country, to think as unfavourably of the general character of Mr. Addington's administration as of that particular measure. I found those persons with whom I had been acting abroad and those with whom I have been connected in the closest friendship, public and private, I may say the whole of my life, entertaining the same sentiments, and we have acted ever since in the most intimate union. Our opinions became gradually more general, and one description of men after another acceded to them. In the meantime Mr. Pitt and his party either counteracted us, or kept aloof, and left us to our own separate strength and exertions. The necessity of removing the weak Ministry that governed the country in such dangerous times became every week more manifest and more pressing. Under these circumstances, and despair-

ing of the natural support which might have been
expected from Pitt and his friends, an opportunity of
employing Fox and his friends, both in Parliament and
the country, in the accomplishment of this object, occurred and was embraced by Lord Grenville and Windham. This measure was resorted to in my absence,
and I confess was neither sanctioned by any opinion of
mine at the time nor acceded to by any subsequent act
of mine. I stated my objections to it, on my arrival in
town, to my friends, as forcibly as I, and probably all
the world, felt them; but I did not deliver these sentiments publicly, nor take any step to distinguish myself
from those with whom, in the public eye, I stood connected on this point—content with the absence of any
occasion which called for a positive declaration or for
any positive act of concurrence in this measure. In the
meanwhile we were all availing ourselves of the powerful, and as it proved of the efficacious, aid which the
accession of Fox's party certainly brought to us. The
efficacy, indeed, of this aid became so apparent that it
seems to have attracted Pitt at last; and encouraged by
the prospect of success from the union of *all*, he came
forward unequivocally, and not only concurred in
common measures, but *concerted* them with all the other
parties, Fox included. The consequence was the defeat
of Addington. Pitt felt the obligations which these
circumstances created of carrying his union with Fox
further, and entered therefore unreservedly into the
measure of an administration which should include him.
Without changing any one opinion with which the

former conduct of Fox had impressed me, I must say
that I came sincerely into the conviction which is, I
think, as nearly universal as such a point can be, that
the union of *all* parties in a Ministry afforded the best
chance of saving the country from its present extraordinary difficulties.   The *present object* is to repel the
enemy; to carry on the war vigorously and wisely, and
to obtain by those means a secure and real peace.   Fox
is as ardent in these objects as any of us can be; and
he is as sensible of the necessity for those purposes of
suspending any of those measures in Parliament or out
of it which would alarm or distract Government in the
country as any of us.   I think it was therefore a great
advantage to strengthen Government at this time by
an accession, which at the same time left no possibility
of division, and consequently of weakness, behind.   I
also think that, to redeem Fox and *all* his friends,
weighty as many of them are in the country, from the
desperate courses of disappointed and irritated ambition, was a great benefit for the time, and was likely
to produce more lasting consequences.   I agree therefore entirely, not only with my own friends, but with
Pitt's and the King's, and, in short, all mankind, that
such an occasion to strengthen the King's hand in this
crisis, and at the same time to insure the perfect tranquillity of what remains of his reign, was singularly
fortunate, and that, in good policy both for the King and
the country, it had better have been adopted.

  ‘ The contrary has happened; and now the question
was, first, what it became Lord Grenville and Windham

to do; next what was fitting for me to do. If they who
formed this connection with Fox had accepted the fruit
of their common victory, and had cast Mr. Fox by as
soon as he had served their turn, what would have been
the language of all the world to-day, even of those
who censure them the most loudly on the opposite
ground for withholding their services to the public on
motives of private combination?

'It is to be entirely ignorant of this country and of
its habitual opinion to suppose this possible. You
will say Mr. Fox should have rejected this sacrifice.
So he has, and his conduct has been perfectly liberal,
and even more than liberal. He reminded them even
before the King's decision was known that there was
no engagement to him, and that he desired not to stand
in the way of any useful arrangement, professing his
intention to support the new Government. When the
King's rejection was known, he observed that it was
only *personal* to *him*, and not to his *friends*. He
therefore proposed to Grey and some few friends to take
a part in the Ministry, and he should consider their
adoption as equivalent to his own and as acquitting all
parties towards him. Grey, &c. refused to come in with
his exclusion. In a word, Lord Grenville, Windham,
and *all* the leading characters took the only resolution
they could, and declined acceding to Fox's exclusion.

'I certainly stood on separate ground myself, not
having concurred in the co-operation, as it is called, and
not being in habits of friendship with Fox, but *just the
contrary*, having suffered the deepest and most un-

merited injury from him, or at least from his partisans, not disavowed as far as I have ever heard of by him. But the point which I considered was, whether my own friends and connections were *doing right*. Was I to separate myself from them merely because I might without positive treachery, and when the result would have been the promotion of my own personal advantage? I may ask how you would feel if I had done so, and I feel confident of what your feeling would have been by my own, whenever I only imagine myself in such a situation. It is much easier to be too fond of office and fortune than too indifferent about them. I do not profess any unmeaning indifference on such subjects; but I have experienced before that it is wise for private happiness to keep these desires extremely temperate, and not to reckon on any of the objects of ambition as our own or essential to us. Keep worldly ambition enough to fill your sail and excite exertion, but do not let it drive the ship before it. I am writing this as hard as I can, &c.'

This letter was forwarded by Lord Minto's son to his grand-uncle, the old Admiral who has been so often mentioned as living on Teviotside, and, in his quiet seclusion there, as listening with keen sympathy to the letters read to him by Lady Minto, which brought before him the interests, the struggles, the passions of political life. With him lived, as has been said before, his sister Jane, who had had some share in directing the early education of her eldest nephew; and both

brother and sister were not only warmly attached to
him, but were sensitive in the highest degree on every
point that touched the family honour. How could the
venerable sailor be expected to believe in political
exigencies which required separation from the chief who
had so manfully asserted the resolution of the nation?
How would the sister with all her old-world loyalty and
faith endure to hear that this was done for one who was
confessedly obnoxious to his Sovereign as having encouraged the vices of the Prince, who at home had taken
part with the son against the father, who abroad had
sympathized with regicides, who had paid his court to
Bonaparte? No! all the waters of the Teviot could never
wash him white. Even Lady Minto's stout heart failed
her when the moment came to tell the news to them.
'Miss Elliot will be *terrible*,' she said. At this junc-
ture arrived Lord Minto's letter to his son, and the
effect it produced is described by Lady Minto in her
next letter to her husband :—' I never saw the Admiral
so moved before. Miss Elliot is apt to express her
feelings strongly. As he gave it me back, he said with
his eyes full of tears: " Put that letter in the strong-
box for ever with the most important papers of the
entail. So much feeling as a father, so much true
honourable feeling as a statesman, do honour equally to
the mind and to the heart."'

In his letters to his wife Lord Minto said: 'These
things are neither refined nor romantic. In this country these feelings of personal attachment amongst

public men, as long as the objects proposed are honourable and not mischievous, form a real solid branch of duty and are a just criterion of character. I confess I look forward with great uneasiness of mind to the possibility, not to say probability, of the case arising when I must part from the line of my friends and follow my own individual judgment. At present I think them right.'

'May 11.

'Many of Pitt's friends are dissatisfied with the present transactions. Several of his most particular friends have either entirely declined or shown great backwardness to take office in this arrangement. Canning is one of these, and it is doubtful at this moment whether he will come in or not. The times are difficult, and to a man who has no other anxiety than to do right, both in point of personal honour and public duty, the choice may not be obvious in such an intricate course. But the more difficult the channel is, the more necessary it is to keep a sure compass to steer by. That compass is a preference of duty to every possible motive, and with this needle I expect to steer safely through. It may very well happen that I may not find myself in a numerous company by and by, as I am more than ever determined to abstain from the violent course to which the approaching warmth and exasperation of parties will probably lead. I shall endeavour to keep my friends, either all or some of them, in the right way, and whether I succeed in that or not, I shall pursue my own notion of public duty if I am alone. This is what

will be called between two stools; but it does not
appear so to me, for then one *sits low*, whereas I shall
feel myself standing on high ground.'

'May 15.

'I have had a good deal of conversation on the most
leading points already with Lord Grenville, and also
with Windham; and notwithstanding the appearances
that gave me apprehensions at first, I have now the
concurrence of both that nothing like a professed and
systematic opposition should take place. Fortunately,
the Session need not be much longer, and the financial
measures have not hitherto drawn any declaration of
opposite opinions from the ins and outs.

'On Mr. Pitt's measure for the defence of the country,
as he opened it lately in the House of Commons, there
has already been a difference of opinion declared in the
debates of the former part of the Session. On these
points the same sentiments will be delivered, but as a
difference on these points, not as a feature of a regular
opposition. I have done all in my power to dissuade
any stir of the Catholic question at present; and on
this I have also Lord Grenville's and Windham's assent to
the propriety of avoiding that source of dissension and
warmth at present; although those who have a strong
opinion on the question, like myself, will have no
choice if it be forced on by others. Whether, in spite
of these moderate intentions, the natural course of human
passions may not lead to more warmth and earlier opposition than I wish or approve, is a point which is not

in my hands, or within my control; but I have already
done something towards promoting another system.'

'May 16, 1804.

'The state of public opinion, I presume, is very different here from the quarter you are in. I never saw a
more general or deeper dissatisfaction and gloom than
at the failure of the comprehensive plan, including Fox—
a plan which was universally, not merely acquiesced
in, but looked forward to as the best, if not the only
chance of saving us; but a plan with which individually
I have had less concern than any in the kingdom—much
less than Pitt and all the present Ministers except
Addington's colleagues. Pitt proposed Fox to the King,
and the only anxiety expressed by him and his friends
is to convince the world that he and his friends were all
sincere and earnest both in wishes and endeavours to
bring this about. They still even talk of its all coming
right with a little time. In this I have no faith; but
it shows that in the capital at least, and in both Houses
of Parliament, and in the Cabinet, and even at Court,
it is not reckoned "infamous" to wish for Fox, not
Minister, but in the Ministry—much less infamous
merely to have acted, and to continue to act, with other
respectable men who profess such an opinion. Never
mind their calling me names unjustly. What part Fox
will take hereafter I don't know, and I don't mean to
answer for him. I am convinced my own friends will
do nothing worthy of censure; and I am still more
certain that I shall not myself. I forget whether I

told you that Lord Pelham was turned out from the Duchy of Lancaster, which is generally for life and was given to him as a compensation for his giving up the Secretaryship of State. The appointment is given to Lord Mulgrave. This is the more remarkable as Lord Pelham went out in consequence of a handsome offer he made at the time of Pitt's negotiation with Addington last year, to resign if it should facilitate the arrangement with Pitt. This offer was afterwards unhandsomely made use of to get him out on a perfectly different occasion, and the Chancellorship of the Duchy of Lancaster given as a compensation. Now Pitt takes that from him, though the whole transaction arose in Lord Pelham's desire to bring Pitt in himself.'

'May 17.

'The arrangements are not all entirely settled, and Lord Pelham's case still strikes everybody as the most remarkable. Lord Amherst is also dismissed from the Bedchamber, and is the subject of conversation. He voted against Addington and for Pitt the last two or three divisions, on the express ground of attachment to Pitt. This the King resents, and has turned him out himself for having supported the person who is now his Minister. The King has always insisted on keeping the places in the household in his own hand; but it is a singular use of that power at present and does not afford a comfortable view of Pitt's footing with the King.'

'May 18.

'The King offered Lord Hobart the Gold Stick in the room of Lord Aylesford, but Lord Hobart declined it. Everything the King does himself shows his dislike of the present Ministry, or rather, Ministers; and the truth is that he has been just as much *forced* as if the whole measure had been carried; while the country and the real interests of the King himself are much worse provided for. The Duke of Montrose is also President of the Board of Trade, in the room of Lord Liverpool, who is turned out. This, again, is done by Pitt against the King's private wishes, as you may suppose.'

'May 19.

'I have just been reading a little publication by Lord Grenville which he has given me, of some letters written by the late Lord Chatham to the first Lord Camelford, then at Cambridge. They are principally interesting from the names of the writer and editor. In other respects there is not much instruction or amusement in this little book; though the zeal of Lord Chatham for the improvement of his nephew was extremely amiable. Praise is the engine with which he chose to work on him and to excite his diligence and caution in study; and it runs into extravagant flattery, enough to turn a young head and make a conceited character for life.

'But Lord Chatham was not a great scholar himself; and if the letters had not been written by Lord Chatham to Lady Grenville's father, Lord Grenville would probably have thought them too superficial for the public. They are curious, however, as true specimens of Lord Chatham's disposition and domestic life. I shall send the book to Gilbert, and in the meanwhile I shall favour you with only one extract from the instructions of such and such to a nephew—"Enclose your letters in a cover; *it is more polite.*"   Avis au lecteur.'

'May 21.

' There is nothing very interesting in London at this moment. The arrangements are nearly completed, both at Court and in the offices of Government. The *opposite* lines of the Court and the Ministry is the subject of general observation, and Pitt is thought to feel his situation already uneasy and embarrassing. The King has done all that relates to the household with his own hand, and it is all *against Pitt.* He has written letters himself to those whom he has removed and to those whom he has put in their places. The slightest failure in the support of Addington is punished without remission, and some singularities are talked of in some of the letters, as well as in other parts of the King's behaviour. With regard to the Prince of Wales, he has conducted himself, or has been conducted, with great prudence and propriety, till very lately; and his course of dinners seems the first false step into which he has been led. If he gave, as perhaps he may still, handsome dinners to the most respectable men of all parties without distinction, including those who are in office and are attached either to the Ministry or to the

King, I should think it quite right and becoming his situation. But to set up for the head of a party, especially with any view to opposition, is always wrong in a Prince of Wales, who should come to the throne, should indeed remain on the throne, without any strong partialities or antipathies. The world will naturally imagine some purpose or other in the appearance of party at Carlton House. To facilitate a Regency is the most obvious conjecture ; and nothing can be more discreditable to himself and to those whom he involves, without any act of theirs, in the same suspicion. As yet no design whatever has been discovered, and .I doubt very much whether there is more in the matter than a little injudicious bustle and busy-ness.

'But *we*—at least some of us—are by no means fond of appearing in this light, and having our conduct, which certainly stands on better grounds, subjected to these imputations.

' He did the honours of his dinner the other day, as he always does, remarkably well ; and his conversation, especially on any matter of public business, was extremely good and clever. The company was a complete jumble of the co-operation, and exhibited a strange assemblage of parts lately so discordant ; the Marquis of Buckingham and Charles Fox carrying about their large dimensions side by side, and looking exactly like Gillray's horses ; Windham, myself, Grey, Sheridan—in short, a *salmagundi*. We walked about half an hour till dinner was served, ate a handsome dinner, drank a good deal of wine, and parted at eleven.

There was another dinner of the same sort on Saturday, at which Elliot was present.'

' I have been all day at the King's Bench, attending Cobbett's trial, who is convicted of a libel, not written by himself but signed "Inverna," on the Irish Government. Windham and I, Mr. Yorke, Mr. Liston, Lord Henry Stuart, &c., were called to his character as a friend of the King and Constitution.

' Our dinner at Lord Fitzwilliam's yesterday was very much the same company, without the Prince ; but I dine there to meet him again on the 30th.'

' May 25.

' Lord Arden and Lord St. Helen's are made Lords of the Bedchamber, both against Pitt's wishes, as it is understood. The King sees a good deal of Addington ; he breakfasted with him at Richmond Park yesterday. Lord Hobart told me yesterday that he and Eleanor thought of a tour to Scotland this summer ; and Mrs. Crewe is just setting out on her annual visit to Minto, on which she will be accompanied, as usual, by Mr. and Mrs. Windham.[1]

' There is to be another trial to-morrow of Cobbett for the same paper, " Inverna," for damages, at the instance of a Mr. Plunkett, Solicitor-General in Ireland. Elliot is summoned as a witness to prove that Mr. Plunkett

---

[1] A playful allusion to the plans formed annually by Mrs. Crewe and the Windhams, and as regularly abandoned.

really spoke the words in the Irish House of Commons imputed to him by " Inverna "; several other witnesses are called upon to prove the same thing ; but there is a doubt whether it is proper to *reveal* what passed in the House of Commons.   On this there is to be a consultation at Adam's this evening, and Windham has just called to desire that I will attend.'

'May 29.

' There is a strong report that the King is worse ; but though there is no doubt that he has never been *well* since the beginning of this attack, yet I do not consider these occasional reports as at all to be depended upon.'

'May 30.

' I dine to-day at Lord Fitzwilliam's, to meet the Prince of Wales—all of which goes very much against the grain with me, and indeed with most of those with whom I consider myself at all connected.   I was at a new subscription concert, supper, dance, &c.—something of the pic-nic kind— at the Hanover Square Rooms, on Monday.   Between the concert and supper the Prince of Wales talked to several men, and at last came to me, laid his hand on my arm, and held me as if by the button, talking a great deal of politics, and, I must say, a great deal of nonsense, especially considering where he was and how loud he spoke.   Nobody can help this.   All that can be done is to take great care of our conduct.   To quarrel without an absolute necessity with the Prince of Wales, at the very moment when circumstances have required that we should make our affairs and views desperate in every other quarter, can be required neither by duty nor prudence.'

'May 31.

'Our dinner went off very well at Lord Fitzwilliam's yesterday. The Prince talked the whole time, and extremely well, on all sorts of subjects, and on several relating to public business—such as the volunteers, militia, &c.—but not a word on party topics. There is another dinner at Lord Darnley's to meet the Prince on June 2. I went last night to Mrs. Robinson's, who gave masks. I had a domino. There was to have been a masquerade at Thellusson's, but the pleasure is reserved for this evening, when I shall attend Lady Carnegie and her party, which includes Fanny Temple. It was intended to have a burlesque representation of Bonaparte's coronation as Emperor. The writing was to have been William Spencer's. Sir Watkyn Williams Wynne was to have been Madame Bonaparte; a very little boy who sings at concerts was to have been Bonaparte, with an immense hat. He was, at the end of the piece, to have sunk through a trapdoor, and to have left nothing behind him but hat and crown. The ghost of Louis XVI. was to have appeared—in short, something extremely foolish and extremely wrong in all respects. Lord Hawkesbury, it is said, interfered, and desired it might not take place; and that being the general wish and opinion, the whole affair is given up; and so we are to have merely a masque.'

' I went last night to the masquerade with Lady
Carnegie's party—Sir David a Chief Justice, having
borrowed the gown and wig of Mr. Osgood, his friend,
formerly Chief Justice of Canada ; Lady Carnegie an
old Scotch wife; Christina and Lady Emily Murray
Scotch lasses ; Lady Landon, Mrs. Beaumont, Fanny
Temple a Russian peasant, Sir Francis Whitworth and
I.   I was a Turk, and never took off my mask nor
ventured to speak to more than four or five people.   It
was very good in its way—many fine dresses, many
good characters, a good deal of beauty, which was not,
like my talents, hid in a napkin.   Mr. Thellusson was
a lady in the costume of the fashion, with painted
pasteboard back and bust—a very good burlesque of
the prevailing nudity.   He appeared afterwards as a
jockey, and rode an ass down the middle of a dance.   I
stayed only till two.   My party remained till six.'

' I have been at the Drawing-room, and fought a more
desperate battle with ladies in front and rear and on
both flanks, than I am ever likely to fight again even in
this coat; for I went in the character of Colonel Mc
Murdo, and kissed the Queen's hand for my commission.
The King, of course, was not there.   The Queen stood
with her back between the windows, and people passed
pretty regularly and were presented.   The Princess
said I was *tondu comme un mouton* ; and then enquired
kindly for you; and I said if I was the *mouton,* you

were the shepherdess, which seemed to amuse the whole royal party.

'The Princess made me promise to go to Blackheath to-morrow.'

'June 7.

'I dined at Lady Ann Barnard's, where I had the happiness to sit next to Lady Eliot—a charming woman, with a great deal of *countenance* and *conversation*. Lord Eliot is a fattish, fairish, silent gentleman—one sometimes sees these sort of people come together.

'William and I went after dinner to Harriet's box at Drury Lane, to see the "Stranger," "The Devil to Pay," Mrs. Jordan as "Nell," and "Robinson Crusoe." We wept plentifully at the first. Bannister and Mrs. Jordan consoled us in the second, and "Robinson Crusoe" composed me after laughing and crying. I wish with all my heart I could say something decided about my coming to Minto. At present nobody thinks of quitting the scene of speculation; but *I* think it will soon cease to be so very critical. There will be a trying division in the House of Commons to-morrow,[1] which will show the strength of the different parties. The King's health will long occasion some doubts; but I think it probable that, with a little time, he will be better—well enough to promise greater permanency, at all events, than can be depended on now. The King's real situation at the present moment is this : he is able to converse reasonably and as much as formerly ; but

[1] On Mr. Pitt's measure for the public defence, called the Additional Force Bill.

the next moment he is entirely wrong. You may depend on this. Still the physicians say he is advancing towards a complete recovery. The Chancellor communicates to the Prince of Wales the reports of the physicians, and the Prince is advised to remain perfectly quiet—advice which I have no doubt he will take. Some people speculate on a dissolution. This is Tierney's idea, from an opinion that Mr. Pitt can hardly go on with the present House of Commons against all the adverse parties.

' It is thought that he will coalesce with Addington in his distress.'

'June 9.

'The division[1] last night in the House of Commons was a signal event, and may lead to consequences. It is a strong and clear indication of the most general disapprobation of the late measures respecting the formation of the new Ministry, and shows that even Pitt's name cannot make it strong.'

'June 12.

' The Ministers added ten more to their majority last night,[2] so they may try to go on with the Ministry as it is. Lord Pelham is to refuse the Stick after all. I think I told you that when he went to resign the

---

[1] Second reading of the Additional Force Bill; the Ministerial majority of 40 was considered very small.

[2]   For the Speaker's leaving the chair .   .   .   219

    Against it   269

                        Majority . .   50

seals of the Duchy of Lancaster, the King insisted on putting Lord Aylesford's stick into his hand. Pelham, being taken by surprise, accepted; but has since determined to decline the degradation of a statesman and Secretary of State into a sort of Polonius.'

'June 16.

' You will see the remarkable divisions in the House of Commons yesterday.[1] Pitt was in a minority on his own bill, the first and principal measure of his administration. This division took place at a period of the debate when it was not expected, when neither side had rallied their forces. The main division which took place last night afterwards, on the question of postponing the bill three months, which meant throwing it out, was carried by Mr. Pitt by a majority of only twenty-eight or twenty-nine, I am not sure which. This was a real trial of strength on Pitt's part at least, and appears very decisive of his not having the sort of hearty and personal support which is necessary in our present circumstances. I am going to escort Lady Carnegie and fourteen young ladies to Vauxhall. Harry and Fanny Temple are of the party, the Duchess of Atholl, Lady Balcarras, Lady Perth, and Miss Drummond.

' I am glad Gilbert sees Cobbett's trial in the light I do. As there are so many thousand libels unnoticed every week, I have always thought that the tendency of Cobbett's writings should have prevented his being

---

[1] On the Additional Force Bill.

singled out for severity and the rigour of a law which neither is nor can be put in force generally.'

'June 19.

'I went to the House of Commons yesterday as soon as I got to town,[1] without intending to stay it out; but I sat on till after four this morning. The majority rose again to 42, which is very low indeed, in such a House and after such an exertion. The numbers were 265–223, majority 42. The minority were in fact 225 including the two tellers. There were 493 in the House including the four tellers and the Speaker. This is the fullest House that was ever known. This division, though not creditable to the Minister, will, however, carry him through for the present, and I return to the opinion, which his very low numbers had lately shaken, that he is established at least for the session and recess; and that being the case, it appears more probable that he should gain than lose strength by time. Addington's people will probably, in part at least, drop gradually in to him.

'Elliot spoke extremely well yesterday. Canning made a clever speech, but indiscreet as he generally is; and he gave Fox and Sheridan many openings which were not lost. Sheridan made one of his brilliant appearances and came prepared for that purpose; for Mrs. Sheridan came under the gallery in a man's frock coat and trousers, under the care of Lord Lauderdale. I was next them all night. Lady Palmerston is much

---

[1] The debate was on the Additional Force Bill.

the same; but she will try hard to get to Broadlands when Harry and Willy return from their tour.'

'June 29, 1804.

'I have seen Lord Melville: as frank, hearty, and friendly as I have always found him.   We talked a little politics, and I regretted I never had the luck to hit his.   He professes to exclude politics altogether from his naval administration. He talked handsomely of Lord St. Vincent, personally, as a man of talents and activity ; but describes the state of the Navy as deplorable, and ascribes it to schemes of false economy and injudicious reforms.   I really believe Lord Melville to be as likely to repair the evil by despatch and activity as any man that could have been placed at the head of the Admiralty.'

'June 26, 1804.

' We were up till two this morning, and you can hardly conceive the heat.   Lord Melville spoke well in his strange barbarous but forcible way.   Lord Grenville excellent as usual.   These were the only good speeches. Lord St. Vincent came on purpose to vote against the bill: he took me by the hand when I went into the House and said, " I am glad that we shall vote together to-night."   The division was the most numerous ever known in the House of Lords ; the majority very decisive for Government, but the minority very considerable.[1]   There will be nothing more in the House of Lords, and this is certainly the last week I stay in

---

[1] Additional Force Bill.

town.   I have a visit to Eden Farm, and a small tour
to Beconsfield, Dropmore, Danesfield, and Park Place
for next week.

'You will see that Moreau, Jules Polignac, and
some few others are acquitted. Armand Polignac is convicted, but it is thought he will be pardoned.'

'June 30.

'I dined at Burlington House yesterday, and had good
cheer and a cordial welcome.

'I learnt a piece of history to-day which I did not
know before : the King was ill in the *same way* in the
year 1765, very early in his reign.   I will show you a
passage in the continuation of Smollett which proves
it, and which was softened down even to what it is at
the instance of Government, and at a good price.

'The invasion is expected more than ever, and quite
immediately.'

The latter part of Lord Minto's correspondence during
the summer of 1804 was chiefly occupied by the narra-
tion of a most painful illness which had suddenly developed itself in Lady Palmerston, and of his own
anxieties and fears about her.   He foresaw that a second
time it would become his duty to break to her son the
loss of a parent.   'To us,' he wrote to Lady Minto, 'she
is the greatest loss possible out of our own family—the
oldest, fastest, safest friend.'   Though attacked with
especial virulence by a most trying disease, she preserved
her cheerfulness and courage throughout all its phases ;
'her cheerfulness being almost more melancholy than

depression would be ; one sees her so exactly herself, one possesses her so entirely, and yet she is lost to us.'

When Lord Minto left London, he knew that he had seen her for the last time, and in the course of the winter Lady Palmerston died at Broadlands. She saw her friends to the last, and one of the hopes so simply and touchingly expressed by her in a letter to Lady Malmesbury, written in December 1804, seems to have been fulfilled :

' I hope I may amend, but if I do not, I trust my spirits will be restored to enable me to bear with fortitude whatever evil I am to suffer ; for there is something to me quite wicked in repining at whatever may be our lot in this world, and I have had my share of happiness and health.'

The coronation of Bonaparte as Emperor of the French took place during the recess, but as he had worn the title for some months before, and had held imperial power longer still, the event produced no material change in the condition of affairs. The assumption of these new dignities by the ruler of France led to an alteration in the styles and titles of the Emperor of Germany, who thereupon transformed his hereditary dignity into an Imperial one, and proclaimed himself Emperor of Austria as well as of Germany—a measure thus commented on by Lady Malmesbury : ' I never heard anything so absurd in all my life, and this, as he says, in order to put himself on an equality with Bonaparte. Two Emperors in one man is like an unnatural birth of two children joined in one.'

CHAPTER XIV.

EARLY in February 1805, the family took possession
of a house in Kensington, not far from Holland House.
'So,' said Lord Minto, 'William can go bird's nesting
in the hedges there, as I used to do in my school days.'
But William, who was at home on leave, was shortly
ordered to join the line-of-battle ship preparing to convey Lord Cornwallis to India; and another parting,
sorely felt by the whole family, took place in
the summer of the same year, when John,[1] Lord Minto's
third son, was appointed to a writership in India, and
soon afterwards left them for his distant destination.
His warmth of heart and playfulness of mind had en-
deared him to his family from early childhood, as they
attracted to him through life the affectionate regard of
all who came in contact with him. George, his elder
brother, was also absent, and the tone of Lady Minto's
letters at this time leads us to exclaim with Madame de
Sévigné, 'Hélas! ces pauvres mères.'

Lord Minto to Lady Minto.

'Pall Mall: July 9, 1805.

'Lord Nelson was landing 2,000 troops at St. John's,
Antigua, on June 12. I imagine he had taken the

---

[1] John Elliot, for many years M.P. for Roxburghshire.

troops on board at some other island. He was in pursuit of the combined squadron, and was to be after
them in an hour after the date of his letter (to Lady
Hamilton, who showed it me). They were trying to
get away from him, but were only one day's sail before
him, and they sailed ill and in disorder. They had
done *nothing*, and besides the reasonable expectation
of some grand stroke, we have the certainty in the
meanwhile that the West Indies are saved, and, indeed,
the East Indies are safe. I know nothing more of the
sailing of the Indiamen, but John is safe till he hears
from me.'

> 'Portsmouth: Sunday, July 14, 1805.
> (To Park Place.)

' We got here on Friday night, admiring the country
cottages with their roses all the way ; next day came
a telegraph order to detain the fleet, and a letter from
George to say he was appointed to the " Aurora," and
should be here the same day.

' The " Aurora " is an excellent twenty-eight-gun frigate, perfectly manned and fitted, and ready for sea.
Nothing could be more fortunate and seasonable than
George's appointment to a ship at Portsmouth just at
this moment. The three brothers are now together before the dispersion, and I don't feel much ashamed of
them collectively or individually. Captain Byng commands the " Belliqueuse," sixty-four, convoy to the
East Indian fleet. There are thirteen ships under convoy, four or five for Madras ; it is a great pity they are
detained now the wind is fair and all quite ready.

But there are certain accounts from London that the reason of the delay is to have information from Lord Nelson, or of the combined fleet. This cannot be expected till the wind changes, and then the fleet will not be able to sail, so they may be here a considerable time ; at the same time they may start at a very short notice. We went to the dockyard yesterday, and saw the newly invented machine for making ship-blocks, which is the most admirable thing I ever saw. It is the invention of one of my Toulonese emigrants, who directs the work and has the contracts ; Government has ensured him 5,000*l.* a year, if his profits should not amount to so much. His name is Brunel. . . I say nothing of John all this time, but what can I say ? He is going in the most promising and pleasantest circumstances, which must be our consolation under so great a privation.'

'August 3, 1805.

'I dined yesterday with Elliot at Holland House and slept there ; the party was Lord H. Petty, the Bessboroughs, Lord Duncannon, Monsieur de Souza, Monsieur Moravioff, Russian Minister for a short time at Vienna before I came away ; Fish Crawfurd, and one or two more. I dine there again to-day with Windham. This is the effect of the Coalition. I like Lord Holland in private extremely. Nothing can be more perfectly natural, good-natured, *moderate* or cheerful. She is grown very fat, but otherwise just as she was. They live remarkably well. Her West India fortune is said to have turned out very considerable.

'Lord Henry Petty's marriage with a daughter of Lord Abercorn's is much talked of, but not declared. Lord Enniskillen's marriage to Lady Charlotte Paget is settled.'

'August 5.

'There is every reason to believe that a proposal is intended to be made by Mr. Pitt to Opposition for a coalition. That is to say, he and his friends have expressly said so. It is to comprehend Mr. Fox and his party. However, although so much is certain, nothing can be less so than the result; and there has often been found a great distance between this sort of general intimation and the actual conclusion of such affairs. Lord Grenville will be in town to-morrow and I shall probably be able to tell you something more precise.'

'August 6.

'I hear that Austria has declared positively she will take no part in any confederacy against France, and assigns her total want of means as the motive of this conduct. I am sorry for it, thinking a continental war the *only* chance of terminating our difficulties, though even that chance may not be good. But the longer it is delayed, the worse prospect of success there will be, as Bonaparte will increase his strength every year, and resistance may come at last when it is too late.

'Lord Grenville was not at home when I called to-day. Why do you suppose he is come to town? For a coalition with Pitt, you will say. This only proves that you entirely mistake the man, and suppose him to think of nothing but politics. A masquerade dress is the business that has brought him from Dropmore at present. This is for the festivals at Stowe.'[1]

'Pall Mall: August 8.

' I met three little children *lost* yesterday in Piccadilly, and after trudging a mile or two through all the bye streets of St. James' parish, in rain, it ended in my being obliged to bring them to the hotel and desiring the landlady to bring them some supper and put them to bed, meaning to advertise them to-day. However, an hour after I was gone to Roehampton, the mother of one of them had discovered them with the help of the Cryer ; and I was very glad to find to-day on my return that I was relieved of this family. I never saw an uglier little boy ; and the two little girls no beauties. They had wandered from beyond Oxford Road ; and are the children, one of a collar-maker, and two of a carpet-maker ; they made me a full hour too late for Lord Buckingham's dinner.

' There is again a great bustle on account of invasion, but there is a general hope in the possibility of Nelson's getting a knock at the combined fleets. It is, however, quite uncertain whether they are gone to the southward, or into some port on the western coast of France. If they are gone to the Tagus, it is against the laws of neutrality to receive so great a number of ships of war,

---

[1] There was to be a large party at Stowe for the Prince of Wales : it was to last four days, and Lord Minto had previously mentioned his having contrived to escape that service.

which would justify Nelson in following them.[1]　I dine
to-morrow at Clifden, Lord Thomond's, and after dinner
go to Dropmore, to stay over Sunday.'

'Beconsfield : August 11.

' I was prevented from going to Taplow yesterday for
want of horses; the Gloucestershire election having
employed them all on this road.　I have by this means
made a longer visit to Mrs. Burke; it is the sort of
thing which gives her pleasure—one passes all the time
between meals just as one likes; either walking or in
the library.　I read indeed yesterday good part of the
day on the grass, which is my idea of summer.'

'Beconsfield : August 12.

' I went yesterday to Dropmore; there was nobody but
Lord and Lady Grenville, and, as I have said before,
there never was a more gallant or attentive husband;
and, to all appearance, a better *natured*, as well as
tempered one.　We walked after dinner to his farm,
where he patted and *poored* an old horse, which they
are keeping alive by mashes and care, a full quarter of
an hour.　This was an old horse he had been used to
ride himself in his youth; but he went half the length
of a field out of the way to do the same by an old cart-
horse.　I mention these traits only because they are
very unlike the notion which is generally entertained
of his character. . . . He seems to have little expecta-

---

[1] All this time the East Indian fleet was detained at Falmouth, not
venturing to sail during such complete uncertainty as to the where-
abouts of the combined fleets.

tion of any successful issue to the attempt at arrangement between Pitt and Opposition. Indeed I suspect that Pitt's hints and insinuations on that subject have been pretty loose and general. I take it the question will be whether he can carry on government alone. If that is found impracticable, he will try to negotiate; and the nature of his proposals will depend on the degree of his necessity. But no serious efforts are likely to be made for that purpose till Parliament meets, or a short time before. I came here from Dropmore after breakfast, Lord and Lady Grenville setting out at the same time for Stowe; and, as the Windhams came this evening, I stay to-night. I have been reading Spenser's Fairy Queen on the grass all the day, and have dined with Mrs. Burke, Mrs. Haviland, and Miss C. Hickey.

'This has been a beautiful day for the Moors.'

'Pall Mall: August 14.

'I called at Bulstrode on my way to town yesterday. From Uxbridge I came by the *canal* to Paddington, and liked it extremely. It runs through a prettier country than canals generally do, and the boat is very clean and clever. There were twenty or thirty passengers, but room enough and to spare. There is very good walking as well as sitting on the roof. I got to Pall Mall about ten at night.

'John has really sailed from Falmouth at last, but I believe only to Cork.

'They will hardly sail till something is known of the combined fleets, supposed to be gone to the Canaries or some southern port, which would throw them rather on the way of our outbound fleets.   John seems to feel his departure, poor fellow, a good deal, and there is a good share of earnest in his jesting on the subject. However, he is both feeling and manly about it.   I do flatter myself he will do well, both by the favour he is sure to conciliate and by his other qualifications.

' The invasion appears to me much in the same state as ever ; always possible that the attempt may be made, but not much more likely now than at former periods of bustle on their side of the water and stillness on ours.'

' August 16.

' Accounts are received from Admiral Cornwallis to-day that the combined fleets are in Ferrol at last.   Sir R. Calder and Admiral Starling have both fallen back and joined Cornwallis off Brest.   There are now thirty-one sail of the line at Ferrol, which is not blockaded, nor Rochfort either.   Cornwallis has between thirty and forty sail of the line, but has both Ferrol and Brest to look to.   Nelson has not yet been distinctly heard of since he came out of the Straits.   The Dutch came out of the Texel the other day, but were prevented sailing, I understand, by the wind.   This is true ; I heard it to-day at the Secretary of State's Office.   The question is beginning to arise whether our naval superiority is still sufficient to guard all these points at once against such numerous fleets.   If not ! ! '

'Saturday, August 17, 1805.

' The news from India makes a strong and unfavourable impression. Immense loss of men and officers,
with a failure in the object. All this is novel in that
country, and seems the beginning of a new era there.
The sensations are also not good on the collection of
so great a fleet at Ferrol, perfectly at liberty for the
present to act as they think proper. All these unto-
ward events, and the public uneasiness they evidently
produce, seem likely to bring forward the ideas of
coalitions, and accordingly it is reported to-day that
overtures have been sent to Lord Grenville and
Mr. Fox ; but I know nothing of them ; it was certainly
not so last Monday.'

'Pall Mall: August 22.

' You will see that George is at last off ; they have
two frigates and a sloop, the " Aurora," " Constance,"
and " Weasel." We may perhaps have another line
from George from Falmouth ; but perhaps not, as he
will only make the signal for the convoy to come out
and push on if the wind is fair. Lord Nelson has come.
I mean to propose myself to dine with him at Merton
on Saturday, or to return and dine with the Bessboroughs at Roehampton. I have taken a great fancy
to Lord Holland (don't tell the Admiral), and find him
the most natural, most good-natured and pleasantest
person in private society that I have ever known ; he
gets the wits of all persuasions about him, and all
ingenious or distinguished foreigners. He is all

obedience to her, who seems to know how to preserve her power without offending him. I have seen most of the Edinburgh Reviewers there, and amongst the rest Mr. Horner, who is, I suppose, Anna Maria's friend.'

'August 24, 1805.

' I went to Holland House yesterday to accompany them to Lord Bessborough's. I found Mr. and Mrs. Fox there, who did not know of the Hollands' dining out. Mr. Fox had been shopping with Mrs. Fox, an amusement they say he is fond of ; they had been buying china —cheap china, I mean ; for they seem great economists. We left them at Holland House, and went to Roehampton, carrying Mr. Horner and Mr. Allen, a domestic physician of Lord Holland's, and a very plain, sensible, studious man, who is writing a history of Spain. At Roehampton we had two Mr. Lambs, the eldest of whom,[1] having been the second brother, was intended for the law, and appeared to me a remarkably pleasant, clever, and well-informed young man ; he is now the eldest son ; the other, George, seems merely a good-natured lad. They are very unlike : the eldest puts me in mind of Windham ; the other has something of the Prince of Wales, only stunted in height, but very like in some points of manner. A daughter of Lady Bessborough's is a lively and rather a pretty girl : they say she is very clever.[2] Monk Lewis was also of the party.

---

[1] William Lamb, afterwards Lord Melbourne.
[2] Lady Caroline Lamb, already married to Mr. William Lamb, though Lord Minto was not aware of it at the time.

Lady Bessborough was, you know, very blue, which will be a resource when all others fail. They talked a good deal and very civilly of our Roehampton play. We got back to Holland House about twelve, and found that Mr. and Mrs. Fox had gone to bed. I breakfasted with them, however, this morning. She has grown fat, and not younger, nor softer-favoured ; but her manner is pleasing and gentlewomanlike. I perceive that Lady Holland does not admire her, and would willingly indulge herself now and then with a fling at her. Fox is himself, always good-natured and simplicity itself in private life. Peace seems the grand ruling principle of his politics and all his party's, and I wish the plot may not thicken so as to make the dangers of peace, great as they are, appear *even* to others still less than the more pressing dangers that are gathering and ready to burst around us. The sailing of a great hostile fleet, of twenty-eight sail of the line, in the direction of Ireland, creates no small uneasiness here ; and if Ireland is not the object, yet we have many great stakes at sea. The Roehampton dinner has led to a Chiswick one next Monday in the same company. So you see I am fairly entered in the Devonshire set, which I know must give *you great satisfaction !* I am going to Merton this moment in hopes of finding Lord Nelson at home.'

'Pall Mall: August 26, 1805.

' I went to Merton on Saturday and found Nelson just sitting down to dinner, surrounded by a family party, of his brother the Dean, Mrs. Nelson, their

children, and the children of a sister. Lady Hamilton
at the head of the table and Mother Cadogan at the
bottom. I had a hearty welcome. He looks remarkably well and full of spirits. His conversation is a
cordial in these low times. . . .[1] Lady Hamilton has
improved and added to the house and the place extremely well without his knowing she was about it.
He found it all ready done. She is a clever being after
all: the passion is as hot as ever.

'I met Nelson to-day in a mob in Piccadilly and got
hold of his arm, so that I was mobbed too. It is really
quite affecting to see the wonder and admiration, and
love and respect, of the whole world; and the genuine
expression of all these sentiments at once, from gentle
and simple, the moment he is seen. It is beyond anything represented in a play or a poem of fame.'

'Pall Mall: August 27, 1805.

'The Brest fleet of twenty-one sail of the line came
out of harbour on the evening of the 21st. Admiral
Cornwallis endeavoured to bring them to action, but as
the first of their ships came within gun-shot, she fired
her broadside and tacked, which all the rest did also,
and they anchored at the mouth of the harbour where
they could not be attacked next day. My account is
not very distinct, as you will perceive; but in substance
the French made a show of coming out, but declined
engaging Cornwallis, and anchored in a situation to come

[1] Speculations on the probable movements of the combined fleets are
omitted as having no interest or value.

out at a short notice.   In the meanwhile John has not
sailed, as you will see by the enclosed letter of the 18th
from Cork Harbour.

‘ The Continental war seems on the point of breaking
out.   There is one great event which might set the
world upon its shanks once more, but which I know of
no reason to expect more now than before.   I mean
Prussia’s joining against France when the other two
Powers are fairly engaged.   All one can say is that the
French have talked less cordially and confidently of
Prussia of late than formerly.   Without this event the
war between France and the two Emperors cannot be
thought very promising.   Yet as the present French
Government can be effectually controlled or opposed only
by the military Powers on the Continent, one cannot help
seeing the contest begin with some satisfaction.   Some
fortunate chance or other may cast up to obtain something like security against this devouring Power ; and
in the meanwhile it will release this country from
constant alarm at home, and afford leisure to increase
our navy so as to keep pace at least with theirs.

‘ I dined yesterday at Chiswick.   Lord Lorne was at
Holland House and accompanied us, as did Mr. Horner
and Mr. Allen.   The party at Chiswick was the
Duke and Duchess of Devonshire, Lady Georgina
and Lady Harriet, Lord and Lady Bessborough, Lord
Duncannon, Lady Elizabeth Forster, Madlle. St. Jules,
Madlle. de Grammont,[1] a very handsome young girl,

---

[1] Corisande de Grammont, afterwards Countess of Tankerville.

daughter of the Duc de Guiche and granddaughter of Madame de Polignac. Lord Ossulston was there, in love with Madlle. de Grammont, who has accepted his proposals ; but Lord Tankerville will not consent, and though much in love, Lord Ossulston has not yet brought himself to marry without his father's approbation. However, it is thought that Lord Tankerville may relent and that the novel will end happily. I sat by the Duchess and am extremely *fêté* in this new or rather old-renewed society. The Duchess looks much better than for some years past ; clearer skin, and her eye not so great a dissight. It is a pity she has faults and blemishes, for Nature meant her to be good and pleasing. The Duke sat an immoderate time after dinner. When the ladies retired, he had the table shortened and seemed to set in for it. I should have mentioned Macdowal of Castle Temple, the mirror of *bon-vivants* and ruler of White's, &c. &c. at the bottom of the table.

'This preparation for jollity, however, proved no extraordinary gaiety, and we should have been very humdrum without Lord Holland, who talks a great deal and always pleasantly. We sat till eleven, then went to the ladies till half-past twelve ; got to Holland House at one ; supped, and to bed at two. I dine at Holland House again to-day to meet the Melbournes, and Baron Strogonoff, the new Russian Ambassador to Spain. Horner and Elliot accompany me to Kensington. I sleep there, and have Frere's room assigned to me as a regular thing.'

'August 28.

' News has been received to-day of the " Phœnix " (I think), a frigate of thirty-two guns, commanded by Captain Baker, having taken " La Didon " of forty-four guns off Ferrol on the 10th inst. after an engagement of three hours, in which the French had 150 killed and wounded. I don't know why this news did not come sooner except that it was brought by the frigates themselves which may have had a long passage.'

'Pall Mall: August 29, 1805.

' We were wrong in supposing that Calder had been heard of off Ferrol on the 20th, as I probably mentioned to you in a former letter; but accounts are just received of his arrival off Ferrol on the 21st, and not finding the combined fleets in that harbour. As they have not been heard of to the northward, there is the strongest reason to believe that they are gone to the southward, and probably to the Mediterranean ; but they *may* be cruising to the westward to intercept our homeward-bound fleets. I do not know what Calder has done or is to do on finding that they had left Ferrol.[1] The interval is anxious, as they may, on the one hand, fall in with some valuable merchant fleets of ours, and, on the other, may meet our squadron and be well beaten .

---

[1] ' As to Sir Robert Calder, he will never catch anything but crabs if he attempts to row about. He puts me in mind of the clown in a harlequin farce, who always lets harlequin slip in and out, and then comes staring about to look for it till he runs his head against a post.'— *Lady Malmesbury to Lady Minto*, August 29, 1809.

By the enclosed letter from John of the 23rd, you will
be glad to see that our outward-bound convoy is not
exposed to this hazard, and that they are safe in port.
I dined yesterday with Lord Nelson at Lady Hamilton's.
It was a family party of brothers and sisters, with their
husbands, and Mr. Greville (Charles).

'Lord Nelson is kinder and more confidential with
me than ever; says all his Mediterranean opinions
and politics have been derived from me; that he has
found all I ever said or wrote to him on that subject
ten years ago fully verified, &c. &c. He tells me all his
present views on that subject, and all that passes between
him and Ministers; hopes to see me Secretary of State,
and so forth. He was with me this morning before I
was up, and left me some papers concerning the Mediterranean which I am to read on my way to Merton to-
morrow, where he will show me all his correspondence
that I may wish to see. It is not the worst point of
his friendship that he says he shall give George a
better ship as soon as he can; and he is to have the
Cadiz station in his command this time if he goes to
the Mediterranean, which I have no doubt he will.'

'August 31.

'I dined at Merton yesterday, and carried some of
my despatches about Sardinia, which is Lord Nelson's
great hobby. He filled my chaise with books of his
own correspondence, to show how his opinion had concurred with mine; and to-day he has sent me another
load.

'The "Victory" is sent to the Channel fleet without him, but if there is anything material in the Mediterranean he will go.'

'Pall Mall: September 2.

'Lord Mulgrave called on me yesterday to propose the Embassy at Petersburgh. I objected my line in Parliament, with which, however, he considered this appointment as perfectly compatible. I of course declined, all sorts of proper things being said on both sides. I collected from Lord Mulgrave's conversation that no offer of coalition is likely to come from Pitt— so much for that.'

'September 3.

'John is fairly off at last. The combined fleets safe in Cadiz. They got in there on August 22. Sir R. Calder was off Cape St. Vincent (within twenty leagues on the 24th), and Admiral Collingwood just at hand looking out for him; so that their junction may be considered as made.

'Sir Richard Bickerton may also join them, and these fleets which we have been gaping after so long are once more blockaded. I have seen Nelson to-day, and there seems no doubt of his going immediately to take command of Calder's fleet.

'There has been the greatest alarm ever known in the city of London since the combined fleet sailed from Ferrol. If they had captured our homeward-bound convoys, it is said the India Company and half the City must have been bankrupt.'

' Lord Nelson has been here to-day.   He is going to resume the command of the Mediterranean as soon as the "Victory" is ready, which will be within a week. Nothing can be more perfectly affectionate and kind. He told me again to-day, as the first point he had to talk on, that he should give George a good thirty-two-gun frigate, at least, as soon as possible.   There is nothing confidential that he does not show me and consult me about, saying that he knows I am in opposition, but that I am a friend of my country and everything is safe with me.

' I have been walking with the Duke of Clarence, who has told me all the arrangements on the Duke of Gloucester's death.'

'September 9, 1805.

' I have been on foot all day, that is to say since breakfast at Holland House.   Lord Lorne is an inmate as well as myself, and sleeps there whenever he likes. He enquires after Anna Maria's letters, as it is his only way of hearing of his family; I like him extremely; one benefit of these Coalitions is to bring people together independently of political opinions ; and I feel very much disposed henceforward to make no exclusive distinctions in private life between parties, however opposite their principles, and to meet even Jacobins and Republicans on fair terms in society, as I should do Pittites on the other hand.   This *thin* time of year, too, contributes to draw people together however unlike they may be in other respects. There is no danger to any of my principles on any subject. I am not so sure of some others whose opinions have been as strong as mine. But I believe myself the least obnoxious to *party* influence on my ways of thinking, perhaps of any public man in the country, having a very strong public feeling of a larger description which counteracts a little the narrower passions of party. I dine to-day at Holland House to meet the young Duke of Leinster.'

'Pall Mall: Friday, September 13, 1805.

' I went yesterday to Merton in a great hurry, as he, Lord Nelson, said he was to be at home all day, and he dines at half-past three. But I found he had been sent for to Carlton House, and he and Lady Hamilton did not return till half-past five. I stayed till ten at night and took a final leave of him. He is to have forty sail of the line, and a proportional number of frigates, sloops, and small vessels. This is the largest command that any admiral has had for a long time. He goes to Portsmouth to-night. . . . Lady Hamilton was in tears all yesterday; could not eat, and hardly drink, and near swooning, and all at table. It is a strange picture. She tells me nothing can be more pure and ardent than this flame. He is in many points a really great man, in others a baby. His friendship and mine is little short of the other attachment, and is quite sincere. I had a curious meeting yesterday, at Merton, with Mr. Perry, editor of the " Morning Chronicle," whom I formerly sent to the King's Bench or Newgate, I think

for six months, for a libel on the House of Lords. When
Lord Nelson came he introduced us to each other.
I told Mr. Perry I was glad to have the opportunity
of shaking hands on our old warfare.'

'King's Arms Yard : Tuesday, September 17, 1805.

'It is a melancholy reflection that the winter theatres
are open again; as for my summer I have lost it and
there is no help for it. The peaches and grapes, to be
sure, sound tempting; yet if I could get *home* once
more, by your side, my dearest love, and amongst the
home department of the family, I should not lament
the season so much; bnt I am now completely losing
all comforts, animate and inanimate, animal and vege-
table. Windham, Elliot, and I dined at Blackheath
yesterday. There was nobody else except Mrs. Fitz-
gerald and Miss Cholmondeley. It was very pleasant
and good-humoured as usual; but she got me into one
of the confidential whispers for the last two hours,
which always distresses the patient, besides making my
head ache desperately. The King is as fond of her as
ever, and has at last given her the rangership of Greenwich Park, which I am very glad of. They used to be
very shabby and blackguard in refusing her half roods
of green under her windows; now the whole is at her
own disposal.'

'Pall Mall : Friday, September 27, 1805.

'We had Sydney Smith yesterday at Holland House.
I had never seen him before and do not admire him,

though he is certainly lively and clever; but his taste is bad, whatever his genius may be.' [1]

On his way North, Lord Minto paid a visit to his favourite niece Lady Buckinghamshire, to whose 'light-full countenance' and cultivated mind there are many allusions in his letters, as also to the pleasure he had in strolling with her through the shrubberies and gardens of her villa at Roehampton, so much more to both their tastes than the life of London. 'There never was more good-humour and good-nature collected in one couple,' wrote he from Nocton, but his stay there afforded no material for correspondence, and the only letters of the autumn worth preserving are two—written to Lady Minto, when on his way to visit Lady Carnegie, at Kinnaird.

(Extract.)   'Edinburgh: November 2, 1805.

'Sir W. Forbes is writing Dr. Beattie's Life, and Dugald Stewart is to write a few passages on the metaphysical part. He took me aside to ask my leave to insert a quotation or two from the correspondence between my father and David Hume which I sent him some years ago. The quotation is from one of my father's letters, of which he spoke with great admiration, and I was happy to find him of my father's side

[1] As an instance of this want of taste when Sydney Smith was new to London society, Lord Russell relates on the authority of Lord Holland that when dining at Holland House to meet the Prince of Wales (lately become Regent), Sydney said somewhat pointedly in the course of a discussion on French morals during the early part of the life of Louis XV., that the *Regent* was the most profligate man in France; to which remark the Prince quickly rejoined, 'No, Mr. Smith, Cardinal Dubois was the most profligate man in France, and *he* was a *priest*, Mr. Smith.'

of the question against David Hume's sceptical philosophy. I met Mr. Horner the reviewer yesterday. He
is here to attend a few of Mr. Playfair's first lectures
on Natural Philosophy. Lord Webb Seymour has come
for the same purpose. . . .

'All the wits, critics, lawyers, judges, authors, pro-
fessors, divines, young men, and pretty Misses swarm
about the Glenbervies. . . . Lady Douglas, Caroline,
Miss Mary, and Giustanielli came yesterday to dinner.'

'Perth : Sunday, November 10, 1805.

'I received this morning, at Forfar, the account of
Lord Nelson's victory and death ; and my sense of his
irreparable loss, as well as my sincere and deep regret
for so kind a friend, have hardly left room for other
feelings which belong, however, hardly less naturally
to this event. I was extremely shocked and hurt when
I heard it, and it has kept me low and melancholy all
day. One knows, on reflection, that such a death is
the finest close, and the crown, as it were, of such a
life ; and possibly, if his friends were angels and not
men, they would acknowledge it as the last favour
Providence could bestow and a seal and security for
all the rest. His glory is certainly at its summit, and
could be raised no higher by any length of life ; but
he might have lived at least to enjoy it. I feel his
death all the more sensibly for having seen so much
of him so lately, and received only yesterday, as it

---

[1] Caroline Douglas, Lady Scott, authoress of *A Marriage in High
Life* and *Trevelyan*.

seems, so many strong marks of his entire confidence and affection. He was remarkably well and fresh too, and full of hope and spirit. After all, the manner and occasion of his fall would be a full consolation for any other death; and since the event, however lamented, must be submitted to, we cannot do better than turn to the bright side of it. The victory is a most important one and comes most seasonably. It is singular that the two most remarkable naval actions that ever were should have been fought so near the same spot, and that they should both have come to cheer us just in moments of the greatest despondency. Nelson, too, was conspicuous in both, and fastened both times on the same adversary—the " Santissima Trinidada," for that was the first ship he engaged on February 14. But great and important as the victory is, it is bought too dearly, even for our interest, by the loss of Nelson. We shall want more victories yet, and to whom can we look for them ? The navy is certainly full of the bravest men, but they are mostly below the rank of admiral; and brave as they almost all are, there was a sort of heroic cast about Nelson that I never saw in any other man, and which seems wanting to the achievement of *impossible things* which became easy to him, and on which the maintenance of our superiority at sea seems to depend against the growing navy of the enemy. However, his example will do a great deal, I have no doubt. What a contrast with two recent events—Mack's capitulation, and Calder's puny, half-begotten victory ! What a contrast, too, is Collingwood with Calder ! The one sacrificing nineteen prizes to the public cause ; the other spoiling all for the sake of two.'

The events of the winter are historical. The great naval victory of Trafalgar, which secured the invulnerability of Great Britain, was balanced by the continental disasters of Ulm and Austerlitz. Within a few months of each other England's greatest hero and her leading statesman passed away ; but not till their work was done. Whatever were the faults of Pitt or the shortcomings of his administration, this truth remains : that by the undaunted front he showed in the hour of his country's greatest peril, he gave, not only to her but to Europe, ' a power and a sign.' He did not live to see the glory acquired by our arms and to share in the loud triumphs of the Harvest Home ; but when, in 1814, our little army marched into Paris, side by side with the mighty continental hosts, it owed its proud pre-eminence less to its military distinction, great as that was, than to the fact that during the long death-struggle with France, the nations of Europe had found in England 'a bulwark for the cause of man.' Of the national qualities which had made her so, of her persistence and heroic self-reliance, they have ever acknowledged a fitting representative in Mr. Pitt.

The first letters of the New Year, 1806, brought to Lord Minto the intelligence of Pitt's increasing illness. Towards the middle of January he heard of its approaching end.

'I am this day,' wrote Lord Grenville to Lord Minto, 'in hourly expectation of receiving the account of the loss of a friend whom, notwithstanding some political differences, I have never ceased to value and to love, and whose loss will be a heavy blow to the country. I think it highly probable that this melancholy, and to me truly distressing, event will delay for some days longer than as now fixed, the discussion, at least in the House of Lords. . . . What is to be done in consequence of this great misfortune few people can even guess ; but the prevailing opinion seems to be that there is to be an attempt to patch together the poor remnants of the present Government. If so we are indeed a nation devoted to destruction.'

Mr. Elliot wrote the same day from Spring Gardens : 'I cannot let the post go without informing you that Pitt has become so much worse as to leave no chance of his recovery, and he probably cannot survive many hours. Thus is extinguished a bright and luminous star which has long shone in our political firmament ; and though I certainly have never considered its influence beneficial, yet it is impossible not to feel a deep regret for the loss of a man of eminence and distinction, whose talents have been an ornament to his country.'

On the following day Mr. Elliot wrote that Pitt's death had happened at half-past four this morning. 'Lord Grenville is so much affected by Pitt's death that he has gone to Dropmore and does not return till Saturday.'[1]

Mr. Pitt died on the 23rd of January. On the 27th the question of his interment with funeral honours was debated in the House of Commons. In these days, when notoriety seems sufficient to secure a place in our Walhalla, it is startling to find Mr. Pitt's claims to a public funeral disputed. The debate is a curious monument of the difference between those times and our own in matters of opinion and of taste. As regards opinion, probably few at the present day would agree with Mr. Fox in placing the institution of the Sinking Fund among the foremost claims of Mr. Pitt to his country's gratitude. As regards taste, that of modern times would have rendered Mr. Windham's speech impossible, in consideration of the long official connection which had subsisted between himself and Mr. Pitt. As a general statement of the sentiments entertained by his Whig colleagues of Mr. Pitt's Administration, Mr. Windham's speech was probably not far from the truth. They joined him at the instigation of Burke; they sympathised with no part of his policy except his war policy. They did not approve of the manner in which he carried that out; their official connection with him never ripened into habits of intimacy; but from first to last, they were clear in their own minds that the progress

[1] 'Exclusive of that concern,' wrote Lord Holland to Lord Minto on the same day, 'that we must all feel for the loss of so remarkable a man, I am one who in a party view do not think this event a fortunate one for the cause or for the country.'

of the French Revolution from Jacobinical to Imperial tyranny was only to be met by open resistance, and that a policy such as would make that resistance effectual, could be hoped alone from a Minister possessing the confidence of both Crown and People.[1]

'February 22, 1806.

' I have been attending Mr. Pitt's funeral in Westminster Abbey. Those who opposed the measure in Parliament did not attend, which I think a pity, as

---

[1] In the Memoirs of Sir James Mackintosh, a letter will be found, dated Bombay, December 9, 1804, in which he, who in 1791 wrote the most able answer to Burke's Reflections, thus expresses himself:—' The Opposition mistook the moral character of the Revolution ; the Ministers mistook its force; and both parties, from pique, resentment, pride, habit, and obstinacy, persisted in acting on these mistakes after they were disabused by experience. Mr. Burke alone avoided both these mistakes. He saw both the malignity and the strength of the Revolution.   But where there was wisdom to discover the truth there was not power, and perhaps there was not practical skill to make that wisdom available for the salvation of Europe.   *Diis aliter visum!* . . . I have lately read the lives and private correspondence of some of the most remarkable men in different countries in Europe who are lately dead.   Klopstock, Kant, Lavater, Alfieri—they were all filled with joy and hope by the French Revolution ; they clung to it for a longer or a shorter time ; they were all compelled to relinquish their illusions ; the disappointment of all was bitter.' To the names enumerated by Sir James Mackintosh might be added others held in high honour by Englishmen.   No history has given or perhaps will ever give a more distinct reflection of the impression produced on thoughtful minds by the fluctuations of the times than the series of Wordsworth's sonnets dedicated to Liberty. We see in them the gradual change from hope to disappointment, from indignation to high resolve, produced by the course of events as they hurried on from that ' too credulous day,'

' When Faith was pledged to new-born Liberty,'
to the evil hour when men had grown

' Impatient to put out the only light
Of Liberty that yet remained on earth.'

after expressing their dissent to the measure, they could not be supposed to adopt an unqualified approbation of Mr. Pitt's political character or conduct by joining in this mark of respect for his person and talents. Windham gave extreme offence by his opposition to it in the House of Commons; but there I am inclined to think as he did : but, the thing being ordered, I think he might as well have attended.'

A change of Ministry was the inevitable consequence of the death of Pitt; and the Administration known as that of 'the Talents' came into office at the end of January.

On February 3, 1806, Lord Minto wrote from London :

' I am to be President of the Board of Control, but not in the Cabinet. So at least it stands at present, but I consider the latter point as open to future consideration. The office is that which I should have preferred almost to any other, in many respects. I have not a moment to write.'

'February 7.

' I am flattered with hopes of getting perhaps a couple of summer months at Minto. . . .

' Lord Eldon sitting, the day before yesterday, rather melancholy, with his feet on the grate thinking of his misfortunes, the loss of his son, and the Seals, was just consoling himself a little with the idea that, as Lord Redesdale would also be out, he might perhaps pass part of his leisure with his old friend. At that moment

a letter was brought to him acquainting him that Lord
Redesdale had died suddenly at Dublin.   Lord Eldon
was so much shocked that he dropped the letter in the
fire, and remembered neither the date nor the signature,
except that the name ended in a y, and it appears that
the name of Lord Redesdale's secretary does end with
that letter.   Lord Henry Petty has carried his election for Cambridge very hollow.   Lord Althorpe was
next to him, and Harry had the smallest number ; but
he had a very handsome support considering his own
age and the formidable opponent he was to contend
with.'

After the death of Lady Palmerston, her son, who
had grown up in habits of intimacy with the Malmesbury family, drew still more closely towards those who
had been attached to her.   When not at Cambridge he
was constantly at Park Place, and there in the society
of the distinguished men who had been so intimately
connected with Mr. Pitt as to have received the denomination of *Pittites,* he received his first political impressions ;—a circumstance viewed with some regret by
his friends at Minto, one of whom not unaptly remarked
that ' political parties might be sometimes treated with
advantage as Joseph II. had treated the convents—
allowed to die out, but not to take novices.' [1]

After Lord Minto's entrance on the cares of office
his letters become less frequent and less full than those
of earlier years.   In one of them he complains that,

---

[1] Letter from A. M. Elliot to her father.

even by rising at half-past seven, he can hardly find a moment in which to give himself the greatest pleasure of his day—a letter to his wife. ' Building cottages and dog-kennels,' he says to her, who was thus occupied, ' are more amusing work than mine ; but one must not show this to those who think they have claims on one's time and attention.'

To the claims of *friends* he ever gave more than ' time and attention '—his entire sympathy and cordial interest; and of friends no man had more. A letter from a very valued one, Lady Glenbervie, expresses very pleasantly the feelings which were by no means confined to her.

'Pheasantry : January 18, 1806.

' Dear Lord Minto,—I cannot thank you sufficiently for the few lines you sent under the cover of *our* daughter's letter, and sincerely rejoice in your emancipation from the doctors and their dread commands. Though they may have deprived you of your lilies and roses, my love is an evergreen, and will out-flourish such fading flowers. If you doubt this come and see. You are, and always have been, the friend we lean upon the most securely. To your wise and kind advice I chiefly attribute the comforts of our present situation. Your friendship has been the source of the greatest advantages, and your society of the pleasantest moments of our lives.

' I have seen very few faces since I came *sooth*, and those few so long that I do not desire to see more of them and am very sorry to leave this place and the improvements we are to make in March, and which afford us sufficient occupation at present. I only feel that we may be building for Bonaparte's valet de chambre.

> ' Most affectionately yours,
>> ' KATE GLENBERVIE.'

The chief topics of the correspondence of 1806 are : the impeachment of Lord Melville, the enquiry into the conduct of the Princess of Wales, known as the ' delicate investigation,' and the differences between the Government and the Court of Directors on the subject of Lord Lauderdale's candidature for the appointment of Governor-General of Bengal.

In a note addressed to Lady Minto, at Park Place, during the spring of the previous year, Lord Minto mentioned the ' business of the Navy Pay Office as making a great noise,' and he added, ' There has no doubt been very great irregularity and abuse, yet an abuse perfectly free from fraud. Lord Melville's concern in the matter seems to be much misunderstood by the public, but when explained does not appear to me likely to affect him seriously, and, indeed, the whole of this inquisition seems so much the effect of party rancour, and so venomous against Dundas personally, that I don't sympathise with it.'

On April 29 (1806) he wrote :

' I went this morning to the trial, where I have been ever since, and I am more fatigued than I ought to be for one sitting. The scene is horrid. Lord Melville looks like death. I never saw anybody more terribly altered. Whitbread spoke almost four hours with great ability, and although he was temperate in his language, and expressed many becoming feelings, it was a most dreadful speech to sit under, and in such a place too. The evidence will begin to-morrow; we meet at ten in the morning and stay till four at least.'

His subsequent letters of this summer contain little more than passing allusions to the progress of the trial; but in Lady Minto's to her husband we gain a glimpse of the excitement it produced in Scotland.

The accession to power of Mr. Fox and his friends, and the impeachment of the man who for many years had been the ruler of Scotland and the sole dispenser of Scotch patronage, were events which filled the Liberals with hope and energy.

In no part of the United Kingdom had the rule of the party which had so long held power been more absolute than in Scotland, and as a natural consequence nowhere was the opposition more *thorough*, though it was confined to a smaller minority.

Lady Minto to Lord Minto.

'Minto: May 30, 1806.

'. . . A dissolution is, I think, quite necessary; for Scotland will be a thorn in the side of Government till it is newly represented. This whole country considers Lord Melville as its *chief*; and well they may, after

thirty years' reign and entire power : even out of power
he has never ceased having the patronage.   You cannot
really form an idea what the state of feeling is here.
There is no such thing as an opinion between one
political party and the other; there are merely *Mel-
villeites*, without an idea that any other man can *serve
Scotland*, as they call it.

'Again, what is done by Ministers from delicacy of
feeling passes here for protection.   Indeed, Ministers
know nothing of Scotland ; and they feel that they have
gained so much through Lord Melville's interest, that
they cannot see any other God to worship.   It only
proves how much too far his power extended.'

Among the most personally distinguished of the
Scotch Liberals was Dugald Stewart.   Though an object of suspicion to those who detected in him 'democratical tendencies,' 'which, however,' wrote Lady
Minto, 'he never brings forward in conversation,' he
had established a considerable influence over the minds
of the rising generation; such as must always belong
to a teacher who inculcates high and generous principles
with the breadth of view and candour of opinion belonging to a highly cultivated intellect.   With him
and Mrs. Stewart the Minto family had established
relations of friendship, and in the summer of 1806
they visited Minto.

'Minto : June 5.

'The Stewarts and Lord Webb came yesterday. The
account they all give of the state of Edinburgh, and

indeed of Scotland in general, from the report spread far and wide of Lord Melville's acquittal and restoration to power, is far, far beyond what I have time to detail. The Land of Cakes has really gone crazy, and they say if he is acquitted they are determined to have an illumination in Edinburgh, Glasgow, &c.   I wish it may be so; as Ministers will then be convinced of the situation of this country, divided against itself by the strongest faction, the majority glorying in their protector having completely defeated the *malice*, as they call it, of Ministers, Lords, and Commons.   I do assure you that *insolent* party-spirit never went so far as on this occasion and in this part of the island.'

'Minto: June 22.

'I find the illuminations in Edinburgh for Lord Melville's acquittal were stopped by the Provost. Clerk went to him and informed him the people from Leith highly disapproved, and there was some apprehension of a mob; and so the candles were ordered to be snuffed out, after he had given notice all good subjects might illuminate.'

It was at a public dinner [1] in honour of Lord Melville's acquittal that was sung a song composed by Walter Scott, which gave just and general offence.

Of the circumstances Lady Minto received an account from Mr. Dugald Stewart.

---

[1] Given in Edinburgh on the 27th June.

From Dugald Stewart to Lady Minto.

' I send you Walter Scott's song, my dear Lady Minto. There was another written by him and sung likewise, but he seems to have taken fright about it, for he won't give any copies. The chorus was : " Since Melville's got justice may the Devil take *Law !* " The applause that followed the song was so great that it was a quarter of an hour before silence could be restored. The Justice-clerk and most of the Judges were present, all the Barons of the Exchequer, all the Commissaries, all the Board of Customs, and most of the Excise. One toast is much talked of; it was given by one of the Judges of the Commissary Court—" May the oppression of the House of Commons ever be repressed by the House of Peers." This was said to be thrice drunk in compliment to its peculiar merit. Some of the party boasted that the songs and toasts would be in yesterday's papers, but they seem to think twice of that.'

' I do assure you,' added Lady Minto, ' that Mr. Stewart's letters are no more than the real truth. England has no idea of the state of Scotland.'

She wrote again :—

' July 6.

' We agree entirely about Walter Scott's song. It is in itself below par. If his place had not been for life he would have saved his character; but it is a proof of the delirium of Edinburgh that he should be so led away by the hue and cry, and so blind to the effects it would produce against him.

' I send you another song of his, worse, if possible, in all respects than the first.   Hugh Scott and all his friends are quite outrageous against him ; there never was anything more wrong-headed or wrong-hearted.'

Some time before the trial of Lord Melville came to an end, it was apparent that the result could only be acquittal; and in the London world the interest it had once excited had been attracted to another enquiry into the conduct of a more exalted personage, and into matters of a still more delicate character.

Lord Minto to Lady Minto.

('Secret.)   'London: June 9, 1806.

' You will be very much shocked and hurt to hear that a most serious proceeding is commenced against the Princess of Wales.   On Saturday last, at nine in the morning, the Duke of Kent arrived at Blackheath and told her that some injurious reports affecting her had reached the King's ears; and that he had thought it necessary to appoint a Commission to enquire into the truth of them.   The Commissioners are Lord Grenville, Lord Spencer, the Lord Chancellor, and Lord Ellenborough ;—that he (the Duke of Kent) had been requested, from delicacy towards her, to be the bearer of this painful intelligence ; and that he was to desire that six of her servants should attend the Commission that forenoon.   Accordingly her own German maid and two other maid-servants, her butler or servant out of livery (Sicand), and two footmen, were sent and were examined.

The Princess, under this shock, had the astonishing courage and fortitude to keep her engagement that very day to dine in town at Lady Carnarvon's, where I was one of the company, and she told me this story in the middle of the circle, though not overheard. Lady Sheffield and Lady Carnarvon knew it, but nobody else. She had appointed a great dinner at Blackheath for the French Princes, on Sunday (yesterday). This dinner took place also, and I was of the party. Windham and I went together. He had heard, though the whole proceeding is extremely secret, that nothing material had come out. Some indiscretions, but nothing serious. There is reason to believe Sir John and Lady Douglas are at the bottom of this attack upon the Princess. Sir John Douglas had obtained a house in Greenwich Park, which the Princess took, or wanted to take, from them, to give, I think, to Miss Cholmondeley, when the Princess was made Ranger. Sir John was furious, and sent her, I hear, a threatening letter at the time. This is fortunate, and may give an odious turn to the enquiry and a favourable one to her. Yesterday she again contrived to give me and Windham these particulars. She imputes the whole to Sir John Douglas and his Lady, and acquits the Prince and Mrs. Fitzherbert. She says there is no sort of question which was not asked of her servants, but as there is no truth in the charge, they had nothing to tell. She seemed more composed than the day before. However, I do not suppose the matter will rest here, and the enquiry will probably proceed. What is most unpleasant in the transaction is, that one can hardly conceive so strong and shocking a step to have been taken without a great deal of consideration and previous information. Yet all one knows of her unreserved and indiscreet manners may make one understand how an unfavourable judgment may have been formed without any *real* foundation.'

'House of Lords: June 10, 1806.

' We are all collected here on an appeal from a decree of the late Chancellor concerning the guardian of Lord Hugh Seymour's orphan child. . . .

'I am sorry that I have not been able to learn anything further of the distressing business of which I told you yesterday. Lord Spencer, who is sitting at this table, could tell me if he would. But I must not even ask him or be thought to know the business. I am apprehensive that the enquiry is proceeding. But I trust nothing will result from it to justify the strong imputations which must be supposed to have given' rise to so shocking and affronting a proceeding. The discussion of Lord Melville's impeachment will end tonight, and judgment will be given in Westminster Hall either on Thursday or Saturday. There is every appearance of his acquittal on all the articles, but it is somewhat doubtful on one or two of them.'

'Arlington: June 16, 1806.

' The town is thinning very fast. Lord Hugh Seymour's daughter is committed to the guardianship of Lord Hertford, who is certainly the natural person, and who will leave her with Mrs. Fitzherbert as much as she pleases. The House of Lords made a very discreditable appearance on this occasion, attending in great numbers, at the solicitation or command of the Prince of Wales. He desired me to attend a good while ago, and I was there the first day of the pleadings; but the affair—I mean the attendance of lay lords in crowds on a judicial business—appeared to me so scandalous that I returned no more, for which the Prince will not soon or easily forgive me. The decision was, however, fI believe, perfectly right. The Prince wanted Mrs. Fitzherbert to be guardian, but that was too strong even for the House of Lords.'

'June 18.

'Another Eden marriage that will give you pleasure —Kitty to Mr. Vansittart, secretary of the Treasury, an excellent man and very clever and pleasant. This broke out yesterday: he is nearly related to Colonel Vansittart, who married Caroline Eden yesterday. There is so much billing and cooing of Vansittarts at Eden Farm, that the family has got the name of *Vansweethearts*. Louisa will be married in a few days. Fitzharris was married yesterday, and is gone to Broadlands for the honeymoon. I dined and slept last night at Holland House, and return there today. Lord Henry Petty was the flower of yesterday's flock, and Miss Fox, who is extremely agreeable, sensible, and I believe good.'

'June 25.

' I fear that the affair of the Princess of Wales is
going forward.   Miss Cholmondeley, who should not be
quoted, told me to-day that yesterday and the day before
she was extremely agitated and talked very seriously
of going back to Brunswick.   Windham dissuaded
her strongly, saying it would be to plead guilty and
abandon her reputation.   For my own part, as nothing
but humiliation and affronts attends her here, or is
likely to attend her, I do not feel so clear that for her
own comfort and tranquillity it would be so unwise a
measure.   I am really grieved for her.   Her treatment
from the beginning has been afflicting and insulting ;
and the prospect, instead of brightening, is more gloomy
and threatening than ever.'

The chief advisers of the Princess at this time were
Lord Eldon—and Mr. Spencer Perceval.   It is well
known that under their auspices was drawn up ' *the
book* '—' A Narrative of the Circumstances and Proceedings upon the Subject of the Inquiry into the Conduct
of the Princess of Wales, with a Statement of recent
Events '—and it is also known that the threat of publication alarmed the Ministry for their existence, and
the Royal Family for their credit.   While this painful
business was going on, Lady Malmesbury, feeling
warmly for the miserable position in which the Princess
was placed, became far more assiduous in her attentions
to Her Royal Highness than she had ever been before.
She paid frequent visits to Blackheath, where she

generally met Mr. Spencer Perceval, and after one of
these visits she carried him to town in her carriage. As
they drove along she remarked with her usual playful
exaggeration: 'I believe, Mr. Perceval, we might be
sent to the Tower for what we have been doing to-day.'
'To the Tower, or to the scaffold in such a cause!'
was the enthusiastic reply. Within little more than a
year, Mr. Perceval and Lord Eldon were in office, and
on the announcement that 'the Book' would shortly
appear in print they, having dropped all sentimental pre-
dilections for the Princess, the Tower and the scaffold,
determined to suppress it without loss of time. Lord
Thurlow, an earlier friend, is said to have advised the
'investigation.' 'Put not your trust in princes' said
the Psalmist, but the second clause of the same verse
was surely addressed to them: 'nor in any of the sons
of men.'

The last topic we have named as treated of in the
letters of 1806 was one which in process of time
effaced all others in interest—the appointment of a
Governor-General of India. On the accession of the
Coalition Government of Lord Grenville and Fox, the
latter desired to send his friend, Lord Lauderdale, to
India, and the Ministry acquiesced in this desire,
though not without hesitation, for they were well
aware that the reputation of Lord Lauderdale, who as
'Citizen Maitland' had made himself conspicuous
for the extravagance of his opinions, was not calculated
to impress the public mind with the propriety of the
selection. The Court of Directors, however, objected

strongly to the appointment ; and after lengthy negotiations, conducted with considerable heat on both sides,
they determined to negative it, should it be made.   Mr.
Fox therefore urgently represented to Lord Grenville
that a persistence in this policy on the part of the
Directors ought to be considered as a decided act of
opposition to the Ministry, and not as one of simple
hostility to Lord Lauderdale ; and that in pursuance of
this view, the Government should refuse to nominate
anybody, leaving the Directors to please themselves.

Lord Grenville, however, demurred to a course of
action which would have enlisted against his administration so important an interest as that of the Court of
Directors ; and it was finally arranged that Lord
Lauderdale should resign his pretensions, (which he did
the more readily from a desire not to agitate Mr. Fox,
already very ill, by further discussion,) and that Lord
Grenville should make a new nomination.   He at once
expressed to Lord Minto his earnest desire to confer
the appointment upon him, coupling this intimation
with the assurance that the nomination would be approved by the Government, the Directors, and the
public.   The offer was on this occasion decidedly refused by Lord Minto ; but when, a few weeks later,
Lord Grenville returned to the subject, assuring Lord
Minto that ' there was nobody else who would thoroughly answer the public wishes and those of the
Government, that he alone could extricate the Ministry from a position of considerable embarrassment,
with a great deal more in the same strain,' the result

of the conversation was an engagement on the part
of Lord Minto to fully reconsider the question in
his own mind, and to take his family into the consultation. Accordingly he wrote to Lady Minto at
length ; and after stating the causes which had made
his acceptance of the proposed nomination a matter of
importance to the Ministry and the Court of Directors,
he went on : 'Now comes the domestic deliberation, and
that is exactly the greatest conflict to which my mind
could ever, or in any possible question, be put. My
own personal comforts, enjoyments, and happiness can
be preserved only at home with yourself and the children. On the other hand, the general benefit of all
those who depend on me for comforts that extend
beyond my own short period, would undoubtedly be
best provided for by this measure ; and the ultimate
happiness of witnessing the fruits of that sacrifice is
certainly not out of possibility, or, I might say, of fair
probability. It is a question so painful to decide, that
it would be natural to wish it might be determined for
me. But I cannot put that task upon you. I must,
however, add that my mind would be entirely settled
by a positive opinion or desire of yours, and that if,
after weighing everything, you express a wish against
it, that will be decisive.' The peculiar painfulness of
the impending decision consisted in the knowledge
that acceptance of the appointment involved a separation of the husband from the wife, and the father
from his family, for a period of several years, and that
at a time when letters from India were six months old,

and occasionally much more, before they came to hand.
In any part of Europe they would have remained together, but it was believed that a tropical climate
would be fatal to Lady Minto and could not be otherwise than most injurious to the constitutions of her
young daughters.   The question therefore of their
going out to India was never discussed.   On the
following day he wrote again, reviewing the reasons
which weighed with him for and against acceptance
of the appointment, and ending thus: 'There is
the hope of becoming the instrument of great and
extensive good. I do not include among the attractions of this object its greatness and splendour; for
I am sure you will believe me when I say that sort
of ambition is no longer new enough to me to captivate
my imagination, and that, on the contrary, all that
belongs to splendour is a real fatigue and annoyance
to me.   But most of all I hope you are firmly convinced
that no personal passion, such as ambition, could weigh
a single grain in the balance against the love I bear
you, my affection for the children, and the delight with
which I have been looking forward to a greater share
of your and their company than I have had for many
years, and the real wretchedness with which I look to this
separation, so much greater in point of time and distance than any former absence.   Amongst the allevia-
tions of such evils I should think of John, and of his
living with me. *Possibly* George might carry me out,
and William say I am a nice old fellow, as he did of

Lord Cornwallis.   To-morrow I shall have your letter:
your clear and positive wish will decide me.'

When the expected letter came, it was seen that
Lady Minto had been unequal to the task of putting
in writing the decision to which her good sense led her.
She had therefore deputed it to her eldest son.   In his
letter, expressing, not a wish, but a clear opinion of
acceptance, was enclosed the following note from his
mother :—

'You will easily believe, wrote Lady Minto to Lord
Minto, that your letter has agitated me too much
for me to be able to collect my opinions so as to
put them as hastily as the post requires on paper.
Gilbert has just left me to write, and will tell you his
opinions, which must be mine, though certainly against
all my natural feelings and wishes.   I see even at this
moment the importance of the request Lord Grenville
has made to you, and all I can say is, that I beg you
to follow your own opinions, placing me entirely out of
the question.   I certainly do consider it as the greatest
sacrifice of private comfort to public duty; and as I
feel perfectly convinced that in acquiescing with Lord
Grenville's request you put all your own feelings out
of the question, I cannot have a right to consider my
own, nor would I on any account stand on that ground,
either towards you, our children, or the public.   I
really cannot write more to-day.'

A few days later Lord Minto was proposed by the

Government, and accepted with flattering readiness by the Directors. On the 30th of June he wrote:—
'This event being now, after much reflection, decided, I will not yield to the feelings which I cannot but experience, but will proceed as manfully and gallantly as I can.'

And he kept his word. The remaining letters written during the session are all occupied, as heretofore, with the subjects of the day, some public, others personal, though the latter are not of a nature to be admissible here.

Lord Minto to Lady Minto.

'London: July 11, 1806.

'I dined yesterday at Sheridan's (the Navy Pay Office) to meet the Prince of Wales, who is as civil to me as ever, notwithstanding my weekly visit to Blackheath, where I dine literally every Sunday. Mrs. Fitzherbert is very ill—considered dangerously so, and the Prince went off to her directly after dinner. Sheridan seemed fuddled at the beginning and drunk at the end; he flummeried me so much that I am clear he wants something. The Enquiry still proceeds; the Princess thinks it is kept going till Parliament rises to prevent discussion there.'

'July 14.

'On Saturday I attended the opening of the West India Export Docks, and we had a very beautiful day. The whole of the work is now finished, and it is a most magnificent one, especially as the enterprise of private individuals. It was to cost 1,200,000*l.*, and answers already perfectly to the proprietors who draw about 8 per cent for their money. It has been exactly six years in completing. The first stone was laid by Mr. Pitt, Lord Rosslyn, and some others, on Saturday, July 12, 1800, and we saw the Export Dock opened on Saturday, July 12, 1806.

'I could not have had a successor (at the Board of Control) more agreeable to me than Tom Grenville.'

'July 26, 1806.

'I dined and slept at Holland House yesterday to take leave. Lord Holland's book on the Spanish Literature is coming out next week and will I daresay be very good and interesting. Mr. Fox is as ill as possible, though they continue to say every now and then that he is better. The Russians have made peace in a hurry and shabbily towards us, who have always refused to treat separately from them. This will either prevent our peace, or increase the difficulties. I flatter myself if we do make peace that it will contain nothing like humiliating conditions or concessions ; but a peace, however honourable the conditions may apparently be, is an experiment not free from danger in the present crisis of Europe.

'I dined and slept on Saturday at Sir George Shee's : a great company with the Duke of Gloucester at their head. As soon as the cloth was removed Windham fell fast asleep ; so sound that an hour afterwards I attempted in vain to rouse him by speaking pretty loud near his ear, " Parish Bill—Limited Service,—Volunteers," &c. &c., but nothing moved him.   This continued till we retired to coffee about nine o'clock, when the Duke of Gloucester singled him out and took him into a corner of the drawing-room.   Everybody immediately withdrew into the next room, with the door open, and left the poor stricken deer to his fate, rejoiced that it was not ourselves.   He remained under this protracted operation till *past twelve*.   We could see him from the other room without being seen by the Duke, and we went by turns to observe the picture of suffering and misery which his whole figure and face exhibited.   He was the very picture of Count Ugolino.   The Duke of Gloucester is famous for inflicting this sort of slow torture.   Sir Evan Nepean dropt down the other day under it on the floor apparently dead, and being revived by cold water sprinkled in his face and by cordials, as soon as he was a little recovered *the Duke took him again.*'

At the end of July Lord Minto was once more, and for the last time, at Minto.   He returned there to find that even the great change which had taken place in his own prospects and anticipations since he left it six months before, was second in interest to another which was about to determine the future lot of his eldest son. There was something almost ominous in the simultaneousness of the events which sent the father to a distant land, and gave the son the headship of the family at home.

On the very day on which the letters announcing Lord Grenville's second and most urgent offer of the appointment to Bengal were received at Minto, others had been sent to London to communicate 'one of the most material events in a man's life'—the engagement of Gilbert Elliot to Miss Brydone. On the following day Lady Minto wrote that 'he was deeply distressed to find that he had added, by what he calls his selfish feelings, to the over-occupation of your mind.' But such regrets were as rapidly dispelled as posts and distance permitted, and a few days only elapsed before she wrote again : 'Your delightful letters have occasioned great joy in the house. The certainty of your approbation doubled Gilbert's happiness, and he went off to Lennel at once. I wrote to " Mary," telling her she cannot be more in love with him than I have been for the last three and twenty years.'

There are affections and tender recollections still clinging round the memory of her who then entered the family to deepen every joy and lighten every burden, which make all that relates to her matter too sacred for publicity. It is not, therefore, to make known a character which, shrinking from observation, was best seen in the light it shed on others, but simply to complete the portraiture of those who received her in their home that we give here the following letter from Lady Minto to her husband :—

'Mary is beautiful, but her beauty is not her principal merit, as she is universally said to have a temper as fair as her face. Her family doat on her and have brought her up with simple tastes, which will not jar with Gilbert's; so that we shall gain a daughter and not lose a son, which might have been the case had she been a London lady, apt to think Scotland a desert. Her life has been so retired that with all the love of a ball which belongs to her age, she has a great many other resources and pleasures, and her education having been carried on by her father and mother, has been much better and more useful in every way than the mere produce of masters and governesses. She is now the teacher of her sisters, which looks well for the future charge of her children. Gilbert might of course have made what is called a more advantageous alliance; but you will agree with me in thinking this a matter of no importance compared to the material advantages of character, of disposition, and similarity of tastes. Gilbert's happiness is the first object.

'Mr. Brydone [1] is a man of first-rate attainments and accomplishments, and his wife, a delightful person, is a daughter of Principal Robertson.'[2]

Lord Minto was present at the marriage of his son in August 1806. The rest of the summer was spent with his family.

No letters remain to record the features of that time;

---

[1] Author of *Tour in Sicily and Malta*.

[2] Author of a *History of Charles V.*, of a *History of America*, and of other works. Mrs. Brydone and Mrs. Brougham, mother of Henry, first Lord Brougham, were first cousins.

but perhaps no letters could record the blending of pain
and pleasure which those last few months must have
produced—pain which none experience but those who
have lived long enough to value what they lose, and to
know that all things may be, save what have been.

He sailed for India in December 1806.

There, for the present, we do not intend to follow
him. Though no biography of Lord Minto could pretend to completeness which should stop short of the
most distinguished and successful phase of his career,
the case is different as regards his correspondence ; the
interest of its European and Indian portions being
entirely independent of each other.

Moreover, Lord Minto's administration of the government of India forms a chapter in the History of
the British Empire. Historians have done justice to
the energetic policy by which he swept England's
ancient rival from the Eastern seas, and added Java
and the Isles of France and Bourbon to British dependencies ;[1] they have related with equal approbation the successes of his internal administration and
his earnest personal sympathy in the labours of those
who were striving to raise the moral and mental condition of the people of India.[2] Hence no injustice is
done to his memory by withholding for a while a correspondence which, as dealing with scenes, men, and

[1] For these services he was created Earl of Minto and Viscount
Melgund.
[2] See Wilson's continuation of Mill's *History of British India*, *Kaye's
Indian Officers*, and other works.

interests totally distinct and different from those which have become familiar to us, is perhaps better fitted to appear as a sequel to the present volumes than to be incorporated with them.

The political career of Lord Minto in Europe ended with the year which closed the lives of England's two great statesmen, Pitt and Fox. The first of these events terminated the peculiar position of the Whigs who had attached themselves to Pitt during the revolutionary war. The second was speedily followed by the break-up of the Administration, and all the purposes and objects for which Lord Minto and his political friends had worked for years seemed for a while defeated. The power of Bonaparte had reached its apogee. The Ministers of Great Britain were henceforth, and for many a day, 'small statues on great bases,' but the policy of greater men had been adopted by the nation at large, and to it their allegiance never faltered.[1] Though fraud and force were all-powerful in Europe, and too many forgot that

> ' An *accursed* thing it is to gaze
> On prosperous tyrants with a dazzled eye,[2]

England and her rulers held on their way, steadfast in resolution, strong in determination, until their efforts

---

[1] 'I have always observed,' wrote Pozzo di Borgo to Lord Minto in 1806, 'that in England, in a far greater degree than elsewhere, a vigorous and energetic policy is that which best commends itself to the nation. A half-hearted pusillanimous policy, such as has unfortunately not been unfrequently adopted by English administrations, has never been popular, and has often led to the overthrow of its authors.'

[2] Wordsworth.

were crowned with success. In the very moment of hard-won triumph Lord Minto returned to England, where the allied sovereigns had met to celebrate the downfall of Napoleon ; but from national rejoicings, from personal honours, and even from the joyous welcome of children and family and friends, his thoughts turned longingly homewards, where his wife waited for him in redemption of a pledge, given when they parted, that their re-union should take place at Minto, thenceforth to become the abiding-home of their remaining years. Vain words ! Such as stir to scorn the unseen powers who dispose of mortal fate.

A chill, caught at the funeral of Lord Auckland, suddenly developed the seeds of a disease already latent in his system. Having hurried away from London in spite of medical advice, he grew rapidly worse, and sank at Stevenage, on the first stage of his journey to Scotland, in the presence of the elder members of his family. It fell to the lot of the son [1] who had accompanied him from India to carry down the mournful and incredible tidings to the country alive with preparations for his reception. In the town of Hawick the people were in readiness to draw his carriage through the streets ; on the hills the bonfires were laid, and under triumphal arches the message of death was borne to her who waited at home.

---

[1] John Elliot, third son of Lord Minto.

APPENDIX.

I.

Abstract of a Speech of Lord Minto in the House of Peers on certain resolutions of censure on the conduct of H.M.'s Ministers moved by Earl Fitzwilliam, June 6, 1803.

THE opening paragraphs of the speech contain an exposition of the views held by Lord Minto in common with the party he voted with on the character and results of the treaty of Amiens.

Describing it as a real and actual continuation of the war, which it only pretended to terminate, 'the measure before them was,' he said, 'entitled to the support of those who had been calling out virtually for war, with the same zeal and in the same spirit as other men invoke peace. When I say in the same spirit, I mean that we have done so for the purpose of terminating what has appeared to us the destructive and ruinous war of Amiens; for we cannot describe by any other word a transaction the sole effect of which has been to cast away our own sword without sheathing for a moment that of the enemy: a transaction which has left us to endure all the disgraces, all the humiliations, all the losses and disasters which might follow successive defeats and lost battles, suspending only the possibility of victory, of glory, or advantage.' Premising that the justification of the war had been placed on narrower ground than he approved, he proceeded to examine 'the immediate and actual occasion of the rupture,' the question relative to Malta :—

'The question respecting Malta may be stated in a very few words; and when distinctly understood, it appears to me entirely free from doubt, and to furnish a certain and even indisputable conclusion. When these two nations, Great Britain and the French republic, met for the purpose of adjusting their differences and restoring peace, each government advanced a principle of its own concerning Malta to which they have respectively and invariably adhered, from which neither has ever departed or even receded a hair's breadth in any moment of the negotiation, nor in any article, word, or syllable of the engagements by which they bound themselves to each other. The principle stated and insisted on by the French government was perfectly simple and could not be misunderstood. They required the departure of the British troops from Malta, and they have never at any period relaxed in this peremptory demand. The French government has, therefore, a clear incontestable right to regard the evacuation of Malta by the British troops as a fundamental condition of peace, without which the treaty ceases to be binding on them.

'On the other hand, Great Britain insisted with the same steadiness on the principle in which we are interested, namely, that Malta should be placed in a state of absolute independence of France, and that we should obtain a full and perfect security against its reoccupation by French troops after the departure of our own. From this principle we have never swerved, and we have been as tenacious of our claim as the other party has been pertinacious in theirs. It must no doubt have appeared difficult to reconcile demands apparently so much at variance with each other. The desire of peace, however, prevailed so far, on our side at least, that this puzzling problem was attempted, and its solution was supposed to have been found in the tenth article of the treaty of Amiens.

.   .   .   .   .   .

'The tenth article, ineffectual as it has proved, the tenth article, of which I may now say without offence, repudiated as it is by its parents, that it has been the laughing-stock of Europe, and has excited from its birth the mirth as well as the wonder of the world, I must candidly admit, appears to me to have been not less adapted to its purpose than any other that could have been framed. For in truth the purpose was unattainable, and manifestly unattainable from the beginning. What was that purpose? It was to keep the French out of Malta without a British garrison. These two things I boldly state to have been from the first absolutely incompatible with each other; I mean the departure of the British troops, and the subsequent exclusion of the French. In the state of Europe as it was left by the peace of Lunéville, and was about to be established by the peace of Amiens, he must have possessed a very singular judgment who could amuse himself for a moment with the imagination that the grand-master and his knights of the Order of St. John of Jerusalem, that a few Neapolitans, and that the signature of a thing called a guarantee by all the courts, kingdoms, and republics of Europe could retard the resumption of Malta by one French demibrigade, one week after the ships that carried them had eluded the British squadron in the Mediterranean.

'Austria, the only Power in which, from similarity of interests, we have any reason to confide, that has acceded to this guarantee, did more than guarantee; she stipulated the independence of Switzerland, and in the maintenance of that article she had herself a deep concern. Your lordships will probably ere long have more experience of the security afforded to countries which come within the scope of French ambition by the guarantee of the sovereigns who still reign in Europe. I respect the sovereigns of Europe, and might confide, perhaps, in the sincerity of some of them, at the moment in which they should contract the loose, undefined, and always illusory engagement called a guarantee to the arrangements made between two other Powers. But who shall promise to this assurance, even such as it is, the stability due to an interest so great and so permanent as that which we are considering? The Power on which we might securely rest to-day, for the protection and even the custody of Malta, is to-morrow, perhaps, engaged in some new or revived quarrel with this country, in some new or revived confederacy with France, to cut up our power by the roots, to shake the very pillars and foundations of our empire. What, then, becomes of Malta? . . .

'But, my lords, if the provision made for the independence of Malta was insufficient at the date of the treaty, it is become yet more impossible to provide for the same object now. What is the foundation of our solicitude concerning Malta? It is an apprehension that the possession of that island would facilitate the projects of the French government, first against Egypt, then against our possessions in India. But against these ulterior dangers we possessed, at the date of the treaty, several securities apart from those of the tenth article. First, the just and moderate character, and pacific and friendly disposition, of the French Consular government; next the express renunciation of the particular designs upon Egypt falsely imputed by prejudice and malice to that government. . . .

'We now learn from H.M.'s declaration that the Consular government has been discovered to have some share of ambition, and that it has even fallen off from its affection for England. We learn also that, instead of renouncing the views on Egypt and India which the First Consul had forsworn at Amiens, an official avowal has been made of them to His Majesty's Ambassador at Paris. To this total change of circumstances, which has fallen so unexpectedly on our Ministers, must be added another novelty which I myself allow to be a change.

' France has made very considerable conquests during the *war* of Amiens, and has extended her dominion more particularly in the Mediterranean, that is to say, in the quarter where her new territories and resources are most applicable to the promotion of those very views which it is most essential to our security that we should counteract. The danger, therefore, against which we are now to provide, being much greater than that to which the tenth article was opposed, that security, even if we could possess it, would no longer be of equal value, and we may reasonably require additional defences proportioned to the growth of the danger.

. . . . . .

' Thus, then, the question stands respecting Malta. On one hand, France is entitled to claim the departure of our troops. I say France is entitled to insist on this demand, but not *by virtue* of the treaty of Amiens. She is entitled to require it, *notwithstanding* the treaty of Amiens. She has not barred herself from that demand, or from making it a condition *sine quâ non* of peace. I entreat the attention of your lordships to this distinction. The demand can be founded only on her right as it stood anterior to the negotiation, and as it still subsists unrenounced by the treaty; but it is equally clear that the pure and simple evacuation of Malta cannot be demanded of us under any of the engagements which we subscribed at Amiens. For, on the contrary, we, on the other hand, are entitled to retain possession of Malta under the clearest and most distinct stipulations of that treaty, since we engaged to withdraw our troops only on conditions which neither have been nor can be fulfilled. What follows? I mean what follows closely and logically from these circumstances? The clear conclusion is, that the conditions of this essential article of the treaty of peace having proved impracticable, and the opposite interests, or views of those interests, entertained by the two nations, continuing by this manner unsatisfied and uncompromised, each party remains, as before the treaty, at liberty to pursue his own advantage according to his own judgment, and both return precisely to the point at which this ineffectual negotiation found them, that is to say, to a state of warfare and hostility. All that can be said on either side is, that these great and clashing interests have been found hitherto irreconcilable; that the attempt which has been made, let us say, sincerely by both parties, to adjust them and to bring about a pacification, has failed. The tenth article has proved abortive, but this miscarriage is fatal to the whole treaty of which that section was an essential and vital part. We may, indeed, begin anew, and look for some other means to adjust our differences, but this is optional, and if declined by one of the parties, no complaint nor any claim of the other can be built on the treaty of Amiens, which, by the loss of one essential member, has expired, or rather may be said to have been still-born, and never to have existed in perfect life or vigour. In truth it appears to me most evident that the affair of Malta could not and cannot be adjusted by nego- tiation. Negotiation can only devise or discover the terms on which the reconciliation of reconcilable interests may be effected, but where the interests are truly opposite and contradictory, then an adjustment can be obtained only by a renunciation of these on one side or the other. Now such a consequence seems rather to be expected from war and its events, than from diplomatic controversies. While the French government retains the design of conquering Egypt and disturbing India, her negotiators cannot consent to our possessing Malta; on the other hand, while we are determined to exclude the French from Egypt, and to defend our empire in the East, we cannot part with Malta. The events of war may induce France to renounce or moderate her ambition, or may compel us to renounce our empire and existence, but until one of these changes is operated, until France becomes just or Great Britain is content to be her province, this point must be contested by the sword. It is not on the individual question of Malta alone that I have formed these sentiments concerning the utter impossibility of a sincere peace with France in the present circumstances. They were founded on a general view of her known character and of her manifest designs, earlier even than the fatal conferences between Lord Hawkesbury and Mr. Otto. When I have been asked whether reports concerning negotiations for peace were true, I remember well that I answered, and answered as I thought, "I cannot believe them, because neither nation appears yet in a condition that makes reconciliation possible. France is triumphant everywhere on the continent of Europe, and is accustomed to think the success of her wildest projects infallible. She is not then sufficiently humbled and distressed to renounce her general scheme of universal empire, or her dearest hope, the favourite passion of her heart, the overthrow of the British empire. Neither is England less triumphant on her element, and in the proper scenes of her exertion. She, too, is yet unhumbled and unbeaten; she is not yet reduced to the last necessity of yielding terms incompatible with the views, character, and present condition of her enemy." '

Upon this part of the argument followed a consideration of the causes which had rendered Malta an indispensable possession of Great Britain, and obliged us to retain it, though the alternative was stated by the French government in plain categorical terms, Malta or war.' But from argu-

ments so universally admitted as not to need recapitulation,
we pass to Lord Minto's view of the 'real justification and
undeniable necessity of the war.' 'I say, my lords, and
I say it in the language of H.M.'s manifesto, it consists in
the immense and still growing aggrandisement of France
since the conclusion of the peace. This is the ground on
which I rest the present rupture. This is the change,
operated as it has been by the other party, which furnishes
the clearest right to reject a treaty assented to in different
circumstances, and to require a fresh adjustment of our
respective interests, adapted to the exigencies of our
present situation, and unprejudiced by former but now inapplicable engagements.

.   .   .   .   .   .

'A treaty of peace which terminates a general and extensive war, has in contemplation the relative condition of the
parties, in power and territory, at the time of concluding
the peace. . . . Nothing is more certain than that the
future security and prosperity of this country was, in
reality and effect, more or less measured by the extent of
power and territory left to France by the peace; and
nothing is more certain than that a considerable addition
to the power of France must of necessity and of course
have operated a proportional diminution of the security and
prosperity of England. . . .' Lord Minto having proceeded
to discuss the examples of interference on the part of
certain of the states of Europe for the purpose of prohibit-
ing the growth of any particular Power, went on to say:
'Society at large is interested in maintaining a balance of
power amongst nations, for the purpose of imposing a check
and restraint on ambitious rapacity, and as a protection of
the weak against the strong. It is by the force of this
principle that small or moderate states, and even single
independent cities, have stood for centuries unshaken in
the midst of great military and ambitious Powers. The

guarantee of the greater Powers, founded on the principle of the balance, that is to say, on their mutual jealousy and apprehension of each other, and not the walls or moats, not the rusty artillery and the train-band garrisons of those free cities, has been their sole defence, and has alone perpetuated for ages their insulated freedom. The principle was that honourable as well as wise one, of a common cause; and that useful and social sympathy amongst nations which made the remotest from the danger thrill with the first aggression against the most distant and the weakest, as if the blow had struck themselves. Of late such blows have indeed been watched, and have excited their due portion of jealousy, but instead of honest and prudent opposition, that jealousy has awakened only the emulation of competitors. If one great Power enslaves a neighbour of the second or third order, none fly to its rescue, none avenge the common wrong, but all start in the same chase and run down each the victim which crosses its way. The balance is disturbed, and must be restored, not by snatching the plunder out of the sinking scale, but by heaping a counterpoise of rapine into their own. Does France seize on Brabant or Luxembourg, Prussia must seize on Munster and dismember Westphalia. Does an elector secularise, that is to say, rob and plunder a Bishopric, a neighbouring Margrave or Landgrave must devour a compensation of abbeys and priories. The balance, therefore, instead of curbing, bridling, and muzzling ambition, acts as a spur to goad and stimulate its fury. It has in effect unhooded and turned loose the eagles and vultures of Europe on its dovecots and sheepfolds. This is not the principle which I reclaim against France to-day: I claim what has never yet been denied, the right to challenge the daily conquests of France, to cry halt! to the conqueror in his career, to oppose it foot to foot and hand to hand, and if I cannot arrest his course in one quarter, to re-establish the impaired security of our own empire at the expense, not of innocent and independent countries, but of that very France herself, and of her subject and vassal adherents.

.   .   .   .   .   .

' France has conquered, annexed to her dominion or reduced to a state of dependence and vassalage, in our own time and under our eye, the Low Countries, the United Provinces, the left bank of the Rhine, Switzerland ; Savoy, the county of Nice, Piedmont ; the territories comprised within the denomination of the Italian republic, including the whole of Lombardy, the Roman legations, and part of the ancient territory of Venice ; the Ligurian republic, that is to say, the territory, the city and port of Genoa, the Duchy of Parma and its dependencies; the duchies of Massa and Carrara, the republic of Lucca, the duchy of Modena, the grand duchy of Tuscany, and in truth the whole Roman state, while the kingdom of Naples, but a little more remote, is scarcely more secure ; and the catalogue might be closed, though but for the moment in which I am speaking, with the island of Elba, if I did not feel that your lordships may perhaps expect me to add to this list of dependents, the whole Spanish monarchy.

' I know the controversy that has always existed in this country on the question of the continental system, and on the expediency of entering into wars, or continuing them, for what is called the balance of power. But while the wisest and weightiest opinions have acknowledged the interests of these islands to be inseparable from the affairs of the continent, and while the nation has sanctioned that system and borne witness to its absolute necessity by frequent exertions and sacrifices, I would ask whether the most sanguine advocate of the insulated system ever maintained, that the total destruction of all balance whatever was a thing indifferent to Great Britain ? . . . Where is the statesman to be found, who, in the spirit of the most insulated policy has ever maintained that the accession of the Netherlands to France was not a danger to Great Britain which it was prudent to repel by arms? When the separation of the Low Countries from France has been thought an interest worthy of being vindicated by war, our main consideration has been that the possession of those countries exposed the United Provinces to a similar dependence on France.

'Shall we then hesitate now in esteeming the subjection of both those countries under the dominion and control of France worthy of a contest? Add to these acquisitions all the many populous and martial countries, and the many fortified places comprised between the whole frontier of France and the Rhine. . . . Next throw Switzerland into the scale, and weigh the danger against the exertion once more. Turn now to Italy. The invasion of Italy by France has been felt in all times to be an event too interesting to admit of our neutrality. Compare the progress of France in that quarter, which has in former periods provoked the resistance of England, with the dominion she has now established there, and the preparation and promptitude in which she stands to extend it. Is not this sufficient of itself to interest this insular commercial country? It interests us deeply in commerce as well as in security. Add, then, this southern empire to her acquisitions in the North, and France presents a mass of power not such as disturbs a nicely-adjusted balance, but such as leaves none whatever. such as becomes formidable to the whole world, and brings the scheme of universal monarchy from the region of dreams and chimeras within the sphere of possible and almost probable views.

.   .   .   .

'It was contended (by the French negotiators of the treaty of Amiens) that because these kingdoms are surrounded by the sea, because this empire comprises some great and important dominions in the other quarters of the globe, because His Majesty commands a powerful and valorous navy, and because he reigns over an active, industrious, ingenious, flourishing, and commercial people : it was contended, I say, I know not by what new logic, that for all these reasons His Majesty and his people were not Europeans ; that they could have no concern in the affairs of the continent ; that the air of the terra firma is an element in which they could not breathe ; that it was impertinent in them to enquire or to busy themselves concerning the conduct of France, or any event that passes beyond the British Channel. These principles, insolent indeed beyond the utmost limits, no one should once have thought of British temper, but excellently fitting both the scope and the character of French ambition, were advanced first in the measures and conduct of their government, but soon (as the ministers now themselves inform us) in express and explicit terms.'

After a clear exposition of the principles and conduct of the two governments during the negotiations for peace, establishing the rapacity and fraud of the French, the speech ends thus :

' Let us negotiate anew as soon as a fit occasion offers. By fit occasion I mean one which may promise such a result as is consistent with our safety and honour ; and the sooner that happy hour arrives, it will be the more welcome.

' But even then, my lords, let us treat as becomes this great and independent nation. Let us conciliate the friendship and welcome the good offices of other governments ; let us concert, if you please, our claims and interests with other Powers ; let us treat in a congress of the world, if it can be done. The interests of the world and our own are in truth common. But let us not abdicate our own sacred trust. Let us not commit our own essential interests to any bosom, and to any hand, but our own. Let us treat, in a word, as principals and as sovereigns, by our own ministers directed by our own councils, not by the most honourable or friendly mediation that can be imagined in Europe. This word mediation is become harsh to my ear, and uneasy to my mind, since the mediations of Switzerland and of Germany. But, in truth, a foreign arbiter can neither be wanted, nor, as I think, be brooked, by this great country, which has wisdom to discern and power and spirit to enforce its own just claims.'

II.

WHILE vainly searching the Minto MSS. for some personal reminiscences of the lighting of the beacons I applied to a lady, a connection and a very intimate friend of the Elliot family, for any information which she might have received and preserved on the subject. In her reply she tells me that she was herself a witness of the scene, and that her memory retains a distinct impression of it at the present day. Herself a daughter of Lady Carnegie so often alluded to in the correspondence, she was at the time on a visit to her great-uncle the Admiral—whose most brilliant service had been performed during the administration of the first Pitt—and to his aged sister, who, in her youth, had sung the sad fate of the 'Flowers of the Forest,' and had lived to tremble lest those of her own garden should be swept away in the storm. With this aged pair their young kinswoman shared the suspense of that memorable January night, and though seventy years have passed since then, there hangs something of the gay audacity of youth about the recollections here recorded :—

'I was staying at Monteviot at the time, and Lord Minto was there for the night, having come over to see his uncle, who was indisposed. They had both retired early to their rooms, when the butler threw open the drawing-room door and made the startling announcement that the beacon-fires were lighted. Lord Minto was roused at once, ordered his carriage, and went off to Jedburgh, but before he went he said he was convinced there was no just ground for apprehension, and that it would prove to be either a mistake, or a false alarm to test the alacrity of the volunteers. This assurance was most satisfactory to the old aunts, but not so to me, for I was wild with excitement at the thoughts of the stirring events which would follow on an invasion by the French.

'Lord Minto found the town of Jedburgh as light as day, for the people had put lights in all their windows. The streets were crowded with volunteers. John Elliot was in command of a company, and, for that night only, his tutor was under his orders. Every man, high or low, was at his post. The people behaved admirably, and when it was discovered that a limekiln on fire had led to the error which had lighted the beacons on the Border hills for the first time for more than 200 years, disappointment was to a certain degree mingled with the more general sense of relief.

'When the excitement was over, a good deal of amusement was caused by the manner in which the news had been received in various places. At Wilton Lodge, where Lord Napier was then living, the butler made the usual announcement—"Supper is on the table—and —the beacons are lighted on the hills." At Selkirk, where Lord Home was in command of the volunteers, he called upon them to sing the old song which never failed to excite their enthusiasm : "Up with the souters of Selkirk, and down with the Earl of Home ; " and finding that none of them was able to do it, he sang it himself, for which he next day was enrolled a "souter" in due form.'
—*Letter from Mrs. Wauchope to Lady Minto.* 1870.

INDEX.

LONDON : PRINTED BY
SPOTTISWOODE AND CO., NEW-STREET SQUARE
AND PARLIAMENT STREET

LORD MACAULAY'S WORKS.

Various Editions kept on sale as follows:—

HISTORY *of* ENGLAND, *from the* ACCESSION *of* JAMES *the* SECOND:—

Student's Edition, 2 vols. crown 8vo. price 12s.
People's Edition, 4 vols. crown 8vo. 16s.
Cabinet Edition, 8 vols. post 8vo. 48s.
Library Edition, 5 vols. 8vo. £4.

CRITICAL *and* HISTORICAL ESSAYS:—

Traveller's Edition, ONE VOLUME, square crown 8vo. 21s.
People's Edition, 2 vols. crown 8vo. 8s.
Student's Edition, 1 vol. crown 8vo. 6s.
Cabinet Edition, 4 vols. post 8vo. 24s.
Library Edition, 3 vols. 8vo. 36s.

SIXTEEN ESSAYS, *reprinted separately:—*

Addison *and* Walpole, 1s.	Pitt *and* Chatham, 1s.
Frederick the Great, 1s.	Ranke *and* Gladstone, 1s.
Croker's Boswell's Johnson, 1s.	Milton *and* Macchiavelli, 6d.
Hallam's Constitutional History, 16mo. 1s. Fcp. 8vo. 6d.	Lord Bacon, 1s. Lord Clive, 1s.
Warren Hastings, 1s.	Lord Byron *and* the Comic Dramatists of the Restoration, 1s.

LAYS *of* ANCIENT ROME:—

Illustrated Edition, fcp. 4to. 21s.
With *Ivry* and *The Armada*, 16mo. 3s. 6d.
Miniature Illustrated Edition, imperial 16mo. 10s. 6d.

MISCELLANEOUS WRITINGS:—

Library Edition, 2 vols. 8vo. 21s.
People's Edition, ONE VOLUME, crown 8vo. 4s. 6d.

SPEECHES, *corrected by* Himself:—

People's Edition, crown 8vo. 3s. 6d.
Speeches on Parliamentary Reform, 16mo. 1s.

MISCELLANEOUS WRITINGS & SPEECHES

Student's Edition, in One Volume, crown 8vo. price 6s.

The COMPLETE WORKS *of* LORD MACAULAY.

Edited by his Sister, Lady TREVELYAN. Library Edition, with Portrait. 8 vols. 8vo. £5. 5s. cloth; or £8. 8s. bound in calf.

London: LONGMANS and CO. Paternoster Row.